The Others

T. C. Weber

To contact the author, visit https://www.tcweber.com/

The Others / Weber, T. C.
Freedom Thorn Press, 2024.
ISBN 978-1-7369017-4-8

FIC028010: FICTION / Science Fiction / Action & Adventure
FIC028100: FICTION / Science Fiction / Cyberpunk
FIC036000: FICTION / Thrillers / Technological

Cover by Thejan @ Ambient Studios

Acknowledgments

Thanks to Jane Knuth, Georgi Prenatt, Miguel Mitchell, and Lucia Cartegni for reading drafts and providing feedback, and the critique groups at the Baltimore Science Fiction Society (www.bsfs.org) and the Annapolis Fiction and Poetry Writers. Special thanks to Andrew Cox for fact-checking on everything Navy-related, and Wayne Martin for feedback on matters both technical and non-technical.

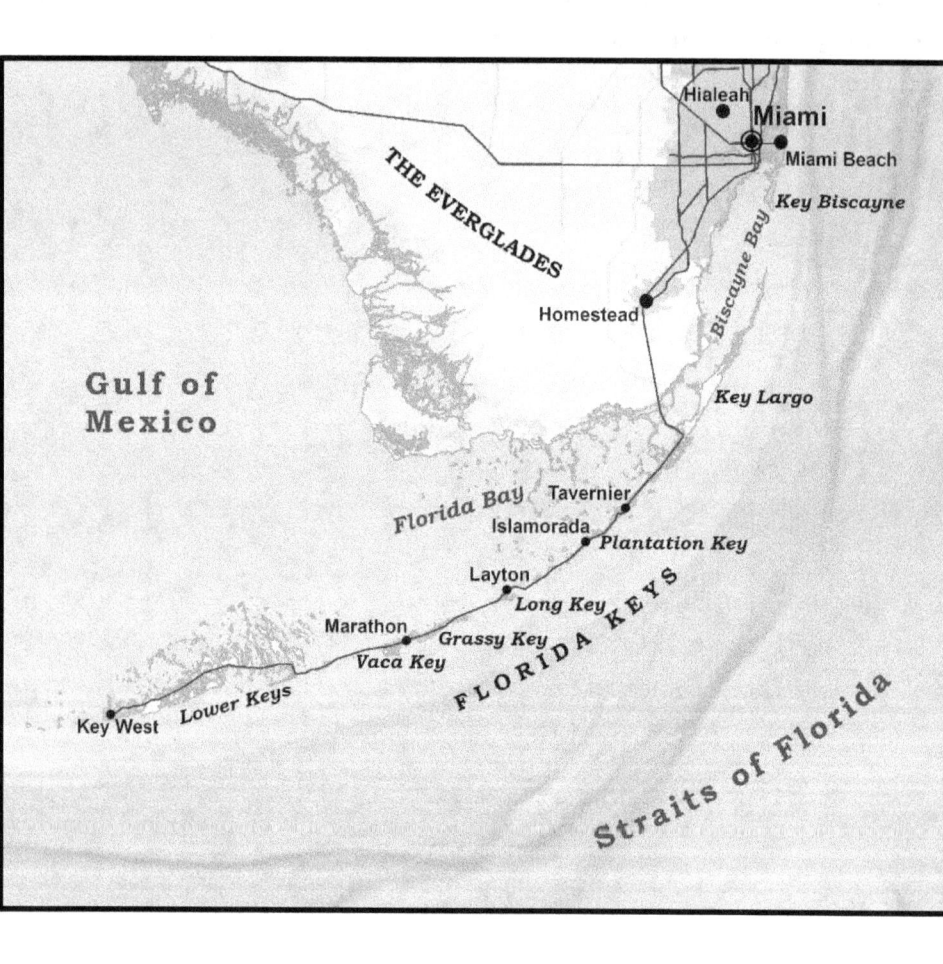

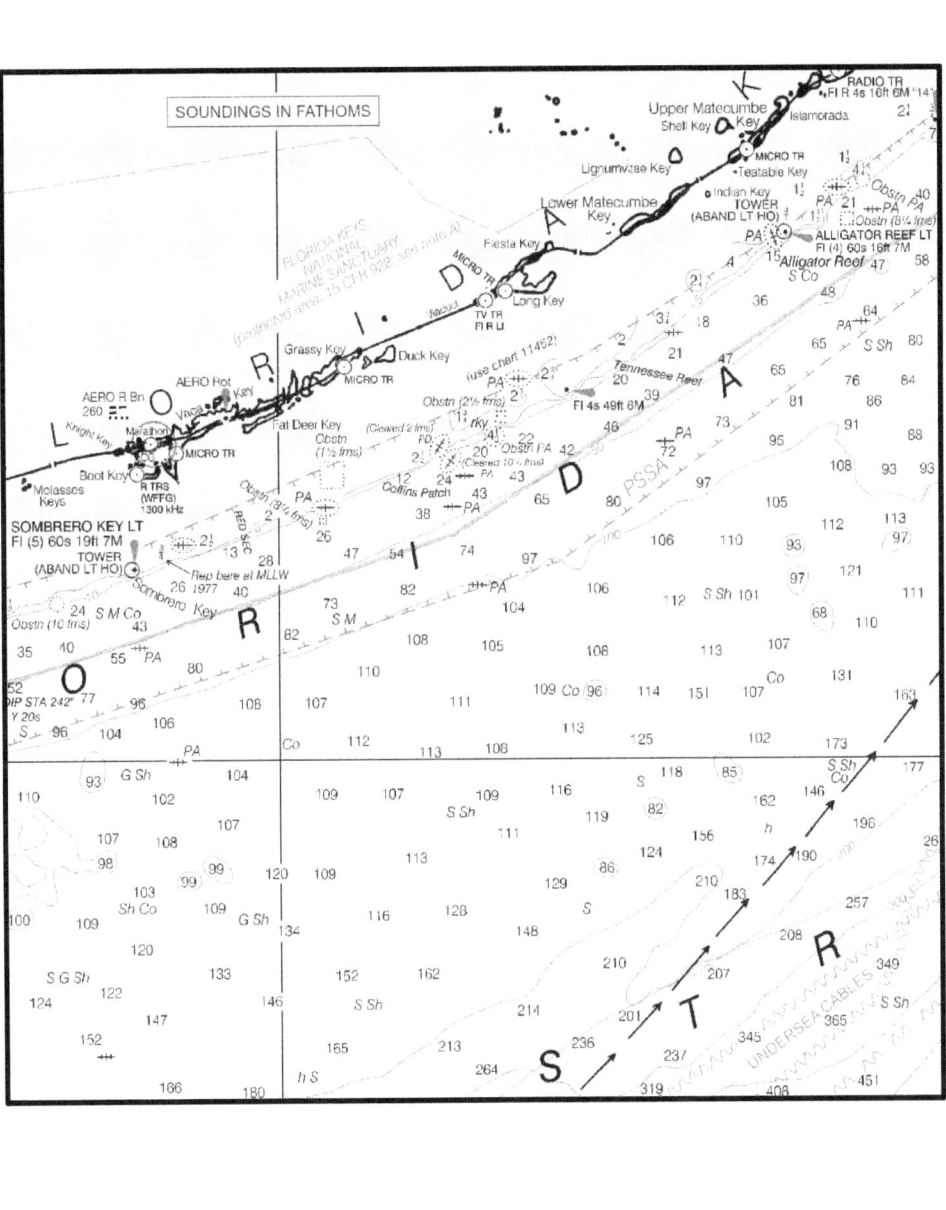

Chapter 1

Will

Will Myers inched his pickup past the downed trees and powerlines scattered along U.S. 1 in the Florida Keys. The drive home had already taken four hours, but he was used to it. The price of living in paradise—albeit a dying paradise—was the yearly onslaught of tropical storms and hurricanes.

Will had left his friend's place in Fort Lauderdale, just north of Miami, as soon as the road re-opened. He hoped his house was okay. It had survived prior hurricanes, though, and this one had unexpectedly veered further west, sparing the Keys a direct hit. Besides, when the mandatory evacuation was announced, he'd packed his most important possessions—his fishing and diving gear—in the 29-foot boat safely hitched to the back of the truck.

He drove onto the low concrete bridge heading into Long Key, where he'd lived since his PhD days—over seven years now. Still roiled by the storm's aftermath, the choppy water was strewn with seaweed, palm fronds, and fragments of wood. The sky was milky gray, the color of rotting fish.

The old-fashioned ringing of a rotary phone sounded over his car speakers. The number on the display wasn't in his contacts, but had a local area code. Will tapped the phone button on the steering wheel. "Hello?"

"Will?" asked a faintly Bahamian-accented voice. "It's Eloise."

Eloise Clark was a friend from the dive club—and the Medical Examiner for Monroe County. Will's fingers tightened on the steering wheel. The aftermath of a hurricane wasn't a time to discuss diving. In her official capacity, she'd only call if she had terrible news. His mind raced through a list of relatives and friends who might have ignored the order to evacuate.

"Are you there?" came her voice.

He swallowed. "Um, yeah, what's up?"

"You're okay?"

"Yeah." He kept his eyes on the road.

"Are you back in the Keys?"

"Almost home." Traffic was speeding up. "Is something wrong?"

"No, no, nothing like that. I need your opinion on something."

Will exhaled and his fingers relaxed. "Can I call you back when I get to the house?"

"Sure."

The bridge turned into a causeway, which widened into the beginnings of Long Key. After another minute or so, he reached the 'City of Layton' sign and turned left. Layton was tiny—about 200 residents. But he could walk to work, there was no crime to speak of, and best of all, he could keep his boat in the water next to the house.

Will pulled into his lot, which was littered with debris. Fronds from the palm trees lay across the gravel, and part of the balcony railing had been ripped away. But the sand-colored house itself—a two-bedroom living section atop an open carport and enclosed utility room—looked okay. The solar panels on the roof were intact and the steel accordion shutters still snugly fastened over the windows. Will exhaled in relief.

He hopped out of the truck and walked around the house. The air was fetid and muggy. His first impression was correct—no major damage—and he started clearing a path between the road and the garage.

It was getting harder and harder to live here. By mid-century, the sea would be two feet higher, most of the island submerged, and hurricanes more intense. The coral reefs, the focus of his studies and his playground since childhood, would die completely, and the economy of the Keys would follow. *And there's nothing I can do to change it.*

Will trudged up the external stairs with his phone. With the windows shuttered, it was dark and stuffy inside. He switched on the lights—his solar kit included a rack of batteries—and was greeted by memorabilia of happier times. His eyes lingered on the wedding photo on the wall. Yoselin, the love of his life since college, holding his arm and smiling. Him, a head taller than her, sweltering in his tuxedo, his brown hair slicked back by the stylist, completely at odds with his normal look.

Yoselin had been gone two years now, victim of a Covid variant and a chain of complications. Every reminder hollowed out his chest and filled it with hopelessness.

I need a drink. But first, he had to call Eloise back.

"Hi, it's Will again."

"Any damage?" she asked.

"The house is fine, more or less. Haven't been to the lab yet." The Keys Marine Laboratory, where Will conducted his research, was a five-minute walk

2

from the house. "We moved everything we could to the top floor," he added, "so hopefully, it's just a matter of cleaning up and putting things back."

"That's good. Listen, can you come over to my office? There's something I'd like you to take a look at."

It took a second for the strange request to register. "Something? Not someone?"

She paused before answering. "It's a someone—a male teenager. No ID."

Not someone he knew. At least, not someone she knew he knew.

"Police found him washed up near mile marker 75," Eloise continued.

Islamorada, Will translated subconsciously. An overdeveloped island he'd passed through on his way home.

"Why me?"

"There are... oddities you might be able to shed some light on. Since you study marine animals and, uh, perform a lot of necropsies."

Will studied sea turtles, five species of which were endangered. Once grown to adult size, they were mostly immune to predation. Their usual cause of death, when someone brought in a corpse, was ingestion of plastic trash— humanity's #1 contribution to the ocean.

He asked, "What do marine animals have to do with... Was he bitten by a shark?"

"No shark damage. Anyway, you're nearby, and I could use your expertise."

"What do you want me to look at, then?"

"Easier if you come and see for yourself. That way I'll get an objective opinion."

Will's coursework at the University of Miami had included comparative anatomy and physiology. But he'd never examined a human corpse. An unappealing prospect. He wasn't the sort to make excuses, though. "Give me a few minutes to unload and I'll head over."

* * *

The Monroe County Medical Examiner's Office was on Grassy Key. With the slow traffic, it took Will nearly half an hour to get there.

He'd never been to Eloise's office before. Two single-story, green-roofed buildings sat connected by a breezeway and surrounded by battered scrub. The hurricane had toppled the electric and floodlight poles, which had been bulldozed out of the way, along with piles of plant debris. The rumbling of a diesel generator sounded from the far side of the buildings.

Will met Eloise in the lobby. She was older than him—about forty—with dark brown skin and close-cropped curly hair, and wore a white lab coat with huge pockets.

"Thanks for coming," she said.

She led him down a hallway and opened a door with a keycard. They entered a tiled room with stainless-steel cabinets, sinks, and equipment trays. Frigid air blew from ceiling ducts, raising goosebumps on Will's forearms. The room reeked of formaldehyde and alcohol.

On the metal autopsy table in the center lay the body of a teenage boy, clad only in swimming trunks. Will recoiled at the sight. He forced himself into scientist mode, and noted no visible damage—at least at first glance.

"I took photos and fluid samples," Eloise said, "but I haven't opened him up. We're hoping to find next of kin, but he didn't have an ID."

The boy had an oval face, large almond-shaped eyes, a slightly broad nose, shoulder-length dark hair, and smooth, golden-bronze skin. He had a thick chest and muscular legs, like an athlete. But his most distinguishing features were large feet, elongated toes, and thin webbing between the fingers and toes.

Real or fake? Will stepped closer to look.

"Gloves on." Eloise passed him a pair of latex gloves. "You might want to take the ring off."

Will twisted off his wedding band, feeling naked and alone without it. He secured it in his pocket, then slipped on the gloves and approached the body.

The feet were wide, especially in front. The toes were at least twice as long as normal—almost like fingers. Bad for endurance running, but advantageous for swimming. The webbing looked and felt like real skin, like that between his own fingers, only reaching all the way to the top joints.

"Take a look at this." Eloise shone a penlight into the boy's nostrils.

Inside the hairless interior, the flesh bulged noticeably. Will poked it. It was pretty solid. "Strong-looking nasal musculature. I bet he can—could—close his nostrils easily."

Eloise handed him an otoscope. "Check out the ear."

The lobe was a little smaller than normal, with an enlarged tragus—the flap people pressed to block loud noises. The ear canal was short and wide. Through the magnifying lens of the otoscope, the tympanic membrane—the eardrum—was also big. It was undamaged—no signs of rapid pressure change.

"Have you ever seen ears like this?" Will asked.

"Never."

The eyes were closed, but seemed a little on the large side. "Do you mind if I lift the eyelids?" he asked Eloise.

She pushed them up herself. The pupils were fully dilated, pools of black staring unseeingly at the ceiling. And there was something strange about the iris.

"Do you have a magnifying glass?" he asked.

She pushed over a hefty magnifying glass mounted on a swing arm, and flipped on its ring light, illuminating the boy's face. Seen close-up, the iris muscles bulged upward, forming a raised berm around the wide pupils.

"It looks like his iris muscles are thicker," he said.

She peered through the magnifying glass. "Agree. Why would that be?"

Will wasn't exactly sure. "Maybe some adaptation to see underwater? I'd have to look into it." He pulled out his cell phone. "Mind if I take some pictures?"

"Go ahead, but you can't share them anywhere."

"I know."

As Will took photos, Eloise asked, "So what do you think?"

He stared at the oversized webbed feet again, one of the most bizarre things he'd ever seen. "He's evolved flippers, either by chance or genetic tinkering."

"At least he doesn't have gills."

"Gills can't provide enough oxygen for warm-blooded animals. You'd need 50 gallons of sea water per minute passing through the gills to keep a human alive." He'd calculated this while an undergrad. "The gills would have to be bigger than the body. That's why dolphins and whales breathe air."

Eloise picked up a data pad and started typing, her fingers a blur.

"What's the cause of death?" Will asked.

"Don't know yet. Drowning, perhaps. No froth around the mouth or nose, but I'm going to check for water in the lungs. Only marks I found on the outside were postmortem, probably from when he washed ashore."

"Did you estimate a time of death?"

"Around the time of the hurricane. The body's past the rigor mortis stage, so it's been more than 24 hours. Sheriff's deputy found him against a house on Sunset Drive. He hadn't been exposed to air long, but the decay rate in salt water is considerably slower. It's hard to tell how long he was in the water until

I run some tests. But decomposition's minimal, and nothing's fed on the body, so he died either during the hurricane or shortly before. My guess is, he's a hurricane victim."

"Could have come from Cuba," Will mused. *Although that's 90 miles away.* "Or a boat."

"That's what I was thinking too. The hurricane passed between Florida and Cuba."

"Does Cuba have genetic engineering labs?"

Eloise shrugged. "Not my area of expertise. I'm going to open him up now." She looked at Will. "You don't have to stay, but it might be helpful."

Seeing the dead body hadn't been as bad as he'd feared. It was almost like examining a dead marine animal, which he'd done a thousand times. "I'm fine," he said. *So far.*

Eloise donned a surgical mask and hair net, and instructed Will to do the same. She switched on an overhead video camera and narrated, "Resuming examination of unknown male teenager," and added the current date, time, and other official details.

With a long-handled scalpel, she cut a deep 'Y' incision from the front of each shoulder down to the pelvis. Eloise peeled back the skin, pulling the top flap over the face.

Will felt stirrings of revulsion. He told himself, *it's no different from dissecting a sea turtle.* He noted the subcutaneous fat layer was thick for someone in such good shape.

Eloise switched instruments and snipped the ribs in half. She set aside the severed sternal plate, revealing the internal organs. With scissors, she cut out the body organs individually and placed them in enamel kidney-shaped pans by the sink at the foot of the long table, narrating her findings as she went.

Next, she sawed open the skull and removed the brain. Will had never seen a human brain before, only props. The bulging folds were yellowish and coated with thick, congealed blood. His stomach turned queasy and he found himself backing away.

Eloise glanced at him. "There's some Vicks over on my desk. It can help mask the odor."

Will flushed with embarrassment. "That's okay." He forced himself to approach the table again.

Eloise proceeded to weigh the organs and narrate the readings. "They're all within the normal range for someone his height and weight," she told Will afterward, "except the lungs, which are slightly larger, and the spleen, which is twice the normal size." She looked at him as if waiting for feedback.

"The lungs are obvious," he said, "to store more air." He tried to remember what he'd been taught in biology classes about spleens. *It filters blood... Holds white blood cells for fighting infections...* "I'll have to get back to you about the spleen," he said.

Eloise resumed her examination, removing and fixing small fragments of each organ for later testing. "There's water in the stomach, but no food material," she spoke to the camera. "Intestines empty."

"So he hadn't eaten for more than a day before he died?"

"Correct. Bodies typically release stool from the rectum after death, but without muscles pushing it along, whatever's in the intestines remains."

She dissected the lungs next. "There's water in the lungs. Quite a bit."

"So he drowned?" Will asked.

"Apparently."

"Isn't that strange for someone with so many... um, swimming adaptations?"

She met his eyes. "If he was caught in the hurricane, it wouldn't matter."

Plausible explanation, but... "Why would he swim in hurricane conditions? It couldn't have been by choice. Even dolphins and sharks leave the area when hurricanes approach."

Eloise shrugged. "That's a question that can't be answered in the lab."

"So what happens next?"

"I write a report and send a copy to the sheriff's office. The remains stay here until claimed by next of kin. If no one claims it, it's delivered to the anatomical board, and I predict a big fight over who gets to use it for research."

* * *

After leaving the Medical Examiner facility, Will drove to the Keys Marine Laboratory, crossing his fingers that the damage wouldn't be too bad. It had survived Irma, after all.

The pastel green, two-story administrative building was still intact. The power lines were down, though. And debris lay everywhere, deposited by the waves. It smelled like dead fish and seaweed.

He parked in front of the building. The only other vehicle was a red pickup with a covered bed and mirrors secured with duct tape. It belonged to David McGee, the facility manager.

Will hopped out and noticed the whine of an engine and intermittent scraping noises. He went around back and saw David driving a Bobcat, pushing debris into a pile by the seawall. Seagulls circled, landed, and gorged on dead fish. Will waved, but McGee didn't notice, too focused on his work.

Will unlocked the lab's back door. The air inside smelled musty and briny, and the industrial carpeting was damp. At least the building itself looked fine, and all the computers, books, and files had been moved upstairs.

He flicked on the lights—the lab had installed solar panels and a sizable array of batteries to keep the refrigerators and aquariums running at all times—then opened all the windows and internal doors to air out the building. His office was upstairs. It looked as he'd left it, every available space packed with chairs and boxes from the ground floor.

He returned downstairs. The lab had a cleaning service, but keeping busy was his key to staving off gloom about Yoselin and the sorry state of the world. It might take weeks to purchase and install new carpeting, and nothing could be moved back downstairs until it was dry. He hunted through closets until he found a shop vac, and started sucking water out of the carpet.

David burst in with the satisfied look of a man who had just cleaned out his garage. He had dark skin and a short, graying beard, and was dressed in a T-shirt, shorts, and a Miami Dolphins cap. He stopped and stared. "What the hell are you doing?"

"Drying the carpet," Will said. "What does it look like?"

"I called the cleaning service. They'll be here tomorrow."

"Mildew sets in quick."

"You are a man for whom every silver cloud has a black lining, Will. Don't worry about it, my man! Taking care of this place is my job."

Will shrugged. "I like to keep busy, you know that. How's everything look?"

David recited a litany of minor damage and tasks to complete. "Made a lot of progress today."

"Looks like the Tequila Sunrise is open. The sign's on." The Tequila Sunrise Bar & Grill was the only bar in Layton, and was conveniently located next to the lab. Will was a regular there.

"If it weren't for the mandatory evacuation," David said, "I bet they would have stayed open during the storm."

Will chuckled. "Grab a beer?" It was just after four, the beginning of the three-hour Happy Hour.

"Naw, wanna finish as much as I can here, then heading back to Marathon. Told the wife and kids I'd be there for dinner."

"Next time, then." They bumped fists.

"Next time."

Will headed to the bar. The Tequila Sunrise was a small aquamarine wood structure in front of the identically-painted Key Lime Hotel. Like the morgue, it was running off a noisy diesel generator. Will entered the covered patio bar, which hosted local musicians on weekends but was nearly empty today. He greeted the other customers—all locals—and sat at the blue-tiled bar.

The bartender, a tanned 34-year-old blonde named Cookie, hailed him with her usual uplifting greeting. "Well, if it isn't the good-looking guy next door!" She was attractive, Will admitted, but married—not that he was interested, anyway.

"Channel Marker?" she offered.

"You know it. Got anything to eat?" His refrigerator was mostly empty—he'd consumed the perishables before evacuating.

"Out of almost everything. Fish sandwich and fries okay?"

"What kind of fish?"

"Whatever's left—I don't know."

He shrugged. "Sold."

Cookie poured him a pint of Channel Marker IPA, a beer brewed in nearby Islamorada, and passed the check through the hatch to the short-order cook in back. Johnny B, the deep-brown, heavyset Bahamian owner and occasional chef, strode out of the kitchen. "Will Myers!"

"Johnny B Good! I'm guessing you stayed again, sitting out front with your shotgun and a bottle of booze?"

"Had to keep an eye on things. Sheriff's department gave me a pass, being an essential pillar of the community and all. Hell, where do you think they eat when everywhere else's closed down?" He grinned.

The owner went to greet other customers, and Will's attention drifted to the TV screen above the bar. A meteorologist was discussing the hurricane's impending landfall in Louisiana. Driven by warm water in the Gulf of Mexico, it had increased to Category 4, with 150 mph winds. *Someone's gonna get it bad,*

Will thought, feeling both sympathy for Louisiana and relief that the Keys had escaped the worst of it.

The channel cut away to a blonde anchor in the studio. "This breaking news," the anchor declared in a no-nonsense voice. "Explosions have been reported throughout Saudi Arabia tonight. We have exclusive video."

On the screen, a massive orange fireball lit the night sky across an expanse of calm sea, followed by a low boom. It was followed by another fireball, then another, then another. Will's stomach sank the way it always did when he was confronted with bad news.

The screen split into two windows, blazing fires on one side and the blonde anchor on the other. "That's footage from just minutes ago," the anchor said. "I want to go to our correspondent in Riyadh, Badawi Wazir. Badawi, what have you heard?"

The right window switched to a dark-haired man standing on a balcony overlooking a brightly-lit city. "Judy," the man said, "social media is literally ablaze."

Will grimaced at the cheap pun.

"There have been explosions all along the Ras Tanura waterfront," the correspondent continued, "which handles 75 percent of Saudi Arabia's oil exports."

Judy the anchor returned. "We've got more live video from the scene."

A low-resolution camera panned from left to right, showing massive fires burning everywhere. It wobbled as it switched to selfie mode, showing a young, nervous-looking Arabic man. "I am Uzair. I study here in Al Jubail." He cut back to the front camera and zoomed in on one of the distant blazes. "That's King Fahd Industrial Port, where the first explosions happened."

The anchor and correspondent reappeared on the left side of the screen while Uzair the student occupied the right, fires burning in the background.

"That's one of the busiest oil loading facilities in the world," the correspondent said.

"What time did the explosions start?" the anchor asked.

Uzair's face returned. "About eleven. Maybe fifteen minutes ago."

"Any word on casualties?"

Uzair scratched his dark hair. "Not that I've heard." He spoke to other people off-screen in Arabic.

The anchor's eyes shifted, then she faced the camera again. "We've just received word that the Port of Yanbu on the Red Sea Coast has also caught fire. Badawi, what can you tell us about that?"

The correspondent bit his lip, then shook off whatever he was feeling. "I… Well, this could be some sort of attack. Yanbu and Ras Tanura account for almost the entirety of Saudi export capacity. It can't be an accident, not on the Persian Gulf and Red Sea at the same time."

"Attack by who?"

"I couldn't tell you at this point. But everything looks normal here in Riyadh."

"How many people would be working at the docks at night?"

The correspondent blinked. "I'll have to get back to you on that."

Will noticed Cookie was also glued to the TV. "Israel?" he asked her. "Iran?"

She shrugged. "It wouldn't be us, that's for sure."

As if on cue, the network put one of its retired generals on camera. The chisel-faced man had traded his Army uniform for a dark suit and plaid tie. "With us now," the anchorwoman said, "is Lt. General Tom Hatch. General, do you think this is an attack, and if so, who's behind it?"

"Well, Judy," the former general replied, "so far, no one has taken credit for the explosions, and the Pentagon is still assessing the situation. The scale of the destruction appears to be massive, though, and if indeed it was deliberate, those responsible will be held to account."

Judy the anchor asked the ex-general to speculate who might have carried out the attack, and how, but to his credit, he continued to state there wasn't enough information yet.

The retired general was replaced by a gray-haired man with glasses. "We now turn to economist Ben Stuhl," the anchor said. "Let me ask you what's on everyone's mind. How will this affect gas prices?"

Will groaned, his dislike of corporate news amplified yet again.

"Petroleum futures are certain to spike…"

On the right-hand screen, behind the Saudi student, a giant fireball—dwarfing the others—exploded into the sky with a loud boom. It was eclipsed by a massive dome of seawater and debris that blew high into the air and expanded rapidly toward the camera. The student screamed something in Arabic. The picture jolted and went black.

Chapter 2

Will drove home two hours and three beers later. He'd been glued to the news. Apparently, the King Fahad facility exported not only oil, but refined petroleum, liquefied natural gas, and highly explosive chemical fertilizers. The place was basically a giant bomb that detonated.

Saudi Arabia was by far the world's biggest oil exporter, and the explosions had crippled their ability to load tankers, maybe for months. They had no overland pipes to speak of. Casualties were not yet known, but limited to isolated industrial areas with late-night staffing.

Tomorrow morning, Will thought, everyone would panic and the price of oil—and everything dependent on it—would skyrocket. The stock market would plummet. Simultaneous accidents at two ports were unlikely, but according to the news, no aircraft or missiles had been detected, nor anyone apprehended. Whoever had carried out the attacks had been incredibly stealthy.

Nothing I can do about it. Will unlocked and rolled aside the window shutters, then went inside and checked the marine forecast on his phone. Skies mostly cloudy tomorrow, ocean a little rough, but bay waters smooth to light chop. With the lab closed for cleaning, it would be a good day to take the boat out. His first choice was always scuba diving, especially during lobster season. He'd been hooked since childhood—diving was like entering another world where nothing on the surface mattered anymore, and there was always something new to see. He'd need a safety buddy, though, and it was too late to start calling around. Besides, the hurricane would have kicked up a lot of sediment.

Fishing, then. Fish were hungry after storms, and easier to catch. *Snapper in the bay or head to the ocean for dolphin?* Dolphin, a large and tasty yellow-and-blue fish that leapt into the air when hooked, had been renamed mahi-mahi for marketing reasons. Americans were understandably averse to the thought of eating Flipper, but Will hated name changes, especially for marketing purposes.

Will sat on the living room sofa and switched on the big-screen TV mounted to the opposite wall. It was great for watching football, and when Yoselin was alive, watching movies together. The nearest theater was 25 miles away, with limited options. They'd make popcorn and snuggle. Often, they didn't even make it through the movie before the closeness turned to desire.

Trying to shake off the loneliness, Will put on an episode of 'CSI.' It was like watching science in action, only with more drama—and occasional silliness. Sometimes he fantasized about being a police detective or performing forensic science at murder scenes instead of on turtles. Observing an actual human autopsy had boosted his fixation.

Ten minutes into the show, Will mulled over the strange corpse he'd seen. He switched on his laptop.

Using an academic search engine, he scoured scientific publications for descriptions of marine mammal morphology. The thick subcutaneous fat layer was obvious—helpful for buoyancy and insulation. The webbing and large feet could potentially double the boy's swimming speed. Presumably his strange eyes and ears were marine adaptations also.

Human hearing suffered two major deficiencies underwater. First, air bubbles in the ear canal reflected sound waves away before they could reach the eardrum, so only vibrations through the skull could be sensed. This severely decreased signal strength. Second, sound waves traveled over four times faster underwater—too fast to detect which direction they were coming from.

Will skimmed relevant papers, bypassing details he didn't need. According to the studies, seals and other amphibious marine mammals had excellent hearing underwater, both in sensitivity and directionality. He guessed the boy's short ear canals and big eardrums precluded air bubbles, improving underwater hearing dramatically. Most likely there would be other differences to keep the pressure equalized, but he and Eloise would have to dissect the ear to learn more.

Taking a break, Will plodded to the kitchen and mixed a margarita. He purposely made it weak, so he could still think properly. Unfortunately, there wasn't anything to eat besides limes and stale crackers.

Returning to the living room with his drink, Will started researching eyes. Human vision, like hearing, was handicapped underwater. Divers had to wear masks so the eyes could focus properly. An article in *Bioscience Review* described how children of the Moken island people in the Andaman Sea could see quite well underwater. Like seals and dolphins, they could decrease their pupil size and change the lens shape, although their lenses lost flexibility in adulthood. According to other journal articles he skimmed, some diving birds, like gannets, were even better adapted, using ciliary muscles to reshape the lens for surface or underwater vision.

That could explain the boy's thick iris muscles. And his large eyes and pupils could be an adaptation for low-light vision. *He's like a human-seal hybrid!*

Will's cell phone rang. It was his dad, so he answered.

"Hey, son. We're headed back to Key West tomorrow. Our hotel's nice, but the cost adds up. How's everything look down there?"

Will gave a quick synopsis. "Power lines down, a lot of debris, but no buildings destroyed. My house is fine, just some balcony damage. I haven't been down to Key West, but it looks about the same on news footage. We lucked out."

"That's good. Mind if we stop by on the way home?"

"Not at all. The lab's closed for cleaning. What time?"

"We'll be there around one or so, if you don't mind a late lunch."

"That's fine."

"Did you hear what happened in Saudi Arabia?" his dad asked.

"Yeah, crazy."

"Ten to one it's Iran. They're the biggest sponsor of terrorism in the world, and they hate the Saudis."

"Geopolitics aren't my forte." It was a downplay, but Will didn't want another lecture about how America needed to throw its weight around more. His grandfather had been a fishing charter captain, but his father was a dentist, and thought going to dental school meant he knew everything about everything.

"I have to call my broker as soon as their office opens," his dad said, "and move our stocks into bonds. Or cryptocurrency—there's a new one out that's getting hot."

"You know, if everyone does that, the economy will tank."

"Well, everyone else is going to sell as soon as the bell rings, and I don't want to end up with worthless stocks."

Just like the tragedy of the unmanaged commons, Will thought. When everyone acts solely in their self-interest, it leads to disaster.

"Besides," his dad continued, "they'll stop the trading before the bleeding gets too bad. I just hope I can get through in time. I didn't bring my passwords with me, so I can't do it online."

"Why don't you invest in solar and wind companies? Or electric car manufacturers?" Will suggested. "If the price of oil goes up, they'll make out like bandits."

His dad's voice turned enthusiastic. "Great idea! I thought you didn't know anything about markets."

"It just seems logical. Do your own research."

After a pause, his dad said, "Your mom wants to talk to you."

Will's stomach hardened. "You mean my stepmother?" While Will was in college at the University of Miami, his dad had begun an affair with one of his dental hygienists. In a small place like Key West, word spread. Will's real mom had taken his two younger sisters and moved to Seattle, as far from Florida as possible while still within the continental U.S. Both parents had remarried, and now most of Will's family interactions were conducted by phone.

"Well, regardless—"

"Unfortunately, I'm busy right now."

"Doing what?"

"Research on mammalian ocular and physiological adaptations for aquatic niche exploitation." Nothing killed a conversation with the parents faster than biology jargon. He said goodbye and returned to his laptop.

Switching his investigation to the boy's oversized spleen, Will pulled out his old *Mammalian Anatomy* textbook. Yoselin had once quipped that it was big enough to serve as a murder weapon.

Besides recycling damaged blood cells and filtering out other unwanted material, the spleen stored red, white, and platelet blood cells until needed. In humans, it reserved up to a quarter-liter of red blood cells, releasing them when oxygen levels dropped too low. For all mammals, diving underwater automatically released oxygenated blood cells.

Seals had large spleens—it helped them stay underwater longer. Returning to the Internet, Will read that the Bajau, a southeast Asian "sea nomad" people like the Moken, had spleens 50% larger than neighboring non-diving people. It was apparently a genetic mutation. Like seals, they could gather food underwater for long periods of time, at depths greater than 70 meters—well beyond the "safe depth" for scuba divers.

Will felt a pang of jealousy. *I wish I'd been born a sea nomad, able to dive without all that gear.*

It was unlikely all these adaptive mutations would have occurred in a single individual by chance. They went far beyond those of the Bajau and Moken people.

Maybe the boy really was genetically engineered. Some sort of experiment. By whom, and for what purpose? Defense Department? They have practically unlimited funding and don't hesitate to throw it at wacky ideas. But wouldn't they have taken the body?

Unless they don't know about it yet.

Will searched for information about genetically engineered humans, and was surprised how advanced the science was. A Chinese scientist had created genetically edited babies back in 2018, and the technology had improved greatly since then. The U.S., along with many other countries, outlawed genetic engineering for reproductive use, although lab research was permitted. Cuba had no prohibitions at all.

Around midnight, Will emailed his findings to Eloise, then downed his nightly pills—the only way he could sleep in an empty bed.

He dreamed about fishing from his boat on a sunny day. Humanoid monsters burst from the depths and clambered aboard, determined to tear him to pieces.

Chapter 3

Will woke at seven the following morning, slathered on sunscreen, threw on shorts, a T-shirt, and running shoes, and began his usual weekday run to Long Key State Park and along the nature trail. The four-mile run kept him in condition and cleared away the morning gloom.

After showering, he downed a banana and a Greek yogurt from the Grab-N-Go, Layton's only source of groceries. He hadn't quite finished his coffee when his cell phone rang. It was Eloise.

"Thanks for the research info," she said. "Any theories?"

"The likelihood of all those adaptations suddenly appearing by chance is as close to zero as you can get. I think this boy was genetically engineered. The question is, by whom, and for what purpose?"

"Sounds like a case for Mulder and Scully."

Will cracked a smile. "You don't happen to have their number, do you?"

"'Fraid not. Listen, the main reason I called was, a relative contacted the sheriff's department and is coming to I.D. the body. If the relative claims it, there won't be any further examinations, beyond the ones I did to determine the cause of death."

A familiar itch surfaced in Will's mind—a question to solve. It was why he became a scientist. *Is it really a relative? Or some operative from the CIA or Defense Department?* "I'm headed over. Stall them if they get there first."

"Seriously?"

"I'll be there in fifteen minutes."

Eloise was waiting alone in the medical examiner's lobby when Will arrived. "Are you hoping to convince this relative to let us perform more tests?" she said. "Because this isn't a med school cadaver we're talking about, it's somebody's loved one."

"I know. But that kid is special—incredibly special. I want to know who comes to pick him up. Don't you?"

"I suppose you're not the only one who's curious," she admitted.

A few minutes later, a woman in her early to mid-twenties entered through the front door, tall and strikingly exotic. She wore a wide-brimmed straw hat and a floor-length, floral-patterned sun dress that hugged her hips.

She removed the hat. "I was told by the sheriff's office… you have the body of a teenage boy." She spoke in a low-pitched voice with a faint, vowel-lengthening accent that Will couldn't pinpoint.

Eloise paused, then nodded. She held out a hand. "I'm Eloise Clark. I'm the County Medical Examiner."

The woman hesitated, then accepted the handshake. She had normal fingers, with no webbing. "Do you work here too?" she asked Will.

"Just helping out. I'm Will Myers, Senior Staff Scientist at the Keys Marine Lab."

The young woman definitely resembled the boy, with an oval face, large almond-shaped eyes, wide sea-green irises, long dark hair, and smooth, golden-bronze skin. She had a straight, slightly broad nose and full, sensual lips.

There could be a whole group of these people, Will thought, like the sea nomads in Asia, but even better adapted. *Where are they from? How many millenia of evolution would such specialization take? It has to be genetic engineering, or someone would have discovered and written about them. If it's a whole group, and no one knows about it, it must be a government black ops project. If so, to what end?*

"Can… Can I see the body?" the woman asked. "My brother's missing, and this is my last lead." She bit her lip.

Will compared their features again in his head, and prepared himself for the reaction when she saw her dead brother.

"Do you have some ID?" Eloise asked the woman. "And a photo of your brother?"

"My name's Andréa," she said. "Andréa Álvarez." She reached into a purse and passed Eloise a Florida driver's license. Her first name was spelled 'Andreia,' a Brazilian variant. The address was in Hialeah, a Cuban-American suburb of Miami.

Andreia pulled out a cell phone and brought up a picture of a smiling teenage boy. There was no doubt it was the victim. She studied their somber faces and flinched, then began to tremble.

"I'm so sorry," Will said.

Andreia's eyes began to fill with tears. Eloise returned her license. "Could you send me a copy of that photo?"

She nodded. "Can… Can I see him?"

"We're not set up for relative visits. Let me get your information, and—"

"Please?" Tears dripped from her eyes. "I have to know for sure."

Eloise sighed and led them back to a small cold room with stacked morgue drawers. Will followed, curiosity overcoming his misgivings. On one hand, Will wanted to study the body in greater detail, and sequence the DNA to see how it differed. But he knew from experience the depth of Andreia's grief. Besides, they had tissue samples to work from.

Eloise pulled out one of the drawers and unzipped the top of a black body bag, just enough to reveal the dead boy's face and neck. She'd closed his eyelids, so he almost looked asleep.

Andreia's eyes widened and her jaw dropped. She stared, motionless, then broke into a loud wail and draped herself over the body.

The poor girl's grief was contagious, and Will's eyes also began to tear up. Eloise stepped away, looking uncomfortable. By instinct, Will placed a hand on the girl's shoulder, knowing exactly how she felt.

As her sobs continued, he realized, *I'm an intruding stranger*, and stepped back.

Andreia struggled out words. "It's him." Her eyes remained focused on the corpse. "I was hoping he'd still be missing, but it's him, he's dead. He's dead."

"Your brother?" Will asked.

Andreia faced him with dripping eyes. "My little brother. Galen. My only sibling."

After a pause, Eloise asked hesitantly, "Do you have a funeral home in mind I should contact?"

Will shot her a look. You couldn't wait two minutes?

Andreia turned back to her dead brother, hugged the body tightly in its bag, and resumed crying.

Eloise whispered to Will, "I'm no good at this. That's what funeral directors are for. I'm a pathologist."

The grieving woman coughed, wiped her eyes with a wrist, and straightened up. "How did he die?"

Eloise edged around her and zipped the body bag closed. "Post-mortem indicates he drowned. No signs of foul play. And no shark bites. I'm very sorry for your loss."

Andreia's sparse eyebrows rose. "Drowned?"

"In the hurricane, most likely."

"He'd know better…" She stopped mid-sentence. "Where was he found?"

"Lower Matecumbe Key. Islamorada."

Andreia's forehead furrowed. "Could you tell me more precisely?"

"Against a house on Sunset Drive, if you know where that is. I don't know the address off hand, but it would be in the police report."

Andreia looked as if she were trying to solve a puzzle for a moment, then she said, "Can I bring him home?"

Eloise's jaw dropped. She looked at Will, as if for support.

"You want to bring your brother… to your house?" Will asked Andreia.

"We have to say goodbye."

"Normally that's handled by a funeral home," Eloise said. "Human remains can only be stored at licensed facilities. I can give you some phone numbers if you like."

Andreia sniffled. "Is it required? I have a van, and can get some ice."

Eloise crinkled her nose. "I'm sorry, Florida law doesn't permit that."

Andreia inhaled loudly and her face tightened. She looked as if she were about to cry again.

Will turned to Eloise. "We know the cause of death—drowning. Do you have authority to fill out a death certificate?"

"As the medical examiner, yes. We can do it now."

Will volunteered, "I can help Ms. Alvarez through the rest of the process."

Andreia exhaled in apparent relief. "Thank you. I would be grateful." She opened an Internet browser on her phone.

Eloise led Andreia and Will to her neatly-organized office, took a seat behind her desk and unlocked her desktop computer. Andreia sat in one of the two guest chairs in front of the desk, tears continuing to slip quietly down her cheeks. Will took the other chair, wishing he had a handkerchief to offer.

"May I see your driver's license again?" Eloise asked.

Andreia passed it to her. Will discreetly glanced at her feet. Her espadrille shoes were distinctly larger than normal, but shorter than her brother's feet.

Eloise typed in the information from the license and returned it. "Your brother's date of birth?"

Sniffling, she gave a date fifteen years prior.

"Your phone number?"

Andreia gave a number with a local area code. Eloise typed some more, then hard copies emerged from a small laser printer.

"You'll need at least three of these," Eloise said as she signed the death certificates. "I'll waive the fees. It's not very much, and more hassle than it's worth."

"I can recommend a funeral home in Miami," Will suggested. "Familia Fernández. They"—he paused to collect himself—"they handled my wife's funeral. They're very good, and can take care of all the details."

"Can I have him cremated and take the ashes?" Andreia asked.

Will nodded. "Any undertaker you pick can do that."

"I… I've never had to do this. I'm sorry to ask, but can you help me? With the calls?"

Will met her watery eyes, remembering how difficult it had been to manage the mundane details while overwhelmed with pain. "Happy to help."

He looked up Familia Fernández on his phone and talked to them in Spanish. He passed the phone to Andreia, who also spoke in Spanish.

After a short conversation, she hung up, stared at the phone, then returned it to Will. "They'll pick him up this afternoon."

Will pulled one of his business cards out of his wallet and wrote his personal cell number on the back. He handed it to Andreia. "In case you have any questions or need anything." He gave Eloise a nod to do the same. "I live nearby," he informed Andreia, "so don't hesitate."

Andreia examined the cards. "What's a marine scientist doing at the medical examiner's office?"

"Eloise and I are friends, and dive buddies. Your brother… Galen… he swam a lot?"

"Yes." Her face tensed. "Did you… *dissect* him?"

The question took Will by surprise. "Eloise performed an autopsy."

"It's standard procedure for accidental deaths," Eloise added.

Andreia started crying again. Will gave in to the overwhelming urge to comfort her, and draped his hand over hers.

Eloise was looking increasingly uncomfortable. "Let's talk outside," Will suggested to Andreia. "Get some air." Eloise shot him a grateful look.

Once outside, Andreia donned her straw hat and stylish, black-framed sunglasses. She led Will through the small parking lot to a dirt-streaked white cargo van with a Florida license plate. She directed him to the front of the van, obscuring any view of—and from—the buildings.

Will wondered if she'd brought others, but the van appeared empty. Nor was anyone lurking in the low scrub bordering the facility. Of course, if they were Navy SEALs or other professionals, he might never see them.

Suddenly, Will felt silly speculating like this. *The poor girl lost her brother.* But beneath the apparently genuine grief, there was something strong, even steely about her. *Everyone responds to death differently.*

Andreia inhaled and stiffened her shoulders as if to brace herself. "There's something… I don't understand. Galen wouldn't go swimming during a hurricane. Something must have happened." She spoke in quiet tones, as if not wanting to be overheard. "He disappeared a few days ago, before the hurricane arrived." She looked into Will's eyes. "I don't know where he went, but it must have been pretty far to the northeast to end up on Lower Matecumbe."

To the northeast from where? Here? Hialeah? Will adopted her quiet tone. "Where'd you last see him?"

After a second or two, she said, "You must know about ocean currents, being a marine scientist."

"Yes."

"And how storms push the water?"

"Around here, yes."

"Could you help me? Help me figure out what happened? After I bring Galen home, I mean."

He couldn't say no, remembering the depth of his despair when Yoselin died. And he had a younger brother too, in the Navy, whom he worried about whenever his ship was sent to a conflict zone. "Of course."

She looked at the back of his card and sent him a text. "You have my number now, so you know it's me calling and not a telemarketer."

Will unlocked his phone with his index fingerprint and checked his messages. He had a text saying 'me' from the same number Andreia had given Eloise. He added it to his contact list.

"I'll give you a call," she said.

"Glad to help however I can."

"Before I go, what did you find in the autopsy?"

She seemed kind of all over the place, but Will remembered how hard it was for him to think and converse coherently when Yoselin died. "Sea water in the lungs and stomach," he replied, "meaning he gulped down water and drowned. Eloise thought the waves overwhelmed him."

She shook her head. "Doesn't make sense."

"And he hadn't eaten at least a day before he died."

"Who goes swimming when they're starving?" she asked.

"I was wondering that too." Swimming required a lot of energy. "Was he a surfer, by chance?" Hurricanes brought big waves to the normally calm South Florida coast.

"No." Her eyes darted, then fixed on his. "What else did you find?"

Will decided to open up. "Eloise called me in precisely because I'm a marine biologist. Your brother Galen has some interesting adaptations. Like the sea nomads of Asia—if you've ever heard of them—only to a much greater degree."

She almost smiled. "The Moken, Orang laut, and Sama-Bajau, yes, they're remarkable. As adapted for underwater foraging as Tibetans and Andeans are for living at high altitudes."

"Is it something you study?" he asked.

"Not particularly. I just read a lot. So, you said he reminded you of them?"

"Yes, but none of those people have webbed toes and fingers. The Bajau, maybe the others, have bigger spleens, but Galen's was twice as large as…" *Don't say 'normal'…* "um, is typically seen." He then described the eyes, ears, nose, and other adaptations they'd found. "Do you mind if I ask, is your whole family like that?"

She stiffened, then stepped closer and grabbed his hands. "Look, my family is very private." Her big green eyes bored into him. "I'm asking you to please let us live in peace."

Will found himself speechless. "I'll keep it to myself," he said as reassuringly as he could.

"Thank you." She squeezed his hands, in an intimate yet vaguely admonishing way. "Did you take samples from my brother? Photos? Record your findings?"

"Well, yes, that's standard procedure. It's confidential, though." He decided not to mention the photos he had taken with his cell phone.

Her face knotted in worry and she didn't respond.

Will wanted to help her, and besides, he had to know more about her people and what she seemed so afraid of. "The samples were logged and will be sent elsewhere for analysis. But they'll only test for things related to the cause of death. That might even answer your questions."

Her face relaxed slightly. "I suppose so."

"And the report, only police and next-of-kin are entitled to see it." He wasn't entirely sure that was true, but it probably was, and no one would go looking for something they didn't know existed.

"Could you ask Dr. Clark to leave out whatever details aren't required?" Like the finger and toe webbing? "I'll ask."

She released his hands and hugged him, her long hair smelling like a fresh near-shore breeze. "Thank you."

He hugged her back. "I'm sorry about your brother."

She let go and stepped back, nodding in acknowledgment. "I'll call you in a day or two. Please pick up if you can. I don't like leaving messages."

Her face was really striking, Will thought. Her large, almond-shaped green eyes had a way of mesmerizing him. And her oval face, full lips, golden-bronze skin—she was downright beautiful.

"You look like you're taking a mental picture," she said.

"Sorry. I've never met anyone like you."

"I'll be in touch." She climbed into the van. "Thank you." Her face contorted in grief again as she drove away.

Will went back inside to ask Eloise what could be left out of the official report—and talk about the strangeness of it all.

* * *

Will couldn't get Andreia out of his head as he waited for his dad and stepmother at the Tequila Sunrise. The patio bar was open, and he'd grabbed one of the raised pub tables and three metal-backed bar stools. *What should I say when she calls? Will she call?* Estimating where her brother's body drifted from would be fairly straightforward, although full of uncertainties. Why he was in the water with a hurricane approaching, was another matter. As for Andreia, she was both beautiful and fascinating, and he found himself hoping he'd see her again.

Will had talked Eloise into limiting her autopsy report to the standard diagnostic pathology, omitting any mention of the eye and ear oddities and finger and toe webbing. She'd recorded the unusual spleen weight along with all the other organ weights, but said the only part of her reports anyone ever read was the summary paragraph at the end. The rest was too technical for anyone without a medical degree.

Cookie dropped a menu on the table. "Hi, Will."

"Hi. Can I have two more? My dad and stepmother are meeting me here."

She grabbed two more menus from the bar. "Got the whole day off?"

"Yeah, lab's closed. I was going to go fishing, but some things came up." Andreia's face flashed into his head again.

"Beer?" Cookie asked.

"Sure."

"Channel Marker?"

"Am I too predictable?" he asked.

She shook her head. "I wouldn't put it that way. You like what you like. Don't we all?"

Will's dad and stepmother Jen arrived an hour and a half, and two beers, later. "Sorry we're late," his dad said.

"Miami traffic," Jen added. She rarely said anything worthwhile. She was only a few years older than Will, with teased-out brown hair, tanned face, and thick makeup. *The complete opposite of Andreia*, Will mused.

"Did you get your stocks taken care of?" Will asked his dad.

"I took a hit when the market opened, but got my changes in before the circuit breaker halted trading the rest of the day."

"Circuit breaker? As in the electricity went out?" *Another attack of some sort?*

His dad laughed. Jen said, "Even I know better than that. They stop all trading if the prices fall too fast."

Aren't you brilliant. Will managed to refrain from saying it out aloud, opting for a wise nod instead.

"I followed your advice," his dad continued. "Bought some renewable energy and electric vehicle stocks—so hopefully I'll make back the morning's loss."

"Does that mean you're buying lunch?" Will joked.

"Don't I always?"

True. He'd always been a generous father, which made his betrayal of the family that much more painful.

They ordered lunch, and Will added another beer.

"Not much room on this table," Jen complained.

"This is Layton," his dad told her. "They're lucky to have a restaurant at all."

"I'd rather live in Layton than anywhere on the mainland," Will said. "What do they do for fun there? Spend the day at outlet malls and complain about traffic?"

His dad chuckled, missing Will's jabs at Jen. "Pretty much. They're like lemmings on the mainland."

"I thought you were getting some sort of job in Miami," Jen said.

"Assistant professor at FIU. They gave it to some guy from Italy instead." He stared at his beer. He was over thirty now, and hadn't even set foot on the tenure track.

His dad changed the subject. "Did you hear the latest about the oil port attacks?"

Will only watched news when someone else had it on, and had no social media accounts. "No, what?"

"The fires are still burning, if you can believe that. But they think it was a cyber-attack."

"Who's they?"

"Got a friend in IT, Nick Coates, remember him?"

Will shook his head.

"Well, Nick says all the security experts are working on it. And guess what? It wasn't a bombing at all. Some crazies infected the plant's switching systems with malware. It was still on computers outside the blast zone. Nick says it opened oil flow valves, but everything looked normal on the consoles, and none of the controls would work. And that's just step one. It looks like this program jacked up the pressure on the natural gas pipes, closed some vent valves, and opened some other valves near storage tanks. Then it sent surges through electrical circuits to ignite the gas vapor and nearby oil. Next thing you know, boom! With all the vapor and bursting pipes, it spun totally out of control."

"Sounds sophisticated," Will responded. "You can cause damage like that through the Internet?"

"No, Nick said the attackers would have needed physical access. My guess is, it was an inside job, or done with inside help."

"The Saudis have some leads and are interrogating people," Jen piped up.

"And they said they'll come up with a workaround," his dad said. "They promised to resume oil exports soon."

"Of course they have to say that," Will said, "whether it's true or not." He gulped from his beer. "What a shitshow."

"Shows why we can't rely on foreign oil," his dad said. "The President is making the whole Strategic Petroleum Reserve available. Of course, that's not enough. We have to tap every oil and gas deposit there is—no exceptions. It's a global emergency."

"Drill, baby, drill!" Jen parroted with an incandescent grin.

Will glared at the homewrecker. "This is like the pandemic in a way," he told them, feeling his heart clench as it always did at reminders of his wife's death. "It's an opportunity to take a more sustainable course, rather than business as usual or, like your appalling suggestion, making things worse."

Jen was no longer paying attention, but Will's dad shook his head. "Let's drop it before… Did you catch the Dolphins game on Sunday?"

Will loved football as much as anyone, but as they discussed the Dolphins' defensive woes, his thoughts went back to the dead boy. And his sister.

Chapter 4

It took Will and the rest of the lab staff two days to move everything back and resume normal operations. Will then settled at his desk to tackle the backlog of emails.

While he was responding to a colleague in Mexico, his phone rang. It was Andreia's number. Electricity jolted through him. He'd dreamed about her the previous night—not a sex dream, more a hanging-out dream with hazy details, but it was the first pleasant dream he'd had in a long while.

"How are you doing?" he asked.

"Better, I suppose," her throaty, slightly accented voice said. "I wanted to thank you for recommending that funeral home. They were nice. My family released the ashes and said goodbye."

That was quick. "Released?"

"Scattered underwater. He'll always be with us, memories in our minds and molecules in the water, the sand, the food we eat. He'll always be part of the whole." She sniffled.

She sounded like a Buddhist—or an ecologist. Will started to ask if she believed in an afterlife, but she spoke first. "Are you free now?"

"I'm at the lab, but I can get away."

"Can we meet? About what we discussed at the morgue?"

He assumed she meant about the autopsy report and figuring out how her brother died. "I'd be happy to. Where and when?" Hialeah, where she'd said she lived, was a two-hour drive from Layton. A long way for a conversation that could be held by phone.

"How about now? I'm parked outside."

It took a second for Will to process that. "As in outside the lab?"

"Against the fence."

"Give me a second and I'll be right down."

Just as she'd said, Andreia's white cargo van was parked in the small gravel parking lot, by the wooden fence that surrounded the lab property. Andreia was sitting behind the wheel and saw him approach. She waved without smiling.

She leaned over to open the passenger door and Will hopped inside. She was wearing a lightweight dress and the black-framed sunglasses. Her features were as striking as he remembered.

"Do you travel at the speed of light?" he asked.

The joke apparently escaped her. "I got here as quick as I could." She started the engine.

"Do you have a computer at your house we could use?" she asked.

"Yes. I have one in my office too, if you want to talk there."

"I was hoping for more privacy. Is anyone else home?"

Sadness gripped Will. "I live alone. Since my wife passed away."

Andreia draped a hand over his. "I'm sorry about that."

"Thank you." He gave directions to his house, feeling awkward. This would be the first time a woman set foot in his house since Yoselin died. He hadn't been entirely celibate since then, but the few alcohol-fueled exceptions had been nothing serious or lasting. Mostly they'd been older female tourists on the prowl, and he never brought them home, where his wife had lived.

They parked the van next to his truck, which he usually left at the house. She eyed the dual-outboard boat tied to the dock. "You said you dive?"

"PADI-certified Master Scuba Diver Trainer. I teach scuba and marine field studies to university students." He loved teaching, but was relegated to assisting short courses until he could get a real professorship. "I also do research on sea turtles, and dive for fun whenever I can." He assumed from her question that she was also a diver. "How about you?"

She looked away. "Um, yeah."

"I'm always looking for dive buddies," he decided to ask. "Maybe we could go out sometime. Diving, I mean."

She smiled, the first genuine smile he'd seen from her. It made her face even more captivating. "Sure, that might be fun." She looked at the house. "Can we talk inside?"

"Absolutely." He led her up the concrete stairs and gave a brief tour of the house—living room, dining room, kitchen, two bedrooms, one of them serving as an office.

They returned to the living room and she sat on the sofa. Will's heart pounded as he cleared the empty glasses and stacks of old mail off the coffee table. It pounded even harder when he sat next to her and powered up his laptop. *Get it together*, he told himself. *You're not a teenager.*

Andreia bit her lip and trained her big dark eyes on him. "Did you talk to the medical examiner about the autopsy report?"

"Yeah. She left out anything not required for the cause of death diagnosis, and said no one ever reads them anyway except the end summary, which doesn't mention anything… out of the ordinary. She said only a medical doctor would understand the rest."

Andreia smiled again, apparently relieved. "Thank you."

"Do you mind if I ask, was Galen the only member of your family with webbed hands?"

She glared at him and he regretted giving in to his curiosity.

"I thought you agreed to respect my family's privacy," she said.

Will had only agreed not to share with others, but decided not to argue the matter. "Sorry, I can't help playing scientist sometimes."

"Forget it." Her eyes filled with moisture. "We held the ceremony, but I'm still a wreck." She wiped her eyes with the back of her hand.

"My wife died two years ago and I'm still sick about it. Grief takes time to transform into acceptance, and it follows its own schedule. The sense of loss, though… I don't think that ever goes away."

"It would help me move on if I knew how he died. It's hard to think of anything else. I looked everywhere when he disappeared, talked to everyone he knew, and read all his messages, but he didn't tell anyone he was leaving, and he didn't leave any clues." She pointed at the laptop. "Could you show me where Galen was found?"

"Sure." Will opened a map program and zoomed in on Islamorada.

"What about where he died?"

Will opened his chartplotter program, which he almost never used. Then he went to NOAA's web site and looked up wind speeds, directions, currents, and tides before and during the hurricane. "The current through the Straits of Florida travels from west to east," he told her. "But the winds go east to west. The hurricane went that way too. I'll assume your brother was mostly transported on the surface, where the bottom currents would have a negligible effect. It's a reasonable assumption, given there were no, um, traces of damage on his body."

After some calculating, he drew an ellipse on the screen, south of Key Largo. "There's a lot of uncertainty, but it would be somewhere in this region."

Andreia frowned. "I don't know why he'd go there."

"Where did you last see him? Was he on a boat?"

Her lips pressed together and she didn't answer.

"Unless you narrow it down, this is the best I can do."

She bit her lip. "I don't know his destination, but he took a sled without permission two days before the hurricane, and could have traveled a long distance."

"A sled? What's that?"

She paused before answering. "Underwater electric vehicle with water jet propulsion and on-board air tanks. They're not very big—you lie on top, steer with your hands and feet, and there's a watertight space for cargo."

"Oh, an underwater scooter?"

"Sort of, but most of those—the type you hold in front—are tiny and don't have much range. These are bigger."

Sounds like something Navy SEALs might use. "Do these sleds have tracking devices, so you can find them?"

"No, otherwise I wouldn't be here."

"What do you use them for?"

She frowned. "To get around underwater, what do you think?"

Will didn't have an underwater scooter, and neither did the lab, although he could see how they'd be useful. But her answer didn't tell him anything. "What's their range?"

Andreia paused again. "They have multiple batteries that can recharge from seawater. So there's no range limit."

"They can recharge from seawater?" Will wasn't an expert on underwater vehicles, but if seawater could be used as a power source, wouldn't it be used everywhere? It seemed implausible.

She took a breath, then stared at him. "I don't know the particular chemistry, but they can travel anywhere in your circle." She indicated the ellipse on the screen.

Mysteries upon mysteries. "I assume these sleds are mostly metal?"

"Some metal, but mostly resin. Like fiberglass, but stronger and lighter."

"That will make it hard to find."

She sighed.

Will examined the chart. "If we know where he left from, when, and how fast he was going, it would help narrow down where he drowned."

"I have the date and time he left," she said, "and know the sleds can travel up to 12 knots without cargo. But that uses the batteries faster than they can be replenished. If you want to travel a long distance, you're limited to 5 knots."

That was a lot slower than his boat, but his boat was mostly above the waterline, and water was much denser than air, ergo harder to move through. "How long is a long distance?"

"At maximum speed, the batteries have a sixty-mile range. We don't usually push the motors that hard, though."

Impressive. They have to be military. "We have to think what he might have been doing. If we know where he was headed, I can draw a line between his origin and destination, then we could search along the portion of the line that falls within the ellipse." *Did I just volunteer to help search?*

"I don't know where he was going. That's part of the problem."

"Where did he leave from? Miami Beach? Key Biscayne?" If they lived in Hialeah, those were the most likely ocean access points.

She didn't respond.

What's the big secret? "Somewhere further south? I assume from Florida, right?" Andreia couldn't have driven her van from the Bahamas or Cuba.

After a couple of seconds, she said, "Biscayne Bay."

Will examined the chartplotter map. "He traveled quite a distance. Past the continental slope. Any idea why?"

"I wish I knew."

"Surely he knew a hurricane was approaching."

"It wasn't due for two more days," she said defensively.

"Then his intended trip would have been short, not all the way to, say, Cuba." He measured the distance from Biscayne Bay. "At a speed where the batteries could recharge, the seas would already be rough before he got there."

She stared at the map. "You're right, he wouldn't have tried going that far."

Will pointed at the ellipse. "I'm afraid this is the best I can do for now. If you're looking for closure, maybe focus on where he was headed and why."

"I thought this would be easier, that you'd be able to figure it all out."

"Unfortunately, real life isn't as easy as things are on TV or movies." *Especially when one side is reluctant to cooperate.*

Andreia frowned and Will regretted his statement. "Do you think he took a sled for fun and got lost?" he asked. That seemed a logical explanation. "Then got caught in the hurricane?"

"The sleds have inertial navigation computers and compasses. And he's not—wasn't—a complete idiot, even for a 15-year-old." Her defensive tone was back. "Everyone knows if you head east from somewhere, you go west to return."

"Maybe the navigation computer malfunctioned."

"If that happens, you can use the compass and clock—just stay on course, keep a constant speed, and convert distance to time. Galen knew all that. And I've never heard of a compass breaking."

"True," Will admitted. "Unless…"

"Unless what?"

"Unless he passed over some sort of magnetic anomaly."

Andreia peered at him. "I'm not sure what you mean."

"Variations in the Earth's magnetic field," he said, "like a deposit of lodestone. I don't think there's anything like that off Florida, though. At least not strong enough to alter a compass by 90 degrees or more."

Then he remembered the locally famous case of Flight 19. "You've heard of the Bermuda Triangle, I assume."

"A triangle connecting Miami, Bermuda, and Puerto Rico," she said, "where ships and aircraft disappear mysteriously. That Bermuda Triangle?"

"The exact boundaries depend on who's telling the tale. Galen's body could have drifted from inside it."

"I thought scientists considered it rubbish."

"They do. And I do. But, ever heard of Flight 19? My brother Joe—he's an engineer on an aircraft carrier now—was obsessed with it as a kid."

"You have a brother in the Navy?"

"He does reactor maintenance. Never sees the water. Anyway, just after World War II, five Avenger torpedo-bombers took off from the former Ft. Lauderdale Naval Air Station, then disappeared without a trace. Two hours into the flight, the squadron leader radioed that both his compass and back-up compass had failed, and so had those of the other planes. A search and rescue aircraft took off after them, but it disappeared too."

"What are the odds of all that happening by accident?" she asked.

"I'm not an expert on 1940's warplanes, but ten compasses all failing at once?"

From the U.S. Geological Survey's website, Will found a magnetic anomaly map. He was surprised to see how much magnetic values varied from place to place. Then he checked the map units. The variance was less than 1% from the mean, which wouldn't have much effect on a compass.

Interestingly, there was a lot of micro-variation off the Keys. *Shipwrecks?* Out of curiosity, he zoomed in more. One of the strongest anomalies—though still far too weak to affect a compass—was not far away: 15-20 miles to the south-southeast of Layton, in 125 fathoms of water.

Andreia stared at the screen, then at him. "What are you looking for?"

"Magnetic anomalies. I had no idea there was so much variation." Will rubbed his chin. "But none of it's strong enough to throw off a compass."

She examined the screen again. "How'd they make these maps?"

Will clicked a link at the bottom of the legend. "Sensors on aircraft and satellites." He examined the metadata. "They recently added declassified Defense Department data with better resolution."

Her eyes lit up. "Do you think one of those sensors could detect a sled?"

"I'd be surprised if that sort of equipment is commercially available." He looked at the metadata again. "Besides, the resolution isn't fine enough to pick up something that small and nonmetallic."

Her shoulders slumped.

Will returned to the question of *why*. "I assume you talked to whoever might have last seen your brother?"

She sighed. "Apparently, that last person was me. Galen said he wanted to move out, and I told him he couldn't."

"Move out? At age 15?"

"That's what I told him. He gets bored—" Her breath caught for a moment. "*Got* bored easily." She laid a hand on Will's arm. "It's my fault he was so adventurous. He always wanted to know where I was going and what it was like and when could he go with me."

Will tried to make sense of her statement. *What* what *was like? Where were you going?* She hadn't responded well to direct questions so far, so he tried an indirect approach. "You travel a lot, I assume?"

"Not that much. Just for work."

"Where do you work?"

"I deal in rare coins and artifacts."

That was the last thing Will would have guessed, and he found himself grinning. "Really?" *Maybe she dives shipwrecks and sells what she finds. And doesn't report it—that would explain why she's so cagey!* In Florida waters, shipwrecks belonged to the state. Will wasn't sure about international waters, but profitable salvages were usually tied up in court for years.

She smiled back. "Yes. The buyers take one look at me and think they can take advantage because I'm young, and a woman. But it's the other way around."

"You certainly have charm," Will said without thinking.

"So do you, actually."

A storm surge of heat rushed through Will and he wondered if he was blushing. Careful. She either works in the black market or she's a con artist. With access to military-grade equipment. Maybe selling treasure is just a front for what she really does.

He changed topics. "These sleds you have, where can I get one for our lab? They'd really help our reef work, being able to move farther from the boats and carry gear and samples."

She blinked. "They're custom-built. Sorry."

"Could I at least check one out sometime?"

"Maybe." She stared at the worn striped rug at her feet and stood, signaling the end of the conversation. "I should go. Can you print out that map with the area marked?"

"Sure." He sent the chart with the ellipse to the laser printer in the next room, then retrieved it for her.

"Thank you. It sounds like I might never find out what happened to my brother, though."

"Not necessarily true. Give it some time. Sometimes when you're working on another problem, a solution to your original question appears. It happens in science all the time."

She met his eyes, smiling. "Thanks. I'll give you a ride back."

They returned to her van. Will's cell phone slipped out of his pocket as he sat. *Always with these pants!*

As Andreia drove back to the lab, Will worried he might not see her again, and his many questions might never be answered. He wasn't sure if he was more concerned that his curiosity would never be satisfied, or that he'd never enjoy her company again.

On a crazy impulse, he casually muted his phone, and instead of returning it to his pocket, he surreptitiously slipped it under the seat. He felt guilty about being so sneaky, but he could track where she went with the phone finder app on his laptop. And retrieving the phone would give him an excuse to see her again.

Andreia parked in the boat lot again.

"Sorry I couldn't be of more help," Will said.

"Thanks for trying." She hugged him.

As he exited the van, Will glanced down to ensure his phone wasn't visible, then asked, "When do you want to go diving?" He could retrieve voice mails from anywhere.

Her sensual lips formed an 'O.' "I'll call you." She waved as she drove off.

* * *

Andreia

After dropping off Will at his lab in Layton, Andreia proceeded west on U.S. 1, the highway connecting the mainland to the necklace of small islands that made up the Florida Keys. Her driver's license listed a residence in Hialeah—in the opposite direction. Were anyone to check, they would find an empty lot.

Would it have helped if I hadn't lied about where Galen left from? Or lied about nearly everything? She had no choice, though. Her people's safety came above all else.

Andreia gripped the steering wheel. *Is his death my fault?* Who but the impressionable little brother of an adventure-seeking Trader would steal a sled and set off alone with bad weather coming in? *The sled.* Another wave crashed against her—she'd told Will all about their sleds, which was secret technology. *What if he tells someone?*

She tried to focus on the future rather than the unalterable past. What about the invitation to go diving with Will? *Why not keep it? He is helpful, and appreciates the marine world more than anyone else I've come across.*

And he was clearly attracted to her.

Her people said she was gorgeous, a useful attribute in a Trader. It enhanced her skills of persuasion. Even surface men found her attractive—but only because her finger webbing had been surgically removed before her move to the surface.

Regardless, she'd never dared a physical relationship with a surface man. If they saw her feet, any potential arousal would disappear as fast as a sailfish fleeing a hungry shark.

What do I do about Will? She couldn't ghost him; he knew too much. Galen's physiology. The sleds. He'd probably already guessed her feet were like Galen's.

She pushed her discomfort aside by escaping into her Land-Dweller fantasy. It was a game she sometimes played on long trips, or when feeling especially lonely. *I'm in my Porsche. I have three children, a swimming pool, a yacht, and a husband who worships me.*

But lately, the game offered little comfort, and failed to lift her spirits. In truth, she was relieved not to be a Land-Dweller, too many of whom were vapid, selfish destroyers of the beautiful earth. Her feet straddled two worlds, but she fit into neither.

Andreia drove past a large complex of battered vacation cottages, then onto one of the long, low bridges between islands. The sky was blue with scattered clouds, the shallow water bluish-green. Small groups of people fished from the pedestrian walkway to the left of the two-lane road.

They appreciate the ocean. So do the beach crowds. Why, then, do so many treat it as a dumpster?

She passed the turnoff to the Medical Examiner's office and turned left onto a curving road, following it nearly to the end. While the truck idled, she unlocked the gate of a tall wooden fence, pulled into a heavily wooded property and rebolted the gate behind her. She parked under the Australian pines and mangroves in front of a small two-bedroom house. It served her clan, the Mazi, who had acquired the property using a shell corporation. It was their trading outpost.

One of the pine trees had fallen on top of her small boat, crushing it. But the house was intact—it was built to withstand anything short of a missile strike. She punched the entry code into the keypad and entered the house.

The heavy curtains admitted only dim light through the thick, bullet-proof polycarbonate windows. The air was stale and hot inside, so she switched on the overhead fan. Tall shelf units lined the tiled living room, filled with books and artifacts she and her predecessors had collected. A wicker sofa and a matching coffee table faced a wide-screen TV, hooked to a satellite dish on the roof. Diving gear and watertight dry bags covered most of the floor space.

There wasn't much for her to do at the house, except wait for more buy or sell orders. And since she was the only current resident and never had visitors, it was a lonely place. *Stefan warned me about that.*

Land-Dwellers had fascinated Andreia since early childhood. Internet videos depicted their world as vast and glamorous. She'd clung like a remora to Stefan, the clan Trader at the time, begging him to take her to Florida with him. Eventually, he—and her parents—finally relented. Enraptured by that taste of freedom, she'd talked Stefan into an apprenticeship, and had eventually replaced him. Lately, the bouts of boredom and loneliness had given her second thoughts.

Andreia kicked off her homemade shoes, which she absolutely hated. She uncurled her long toes and spread open the webbing between. Feet relaxing in freedom, she dropped the car keys on the coffee table, plopped onto the sofa, and switched on the TV.

A news anchor was in the middle of a story. "No suspects have been named yet, but the Saudi government said that they are pursuing leads…"

Andreia switched to one of the music video channels, Tempo Dance Hits. Normally, she sang along and replicated the moves. She wasn't in the mood, though, and went into the kitchen to make a tuna sandwich.

She had to know how her brother died. Something had happened to him, and it probably wasn't a simple accident. In her mind, she drew a line between Galen's real point of departure and the ellipse Will had drawn on the computer. She'd follow that line and look for any sign of the sled. What else could she do?

When night fell, Andreia took off her dress and hung it in the bedroom closet next to her other surface clothes. She tossed her bra and panties atop the pile of dirty clothes next to the bed. She put on her black bikini and strapped a dive knife to her calf, then slipped on her swimming gloves. They were custom-formed and painted to resemble real Sea-Dweller hands as closely as possible. At a casual glance, other Sea Dwellers couldn't tell she'd been mutilated.

She exited and locked the house, and followed a narrow trail between the mangroves, which were otherwise completely impenetrable if you were bigger than a crab. The short pathway ended at a narrow, canopy-covered channel that led out to one of the boat canals that crisscrossed the island. Andreia slipped into the warm water. Her bare skin reveled in its caress.

Her sled rested on its skids at the bottom of the dark, muddy water, beneath a sandy white camouflage tarp cut from sailcloth. She took a deep breath, closed her mouth and nostril flaps, and dove the short distance to the sled. The channel water was murky from suspended silt. Even though she had perfect vision underwater—even in dim light—she could only see a few feet.

Andreia pushed the rocks off the tarp edges and rolled up the sailcloth. Beneath, the sled was painted ocean blue—darker on the top, lighter on the bottom. It was about three meters long, with a rounded nose, glass shield to deflect water away from the pilot's eyes, a contoured rubber deck to lie on, and a long, cylindrical jet-pump motor on each side. A rudder in back controlled horizontal movement, and flaps controlled vertical direction and pitch.

Beneath the deck, multiple sets of batteries sat inside the streamlined hull. The sled had two rebreathers, two air tanks, and two oxygen-only tanks, with built-in compressors and membrane gas separators. The rebreathers absorbed carbon dioxide and recycled the nitrogen and unused oxygen, while adding more oxygen as needed. As an added benefit, they didn't produce air bubbles, which could reveal her presence. Andreia could hold her breath for half an hour when not exerting herself, and usually reserved the rebreathers for deep water.

Andreia stuffed the rolled-up tarp in the bow storage compartment, then lay atop the sled. She pushed the power button and checked the indicator gauges to ensure everything was working properly. Once satisfied, she entered her starting and destination coordinates into the inertial navigation computer. It didn't save any information when the power was turned off; while inconvenient, it prevented sensitive locations from falling into the wrong hands.

She purged ballast water until the sled was neutrally buoyant and the skids lifted slightly off the bottom. Gripping the twist throttle and buoyancy control on the steering bar, she eased out of the mangroves and into the adjacent canal.

Then she headed for home—her real home.

Chapter 5

Will

As Will re-entered the main lab building, he cursed his impetuous decision to bug Andreia's van.

"Where were you?" the lab receptionist asked.

"Left something at the house."

She didn't pursue it, and Will went up to his office. He closed the door and brought up the phone tracking program on his laptop.

The GPS display showed the van moving west on U.S. 1. Not east, toward Hialeah. He watched as the dot turned left when it reached Marathon, then followed the road as it curved back east. It stopped, then exited the road.

Will brought up satellite imagery, which showed an island created from dredge material but only partly developed. His phone—presumably still in Andreia's van—stopped next to a small, isolated house surrounded by 4 to 5 acres of trees with canals on three sides. The imagery showed a boat on a trailer in front of the house, but no dock, ramp, or other water access. *Makes no sense. Why have waterfront property and a boat, but no place to put it in the water?*

He decided to wait until the end of the day before investigating in person.

* * *

Andreia

Andreia touched the end of her nose and bowed to her relatives gathered in the small forest clearing. "Grazi itas merid." *Thank you for coming.*

Used for discussions, meditation, and classes, the clearing was carpeted with soft moss, punctuated with seedlings and grass tufts that had found opportunities to root and needed periodic removal. To her right, painted limestone statues of a man, a woman holding a baby, and a child stood with linked hands. They didn't represent anyone in particular; rather, the clan as a whole.

The clearing was surrounded by large trees covered with vines and bromeliads, slender palms, and layers of tree ferns, shrubs, and ground plants. Parrots, parakeets, and songbirds squawked, chirped, and whistled from the trees. Insects buzzed through the humid air, and water rippled down a nearby brook. Sea-Dwellers had a poor sense of smell compared to Land-Dwellers, but the flowers, leaves, and moist soils gave off a faint earthy scent that Andreia liked.

Andreia and her ten relatives sat in a circle on bamboo chairs. Her mother, Diasiaka, Mazi by birth, showed few signs of age, and wore the grease-stained, dark-gray coveralls of a mechanical technician. Her father, Nauti, originally from the far-off Widin clan, had cast aside his painter's smock for a *prothos*— a traditional vest and kilt. The others included uncles, aunts, and cousins, all adults in good health.

Andreia turned on her laptop and showed them the map Will had generated. "The supply commission has authorized the use of six sleds. Who would like to come with me to find Galen's sled?"

Her uncle Thanost placed a hand against his heart. "Galen is gone from us. We must accept that. We have already searched for explanations—it was the top priority of the entire clan—but we are unlikely to learn anything else."

Andreia's jaw clenched in irritation. Thanost had always thought her overly impulsive and childish. Why did she have to constantly prove herself to people?

"Galen's death makes no sense," she said. "I have to know what happened." *Or my mind will be trapped forever.* "We must do this for him. We are family." For her, as his older sibling and the person he most looked up to, the obligation was stronger than barnacle glue.

"What if the sled malfunctioned?" her aunt Sophia asked Thanost. "What if that contributed to Galen's death? We wouldn't want that to happen to someone else."

"True," he admitted.

Andreia's mother reached over and held her hand. "We support you, all of us, even my argumentative brother."

Thanost grunted.

"Who will search with me?" Andreia asked again. It meant days away from home and work, and in some cases, children.

"We will stay beneath the surface, I assume?" Thanost said.

"Of course. We're searching the bottom. No Land-Dwellers will see us that deep."

All ten—even her uncle Thanost—placed fist against heart, signaling assent. Andreia hadn't expected unanimous support, although maybe she should have. Tears of gratitude sprang into her eyes. Her relatives nagged her incessantly to train a replacement Trader and return home to bear children—supposedly her most important duty as a woman. But now they showed how much they all loved her and supported her.

"Thank you. I wish we had that many sleds available." She picked five of the volunteers: her parents, her aunt Sophia—one of the best dolphin communicators in the clan—and her cousins Kuane and Saba, who were young and strong. "The rest of you can come next time if needed."

* * *

Will

Will's phone still hadn't moved by 5:00, so he walked home to get his truck, skipping the usual beers and dinner at the Tequila Sunrise. It was about a twenty-minute drive to where Andreia had stopped. He brought his laptop so he could keep tracking her if necessary—there were plenty of free Wi-Fi hotspots in Marathon.

Will had prepared a cover story in case Andreia was there. He ran through the basics. I lost my phone. I looked everywhere and couldn't find it, but then I turned on the tracker on my laptop and saw it was at this location. It must have fallen out of my pocket; I hate it when that happens.

He was greeted by a tall wooden fence with a locked gate and a NO TRESPASSING sign. No buzzer or intercom, not even a mailbox. No vehicles parked on the road. The fence was taller than his hands could reach, with nothing to grip and no overhanging trees.

Will knocked on the gate. No one came.

Now what? He returned to his truck and scribbled a quick note, 'Think I dropped my phone in your van.' He added his email address and stuffed the note between the two halves of the gate.

He drove back to U.S. 1 and pulled up to a nearby seafood restaurant with Wi-Fi coverage. The food there was at least a notch or two above the Tequila Sunrise, so he might as well take advantage.

The restaurant wasn't crowded, and he took a booth seat so he could work semi-privately. It also had a clear view of the TV over the bar.

As his laptop was starting, a waitress arrived. "Can I start you off with something to drink?"

"Channel Marker."

Her face formed a pout. "I'm sorry, we don't have that."

He named some other local beers and finally settled for a Corona with lime. As soon as the waitress departed, he brought up the tracking program.

His phone still hadn't moved from the mystery house. *Maybe she lives there and lied about Hialeah.* It was about as off the beaten path in the Keys as you could get and still have highway access. *But why lie about it?*

The TV was tuned to cable news and had caught the attention of the people sitting at the bar. Will couldn't hear it, but the banner beneath the talking heads read, 'STOCK MARKETS TO REMAIN CLOSED.'

Another recession on the way. Will didn't give a crap about Saudi Arabia, a harsh feudal dictatorship with too much global power. But recessions meant cutbacks and people would lose jobs. The state would probably freeze funding to the Marine Lab, or even reduce it.

Will ordered freshly-caught grouper, grilled, with rice and sautéed vegetables, along with another Corona. While he waited for his food, he pulled up the Monroe County Property Appraiser web site and entered the address Andreia had parked at.

The property report listed the owner as RZA REAL ESTATE, LLC. The lot was listed as unimproved, even though aerial photos showed a house on site. *Strange.*

Will looked up RZA Real Estate and found they were owned by RZA Investments LLC. This company in turn was owned by Blue-Tang Group LLC, with an address in the Cayman Islands. Will chuckled. It sounded like someone had combined a reef fish name with the hip-hop group Wu-Tang Clan. He searched for more information about Blue-Tang Group, but there was nothing publicly available. *A front for someone, somewhere.*

Having hit a dead end, he searched the Internet for people with webbed hands and feet. The closest he could find was an inherited birth defect called syndactyly, but it was entirely different—two fingers or toes fused together. He found nothing resembling Galen's webbing, extending all the way to the top joints yet allowing full finger flexibility. He hadn't seen Andreia's feet, but her brother's looked almost like flippers. It was like he belonged to an entirely different species.

Will's food arrived. By the time he was finished, his phone still hadn't moved, so he headed home. *I'll try a different approach next time.*

* * *

Andreia

The next morning, Andreia awaited the search crew at the rendezvous point: the southeast corner of the tidal generator array. Large camouflaged funnels, anchored to the sea floor, directed moving water across turbine blades. Heavy screens prevented fish and other organisms from being sucked inside.

The volunteers had prepped six sleds for an extended trip, and each wore an insulated suit. The water was warm at the array, but once they ventured below the thermocline at 200 meters or so, temperatures would drop to 20 °C—not exactly cold, but cool enough to suck the heat from their bodies.

Andreia's cousins arrived first, then her parents. They communicated with hand signs—a primeval, complex language that Sea-Dwellers began learning in infancy.

Finally, her aunt Sophia descended from shallower depths, accompanied by a pod of bottlenose dolphins. Sea-Dwellers had partnered with dolphins and other marine mammals since before recorded time, with each clan cultivating close relationships with the populations in their territory.

Sophia signaled with her hands, #The dolphins will help as much as they can.#

Andreia's mother led the sacrifice ritual. Andreia doubted such rituals could actually help their search, but kept her opinion to herself. They each held something of value—a bracelet, a food delicacy, a statuette… Andreia had brought the silver hand mirror Stefan had gifted her on the first day of her Trader apprenticeship. It was for studying her microexpressions, but she'd long ago mastered them, and now the mirror was merely a keepsake. Her mother waved the ancient sign-language incantations, then they released their treasures. They pirouetted to the sea floor, never to be retrieved.

Lying on their sleds, the group ascended to ten meters to reduce decompression time, then headed at maximum speed to the area Will had circled. Once there, they descended to the bottom and fanned out, barely within sight of each other.

The dimly-lit seafloor was a mosaic of sand and eroded carbonate, colonized by tubeworms, sponges, and deep corals. The fish community was sparser and less diverse than in shallow waters—which Andreia much preferred, even though it broke her heart to witness the inexorable death of the coral reefs from bleaching, acidification, and disease.

An adult dolphin approached and swam next to her, making squeaking and clicking noises. The twin mammary slits revealed it to be female.

Andreia had never mastered dolphin communication, having been more focused on learning everything possible about Land-Dwellers. She clicked her tongue against the roof of her mouth, indicating that she didn't understand. Then she undulated her hand toward her barely visible aunt Sophia and made the sound for "go there."

The dolphin shook her head and swam loops around Andreia as if bored, then swam off toward Sophia. Andreia followed on the sled.

Sophia exchanged grating throat noises with the dolphin, then flashed hand signals to Andreia. #Too deep for dolphins here.#

It would only get deeper. Most of the search area was below 200 meters, and even though dolphins could dive deeper than this, they couldn't stay down long before needing more air. Andreia signaled, #Tell them they can leave. Thank them for helping.#

After the dolphin left, Andreia signaled her aunt, #Thank you for joining me.#

#Of course. We are family.#

Andreia started to grow hungry. They'd brought food—nutritious but bland mush inside squeeze packets—but Andreia hoped to reserve that until necessary.

She scanned the nearby sea bottom until she spotted a flounder. *Delicious.* She stopped the sled and unhooked her speargun, which was powered by compressed air. She pointed the gun at the flounder and pulled the trigger. Trailing line, the spear impaled the fish. She reeled it in.

She slid her dive knife into the struggling flounder's brain. *Thank you for giving your life so I may eat. I honor your memory.* She cleaned it with her knife and ate the flesh raw. She swallowed some seawater in the process, but her kidneys were adapted to handle it.

Hunger pangs gone, she dropped the carcass to the bottom, where fish and crabs would feast on it. In a few days at most, nothing would remain but bones, and even those would eventually dissolve.

Andreia and her relatives searched methodically for Galen's sled all day without success. When night fell, they gradually ascended to ten meters again. They inflated the balloons of their air snorkels—long hoses with waterproof intakes on the top—and released them to the surface to recharge their oxygen tanks. They slept beneath the waves until sunrise.

They gulped down nourishment from squeeze packets and resumed the search. Shortly before dusk, Andreia heard loud tics—a team member beyond visual range tapping a message on their sled. They'd found something!

Andreia and the others hurried toward the source of the tapping. It was her cousin Kuane. He waved his arms. Just past him was an abandoned sled, of Mazi design. *The one Galen took?* They all looked the same, but only one was missing.

Everyone gathered around the abandoned sled, flashing hand signs to each other. Andreia examined the sled, which had a big dent on the bow. The regulators and hoses were intact, with no rips or punctures. She pressed the power button, but nothing happened; the batteries were dead. The compass was pointing in the correct direction, so Galen shouldn't have gotten lost.

Andreia laid a hand on the bow dent, which was coated with grit. *Collision with the sea floor, most likely.* Memories of her brother flashed before her— celebrating his birth, the festivities on his naming day, the lessons she taught him, their travels together… Her stomach cramped and her arms shuddered. She screamed into the dark blue water.

Her parents pressed outstretched hands to her and began to cry. Andreia collapsed in their arms.

Chapter 6

Andreia

After a pause to regain their composure, Andreia and her relatives conferred.

#It looks like he was forced to abandon the sled# Andreia signaled. One drawback of Mazi sign language, even though it was nearly as comprehensive as their spoken language, was a lack of personal names. She didn't need to trace Galen's name in the water, though—it was obvious.

#Then he was caught on the surface by the hurricane?# Kuane asked.

Andreia was unable to answer. Her father responded instead. #Thus it appears.#

#Let's return#, Andreia proposed. #I'll tow the sled back.#

* * *

Will

Will's phone still hadn't moved by the weekend, and its battery was probably almost dead. At this point, he felt pretty damn foolish. He wished he could unwind his boneheaded move. But stuck in this uncomfortable reality, he had to retrieve his phone somehow.

He loaded his boat, took it into the bay, and headed southwest. The weather was nice, partly sunny with minimal wind and no chop. Even if the phone retrieval was a bust, he could get in some fishing. *What if Andreia's trying to call me right now? What a disaster.*

He continued south beneath the highway bridge and entered the Atlantic. After another four miles, he took another channel into the network of canals where Andreia apparently lived.

The starboard shore of the main canal was covered by dense mangroves. The port side had been converted to dredge-and-fill properties with water access, but it appeared mostly vacant near the channel entrance.

He pulled into the canal on the east border of the RZA Real Estate property where Andreia had parked. The shore was a solid wall of trees.

Near the house location, he spotted a small channel entering the mangroves. It was too narrow for his boat. He dropped anchor, pulled off his

T-shirt, and jumped in the water with the bow line. He tied the boat to a tree trunk and swam into the channel.

The water was deep and overhung by branches. After a short distance, the bottom sloped sharply upward and ended in a muddy trail through the dense trees. The thick canopy shrouded the footpath in shadow.

Will followed the trail to a patchy clearing covered with broken branches and leaves. In the center stood the house visible in the satellite imagery, a single-story white bungalow squatting atop concrete blocks. Andreia's white van was parked out front. Beyond, a small boat had been crushed by a storm-toppled Australian pine.

As he approached the house, he noticed all the curtains were drawn, and security cameras had been positioned beneath the gutters. The roof was covered with solar panels, and a small satellite dish was perched on one end. He saw no phone, cable, or power lines. *Completely off the grid and as hidden as you can get.* A doorbell camera and a keypad—usually found on rentals—was mounted by the front door.

I'm trespassing and acting like a creep. But I'm here now, and I'm almost certainly being recorded. He took a deep breath and rang the doorbell.

No answer. No dogs barked either.

He rang the doorbell again, then knocked.

Still no answer.

Will knocked on the door one last time, then went to the van and peered inside. The passenger door was unlocked—not surprising, considering its inaccessibility and minimal resale value. He made a show of searching for his phone, then retrieved it from beneath the seat. The battery was almost dead.

He returned to his boat and plugged his phone into the console to charge it. *Where's Andreia? Her van's here. Either she walked somewhere, or took one of those underwater sleds.* He resisted the urge to search for the sled. *I should get out of here.*

Will drove his boat back to the ocean. Before heading home, he decided to check out some of the magnetic anomalies he'd shown Andreia, ones that didn't correspond to known shipwrecks. *Maybe that's where she is, following up.*

The strongest anomaly was 20 miles to the southeast, in 125 fathoms of water. Recreational divers were limited to 130 feet, or 22 fathoms. But with the right equipment and training, people could go much deeper. He suspected Andreia and her family had both, especially if they indeed salvaged shipwrecks for a living.

He entered the location into the GPS and pushed down the throttle. The twin engines whined as the boat lurched onto a plane and cut across the calm surface.

It took about 40 minutes to reach the location. Will pulled back the throttle and the boat settled into a slow crawl, the motors gurgling. He switched on his fish finder sonar and set it to ping at 50 kHz, which was better able to penetrate deep water than higher frequencies.

Disappointingly, the sonar showed nothing unusual. The bottom varied, but nothing strange popped out.

A group of bottlenose dolphins broke the surface next to the boat and swam next to it, occasionally leaping partway out of the water and eyeing him.

Will almost waved to them. He'd always loved dolphins—everyone seemed to. Maybe because they had a permanent smile, were playful and sociable, and were one of the smartest animals on the planet. His fish finder showed them moving beneath the boat also.

Then it detected a large object—maybe ten feet long—moving far below. Another dolphin? More likely a nurse shark. But what if it's one of those sleds Andreia mentioned?

He turned to follow the object. It dropped to the bottom and stopped moving.

What now? It was too deep to dive—he'd need trimix and a buddy. He saved the position on his GPS and kept poking around.

After about an hour, he gave up and headed northeast to a subsurface mound that made a good fishing spot. Two of the dolphins accompanied him, riding the bow waves on either side, leaping in and out of the water.

He dropped the boat into neutral and cast a couple of lures. "Go away," he shouted to the dolphins. They wouldn't go after his lures, but they'd almost certainly eat any fish he hooked.

The dolphins kept shadowing him until he reeled in his lines and headed in.

* * *

Andreia

Standing before the Council of Elders in the Assembly Chamber, with half the clan in attendance, Andreia was more nervous than she had ever been in her life. Her nose muscles clenched her nostrils shut—not just an involuntary diving adaptation, but an idiotic fear reaction too. She had to focus to keep them open.

The Assembly Chamber was a large circular room adjacent to the living quarters. The curving walls and support arches had been decorated nine decades ago with depictions of nearby reefs: colorful corals and fish populating the bottom half, and blue water with circling dolphins, sharks, and pelagic fish above. The real reefs were nearly dead now, and the fish far less abundant—an inexcusable Land-Dweller crime that her people profoundly resented, but deemed themselves powerless to prevent.

The chamber was ringed by tiered limestone benches, painted to fit the wall tableau. The twelve Elders, clad in silk ceremonial robes and necklaces of coral, shells, and shark teeth, sat in the section before Andreia. Around eighty other adults, wearing their finest clothes and ornaments, sat to either side. They included her parents, maternal grandparents, and other close relatives. The others were also related by blood or marriage, although distantly. Even with over half the clan present, the room felt empty—the Mazi were once far more numerous: over 400 when the habitat was constructed, and in the thousands in ancient times.

Stefan, her predecessor as clan Trader, had come, sitting with his much younger, visibly pregnant wife, Sijaesiaka. Stefan and Andreia had kept in touch after he switched jobs. He met her eyes and clasped his hands—which were webbed again—indicating his full support.

Andreia touched her nose in thanks. His wife scowled. *Ever jealous, even though Stefan and I haven't had relations in years.*

Andreia's mother smiled and waved an arm. Andreia started to wave back, but one of the Elders rang the ancient brass bell that signaled the start of the meeting. The clan Historian, a man with silver-streaked hair, sang tenor-pitched verses from one of the sagas everyone knew, about the mythical arrival of the first clans to the Americas, long before writing was invented. Andreia joined the others in singing the refrains, loudly enough for the Elders to hear her.

The bell sounded again. This month's First Speaker, an Elder woman named Kitane, stood and scanned the crowd. Her thick gray hair was braided with small seashells, and her wrinkled bronze skin adorned with tattoos. She opened her palms. "Thank you all for coming. We gather today in the tradition of our ancestors, where all voices are equal..."

Some more equal than others, Andreia thought. The Elders ran the meetings, and, with no other jobs, had more available time to prepare for them.

After finishing the ceremonial preamble, Kitane said, "I will now summarize the facts according to video recordings and the recollections of those present."

She read from a sheet of handmade paper. "Andreia, Trader of the Mazi Clan, initiated a friendship with a Land-Dweller marine scientist named Will Myers in an effort to learn how her brother Galen died. Will Myers showed excessive curiosity about our people, trying to elicit information from Andreia. The cameras at our trading post showed that he then entered the property, apparently accessing it by boat; knocked on the house door, and searched the vehicle that Andreia uses for land travel. He then piloted his boat to our home area and deployed sonar equipment. We heard the propellers of his boat and detected the sonar signals, and asked our dolphin friends to surveil him. The dolphins later matched the boat pilot's face to a website photograph of Will Myers."

Kitane put down the paper. "Speaking is now open to all, in the manner of our ancestors, until we determine a collective course of action." She cupped her hands and sat, ending her turn.

The Mazi clan, and most other Sea-Dweller clans, reached decisions by consensus. But the *okonoi*—adults of reproductive age—would ultimately defer to the Elders, who had accumulated more experience, knowledge, and wisdom—at least in theory.

The calcite-haired, stern-looking Elder named Meltha stood and fixed Andreia with piercing eyes. She wore golden necklaces and earrings crafted from the clan's remaining stock of salvaged shipwreck treasure. Meltha was one of the oldest members of the clan, and one whose opinions were hard to budge.

"Grief at losing a loved one is understandable," Meltha said. "But you allowed your grief to control you, and put our entire clan, and perhaps Sea-Dwellers everywhere, in danger."

Andreia placed a hand over her heart. "I'm sorry. I did inform you when the house cameras alerted me."

"Will Myers is not a treasure broker, nor a provider of technology. You should not have contacted him again after retrieving Galen's body."

Andreia glared at the woman. Meltha had never set foot on land, and had no business trying to micromanage her. Although it was true she'd screwed up. "I apologize again. But if not for Dr. Myers, we wouldn't have found his sled."

"Was that worth the consequences?" one of the other Elders asked.

Andreia had even more questions than before. Why did Galen travel so far? Why did he let the batteries drain?

Kitane stood again. "So that all know," she addressed Andreia, "can you explain the magnetic detectors?"

Andreia repeated her explanation about magnetic anomaly flights by the Land-Dwellers, and how the Mazi home appeared on a map. "I told the metallurgy engineer"—who was in the audience—"and she said she'd confer with other clans about a solution."

A man to Andreia's left stood. "Will we have to move?"

"That remains to be determined," Kitane replied.

The metallurgy engineer stood. "I apologize for the oversight," she said in a stuffy nostril-clenched voice. She exhaled forcefully. "Land-Dwellers have developed more sensitive equipment, and our demagnetizing and shielding is decades-old. We are working on an upgrade."

"And what if more intruders come?" the man to Andreia's left asked. "We should move."

"A massive undertaking," Kitane reminded him. "And one that must be done with great stealth."

Meltha addressed Andreia. "This surface contact of yours, was he acting on his own or on behalf of others? He works for a Land-Dweller government, which is worrisome."

"Dr. Myers is a man of science who studies sea life," Andreia said. "He works for a university, not the police or military." *He's friends with the county medical examiner, though. And he has a brother in the Navy.*

Xitaros, a gray-haired, diminutive Elder, stood, anger on his face. Xitaros had been the chief opponent of appointing Andreia as clan Trader, claiming she was too young and unreliable. Stefan—who'd battled the man for twenty years—had disputed that, testifying that Andreia's perception and persuasion skills were even better than his. The majority of Elders had accepted Stefan's endorsement, and voted her in.

Xitaros fingered the necklace of shark teeth he wore everywhere. Supposedly they'd come from a dead shark whose dorsal fin had been slashed off for the soup trade. "You have put us all in danger. We should never have allowed a so-called 'freethinker,' someone polluted by Land-Dweller culture, to be our representative on the surface."

Plugged anus of a barnacle! Andreia yearned to shout it out loud.

Stefan leapt to his feet. "As usual, Xitaros, you have no idea what you're talking about. You have to know Land-Dweller culture to make deals with them."

Her father joined the defense. "Family and clan come first for Andreia!"

"Another part of the problem," Xitaros replied. "Family before clan? We are all family. Lineage closeness should not matter, but Andreia put her feelings for her brother before the safety of the clan."

"Not true," Andreia interrupted. "I put clan safety first, as I always do. And I never once called myself a freethinker." Although she had much more in common with the freethinkers at Aux than she did with the Elders here at Katiki, with their slavish adherence to Bronze Age traditions. Her independence and "adventurous streak," as her parents put it, were essential for her job.

"I was not done speaking," Xitaros said.

Here, Andreia was supposed to bow in apology, but that might imply he was right about his accusations too. Instead, she cupped her hands together in receiving mode.

"Why do we need to interact with Land-Dwellers at all?" he continued. "They are dangerous."

"We can't manufacture microchips, for starters," Stefan responded. They argued until the blaring of a conch shell quieted the room. Nanitaan, this month's Signaler, kept blowing the horn until everyone resumed their seats.

Meltha stood and broke the embarrassed silence. "Let us focus on our most immediate task. We must know what Will Myers knows, what he has told others, and what his intentions are."

The other Elders nodded.

The discussion continued another two hours, with no further need for order enforcement. Finally, a consensus was reached.

By tradition, the First Speaker was also the last. "I will now recite our collective decision," she said. "The clan shall prepare a relocation plan in case it becomes necessary. Andreia shall return to the surface and question Will Myers. We must know why he sought us out, what information he gleaned, and what he passed to others."

Thankfully, the Speaker said nothing about appointing a new Trader. Andreia placed open hands next to her ears and bowed, bound by the collective command of her clan and angry that Will had put her in such a position.

* * *

Will

At work on Monday, Will received a news alert saying the president had announced a state of emergency. Anxiety roiling his gut, he clicked the link to the press conference.

"I have directed our intelligence and law enforcement agencies," the president announced, "to intensify their cybersecurity mitigation to prevent attacks on American interests such as the crippling event in Saudi Arabia. I have made every resource we have at their disposal."

That sounds reasonable, Will thought. Unless it means more surveillance of ordinary Americans.

"To control inflation," the president continued, "keep our country out of recession, and keep Americans employed, emergency measures will also facilitate oil and gas drilling and pipeline construction by waiving burdensome review processes. We need those resources as soon as possible, as do our allies. I am also working with our friends in Congress to provide funding for a coal liquefaction program. We have abundant coal resources in this country, not only for electricity generation, but to produce methanol and gasoline. There are already fifteen coal-to-liquid-fuel plants on the books that were never built. This funding will allow them to go forward."

Will banished the news window. *Morons!* So much for trying to slow climate change—now the president and Congress were flagrantly accelerating it. A scan of the web showed that other major countries were doing the same thing. Throwing away the future for short-term politics.

Furious, he went out to the second-floor balcony and stared at the placid blue-green waters of Florida Bay. Once his mind was clear, he returned to his office and pulled up a work in progress on the neurological effects of red tide brevetoxins. He and his colleagues planned to submit their findings to the journal *Aquatic Toxicology*.

A little after 4:00, Will was interrupted by a phone call from his dad.

He sounded angry. "I lost a fortune today, thanks to you! I should have known better to listen to someone who studies turtles for a living."

"What are you talking about?"

"Investing in renewable energy. The stock market re-opened at noon today. Fossil fuel stocks jumped upward and renewable energy stocks dropped."

"That's because the president's an empty-headed jackalope," Will said. "Don't worry, it's just a blip." *I sincerely hope.*

"Blip my ass."

"Sorry. I don't know what else to say."

"The people who invested in that new cryptocurrency, Currentsea," his dad said, "are the ones doing the best. That's what I should have done."

"Currentsea? Never heard of it. Sure it's not a scam?"

"Not according to the financial reporters."

They talked about the weather and sports for a while, then Will said he had to go.

At five, he shut down the computer. *Happy hour time.* He said goodbye to those colleagues still in the office, but as usual, didn't get any takers to join him at the Tequila Sunrise. The other full-timers had to commute and the visitors were too busy.

To his surprise, Will spotted Andreia's white van parked across the street, in the parking lot of Layton's tiny post office. She waved.

It's like we're stalking each other. His stomach tightened. *Am I busted? Did she see the house camera video? I can't believe I did that. Better dust off my cover story.*

He walked across the street to the van. Andreia opened the passenger door and he got in.

"Hi, Will. How have you been?" She didn't look angry, so maybe she didn't know about his trespassing.

"Fine. I assume you're waiting for me and not here to buy stamps?"

"I wanted to thank you for your help. We found the sled Galen took." She started to smile, then her lips slid downward.

"You did? Where was it?"

"In the ellipse you drew, along the direction from his origin. It took a while, but we found it."

"I was on my way to grab some dinner," he said. "You're welcome to join me."

Her lips pressed together, then she said, "Won't all your friends want to know who I am? Why you're having dinner with me?" She smiled.

"You are a head-turner."

"Thank you. So are you." Her eyes scanned his face. "You have a strong jaw, like a statue of a warrior. But blue eyes. You're the only person I know with blue eyes."

"Now I really want to have dinner with you. We can go wherever you want."

"How about takeout? We can talk in private that way."

Not the answer he was hoping for. "Layton only has one place to eat, unless you don't mind convenience store sandwiches."

"Sandwiches are fine. I'm not a foodie."

Ugh. Will pointed west. "Take a left on U.S. 1, and it's less than a quarter-mile on the left. Tan two-story building with a "Grab-N-Go" sign.

"I've seen it." She started the van.

The drive took only a minute. "Coming in?" Will asked as he opened the passenger door.

"I trust you to pick something edible. No dairy products, please."

As the only store in Layton, the Grab-N-Go was fairly sizable, containing several aisles of food, a halfway decent stock of beer and wine, and a bait & tackle section. They also sported a collection of bongs, flavored cigarettes, and every hemp product imaginable. Will had smoked a lot of weed growing up in Key West, but quit when starting grad school—it stunted his motivation and was bad for the lungs.

Will scanned the contents of the sandwich cooler. The chicken subs had no cheese. He grabbed a couple and proceeded to the booze section.

Does Andreia drink? And if so, what? In Will's experience, most women seemed to prefer white wine. His wife had been a beer drinker like him, but she was somewhat an exception.

Will didn't know the first thing about wine, so he picked a bottle more or less at random, with a screw-off top rather than a cork, and bought a couple of plastic wine glasses—slightly classier than paper cups.

He returned to the van. "Where to?"

"Across the street?"

There was a grassy strip on the other side of the highway that slanted down to the water. Layton was small, but it had plenty of ocean views. Andreia moved the van there and parked facing the blue-green water. The clouds were gray, but not dark enough for rain yet.

Will handed her a sub and opened the bottle of wine.

She stared at him. "Wine?"

"I didn't know what else to get."

She accepted one of the plastic glasses. "I'm a lightweight, so make it small."

Will filled her glass halfway, and his the same.

"That isn't small," she said.

"It's only half full."

"But these are big glasses."

Realizing his mistake, Will apologized. "Sorry. You don't have to drink it."

She waved his apology away and took a small sip.

He tapped his glass to hers. "Cheers."

"Cheers." She took another small sip, then a bite of sandwich. "Good enough."

"We should get real food sometime. My treat." A wave of guilt hit him. He was flagrantly pursuing a woman who'd just lost her brother. And that was the least of his sins. "I have an embarrassing story to tell you."

Andreia put her sandwich down and stared at him. "Yes?"

Will launched his cover story of losing his phone and tracking it to a spot near Marathon. "It was behind a huge fence, with no buzzer or anything. I left a note, but no one ever responded."

She kept a neutral face and didn't speak, apparently waiting for him to finish.

"I waited a couple of days, then decided to try from the water side next time I went fishing. I saw your van there, in front of a house. No one answered the door, but thankfully the van was unlocked and I found my phone. I must have dropped it."

Andreia tapped a finger. "Did you try calling your phone as soon as you realized it was missing?"

"To listen for the ring? I only have one phone, so I couldn't; I used the tracking program instead."

"Well," Andreia said, "I'm glad you were able to recover it. Did you leave a note? I didn't see one in the van anywhere."

"No, sorry. I was trespassing, to be honest, and wanted to leave as fast as possible."

Andreia nodded. "Did you catch any fish, at least?"

Will let out a breath. He'd gotten past the phone fiasco. "Got skunked. A pair of dolphins followed me around and scared off all the fish."

"Maybe they were just being friendly." She edged closer. "Have you talked to anyone about me or Galen? Family or friends, maybe?"

Will felt a collision imminent, approaching in slow motion but with too much momentum to avoid. "No, I promised I wouldn't. You can trust me to keep any secrets you might have."

"Trust," she said, "is one of the rarest commodities on the planet." She gulped from her cup of wine, grimacing as it went down.

It's not that bad, is it?

She put the wine cup on the dashboard and stared at him. "Did you take your boat to the magnetic anomaly you noticed on the map, the one that's 15 miles offshore?"

The directness was unexpected. "Yes. I was curious after our conversation. How did you know?"

"I was told about it. Your boat and fishfinder make a lot of noise. Did you find anything interesting there?"

Will decided not to mention the sled he'd possibly detected. "Normal seafloor, that's it. I was hoping for an uncharted wreck, even a sea mound." He changed topics. "Those dolphins shadowed me for three hours. That's a long time. Do your people work with dolphins?" *Maybe they're with the Navy's Marine Mammal Program.*

Her face grew tense. "You ask a lot of questions."

"Of course I do. I'm a scientist. It's in my nature." Andreia didn't seem dangerous—but Will didn't have much experience with criminals. And what about other family members or associates? If she sold salvaged valuables on the black market, she might be connected to organized crime. Or if she was a government operative, what would they do to him?

She relaxed, then met his eyes. "Where in the van did you find the phone? I'm surprised I didn't see it."

Will stiffened. *Back to the phone. Why?* "It was under the seat."

"How did you manage to drop it beneath the seat without noticing?"

"I don't know, it just seems to happen sometimes. Falls out of my pocket and bounces in the worst possible direction, like it's trying to hide."

"Show me," she said in a calm but firm voice.

She knows I'm full of shit! "What do you mean?" In his head, he tried to construct a series of trajectories that wouldn't violate the laws of physics.

"Show me how that could possibly happen."

Should I come clean? Or... The most plausible path was to start from the left pocket instead of the right, then fall between the two seats, and...

Andreia's hand flew out like a blur and struck Will hard in the neck.

His neck erupted in blinding pain. The world swirled into blurs of color and jagged bright lines, with angry, accusing green eyes in the center. He gagged and fought for breath.

Andreia's hand reached out again, a needle in it. He tried to block her hand, but couldn't coordinate his body. The needle pricked his neck, not far from where she'd struck it.

He disappeared in blackness.

Chapter 7

Will

Will drifted into wakefulness with the sensation of sitting, his arms fastened behind his back, bare feet flat against a hard floor. A faint breeze rustled his hair. Blackness lightened into blurry gray shapes that gradually gained color and focus.

He was in a wooden chair in a dark room, wrists secured behind his back and ankles duct-taped to the chair legs, wearing nothing but underwear. As the fuzziness evaporated from his vision, he saw that he was in a dimly-lit living room with drawn curtains. An overhead fan turned sluggishly. Beyond the curtains, it was dark outside. Tall bookcases, stuffed with books and an eclectic assortment of knickknacks, lined the walls.

Andreia rose from a wicker sofa and stood in front of him. She'd traded her dress for a black bikini bottom and a loose tank top. A dive knife was strapped to her muscular right calf. Below, on her ankle, was a tattoo of an equal-armed cross surrounded by a circle. Like her brother, her bare feet were long and wide, with hyper-elongated toes connected by webbing.

"You're awake," she said.

"Where am I?" He tensed against the ropes and duct tape, but they were too tight to move.

"Why'd you do it?"

"Do what? Why am I tied up? Where are my clothes?"

She let out a huff. "Why did you track where I was going? Why are you spying on me?"

Will cursed his idiocy. "I told you, I was looking for my phone." He switched topics. "Why was your van at that house anyway? I thought you lived in Hialeah."

Andreia's long toes tapped the floor in prehensile rhythm, undulating the webbing between. It was mesmerizing, like watching an octopus or some other order of life utterly different from his own.

"Do you find my feet appalling?" she asked. Her toes splayed out fully, forming impressive-looking flippers.

More questions for questions. "Not at all. I'm guessing they improve your swimming speed dramatically, but hurt when scrunched inside shoes."

The corners of her mouth nudged upward. "Correct on both counts. Now, let's dispense with the bullshit. Why did you hide your phone inside my van? And don't bother lying, you're terrible at it."

Will began to feel the full force of his situation. Fear oozed from his stomach. "You drugged me!"

She reached down and pulled the knife out of its scabbard. The blade looked razor-sharp, and big enough to gut a shark.

"I'm not enjoying this one bit," she said, "but I'm under orders. Again, why did you hide your phone inside my van?"

Eying the knife, Will decided to give in. He hated lying, anyway. *No wonder I'm so bad at it.* "It's true, my phone fell out of my pocket. But you're right, I helped it go under the seat."

"Why?"

"I've been curious—obviously too curious—about you and your brother, your adaptations and technology. But besides Eloise, I didn't share the information with anyone, not even my dad. And it's been a week since I last talked to Eloise."

"Who did you tell about the place where you trespassed?"

"No one. Am I in trouble? Do you work for the CIA? Defense Department? Another country?"

She peered at him. "No. What about you?"

"They would have just followed you with drones."

She nodded.

Will decided to ask about the more far-fetched possibility he'd pondered. "Do you come from another planet?"

Andreia broke into laughter. "Another planet?" She laughed more. "Am I that weird? No, I'm from Planet Earth."

"Genetically engineered?"

Her laughter died. "I didn't come from a test tube, either. There is a saying I never quite understood—that curiosity killed the cat."

Goosebumps rose on Will's exposed skin. Did she plan to kill him? *Why did I have to be so stupid?*

"The fault is mine," she said. "You mentioned trust earlier. I trusted you and let my guard down. I was upset about my brother and not thinking carefully." Her voice dropped and she added, "And to be honest, there was electricity between us, which also affected my judgment."

I sure fucked up. "I guess I was overly obsessed. I wasn't thinking straight, either."

"I looked through your phone," she said.

"How?"

"When we first met, I saw you unlock it by fingerprint, so I touched your finger to the screen while you were knocked out. Obviously, you're not a real spy, or you'd have disabled that option and used a code."

"And what did you learn from my phone?" *Hopefully enough to let me go.*

"Nothing incriminating. No texts or emails or phone calls to anyone other than relatives, and no mention of me or my brother—unless of course you erased it. Of course, you could have used some other route."

"I didn't talk to anyone about you or your people, period. Except Eloise, but you already know what she knows."

"My friend did some background research," Andreia said. "Nothing unusual came up. You really are a marine biologist born and raised in the Keys. And your brother's an engineer, like you said."

Will let out a breath. "Then can I go?"

"If you go to the police," she said, "I'll file a complaint for trespassing—I have video—and say you were stalking me, maybe planning to attack me."

"Trespassing is a misdemeanor. And since I didn't break into your house, it's unlikely I'd get jail time. Kidnapping, on the other hand, is a felony. Drugging someone is also a felony, I'm pretty sure."

She frowned. "Point taken. Still… please don't go to the police."

"So, what about my clothes? Why am I sitting here in my underwear?"

"I had to check for mics. Didn't find any, luckily. I guess you can have your clothes back, although it would serve you right if I dropped you off naked in downtown Key West, with 'asshole' tattooed on your forehead. You caused me no end of trouble with your little escapade."

"Just let me go and we can forget all about this."

"I doubt that." She gave his chair a little kick. "I have to check in. I wish you hadn't been so obsessive, but it could have been worse—I was sloppy, and it could have been someone dangerous."

Will wondered if that was that intended as an insult.

She circled around behind him. "What kind of tunes do you like?"

The question seemed totally out of place. "What?"

"Music. I have to check in, but this is a small house. I can't have you listening in."

Music was a far better option than putting him under again. "I'm partial to reggae. The classics—Bob Marley, Peter Tosh, Toots and the Maytals…"

"That's easy to find. Hold on, I'm loading a station."

From behind him, the staccato guitar opening of Bob Marley's "Stir It Up" blasted his ears, followed by the drums and the rest of the instruments.

Andreia returned to face him. "I don't suppose you listen to anything from this century."

"Nope," he had to admit.

"I assume you're a Jimmy Buffet fan too?"

Despite his predicament, Will scoffed. "It's mandatory for Keys residents, but you can only listen to 'Margaritaville' and 'Why Don't We Get Drunk and Screw' so many times."

Andreia gave a hint of a smile. "Don't go anywhere." She strode to a door and opened it, revealing a messy office of sorts. She turned back to him. "I mean it." He could barely hear her over the music.

She shut the door behind her, leaving Will listening to loud groovy tunes that were completely at odds with the ropes and duct tape binding his arms and legs.

* * *

Andreia

Andreia opened her custom videoconference program and entered the address and password for the Assembly Chamber. The tiered Council benches appeared onscreen, with eight of the twelve Elders present.

Andreia summarized Will's interrogation and what she had learned. "He acted on his own and did not share the information with others. The background check was clean; Pijasiros and Zoze found nothing incriminating. To be safe, they deleted his phone's location data. And I purged the phone number I gave him. It wasn't one I use with other contacts."

Meltha leaned toward the screen. "Our clan has never faced anything like this in recent memory. The Codes prohibit killing, but that only applies to Sea-Dwellers. If it's a matter of clan survival, we have that option regarding a Land-Dweller."

Andreia froze. *Murder? A good-hearted person like Will?* She'd met some unsavory people while selling treasure on the black market. Some of the buyers, despite being pre-screened, had brought bodyguards with the cold probing eyes of a seasoned killer. But Sea-Dwellers were supposed to be different.

"Are you suggesting we murder a fellow sentient, one who harbors no ill will toward us? Aren't we taught life is sacred?" she asked.

Meltha stiffened. "Of course. But—"

"I think we can trust Dr. Myers to keep the secrets he's uncovered. He has so far."

Meltha frowned at the interruption. "The danger of exposure is too great. Land-Dwellers don't even follow their own codes, let alone ours. They could annihilate us the way they annihilate each other."

"They're not all like that, obsessed with power or wealth. Dr. Myers discovered our existence, but he's not malicious, he's just antennae-waving."

Xitaros, her nemesis at the prior meeting, interrupted, "This mess is all your fault."

"I know, and I've apologized. Can we be civil?"

"What would happen if that man went missing?" he said. "How thorough would the search be?"

"Very thorough. He has many friends." *And a brother in the military.*

Xitaros addressed the other Elders. "We are in existential danger, and that consideration comes before all else. I have prayed to the ancestors for guidance."

Most Mazi believed in an emergent essence that all were connected to, but Xitaros belonged to the ancestor-worship minority. *As if ancient kings would waste their afterlife talking to that spirit-sucking louse.*

"Our only course," he continued, "is to arrange a fatal accident for Will Myers. Since Land Dwellers kill each other freely, they exempt themselves from our maxims."

"That's ridiculous—" Andreia began.

Xitaros ignored her and kept speaking. "You already hold him captive. You can put him down quickly and painlessly, then dispose of the body far away."

"Make sure the cause appears natural," another Elder added.

Andreia shrank inside. She couldn't imagine ending Will's life merely because he *might* pose a threat in the future. She couldn't imagine committing murder, period. She even apologized to fish before eating them.

"We're not Karsk," she said, "and Dr. Myers isn't a sicario." The Karsk clan of Sea-Dwellers smuggled drugs into the U.S., a lucrative business accompanied by astonishing violence.

"The decision is for the clan to make," Meltha admonished, "not you."

Andreia knew something that might stop them. "The county medical examiner is Will's friend. She'd perform every test imaginable to determine his cause of death, and I don't have the skills to fool her. If she suspects murder, the police would look into me and who knows what they'd find."

Meltha grimaced. "We'll have to come up with something convincing, then."

"I can't believe you're contemplating murder!" A more consequential reason came to her. *This is an opportunity! We can work with the Land-Dwellers instead of cowering in fear and dying off with a whimper.*

"He could be an important ally," she said, "once we satisfy his curiosity. The ocean is dying, but we are too few and powerless to stop it. Only the Land-Dwellers can fix the problems they've caused, but there is so much we know that they don't. Through someone like Will, a marine scientist, we could collaborate without revealing our existence."

Xitaros shook his head. "The Land-Dwellers must be neutered, not assisted."

"They are a disease," an Elder in the back added, "the deadliest that ever evolved."

Andreia tried to remain calm in the face of such astonishing inflexibility. "If you are unconvinced of Dr. Myers's good intentions, why not question him in person? I can put him on camera."

"I propose a middle path," Kitane said. "It is clear you are unwilling to kill Dr. Myers. I understand and empathize with your reluctance. Bring him here, so we can evaluate him in person and give him a fair opportunity to explain himself. Ensure he can't communicate with the surface, and concoct an excuse for his absence."

"For how long?" another Elder asked Kitane. "Are we to feed and monitor him for the rest of his life?"

"He could escape," Xitaros said. "And he'd know everything about us. It's a terrible plan."

"He already knows too much about us," another Elder said.

An Elder woman proposed, "Perhaps we could dissect this man after we bring him here. I've never examined Land-Dweller anatomy, and neither has anyone else in the clan."

"He's not a fish!" Andreia objected. "He's sentient, like us."

On the screen, Kitane and several others nodded. "Their anatomical details are available on the Internet," Kitane said. "What's more important is to study a Land Dweller's reactions upon learning about us. This is something we need to know."

"And we should discuss the possibilities of working together," Andreia repeated. Kitane's proposal would be dangerous for Will, but it could shake up the fossilized Mazi ideology and help them adapt to the changing world.

"What have you done with his phone?" an Elder asked.

"It's in the safe, along with his wallet. I took out the battery and SIM card."

"Is there a chance someone will find it?"

Didn't I just explain that? "No. It has no power source and it's surrounded by thick metal."

"Is he free of disease?" Meltha asked.

"He's given no indications of being ill, and I haven't caught anything, but I'll take his temperature."

Her people were terrified of Land-Dweller viruses and bacteria from which they might have no immunity. Perhaps overly so, but back when they lived mostly on islands, diseases brought by Land-Dwellers had all but wiped out the clan. And there was no guarantee that human vaccines and medicines would help Sea-Dwellers. During her six years on the surface, Andreia had caught colds, flus, and gastroenteritis, with worse symptoms than Land-Dwellers typically suffered. However, she'd survived them all, and actually seemed to be immune to some of their other diseases.

"He'll have to wear a mask at all times," Meltha said, "and eat in your quarantine chamber. And he can't be allowed to wander unaccompanied."

"Yes, yes, I know that."

"It is overly risky," Xitaros objected.

Exasperated, Andreia replied, "I've walked among the Land-Dwellers for six years and am still alive. Our precautions will be more than sufficient."

"I was also thinking of your attachment to them." Xitaros turned to the other Elders. "It's not sufficient for Andreia, who is young and impressionable, to accompany this Land-Dweller within our home. We must supervise him ourselves."

"Agreed," the middle-aged woman named Siaduare said, holding up one of her flipper hands, the fingers fused solidly together from birth.

Andreia fought to control her temper. She had to show she was a part of the clan, someone to be trusted and supported. An outburst wouldn't help her.

The Elders argued and discussed, and finally came to a consensus.

"You will bring Will Myers here tonight," Kitane spoke, "taking all possible precautions to prevent his communication with other Land-Dwellers. Meltha and Briares will meet you tomorrow at 0700 in the Trader zone. The Land-Dweller is not to leave the airlock until then. He will have one week to convince the clan that he will keep our existence secret. If we can't reach consensus, we will have no choice but to ensure his silence."

Andreia bowed with hands next to ears, worrying the odds were against him.

Chapter 8

Will

After about twenty minutes, Andreia re-entered the room, gripping her big dive knife. The razor-sharp bottom edge curved to a point, and had a notch in the back for cutting lines. The top was serrated like a saw.

She shut off the music. "What would you do if I answered all your questions about me and my people?"

An opening. "I assume you'd want me to keep it to myself?"

"Would you?" She stared into his eyes.

"You've more than made your point about it. There was no need to drug me and tie me up."

"Are you fully vaccinated?" She listed everything from measles to seasonal flu.

"Yes, why?"

"We're going someplace and I need to know," she said.

"Where?"

"I'll get to that. Are you sick, or have you been sick recently, even something minor like a cold or stomachache?"

"No, I can't remember last time I was sick."

She half-smiled. "Sunshine and healthy living?"

"I suppose."

"Can you take a week off work, starting now, and cancel any other plans?"

"I have students coming in two weeks and need to prep. And what would I tell my colleagues?"

"Tell them you're sick. You're smart, you can think of something. The question is, will you do it? Will you accept my offer to satisfy all your curiosities in exchange for silence?"

The decision was easy, especially since the alternative might be fatal. "Absolutely."

Andreia knelt in front of him with the knife. "Silence about my people, but there is much we can teach you about the ocean, and to truly know is to truly love."

"I do already."

"You'll love it even more when we're done." She sliced through the duct tape holding his ankles to the chair, then went behind him and untied his wrists. "Maybe we can work together and heal the damage your people have caused." She sheathed her knife. "It's an existential issue for us, and it's an issue you understand."

Will shook out his aching arms. He understood her less and less. "From captive to colleague?"

Andreia let out a huff. "I thought you were a danger. You were spying on me. I am answerable to others." She tossed him his clothes.

He put on his pants. "We could have talked it out without tranquilizers and rope."

"I apologize. Now can we move on?"

Will finished dressing and decided to play along. "So, you're going to answer all my questions, and we're going to save the world together?"

"You don't have to be sarcastic. I'm serious."

"How? We wouldn't be the first to try."

She shrugged. "Good question. And I'm still not completely convinced I can trust you."

"Same here. You kidnapped me."

"I had no choice. Now are we going to sit here and argue until our hair turns gray, or can we do something productive?"

Will decided to stop arguing and embrace the situation. "Okay. I'm sorry about hiding the phone in your van. I had no right to invade your privacy. I let my curiosity overwhelm decency."

Andreia's eyes softened. "Thank you. But you will need to follow instructions. This is a big deal for us." She gave him his phone. "First, call your workplace."

According to the phone, it was after 8 PM. "No one will be in."

She let out a huff. "Leave a message. Put it on speaker."

The lab's main number was on his contact list. He called it and selected the option to leave a message for the receptionist. "Hi, this is Will." If he claimed he was sick, his friends and relatives would make sympathy calls, maybe even drop off food. "I'm going away on a dive trip. Kind of spur of the moment. I'll be back before classes start." He hung up.

"Now text your relatives and anyone else who might wonder where you are the rest of the week."

Will complied.

Andreia took the phone back. "As a matter of fact, we are going on a dive trip." She removed the SIM card and battery, and locked it in a safe. "This has to stay here. In case you're wondering, one of my friends wiped anything pointing to me or this place, and your call just now was ported through a tower in Layton."

"How?"

"They're pros. Maybe you'll meet them."

Will didn't like the idea of being in unknown circumstances without a phone. "What if people call?"

"You can apologize later for not returning their calls. Tell them you were out of range—completely plausible."

"I'll get it back later, right?"

"Of course." She pointed to the mishmash of gear piled in the corners, which included deep-water rebreathers, tanks and regulators, and an electric pump. "There's a diving mask and fins. Grab some swim trunks, BCD, and whatever weights you need. And a dive light. You won't need tanks or a regulator, the sled has all that."

Will picked up a pair of swim trunks, one of several. "I take it these aren't yours?"

"A relic from my predecessor, like most everything here."

"Do I need a wetsuit?" He didn't see any.

"No, we'll be near the surface most of the trip."

Once Will was fitted, Andreia pulled off her T-shirt, revealing a black bikini top. She put on webbed gloves that closely resembled Galen's hands: fingernails, creases, and all.

Maybe Galen's webbing was artificial, too. No, he decided—he'd examined the skin closely, and so had Eloise.

Andreia searched through the piles of gear and picked up a mirror attached to a clamp. "So I can see how you're doing. You can signal me if you need anything."

He made an "okay" sign.

"Follow me." Not bringing a mask, fins, or light of her own, Andreia locked the door and led Will down the trail through the mangroves.

Will had to use the flashlight to keep from tripping on prop roots. "You don't need a light?"

"I can see fine in the dark."

When they arrived at the narrow, canopied channel leading to the canals, she said, "I have to start the sled and calibrate the air mixture for you. I'll be right back." She dove into the dark water.

A few minutes later, her head emerged. "I'm going to pass you a mouthpiece. It's connected by tubes to the secondary air system—the sled has two, each independent. Strap on the mouthpiece, then grab the tow bar. This will be a long trip—I can't go more than 4-5 knots while towing you. We'll stay at 10 meters until we reach our destination."

That made sense—the shallower the depth, the less pressure from the water above, meaning less chance of issues like 'the bends'— nitrogen accumulating in body tissues and forming painful, potentially fatal bubbles when the diver returned to surface pressure.

"Then we'll descend to 180 meters," Andreia continued.

That was damn deep—over twice his personal record. But he appreciated that she shared the dive plan. "What kind of air mix are we using?" Commercial divers typically added helium for deep-water work to reduce the proportions of nitrogen and oxygen, and the chances of nitrogen narcosis or oxygen toxicity.

"Atmospheric until we descend," she answered. "Then it'll vary, mainly for you, but don't worry—the regulators adjust the mix automatically."

Sophisticated. "You're not with the Navy?"

"I'm not. So, this is your last chance to back out."

"No way." He put on his mask and fins.

She smiled. "I thought you'd say that. I'm glad I was right." She dove back below the surface.

Will took a breath and followed. Shining his light through the murky water, he spotted Andreia sitting atop a dark blue vehicle, about ten feet long, with long cylinders on either side. She passed him the promised mouthpiece, attached to two tubes—presumably one for inhaled air and the other for exhaled. As part of a rebreathing system, the exhale tube would go to a CO_2 scrubber and recycle the oxygen and nitrogen.

Will strapped the mouthpiece around his head and gripped the tow bar. Andreia motioned for him to turn the light off.

Guess she doesn't want to be seen. He followed her instructions.

Andreia lay on the sled and eased out of the channel, pulling Will about six feet behind. The water jets were silent and created no bubbles. They entered the much wider canal and Andreia glanced in the clip-on mirror. Will gave the okay sign.

Keeping near the bottom, Andreia steered into a cross canal. Will heard the rapid gurgling slaps of a motorboat propeller in the distance. The volume grew, then diminished.

They turned again and, judging by the gentle cross-flow, entered the shallow, warm sea off the coast. In the moonlight, he could only make out vague shapes of corals, waving turtle grass, and fish. But he heard the clicks of shrimp and the low-frequency grunts of squirrelfish, then the rasping sound of a lobster.

After a while, the bottom dropped away. He drifted into a haze of boredom. Every now and then, Andreia touched her fingers to the top of her head, the dive signal for "are you okay?" He responded with the okay sign.

Will's hands began to ache from gripping the tow bar. Finally, Andreia pointed her thumb down. He gave the okay sign and she began a 45-degree descent.

It grew even darker. Will cleared his ears as the pressure built up, pinching his nostrils shut while forcing air out of his lungs. The temperature dropped, but was still tolerable.

After a couple of minutes, Andreia slowed the sled, then stopped a few feet above a wide knoll. Will looked around, but could see nothing unusual, only the dark profiles of low ridges and gullies shaped by the currents.

Still facing forward, Andreia pressed a button on the sled console. Will heard low clanks and a flushing sound. Andreia maneuvered the sled forward.

After about a minute, the sand-covered surface parted, exposing a pitch-black hole beneath. They descended into it.

Thick panels above them slid together with a clank, followed by clicks, leaving them in complete darkness. The surroundings grew gradually lighter, revealing blue curved walls with a perforated floor beneath. On either side of the sled, tied to the walls, were parked two platforms with straps and netting—presumably for towing cargo. Above, the rippling surface of the water was only a few inches from the ceiling.

With a hum and another flushing noise, the water level dropped until it was completely gone. The sled rested on the floor.

Andreia took out her air mouthpiece. "Welcome to Sealock 12."

Will removed his mask and breather. "Where are we?"

"Katiki, which means 'Home' in my people's language. I was born here." She secured the sled with metal cables and plugged in a charging cord. "You can take off your gear, but bring it with you so we can stow it."

At the far end of the chamber was a watertight door with a wheel in the center, like the hatches on old warships. The number '12' was stenciled above in white paint. A cross inside a circle—like Andreia's ankle tattoo—was etched into the metal above that.

Andreia rotated the wheel and swung open the hatch. Accompanied by the faint hum of unseen fans, cool air with an antiseptic odor blew into Will's face.

On the other side was a suite with olive walls, a rounded ceiling, curving wall struts, and perforated rubber matting. It contained several deflated air mattresses, a plastic table and chairs, a kitchenette, four sliding-door closets, a normal-looking door, and another watertight hatch. According to a clock mounted on the far wall, it was after midnight.

"This is part of the decompression chamber," Andreia said, "but it's more comfortable than the sealock." She turned a timer dial beneath the clock and pressed a metal button beneath. Will heard a faint hiss.

"The pressure inside is the same as the surface, but it's eighteen atmospheres outside. We weren't at depth long enough to really need it, but I set the decompression for an hour to be safe. We have to meet our chaperones at 7, so I suggest we get some sleep."

"Chaperones?"

"Not my idea." She inflated two of the mattresses, found him some sheets, then showed him a bathroom with a shower, toilet, and sink. "To warn you, there's no hot water. Cold water doesn't bother us."

Will remembered the surprisingly thick fat layer beneath Galen's skin. Andreia was presumably the same. But they were sculpted like dolphins: streamlined, strong, and adapted for ocean living. And Andreia's curves and face could lure a treasure ship onto the rocks.

"You're staring," Andreia said.

Will felt his cheeks flush. "Sorry. You can shower first."

She opened a refrigerator in the kitchenette. It was full of water jugs and an assortment of food. "Help yourself to whatever you want to eat or drink. There's crackers and noodles in the cabinets."

"Thanks." Will was thirsty after the long salty trip, and gulped down a glass of water. He was hungry too, and started peeling an orange. "I assume you bring food down here?"

She shook her head. "Only electronics and the like." She strode into the bathroom without explaining further.

As Andreia showered, Will investigated the room. One closet was full of hanging shirts, pants, kilts, blouses, and long skirts, seemingly a random assortment. Two closets were full of neatly organized diving gear, and the final closet contained an air compressor and cylindrical tanks. It reminded him of the shallow underwater lab off Key Largo where he occasionally took students, only more spacious.

Andreia emerged from the bathroom, wrapped in a towel, hair wet but combed. "Your turn."

While showering, Will rinsed the salt off the mask and fins he'd borrowed. The water was the same temperature as the sea floor, neither hot nor cold. There was no soap or shampoo.

When he returned to the main room, Andreia was wearing a ruffled white blouse and a black-and-tan patterned skirt, and had pinned her dark hair back with a golden band. She smiled and hooked a thumb toward the closet. "Pick anything that fits. You'd make a poor ambassador wearing a towel."

"Ambassador? Am I the first visitor?"

"No, but you're the first from the surface."

So they have other bases, all secret? "Who am I going to meet?"

"Almost everyone in the Mazi clan."

"That's your people? They're called the Mazi?"

"That's our clan name. As a whole, we're *Ahta*. In English, Sea-People or Sea-Dwellers, to differentiate from Land-Dwellers."

A whole people that live underwater? He'd been plunged into a world of bizarre, where nothing made sense. He tried to maintain his sense of academic enquiry. It gave him a sort of refuge. "So, that means there are other clans?"

"One thing at a time."

The clothes were odd, like they came from another continent in a previous century. Will found a hexagonally-patterned black-and-yellow shirt and dark blue slacks that fit reasonably well. There were no shoes.

The lack of shoes was the least of his questions. "You're not from Hialeah, obviously. And Galen didn't leave from Biscayne Bay."

Her face drooped. "Yes. I don't like to lie, but on the surface, I often have to. My people are very strict regarding secrecy."

"Why?"

She paused before answering. "Your people have a long tradition of violence. We don't want to be wiped out like the Native Americans. Or any of the other genocide victims—tens of millions in the last century alone."

"We're not all like that."

"I see your point, having met all kinds of people in Florida, most of them friendly. But you have to admit, your history speaks for itself. Most Sea-Dwellers believe violence is a genetic trait of yours and you'll never change."

"That's a depressing outlook." Not that he held much hope for a better future.

"I'm not as pessimistic as most of us," she said. "It's more a societal issue than a genetic one. Your societies have laws against harming others and religions that promote peace—they just need to be followed more consistently. Anyway, while you're here, maybe you could help me some more with Galen. We found his sled, but that doesn't explain why it was so far away, or why he let it run out of power and abandoned it."

Will nodded, while feeling frozen in place. He was among an undiscovered race of people beneath the sea floor. *Does anyone else know about them? If not, will they ever let me leave?*

* * *

Monroe County Medical Examiner's Office

Eloise Clark was filling out reports when the phone on her desk rang. "You have a visitor," the receptionist told her.

"Who?"

"A Dr. Hernandez from the Naval Criminal Investigative Service."

That's weird. "I'll be there in a minute."

Eloise locked her computer screen and went to the lobby to meet the visitor.

Dr. Hernandez was a middle-aged Latina with sharp features, short dark hair, and thick, practical-looking glasses. A black briefcase was strapped over her shoulder. She flashed a badge and held out her hand. "Ana Hernandez, NCIS."

The handshake was firm. "Eloise Clark. How can I help you?"

"I'm with the Office of Special Projects. May we speak in private?"

"Certainly." Eloise led Dr. Hernandez to her office, gestured to a guest chair, and closed the door.

Dr. Hernandez pulled out a tablet out of her case and turned it on. "You filed an autopsy for a 15-year-old male named Galen Álvarez?"

"Yes." Why does the NCIS Office of Special Projects care?

"Do you still have the body?"

"The Familia Fernández Funeral Home took it. It's probably been cremated by now."

Dr. Hernandez gave a look of disappointment. "Do you have their phone number?"

Eloise looked up the number on her computer and wrote it on a sticky note. "What's your interest in it?"

"According to the sheriff's deputy who found the body, it was quite unusual, with webbed feet and hands. Word traveled, and I was informed because of a case I'm working on."

"Oh? What's that?"

"You may or may not know, but the Chinese are extremely... aggressive regarding seafloor resources. Sand, strategic minerals, fish, anything they consider valuable, they try to harvest before anyone else can. But apparently someone has been sabotaging some of their dredging and mining operations in the South China Sea. Naturally, they blamed us and deployed their navy."

"Why naturally?"

"They claim the South China Sea belongs to China alone, contrary to international law and freedom of navigation." She gave Eloise a careful look. "Thing is, we didn't commit the sabotage, nor did any of our allies. The Navy is trying to figure out what went on, in the interest of keeping the peace. We found a half-dead young man, ear drums blown out and internal pressure wave damage, presumably caused by Chinese depth charges. The man had a number of interesting aquatic adaptations—webbed toes and fingers, outsized spleen, altered physiology..."

"Like the body recovered here."

"Precisely. Unfortunately, we were unable to communicate with the man and he died soon afterward. But you can imagine how excited I was to hear about this similarly adapted boy who washed ashore in the Keys, on the other side of the world."

"Well, I'm afraid you're too late," Eloise said.

"Your autopsy report on Galen Álvarez was quite superficial, with only the unusual spleen weight recorded as an oddity. Why did you leave so much out?"

"Listen, I have a whole county to cover, with only one assistant, and he was away at the time. It was an accidental death, not requiring a detailed report."

Dr. Hernandez nodded. "I understand. But I assume you took photos? Notes? Tissue samples?"

"I sent the tissue samples to a toxicology lab. As for what I have here, I need paperwork before disclosing. Do you have something signed by a judge?"

The NCIS agent reached into her carry bag and handed Eloise a signed and stamped document. "This covers anything I might ask for."

Eloise scanned the document. It was signed by a federal judge in Miami. "I recorded the autopsy on video, and took pictures. I'll make copies for you."

"Great. Now, one last thing. Do you have the boy's next of kin?"

"Yes, his sister."

"I'll need her contact information."

Chapter 9

Will

The next morning, Andreia handed Will a cloth mask. "You'll have to wear one of these at all times except in my chamber. I wear one too, since I live mostly on land, and follow quarantine protocols to protect the others."

"I'm vaccinated for almost everything, and haven't been sick in years."

"We don't have the same immunities as you, and have to be careful."

Will slipped on the mask, which was made from layers of silk, and much more comfortable than N95 masks. Somewhere he'd read that silk was an effective moisture barrier and contained copper, which killed bacteria and viruses upon contact. He had a surreal sense of a space explorer making first contact with aliens. He wondered if those he was about to meet felt the same way.

Andreia donned her mask and turned the exit hatch wheel. Will followed her into a yellow corridor with watertight doors on both sides and an archway in the middle. A breeze tinged with the scent of disinfectant blew from the far end.

Two people stood just past the archway: a large, wide-shouldered man in a checkered kilt and vest, and a thin elderly woman in a patterned blouse, long skirt, and fringed shawl. Both had webbed hands and feet, large almond-shaped eyes with wide irises, and golden-bronze skin. Both wore silk masks like Will's.

"You must be Dr. Will Myers," the elderly woman said in a stronger accent than Andreia's—a sort of blend between Italian, Spanish, and Caribbean, but low-pitched and a little raspy. The woman's silver hair was braided with seashells, and she wore golden necklaces and earrings.

"Yes." Will started to offer a hand, then remembered their concerns about viruses and withdrew it.

"I am Meltha. On behalf of the Mazi Clan, I welcome you to Katiki as an honored guest." She opened her palms and bowed slightly.

"Thank you." He tried to match the bow.

"I am Briares," the man said, and bowed with open palms. He wore a necklace of shark teeth, and silver armbands depicting moray eels and barracudas eating their tails. His right ankle was tattooed with a circle and cross like Andreia's.

"Why Briares?" Andreia asked Meltha. "I assumed you'd bring Stefan. He knows Land-Dwellers as well as I, maybe better."

"Briares is more objective," Meltha replied.

Will wasn't sure what dynamics were at play here. He bowed to Briares. "Good to meet you." He had so many questions, he wasn't sure where to start. "I understand I'm the first surface person to visit?"

"Yes," Meltha said.

"You are very lucky," Briares added.

"We are all very curious," Meltha said, "about your interest in us."

"I'm a Keys native and a marine biologist. I thought I knew the waters around here as well as anyone. But I'd never heard of people with webbed fingers and toes who live underwater. It's kind of like learning the Bermuda Triangle myth is real and there are submerged alien spaceships off the coast of Florida."

Andreia made a popping noise with her mouth. "A funny notion coming from a scientist."

"We are not aliens," Meltha said.

"I didn't mean it literally," Will responded, "it's just an analogy."

"It's one matter to be curious," Meltha said, "yet another to trespass and search with sonar equipment."

Will's feeling of guilt returned. "Curiosity is why I became a scientist." He glanced at Andreia. "But nothing I did compares to hitting, drugging, and kidnapping me."

"Let's call a truce on that," Andreia said. "The subject has become tiresome."

"Agreed," Will said.

"Whom did you tell about us?" Meltha asked him.

"I already questioned Dr. Myers, and gave a full briefing," Andreia said.

"First-hand knowledge is always better than second."

"No one," Will said.

Meltha continued to ask questions, most of which he'd already heard from Andreia. Will did his best to suppress his exasperation as he repeated his answers.

Andreia finally intervened. "Dr. Myers must be thinking this corridor is our entire habitat. I was planning to show him the forest."

"The elders are eager to meet our guest," Meltha said, "and we must schedule a clan meeting."

"Dr. Meyers is probably tired from the journey. It would be best to have a relaxed first day."

Will wasn't tired, but didn't object.

Meltha stared at her. "You grow more presumptuous every year you spend on land."

Andreia stiffened. "Living in different environments broadens one's thought horizons."

Briares held up a hand. "That's enough."

Andreia placed a gloved hand against her heart, but didn't bow. "We don't want our 'honored guest' to feel uncomfortable."

Obviously Andreia knows how to handle this. Observing the simmering tension between the two women, Will figured the less he said, the better.

Andreia briefly met his eyes, then stared at Meltha.

Meltha sighed. "Very well, Andreia, I yield to your expertise. But we will accompany you."

Showing no signs of gloating, Andreia led them to a stairwell. They descended several flights and followed a light green passageway with curving walls.

She opened another waterproof hatch and they entered a thick, humid tropical forest, lush with greenery; noisy with bird calls, buzzing insects, and running water; and fragrant from flowers. Thick tree trunks, covered with vines and bromeliads, rose high into the air, letting through dappled light. Beneath them were layers of palms, tree ferns, and other plants, covering nearly every square inch of ground.

This was the last thing Will had expected to see. An entire rainforest more than 500 feet beneath the surface! A pair of scarlet macaws flew overhead and squawked. "This is incredible!"

"The forest dome," Andreia said. "My favorite place here. From a practical perspective, it converts carbon dioxide to oxygen and purifies wastewater." She led them onto a bamboo walkway.

"How long has this place been here?" he asked.

"Since Flagler's railroad opened the Keys to influxes of Land-Dwellers. We've improved it over time, obviously."

That long ago? Before my great-grandfather was born? These people had the technology for deep-water construction when Flagler was struggling to build bridges? "You're kidding."

"We'd prefer islands or shallow water, but this is safer."

"How have you kept this place secret for so long?" *It's only 15-20 miles from my house!*

"We're careful," Andreia said.

Still feeling disoriented, Will asked, "Before that, did you interact with the, uh, native Land-Dweller civilizations?" The Caribbean islands were once highly populated by indigenous people like the Taíno, until the Spaniards wiped them out.

Andreia looked at Briares, who answered, "We stuck to small islands uninhabited by Land-Dwellers. We traded with the Taíno and others, had peace agreements, and met often, but there were no contagion problems until the Spaniards brought smallpox, measles, bubonic plague... at least thirty different diseases that killed most of the Sea-Dwellers and native Land-Dwellers. We had to isolate all our communities where diseases appeared. Everyone on those islands died."

No wonder they're so worried about diseases. "It sounds tragic," was all Will could think to say.

"After that," Briares continued, "we decided to avoid Land-Dwellers. Eventually, we moved permanently underwater. Katiki is just outside U.S. territory, in international waters, exempting us from your laws. At least, until you added an additional control zone beyond it. Now we're not sure what our legal status would be."

"Land-Dwellers should have no claims over the ocean," Meltha remarked.

Andreia nodded. "If we revealed ourselves, we could make such a case."

"Ask the Land-Dwellers to give up something?" Meltha said. "They'd never agree."

"You could claim to be a country and join the United Nations," Will suggested. "That would give you legal rights as a sovereign entity."

"I've wondered about that myself," Andreia said.

"Throw ourselves on Land-Dweller mercy," Meltha responded, "on their terms instead of ours?" She made a spitting noise.

The walkway curved through the thick plant growth and intersected other trails. Two young boys and a girl, maybe four or five years old, came running down one.

"Careful!" Meltha warned them.

They slowed, then stopped and stared at Will. They had the same general features as the other Sea-Dwellers Will had seen. One of the boys pointed at Will's feet and whispered in the other boy's ear.

"Keep a two-meter distance," Meltha told them.

"You use the metric system too," Will remarked.

"It's more consistent than our old system," Andreia said, "which used the height and finger-joint length of a long-dead mythical king. I don't know why you Americans are so stubborn about converting."

"Agree."

Will introduced himself to the Sea-Dweller children. "I come from above, from the Florida Keys."

"What are you doing here?" the girl asked.

"Visiting. I was invited."

"By who?"

"By me," Andreia said, then made a shooing motion with her hand.

They continued down the walkway. The children followed, undeterred, but keeping six feet away.

"Andreia's marrying a Land-Dweller!" the girl's voice chimed behind them.

Andreia snapped her head around. "I am not!"

Meltha placed her hands against her forehead, then pointed them at the children, palms up. "What have you been told about idle gossip?"

"Em… don't do it?" one of the boys responded.

"Exactly. Think before you speak."

They resumed walking. "Children are actually our greatest joy," Meltha said. "I wish we had more." She eyed Andreia, who sighed.

They crossed over a narrow, slow-moving stream. "We circulate water and air throughout the habitat," Andreia told Will. "Here, the soil and plants remove impurities."

"We spray mist from above twice a day," Briares added, "which the epiphytes and some of the frogs need."

"How has this place lasted so long at 18 atmospheres of pressure?" Will asked.

"Organometallic materials 20 times stronger than steel, plus clever engineering," Andreia said. "Land-Dwellers built giant pyramids thousands of years ago; Sea-Dwellers have been building underwater structures even longer."

A small orange-furred monkey peered at them from a tree branch and diverted the children's attention.

"It's remarkable you were able to remain hidden all this time," Will mused.

"Our home is beneath the sea bottom," Andreia said. "And there are no shipwrecks or mineral deposits here worth the expense of deep diving. Before that, we had our own islands and no one bothered us."

"We don't want to be exterminated like the Taíno," Meltha said. "We have no military forces and could not compete with yours even if we did. There aren't enough of us. So, we have to stay hidden."

"Things are different now," Will said. *Sort of.*

"Land-Dwellers still perpetrate genocide on each other," Briares said, "and ecocide against other species and the planet itself."

"Not all of us."

"Those who don't," Meltha said, "do little to stop it. And there's no reason to believe you'll change."

"And yet," Will said, "Andreia lives peacefully on the surface."

"We trade with you for things we can't easily make ourselves," Andreia said, "but traders, like me, pretend to be human."

It took a moment for her comment to sink in. "You're not human?" *Is she joking?*

Andreia shifted on her feet. "We're pretty similar, but as you've seen, there are some differences."

Meltha said, "We're a different species. *Homo aquaticus*, one might say. We've run genetic tests, and seem to have diverged from *Homo sapiens* about 200,000 years ago, although there was a fair amount of interbreeding for a while. We also have a lot of Denisovan DNA."

Will glanced at Andreia, who not only looked human—if forgetting the large webbed feet—but was downright beautiful. "A whole different species rather than a sub-species?"

"We have no records of viable offspring with you," Meltha said. "Our DNA is too different."

"We may look similar, at least from a distance," Briares said, "but our physiology is significantly different."

Will's excitement grew. *This is incredible! Another Homo species that still exists!* "Your clan has been in the Caribbean since before the Spaniards arrived—"

"Long before," Andreia said.

"Did you arrive from somewhere else? Or did the Sea-Dwellers originate here?"

"We're pretty sure our species originated along the east African coast, and spread out from there. Our written records only go back 4,000 years, but our sagas and artifacts go back much further. For most of our history, we had the ocean to ourselves."

"Are you related to the ancient Sea Peoples," he asked. "The ones that caused the Bronze Age collapse?"

Andreia looked at Briares as if for guidance.

"Those so-called 'Sea Peoples' were just Land-Dwellers using boats," Briares said. "We traded with them, but never took part in their wars—we never developed humanity's love of violence."

Again with the 'humans are violent.' "So you're like bonobos and we're chimpanzees?"

"Not a bad analogy," Briares said.

Will wondered about it. Andreia had incapacitated him before he knew what was happening. Maybe they were just non-violent toward other Sea-Dwellers, and had a different standard regarding humans.

"You can probably guess my next question," Will said.

"Atlantis or mermaids?"

"Atlantis—any connection?"

"Atlantis is entirely fictional. Plato invented it."

"Oh." Will had assumed it was a myth based on fact, and felt a little foolish.

"As for mermaids," Andreia volunteered, "that myth could be loosely based on reality. A torrid affair between a beautiful young Sea-Dweller and a lovestruck mariner." She smiled at him, halting his heart for a second.

"Briares," Meltha told Will, "is not only a gifted glassblower, but an expert on water-being mythology."

"From what I've read," the big Sea-Dweller man said, "the merpeople myth is widespread among Land-Dwellers. We don't have fish tails, obviously, but some stories include mermaids altering their form to resemble humans, and our webbed feet could have morphed into tails as stories changed over time."

Andreia led them down bamboo walkways, the three children following behind, until she found an elderly man wearing a button-down khaki jumpsuit, clipping vines and pruning shrubs. She introduced him to Will. "Yidini is our senior botanist."

Yidini told them that he tended the forest with a rotating group of assistants. "They like doing it. It relaxes the mind."

He took them on a tour, pointing out different plants and their uses. Every species either provided food, medicine, or fiber, or contributed to the smooth, stable functioning of the ecosystem. The insects pollinated the plants and the birds kept the insects from overpopulating. "Plus, birds and butterflies are nice to watch," he added.

"Does everyone speak English?" Will asked Andreia.

"We all learn English and Spanish as children," she said, "but most of us don't practice it as often as Yidini or Briares."

They ascended spiraling wooden steps to a walkway just below the canopy. There were more birds up here, and through a small gap between trees, a ceiling of translucent panes was visible, glowing from lights behind.

"We use diffuse lighting favoring the blue and red spectra," the botanist said, "to optimize plant growth compared to the energy required."

"Where does the energy come from?" Will asked.

"Deep geothermal, supplemented by tidal turbines," Andreia said. "It's another area we're ahead of you on."

Meltha frowned, but Andreia ignored her.

"If it has to do with the sea," Briares told Will, "we know far more than your people."

"You probably know more about Mars than Earth's ocean," Andreia added.

Will tensed at the insult. "That's not true, although clearly we have much to learn."

"Forget I said that, you're a marine scientist."

"Why not share what you know?" Will asked. It would be the biggest knowledge leap since Newton or Einstein.

"I agree. We should."

"We can't," Briares said. "Too risky."

Andreia glanced at Meltha and Briares, then told Will, "Should we choose to share what we know, it must be done in a way that protects our secrecy and benefits the ocean. Maybe you can help."

"How?"

"We can discuss it later."

Meltha glared at her.

They took another staircase back to the ground and proceeded through a massive archway to a similar, but smaller, dome. It was full of cultivated fruit trees, with aromatic herbs beneath. A young woman was manipulating shears at the end of a long pole with a basket to clip leaves off a mulberry tree.

Yidini picked three guavas and tossed them to the children. "We can store vitamin C," he told Will, "but not produce it. Citrus and guava fruits contain much more than seaweed."

"We can't even store vitamin C," Will said.

"One of our ancient adaptations to life at sea, I presume."

The children finally got bored and drifted away. Yidini ended the tour at a quarter-acre vertical farm, with ten layers of interlocking platforms of leafy greens and other vegetables, fed by a system of drip pipes.

"This is for variety," Andreia told Will. "We get most of our calories from seaweed and shellfish."

Andreia led him down another hallway, Meltha and Briares behind. They passed through a sprawling metalworking shop with furnaces, industrial machinery, and modern 3-D printers. It was noisy and hot. The workers stared at Will and spoke to each other in an unrecognizable language. Andreia and Meltha addressed them in the same language, then they continued onward.

As they exited, Will spotted a middle-aged man placing a gold bar into a crucible. An adjacent table contained a press and a pile of gold coins.

They entered a large circular room with a curved ceiling, full of brightly-lit tanks of tall seaweeds interspersed with hanging mesh bags of scallops, mussels, oysters, and clams. The shellfish rested on gratings stacked inside the bags. Shrimp swam between.

"The plants are all domesticated," Andreia said, "cross-bred over thousands of years for optimal production and nutrition. The mollusks and shrimp are also domesticated, and provide protein while keeping the tanks clean."

"Do you raise fish, too?" Will asked.

"We catch fish outside—tradition, I suppose—but mostly we're mariculturalists, with surface plants as a supplement."

Andreia led them to another chamber dominated by a huge aquarium, bigger than the one at the Miami Seaquarium, full of corals and fish. Thin tree-like structures held growing coral fragments, much like the coral nurseries in

South Florida that Will had seen. A female Sea-Dweller inside was seemingly conducting an inspection.

"We've been trying to regrow the reefs in various places," Andreia said. "And develop cures for all the coral, fish, and invertebrate diseases. We have a propagule freezer too. Unfortunately, it's a losing battle."

"You proposed working together. You can teach us restoration techniques and disease cures that we can deploy at scale. And yes, for restoration to work, we have to stop heating and acidifying the ocean."

Meltha glared at them.

Andreia held up a hand. "If there's a way we can remain hidden. I'm not convinced we'll be intentionally exterminated, but we don't want to become a Disneyworld attraction, either." She addressed Meltha and Briares. "Will is tired from his trip. I'll bring him to any meetings you schedule. Give us at least a day's warning."

Meltha started to object, but Andreia whisked Will away down a corridor. "You're not ready to be questioned by the Council yet. They'll assume the worst."

Will's stomach contracted. "What do you mean? What's the Council?"

"The Council of Elders. Meltha's one of the most influential. In theory, Sea-Dweller clans don't have leaders—we make decisions collaboratively. But in our clan at least, the Council interprets our codes and customs—our unwritten laws that have been passed down for millenia—and the rest of us defer to their opinions. They want to question you, and I have to prepare you for it."

"So, they're like judges and you'll be my attorney?"

"Kind of. Interesting comparison."

Chapter 10

Will

Will followed Andreia back to the yellow corridor where they'd started, still in awe of all he'd seen.

"My quarters are just past the sealock," Andreia said as they entered. "In case I carry a surface disease. Even when I'm perfectly fine—which is almost always—I have to live in the designated clan trader quarters, and wear a filtration mask everywhere else. Complete overkill." Her face fell. "It makes having a relationship down here nearly impossible."

"I can imagine."

"You have no idea. If I'm in the mood for physical relations and someone else is willing, we have to do it outside in the water." Her expression was matter-of-fact. "And Mazi boys have lost our ancestors' talent for underwater coupling. Totally clumsy."

Will had never tried it, and made a note to ask about her preferred techniques if the opportunity arose.

"And afterward," she continued, "my partner has to wear a mask for ten days, and everyone knows why. I have to beg for partners, and there aren't a lot of suitable choices. It's become too humiliating to bother anymore." She looked down instead of at him.

"You're stunning," Will decided to admit. "I think it would be well worth it."

Her eyes flickered down his body and back up. "Thank you, but I see why Stefan—my predecessor as clan trader—resigned. He works in the sewage systems now—went from the best job to the worst. He wanted to marry and have children, and that was the only way."

"Why sewage systems?"

"Punishment from the Council for a lifetime of thwacking their noses."

Andreia opened a side hatch and flicked on a light switch. They entered a deep space of spectacular chaos. The floor was varnished teak, partly covered by overlapping Persian rugs. Rope nets, holding wooden carvings, bottles, pottery, and other relics, hung from the ceiling. The walls were obscured by shelves, cabinets, and a narrow balustrade from which hung old glass floats, brass lanterns, and antique life preservers. The shelves were crowded with statuettes, bottles, silver and porcelain dining sets, and every nautical knickknack imaginable. Wooden crates with cluttered surfaces turned the room into a maze.

Andreia closed the door. "You can remove your mask now."

Will slipped it into his pocket. The air entered his nose more easily now. It smelled faintly of varnish, salt, and wax.

"This is where you live?" he asked.

"It's mostly storage for trading items."

"Where do you sleep?"

She pointed to the far wall. "There's a bedroom back there."

They threaded their way past artifacts ranging from the Spanish conquest to the modern age. Will recognized the ship name on one of the life preservers hanging above: *SS Marine Sulphur Queen*, a converted tanker that had disappeared without a trace off Florida in the early 1960's. He pointed at it. "Do you know where the wreck is? Relatives of the lost crew might want to know."

She shook her head. "Most of this stuff was recovered before I was born."

He changed topics. "Do you mind if I ask about the ankle tattoos and the hatch design?"

"Oh, that. It's our clan symbol. All Mazi receive it during our adulthood ceremony. The circle represents interconnectedness in space, time, and spirit, and the cross represents strength, resilience, and wisdom. The circle and cross are joined because they support each other."

She brushed aside a curtain of hanging beaded shells and led him into a room with a large iron-scrollwork bed, a tall dresser, racks of clothes, and more shelves loaded with shipwreck salvage. An old-fashioned ship intercom was attached to one wall. Beneath it, an open chest was stuffed with polished gold coins. Another chest was filled with gold bars, and a third filled with silver.

Earlier thoughts displaced, Will eyed the chests. "That's a pirate's dream." The gold and silver bars looked contemporary, with their weight and purity engraved on top. He picked up one of the coins, which was worn, but stamped with a Spanish coat of arms. Will recalled the gold coin production in the machine shop. *Is this legit or counterfeited?*

"That's a doubloon," Andreia said. "Seven grams of gold. Minted by hand in the Americas in the late 17th century, worth about $4,000 on the open market."

Will tried to estimate the total value in the chest. *In the millions.*

"Nothing here is mine alone," Andreia continued. "Everything is owned in common. We sell the coins and other valuables to buy things we can't make ourselves. Unfortunately, our stash is running low, and it's been years since we found anything new."

"Where's the treasure from?"

Andreia paused a moment. "There are over a thousand shipwrecks off the Keys, and in our wider exploration area, tens of thousands. Plus plane wrecks. They're still great sources of metal and wood, but as far as gold, silver, and jewels, it's all been found. We used to work with Land-Dweller treasure hunters, but these days, we sell to brokers who fake the origin."

Dodgy. "You mentioned planes," Will said. "Do you, uh, sell recovered drugs?" He hoped not.

"That's a lot more dangerous than selling treasure. We give any drugs we find to the Karsk clan, who have Land-Dweller contacts in high places. They give us a cut." She studied his face, seeming to sense his disappointment. "Don't worry, it's not a regular practice anymore. We mostly stick near our habitats these days."

"The Karsk clan are nearby?" he asked.

"On the other side of Cuba. I've never been there."

"Their contacts, cartel? Corrupt officials?"

"That's not information they share. And it's best not to know." She pointed at a side door, apparently wanting to move on. "Toilet, sink, and bathtub are in there." She indicated a door in the opposite direction. "Kitchen and eating room are there."

"You said these quarters are for the clan trader?"

"Yes. I moved in when I was appointed. It's by far the biggest living space, but I'd happily trade it for a tiny room in the common quarters. The rest of Yellow Section—yellow for gold—is for storage. There's more items for trading, although not much of it's valuable on the surface. And whatever I bring down has to be quarantined in one of the rooms for ten days."

"How long have you been doing this?"

"Three years. Plus three as an apprentice. I see things no one else in my clan does. It's exciting—something new every day—but a lot lonelier than I thought it would be."

She led him back into the main room, around a stack of crates, and opened a wooden door with a barnacle-covered wooden steering helm attached. Beyond was a wood-paneled office with a faded Persian rug, full bookcases on three walls, and nautical charts tacked to the fourth. A massive desk in the middle had been constructed from old planks, fastened together and varnished. On its surface sat two laptops, extra keyboards, two flat-screen monitors, a headset and external speakers, a laser printer, stacks of papers, and randomly scattered office supplies.

Andreia sat at the desk and powered up one of the laptops. "You helped me find Galen's sled, but I have even more questions now." She pointed at one of the wooden chairs half-hidden beneath more stacks of paper. "You can clear that off and bring it over."

Will moved the papers to the floor and moved the chair next to hers. The external keyboards were big, with several rows of unrecognizable symbols made from lines and occasional curves arranged in varying combinations. "Is that your native language?" he asked.

"A standardized version for communicating between clans. We have a mostly common sign language, too. When it comes to speaking, Sea-Dweller languages are all related—like Spanish and French, for example—but different enough to cause embarrassment if you aren't careful. The closer the clans, the closer the dialects. Karsk, for example, sound full of themselves—their grammar is overly formal—but otherwise, no problem. Now if you asked me to talk to someone from the Mana Hemisphere—the Pacific Ocean—we'd sound like swollen-tongue idiots to each other."

The enormity of the find—a cousin species spread throughout the world, but hitherto unknown—exploded through Will's mind, pushing aside all else. It changed everything, too much to process, like if he'd assumed the world was flat and suddenly discovered it was round. Or if, like most people prior to the Enlightenment, he'd been taught Earth was the center of the universe, then learned it was an insignificant speck.

Andreia fixed her wide green eyes on him. "Are you alright?"

"Sorry. I'm having trouble adjusting to everything you've told me."

Andreia held his hand. "I wonder if one week is too quick. Could you stay a little longer?"

Will sighed. "I told you—"

"Okay, absolute deadline is two weeks. We can talk about it later." She showed Will on a map where they'd found his sled, then brought up a spreadsheet marked with Sea-Dweller symbols. She pointed at one of the rows. "The batteries were drained. To do that, he'd have to be in a hurry and careless.

Even so, Aux—that's our communications outpost—is well within range, and I can't think of anyplace else he'd go."

"You told me the sleds have navigation computers. Did it save Galen's waypoints or track?"

She shook her head. "They don't save any information when the power goes off. It's a precaution to keep our home location secret."

Makes sense.

She pointed at another row. "He had plenty of oxygen. When I plugged in the sled, the gauges indicated that the primary tank was two-thirds full and the secondary completely full. If he ran out of power, he could have waited for the batteries to recharge, at least enough to make it home. The air systems are automated with microcontrollers, but can also be controlled manually."

"I assume you brought his sled back?"

"Yes. Follow me."

They put their masks back on and she led him down a series of corridors to a sealock, stenciled with the number 10. A sled resembling Andreia's, but dented and scratched, was secured to the floor grating, with an electrical cable running to a wall socket. A sign in Mazi script was taped to the side.

"Do not use," Andreia translated. "It's been reserved for spare parts—no one wants to ride a sled someone died on. I recharged the batteries, but otherwise, everything's the same as we found it."

"Did you check the sled for malfunctions?" Will asked.

"A mechanic did. He said nothing was wrong with it."

"Maybe we could take a second look," he suggested. "Take it apart if we have to. It's been relegated for spare parts anyway."

Andreia retrieved a large toolbox from the decompression chamber and removed sections of exterior shell, which were molded from resin. Thick interconnected batteries formed a layer on the bottom. Wires ran to the motors and console. Hoses ran from the rebreathers and CO_2 scrubbers to metal cylinders, marked in Mazi script and the symbols O_2, N_2, and He/H_2.

Will looked for loose wires, but they were all secure.

At the same time, Andreia tested the circuits with a multimeter. "So far, everything's the correct voltage," she commented. "No internal shorts."

As Will checked the motors, Andreia said, "This doesn't make sense."

"What?"

She had pressed the positive multimeter lead against a gas valve connector. "This is the output from the primary oxygen tank sensor. It goes to the microcontroller, which manages the gas mixture and displays the fraction remaining in each tank. There's no voltage, meaning zero oxygen." She pointed at the console display. "Here, it's reading two-thirds full, like last time I looked."

She tested the secondary oxygen tank. Her face tightened. "Same with this one."

Will rapped a knuckle against the gas cannisters. The inert tanks sounded full, but the oxygen tanks echoed inside. "They're empty, alright."

"There must be a fault in the microprocessor." She sniffled. "Poor Galen thought he had plenty of oxygen, when in fact he had none. He might have only realized something was wrong when he started to lose consciousness." Her eyes grew watery and her lips trembled.

Will held her and she cried against his shoulder, warm tears dripping down his neck.

"I'm sorry," he said, unable to think of something else to say.

After a few minutes, Andreia sniffled and let go of him. "Our sleds are so reliable. They're hand-built and receive regular maintenance. How could this have gone unnoticed?"

"Do you have a way to test the microprocessor?" he asked.

She wiped her eyes. "Not here. We have to go to Aux."

"You said that's your communications outpost?"

"Yes, it's how we connect to the Internet."

"Did you tap into an undersea cable somehow?" Will asked.

Andreia paused before answering. "Our engineers are very good at their jobs. They ran a feed from an undersea Internet cable to Aux, and another from Aux to Katiki, all without leaving a trace. The outpost also serves as an emergency habitat in case something catastrophic happens here."

Andreia removed the controller box and some of the attachments from the sled. Then she led Will back to the office in her quarters. She sat behind her computers and began speaking in Mazi to someone.

She looked up. "Zoze wants to meet you." She motioned for Will to join her.

Will went behind the desk and squatted next to Andreia. A young woman with bright pink hair—the first dyed hair Will had seen on a Sea-Dweller—was onscreen.

"This is Zoze," Andreia said. "My most trusted friend."

"BFF's, they say on the surface," Zoze said onscreen.

Will introduced himself, and Zoze bombarded him with questions. "How long are you down here? What's your job on the surface? What's your favorite TV show?"

Will answered her questions, including admitting that he was a 'CSI' addict, then asked, "You're on Aux, I presume?"

"Obviously."

"What's it like?"

"Smaller, with no trees. But all the cool people live here. We can do what we want here."

Andreia made a slicing motion with her hand and leaned toward the camera. "Can Sama look at the controller box? It's not just about Galen—it could happen to someone else."

"Yes, yes," Zoze said, "I'll tell him."

"I'll see you tomorrow, then."

"Be sure to bring Will, so we can all meet him."

Andreia ended the call and said, "Sorry I had to cut you off. Zoze would have you talking until your vocal cords gave out."

"No worries. I understand her curiosity."

"There's another matter I wanted to discuss—why Galen ran out of oxygen in the first place. The sleds have two air systems in case there's a passenger. For one person, they should last about six days before recharging from the surface. But both were empty."

"How much did he start with?"

"The tanks are refilled in the sealocks," she said, "so they should have been full. I checked; the prior user confirmed doing this. The oxygen can also be replenished by running a hose to the surface. We did that when looking for his sled. The batteries must have failed at the same time, or maybe earlier. Possibly the worst luck ever." She gulped. "He would have swum to the surface, desperate for air, and got caught in the hurricane."

"That many mishaps at one time," Will said, "what are the odds?"

Andreia turned rigid. "What do you mean?"

Will decided not to use the word 'sabotage,' not without proof. But the simultaneous and specific failures were awfully suspicious. The question was, *why?*

"I think we need to consider again where he might have been going, and why," he said. "He left from here?"

"Yes." She opened a bathymetry map on her computer and displayed their location and where they found the sled. "You must promise not to tell anyone where we are."

"I promised secrecy." He planned to keep his vow. "Do you have police? On the surface, the police handle disappearances."

She shook her head. "There's not that many of us, so we handle everything together. When Galen disappeared, we all searched for him. Even Meltha. Even Xitaros!"

"Who's Xitaros?"

"An asshole. Unfortunately, he has plenty of company."

"Could Galen have been headed to Aux? Did he have friends there?"

"That was the first place I thought about. Everyone there's older than him, but yeah, my friends liked him and taught him some of their computer tricks. He had a knack for it." She looked down. "It's too bad he died so young. Completely unfair." Tears formed in her eyes.

She wiped her eyes with the back of her hand, then continued, "He's been there with me, but wasn't old enough to go anywhere by himself, a rule he obviously ignored. He never arrived there, though, and didn't tell anyone he was on his way." She pointed at a triangle on the map about 10 nautical miles east-south-east of their position. "That's Aux." It was near a sinusoidal purple line, which on standard nautical charts, indicated an undersea cable.

"Was Galen interested in moving there?"

Her eyes drifted down. "No, Galen wanted to live on the surface with me. The day before he disappeared, he brought it up again. I said he was too young and it turned into an argument. He called me a hypocrite, and he was probably right." Tears formed in her eyes. "That's the last time I saw him. I keep thinking it's my fault he died."

Will held her gloved hand. He'd gone through counseling after Yoselin died and had found it a tiny bit helpful. "Grief can be a terrible monster. It fills you with guilt, that you did something wrong, somewhere, somehow. But just because you feel guilty, doesn't mean you are guilty. Your brother made his own decisions, like to run away, a typical adolescent reaction to an argument. A day or two later, you probably would have been buddies again. You know, from what I've observed, he couldn't have asked for a better big sister."

She smiled at him and squeezed his hand. "Thanks Dr. Myers," she said with a twinge of sarcastic humor.

After few moments, she let go, sniffled, and wiped her eyes with the back of her hand. She looked at him. "I lost my thought current. Where were we?"

Will racked his brain for ideas. "Did your brother have some sort of Internet or internal account that might give us more clues?"

"He wasn't old enough to receive Internet access. My hacker friends searched outgoing data for any indication Galen was communicating externally, but found nothing."

"You said there are other clans. Could Galen have talked to one of them—the Karsk, maybe—and headed to one of their habitats?"

She blinked at him. "You'd have to go all the way around Cuba. The Bahamas clans are closer, but he didn't know anyone from there. And no one would have given him directions or encouraged him; it's a huge violation of custom to accept a juvenile from another clan, and we Sea-Dwellers stick to our customs."

"If there are clans in the Bahamas, Andros is only 150 miles or so from here."

"They're on the far side, so again, it's a circuitous trip. The waters between the Keys, Cuba, and Andros are exclusively Mazi."

"That's a big area."

"It is, but there used to be a lot more of us—tens of thousands. All the clans were much bigger. Some disappeared entirely." Her eyes fell.

"What happened?"

"Diseases, mostly. Then we hid in isolation, and fertility dropped. We encourage inter-clan marriage now, but the men still have sperm troubles and the women have a lot of miscarriages. It's very sad—we are dying like the rest of the planet."

"The rescue effect was insufficient?"

"Rescue effect?"

"Sorry, I'm too used to talking to biologists and students. Small, isolated populations have lower genetic diversity and tend to accumulate"—*how do I explain detrimental alleles?*—"problematic traits like decreased health and low sperm counts. In the Eastern U.S., panthers were persecuted and hunted almost to extinction. Only a few dozen remained, in southern Florida, but their health and reproduction were so bad, they'd have died out if not for the introduction of eight females from Texas."

Andreia held up a hand. "Everyone knows inbreeding is bad. Sex with siblings is forbidden. But it's still mostly within the clan. Girls and boys who grow up together experiment and fall in love, you know how it is. So not many of us end up with husbands or wives from other clans."

She was quiet a while, then said, "Let's get back to Galen. One problem at a time."

Will arranged the pieces of information Andreia had given him. "Most likely, Galen was headed to Aux."

"Then why didn't he tell anyone there he was coming?"

"He might not have planned out his actions. From everything you've told me, he seems adventurous and a little impulsive."

"That's Galen."

"The question is," Will asked, "why didn't he arrive? Why did he go so far away?"

"While we're waiting for Sama to check the air controller," Andreia said, "we can talk to the Aux residents and try to figure that out." She shut down her computer. "Here's the dive plan. I'm towing you again, so all you have to do is hold on. We'll ascend to 10 meters and travel at that depth, then descend to Aux when we get there. It's in deep water—a thousand feet."

"You're kidding."

"The Internet cables are in deep water. Aux is pressurized, five atmospheres to reinforce the shells, but not enough to need helium or hydrogen."

That much helium would be difficult to obtain, Will mused, and hydrogen could explode from a single spark.

"And," she continued, "if the air inside was at the same pressure as the water outside, it would take days for anyone going to Katiki to decompress when they arrived. The Aux maintenance crew works rotating shifts, and can't spend half their life in decompression."

Makes sense. "What about coming back?"

"Ascend to 40 meters—five atmospheres of pressure, same as inside Aux. But we'll have to decompress to one atmosphere when we get back. And the longer we stay at Aux, the longer that will take."

Andreia set up a hammock in the main room, hanging between a net full of bales and a model sailing ship suspended from the ceiling. "Get some rest," she said, and went through the shell-bead curtain into her bedroom.

Will climbed into the hammock and went over everything he'd seen, trying to commit it to memory.

* * *

Baytown, Texas

At her station in the Gulf Coast Baytown refinery control room, Operator Maria Castillo struggled to keep her eyes open. She hated the 12-hour rotating shifts. She just couldn't get her body to adjust; even using sleeping pills didn't help. At least it offered plenty of days off with the kids. And a nice paycheck—much higher than her husband's, a thought that brought a grin to her face.

On one of the many screens at her workstation, a high-pressure indicator began to flash. She checked the readings. Pressure was increasing in a large number of pipelines in the refinery, the indicators moving steadily upward.

She called out to the shift supervisor. "Vance! Got a pressure buildup, multiple lines!"

The supervisor hurried over and stared at the screen. "What the hell? Shut the inflows before something bursts!"

Maria stabbed at control buttons, but nothing happened. The system wasn't responding.

"Shut everything down!" her supervisor shouted.

"I'm trying!"

More indicators turned red on the screens. Alarms began to sound.

"We've got a breach in line 23!" one of her co-workers shouted from another workstation.

That was in the gasoline section of the refinery. *Not good.*

The supervisor picked up a phone and shouted orders in it. Maria hit the manual override switch, but no matter what she tried, she couldn't stop the upward climb of the pressure indicators.

One of the camera monitors above the status screens flashed orange. Maria glanced up. Fire was climbing up one of the towers in the gasoline section.

On the status screens, more breaches. On another camera monitor, a storage tank exploded in a huge fireball. It was followed by another.

The room shook as if from an earthquake. Every alarm in the room blared.

Maria gripped the crucifix around her neck. *Jesus, help us.*

Chapter 11

Andreia

The intercom buzzed Andreia awake the next morning. She stumbled out of bed and pressed the talk button.

"Good morning," Meltha spoke in Mazi. The ancient wall speaker made her voice sound flat and tinny.

"Good morning."

"The Council of Elders requests a meeting with Will Myers at six hours past noon today in the Assembly Chamber."

Andreia had hoped for more notice. She glanced at the brass clock on the opposite wall, a restored relic from a sunken freighter. The hands indicated 8:40. She'd slept late, over ten hours. Which meant they'd have to scramble to get to Aux and back. *Should I postpone it?*

"And the purpose of the meeting?" she asked.

"To learn everything we can. Be sure he arrives on time, and is properly masked."

"Why today? Why not tomorrow?"

"Because we decided today is better than later."

Andreia had expected an answer like that. She signed off and ran fingers through her tangled hair.

She had dreamed about sharing her bed with Will. *Am I so desperate that I would couple with a Land-Dweller?* She instantly condemned her thought as racist—or was it speciest? Her clan respected even crabs more than Land-Dwellers, but that was ignorance born of fear. *Or is it fear born of ignorance?*

She took a deep breath. Wanting companionship is natural. And it's stupid to rule someone out just because they're a Land-Dweller. Especially a Land-Dweller who admires my differences. Plus, Will was ruggedly handsome, despite his small eyes and swimming-handicapped hands and feet. He was well-educated and concerned about the declining state of the ocean. She was still mad at Will for tracking her van, but he had mostly been sympathetic and helpful.

Andreia brushed her long hair, a ritual that cleared her mind. She put on a one-piece swimsuit—Aux was below the thermocline. They'd need wetsuits too, but those were in the sealock.

She pushed through the shell-bead curtain into the main room. Will was already awake, examining the myriad shipwreck artifacts.

They greeted each other, then Will asked, "Do you have any coffee? I had trouble sleeping."

"No, sorry. We don't drink coffee. Caffeine bothers our stomachs." She led him into the kitchen and poked through the refrigerator and pantry.

She hadn't been taking care of the place, and was greeted by half-dissolved seaweed, rancid shrimp salad, and moldy cassava bread. *Yuck*. She dumped it all down the compost chute. But all was not lost—she found some dried sweet potato slices, shrimp paste, and cashew nuts, and plated them with her favorite condiments: chili-infused squid ink, fish sauce, and vinegar.

They sat at the small wooden table along the wall. "Help yourself," she told him, slathering a sweet potato slice with shrimp paste and dousing it with squid ink. "Eat plenty—you'll need the calories."

Will eyed the food suspiciously, then shrugged and started eating, sans condiments.

"I dreamed about you last night," she admitted.

Will put down the cashew he was about to eat. "A good dream, I hope."

"I don't remember all the details," she half-lied. "But good."

He smiled. "I've had a lot of dreams about you since we met. Better ones than usual."

"Glad to be of help. Do you normally have nightmares?"

His face fell. "Yeah. Usually I'm drowning, or caught in an old fishing net, or watching my wife die and not being able to help…"

Andreia draped a hand over his. "I'm sorry." She squeezed his hand and he squeezed back.

Will met Andreia's eyes. "We're a lot alike, you and I. It's hard to believe we're different species."

After breakfast, Andreia went into the office and messaged AUX_LOCK_CONTROL over the encrypted chat line.

MaziAndreia: Heading to Aux w/guest. Which lock has space?

AUX_LOCK_CONTROL: 6. Looking forward to seeing you.

She returned to Will. "Ready?"

"Yep."

They suited up in the sealock. Andreia unhooked the sled from the walls and checked the instruments. She attached one of the cargo platforms with a pair of heavy cables.

"We need to move fast this time," she told Will. "We'll use most of the battery power, but that's what the wall chargers are for." She pointed at the attached platform. "Lie on that, stomach down."

"I held onto the tow rope fine when coming here."

"At a slow speed and shallow depth. I can't take any chances."

"You sound concerned." As instructed, Will lay on the cargo platform.

"You're my responsibility while you're down here." She strapped him in and passed him one of the rebreather mouthpieces. She hit a button on the wall, and the lock began filling with water. Once full, the outer doors slid apart, and she piloted the sled into the dark blue water.

She followed the dive plan, ascending at the fastest safe speed for Will—around ten meters per minute. She leveled off at 10 meters and continued toward Aux. When they reached its position two hours later, she looked back at Will and gave the thumbs-down sign to indicate they'd be descending.

Will responded with the okay sign. Andreia faced the sled downward and descended rapidly, keeping an eye on her passenger in the mirror.

Aux was nearly 300 meters down. The water was chilly and dark. Behind her, Will was shivering despite the wetsuit.

Andreia steered to Sealock 6, located above the hackers' quarters. Irritatingly, the sled's remote opener, which sent a coded signal to open the sealock, only worked at Katiki. Aux didn't have that feature.

She parked the sled atop the camouflaged portal, jumped off, typed the code on the hidden keypad, and hurried back before the doors opened. The sealock doors slid aside and the sled sank within. Sealock 6 had a typical layout, with a storage space for sleds and a decompression suite beyond.

Will was still shivering as the pump removed the sea water. After plugging the sled into the wall charger and attaching the oxygen feed, Andreia helped him out of his wetsuit, led him into the inner suite, and draped him with towels. "Sorry," she said. "I misjudged your temperature tolerance."

"It was like being dunked in ice water," he forced out through chattering teeth.

"Maybe 12 °C, not cold enough to kill you."

Will rubbed his arms and legs with the towels. "That's a lot colder than normal diving depth."

Fair enough. "I'll find a dry suit for the way back."

When Andreia traveled to Aux by herself, or with another Sea-Dweller, there was no need to decompress after quick descents; she'd just let the water-purging pump dictate the pace. But Will lacked her physiology. To be safe, she set the decompression timer for an hour, decreasing one atmosphere per minute until the chamber was at five atmospheres, but including periodic pauses.

They showered and rinsed their gear. Andreia threw on a blouse and short skirt, revealing her legs and feet. Will was shivering again after emerging from the bathroom, and put on three layers of clothes.

They sat at the small table and ate smoked fish on seaweed crackers. "What are your hacker friends like?" he asked.

"As a whole, we Sea-Dwellers are stuck in our customs. We live in an idyllic past and don't like change, risk, or conflict. Each clan is a tightly-knit group—it probably comes from the challenges of living underwater and avoiding Land-Dwellers. We live for the clan and make decisions by consensus.

"Naturally," she continued, "there are those who are more adventurous and individualist. It's more common among young people; then they become more conservative and group-oriented as they grow older. I fall into the individualist category, I suppose, and Galen did, and certainly my friends at Aux. They use the term 'freethinkers.' Which in Katiki, is considered derogatory."

"It's considered an insult to think for one's self?" he asked.

"More, to put one's self ahead of the rest. And to be obsessed with surface people. Like you apparently are with my people."

"Of course I am! A cousin species no one knows about!"

"We're more alike than different," she said. "We have adaptations for living at sea, but on land, it's easy to pass as human. No one expects otherwise."

"Did Galen ever say he wanted to move here?"

"I think he was more interested in living on land, like me."

When the timer dinged, Andreia put on a silk mask and gave one to Will. Then she opened the hatch to the rest of the outpost.

* * *

Layton, Florida

Dr. Ana Hernandez, Supervisory Special Agent at the NCIS Office of Special Projects, pulled her rental car into the gravel parking lot of the Keys Marine Laboratory. The laboratory grounds were surrounded by a wooden fence, with sole visitor access via a two-story sea-green building. Dr. William Myers, who according to video records, had assisted the autopsy of Galen Álvarez, worked here as a marine biologist.

The Álvarez boy had nearly identical aquatic adaptations to the body recovered from the South China Sea, which she'd examined three months ago. A preliminary analysis of tissue sample DNA found a 0.2% difference from the first body, which was significant, but a 0.5% difference from the standard human genome. This was greater even than the difference between humans and Neanderthals. It was astonishing, especially since no obvious signs of genetic tinkering were present. Yet according to the lab experts, the chance of random mutations creating such a coherent set of adaptations was almost zero, at least over a single generation—or even ten. The facility that had engineered these amphibious humanoids—assuming they were engineered and not natural—was apparently more capable than any other lab on Earth.

The boy's sister, Andreia, was practically a ghost, possessing a driver's license, vehicle registration, and credit cards, but no valid social security number, passport, or school records. Ana had driven to her address in Hialeah, which turned out to be an empty lot. A security camera at the Medical Examiner's building had captured video of Ms. Álvarez leading Dr. Myers behind a white van in the parking lot, where they disappeared from view. Unfortunately, any conversation was inaudible.

Ana introduced herself to the elderly building receptionist and flashed her badge. "Is Dr. Myers in?" She'd called his cell number twice without a response.

"Ooo, he didn't do something wrong, did he?"

"No, I just need to ask him some questions."

The receptionist nodded. "He's out of town. Dive trip if I remember right."

"When's he due back?"

The woman shrugged. "He said before his classes start." She checked the staff schedule and provided the date. "Sometime before then."

Ana showed her an enlarged photo of Ms. Álvarez from her driver's license. "Do you know this woman? I'm trying to reach her, as well."

The receptionist peered at it. "Quite the looker. I've been telling Will he needs to start dating again."

"So have you met her?"

"Never seen her before, sorry, though I'm only here part time."

Ana thanked the woman and left. Out of curiosity, she drove to Dr. Myers's house, a few blocks away. His truck was parked out front, and his boat tied to the seawall. *Did someone pick him up?*

The street-facing side of Dr. Myers's house had no doors. The enclosed part of the lower section was probably for storage, so she climbed the concrete stairs next to the car port, where she found a door. After knocking three times without response, she peered in the windows and the sliding glass doors in back. All the lights were off. No one here unless they were hiding. No nearby cameras.

Ana had compiled background data on Myers. No criminal record. Wife deceased, no children. Lived here alone unless he had a roommate or girlfriend.

The back of her neck began to itch—her body's way of telling her something was off. She called a number and requested the phone data of Álvarez and Myers. Then she began to knock on doors, asking the neighbors if they'd seen Álvarez or her white van.

Chapter 12

Will

The hatch at the communications outpost—which also bore the Mazi circle and cross—opened onto a stairwell landing. The air was considerably colder than in Katiki, and Will was glad he'd found a jacket to wear.

Zoze, the young Sea-Dweller woman with bright pink hair, greeted them. She was a foot shorter than Andreia, and wore a short skirt, white blouse, and a tan, midriff-grazing jacket with a double-wing patch on the left pocket and sleeve. No mask.

She hugged Andreia. "Welcome back! Are you sick?"

"No, neither one of us." Andreia pocketed her mask and told Will, "Aux rules are looser than Katiki's. But it's best if you stay masked, at least around others."

Zoze stared at Will's bare feet. "How do you swim with those things?"

"We wear dive fins."

She laughed. "LOL, I know! Come on, joke!"

Who says 'LOL' out loud? Will felt foolish and out of place. It was enlightening being the strange one. *This is how Andreia must feel all the time on land.* "No offense taken," he said.

"Did you bring your glowline kit?" Zoze asked Andreia.

"No, sorry, I'm really pressed for time—the Council scheduled a meeting with us, and they get mad if you're late."

Zoze waved her hands. "Masters and servants."

"It's not that bad."

"What's a glowline kit?" Will asked Andreia.

"For making temporary tattoos, like henna, but they glow."

Zoze led them down two flights of stairs and into a light-blue hallway with doors along both sides. They turned left, opened two watertight doors, and entered a circular room ringed with curving desks full of computers and monitors, and doors labeled in Mazi. Large flat-screen TVs lined the walls. The air was almost warm, presumably heated by the electronics.

Four men and a woman sat in swivel chairs talking to each other. The computer monitors had been turned off, but the screens mounted on the circular wall played news broadcasts with text in different languages. Most showed fires and explosions. The narrators were drowned out by bass-heavy hip-hop. The rapper had a distinct Caribbean accent.

"Ain't no more deceived by the lies I was told
Just 'cause something glitters don't mean it be gold
Hangin' with my homies, that's the way I roll.
Ain't no day-long boss slave, that just ain't my role."

As Will entered, everyone turned and stared. Someone turned down the volume, and Andreia introduced Will to the group. Sama was Andreia's age— early to mid-20's—with spiky green hair and a vest covered with pockets from which assorted tools peeked out. Duripi was slightly older, had dark hair like Andreia, and was chubby compared to other Sea-Dwellers Will had met thus far. Pijasiros was in his early 30's, tall, and had braided black-and-red hair cascading past shaved sides. He was dressed in black and wore dark augmented reality goggles.

The other two, Maia and Yissharu, were a married couple in their early thirties. Maia was also dressed in black, with black lipstick and heavy eyeliner. She had a slight stomach bulge. Yissharu, whose head was shaved, wore a colorful silk shirt, striped slacks, and gold earrings. The couple stared at Will while pretending not to.

"What's the matter?" Zoze asked the others. "Haven't you ever met a Land-Dweller before?"

"Neither have you," the black-clad man named Pijasiros said.

"I got a sneak preview. He's not as weird as he looks."

Andreia placed her gloved hand on Maia's stomach. "Kicking yet?"

"Not yet," the goth woman said. "Should be soon. Have you thought about settling down like Stefan? You only have so many years to bear children. You don't need a husband; we can all help raise them."

Andreia's eyes narrowed. "I hear enough of that from my relatives. I like what I do, and someone has to do it."

"Sorry. It's just that males are better suited for jobs away from the clan. They're more expendable."

The four men turned toward her. "Hey!" Duripi, the chubby guy with baggy pants, responded in semi-mock anger.

"It's true," Maia insisted. "Nothing's more important than continuing the species and clan. We need all the females for that, but not all the males."

Zoze leaned toward Will. "She didn't used to be like that."

Will addressed the group, "What do you do here?"

Pijasiros, the tall man with braided hair and AR goggles, answered first. "Write the tightest, most innovative code on the planet, for starters."

Andreia rolled her eyes. "They maintain communications with other clans—"

"Hard to believe," Zoze interjected, "but our ancestors used to communicate with instruments that imitated whale songs. 10,000-mile range, but only a few dozen bits of information per second."

"We also monitor what's happening on the surface," Duripi said, "and protect the clan from detection and malware. There's been an onslaught of new ransomware and viruses lately."

The green-haired guy named Sama held a fist toward the floor, an unfamiliar gesture. "It's always been bad, but this is like a tsunami. Biggest worldwide spike ever seen. Most of it zero-day—no patches available."

"Keeping us busy," Duripi added.

Andreia turned to Will. "They also help me if I need it."

"Which is often," Zoze said with a smirk.

Andreia blew air into her pink-haired friend's face, but it evoked more smiling.

Duripi fingered a seashell necklace and stared at Will. "We watch your news a lot. Why do your people consume so much? The planet can't support it. And why do you fight all the time?"

"Why ask me?" Will said.

"You're the only Land-Dweller in the room."

Will felt a little guilty. He hated ads as much as anyone, not to mention the concept of shopping for fun. But considering how much diving and fishing gear he owned, and that he bought a new smartphone every two years, he was as big a part of the problem as anyone.

"The United Nations is trying to promote sustainable development," he said, "circular economies instead of linear. It's not my specialty, but what I've read makes sense."

Zoze opened her mouth, but Duripi spoke first. "What about my other question, why do you fight so much?"

"Don't be rude," Andreia told him.

Rude or not, Will was accustomed to debating. "Are you saying your people never fight?"

"We don't kill each other," Duripi said.

So they do have fights, just not to the death? "Fighting isn't confined to humans. That's how life evolved—using resources to grow and reproduce, and if resources are limited, competing for them, with the fittest surviving. There's cooperation and mutualism too, but male animals compete for females, plants compete for sunlight and water, and so on."

Duripi gave a hint of a nod, then said, "Both our species are sentient, though. Yours should know better. Even animals—dolphins and schooling fish, for example, know better. Cooperation is more productive than competition, especially when it involves death and destruction on huge scales."

Will tried not to take it personally. "We cooperate, that's how we survive. As for dolphins, they exhibit some pretty violent dominance fighting sometimes."

"True," Duripi admitted.

"And," Will continued, "killing isn't as common among humans as you seem to think. Most of us abhor the thought. I'd put the number of murderers between 1 in 10,000 and 1 in 100,000. Murders receive a lot of news attention precisely because they're so abhorrent."

"What about your wars?" Maia asked.

Will struggled to come up with an answer. Humans had been fighting wars since the dawn of recorded history, and showed no signs of letting up. But since he was essentially an ambassador for humanity here, he had to say something.

"I agree," he began, "wars and violence are huge problems. A lot of us try to stop them." After Yoselin died, he'd given up trying to make the world a better place, but all his perspectives prior to entering Andreia's world seemed like the uninformed musings of a child. "I welcome any suggestions."

Maia stared at him. "That's nice to hear, but given that all your countries and cultures engage in war and violence, it must be a genetic problem, not just a social one."

Flawed logic. "We're social beings. Mostly it has to do with allocation of resources." He wasn't an expert on the topic, though, and decided not to prolong the argument.

"We're on a tight schedule," Andreia said, "so—"

Duripi kept speaking, his face animated. "They're attacking each other even now, blowing up the world's biggest oil refineries."

"Are you talking about the export terminals in Saudi Arabia last week?" Will asked. "A small faction could have been behind that."

"Not that," Sama said. "The attacks last night. Big refineries in the U.S. You didn't know?"

Andreia stared at him. "Last night?"

Stunned, Will asked, "What happened?"

Pijasiros sat in front of one of the computers and began typing. A serious-looking man in a dark suit and striped tie spoke to the screen, with 'BREAKING NEWS' in a red caption box beneath.

"This breaking news," the anchor intoned, "massive explosions and fires at three Texas oil refineries."

The screen showed flames and smoke billowing into the night sky amid a sea of industrial towers. Judging by the intervening trees and fence, the video had been shot from outside the facility.

"At least five people were killed," the anchor continued, "with dozens injured and transported to area hospitals. Firefighters have been dispatched from around the region, but the fires have not yet been completely extinguished…"

Pijasiros brought up another news video. "This is from this morning."

"Our lead story again," a different newscaster began, "apparent attacks on five of the world's largest oil refineries. Five refineries in total, three in Texas, one in India, and one in South Korea exploded and caught fire at 2 AM Central Time last night. Government officials indicated that an investigation is ongoing, but whether or not the incidents are linked is not yet known, and the causes of the incidents have not yet been determined. However, due to the simultaneous nature of the explosions and their similarity to the catastrophic cyberattacks in Saudi Arabia, terrorism is the most likely explanation…"

Pijasiros announced, "Hackers again, I bet."

"The same way the Saudi facilities were destroyed?" Will asked. "Malware that took over the switching software?"

The black-clad man smiled. "That was my guess too. I'm impressed you are familiar with the likely cause—the media hasn't reported those details. How do you know so much about it? I thought you were a biologist."

"My father had inside information."

"Impressive work by the hackers, in any case. Here's the press conference from yesterday, before the attacks last night." Pijasiros pointed at the wall screen above him. He fast-forwarded past an ad for Currentsea, until reaching a balding man with glasses speaking at a podium. Captioning identified him as the U.S. Director of National Intelligence.

"We've completed the initial phase of our investigation of the sabotage of Saudi Arabia's ports," the Director said, "a heinous attack in which many lives were lost, including several Americans and an unknown number of Saudis. This attack was carried out by saboteurs who planted customized malware into the control systems, requiring physical access to the sites. The prime suspects, two contract employees of the Saudi Ports Authority, have since disappeared, and Interpol has issued a Red Notice for their capture. The FBI has also issued a half-million-dollar reward apiece for information leading to their capture."

Pijasiros paused the video. "We learned more from our contacts in the cybercommunity. The malware—a worm with the attack routines and a rootkit to hide it—was embedded in a software patch that was manually installed to get past the air gaps. The programmers must have had detailed knowledge of the port systems. An inside job, at least partly."

Andreia imitated a fast-moving swimmer with her fingers, and Pijasiros resumed the video.

"The sophisticated nature of the attack points to significant resources and planning," the Director continued. "The forensic evidence suggests Iranian state sponsorship."

Will wasn't surprised, at least regarding motive.

"First," the Director said, "some of the malware routines were used previously by Iranian hackers affiliated with the government..."

"Seems sloppy for an otherwise sophisticated attack," Pijasiros commented.

"The suspects received large payments of cryptocurrency that we have traced to Tehran..."

"How'd they trace it?" Zoze asked the others as the video continued.

"Blockchain analysis tools," Pijasiros replied over his shoulder. "Any more dumb questions?"

Zoze curled one hand and thrust a knuckle from her other hand inside— an obscene gesture, Will assumed.

On the wall screen, the spy director finished his statement and began taking questions.

"What are you doing to control the increasing gas prices?" a reporter asked.

"Are there plans for retaliation?" called out another.

"The president has made it clear that we will take action to protect America's interests and people, and we will do so at a time and in a manner of our choosing. Consistent with the practice we have adopted in the past, the public should not assume that they will necessarily know what actions have been taken or what actions we will take. But no options are off the table."

"Holy shit," Will blurted. It felt like a major war was starting. "Do they think Iran was behind last night's attacks too?" *Will my brother's carrier group be sent in?*

"They just occurred last night," Pijasiros said, "so no one knows yet. But programmers from different countries leave cultural fingerprints in their code. Your NSA probably has them all mapped out. It would be foolish to think it's a coincidence, however."

Andreia interrupted. "You have a knack for discovering interesting news about the Land-Dwellers, but Will and I can't stay long, and need to get started." She gave Sama the air controller box from Galen's sled. "See if you can figure out why this is giving incorrect oxygen readings."

"Zoze filled me in," Sama said. He took the box into an adjacent room.

An idea occurred to Will. "Do all Sea-Dwellers live in stationary habitats? Or do some move around in submarines?"

"We just have the shuttle and sleds," Andreia said. "Some clans have bigger transports. But as far as I know, none live as nomads. Not anymore, anyway."

"What's the shuttle?" Will asked.

"It's for transporting the shift workers back and forth."

Yissharu, the colorfully-dressed bald guy with earrings, addressed Will. "Why do you ask?" His accent was different from the others, gravelly and slurred like Cuban.

"We're not sure what Galen's intentions were. Was he planning to come here? Was he planning to rendezvous with someone on a sled or some other kind of transport?"

Everyone stared at him. "If so," Andreia said, "he didn't leave any trace of his plans."

"You said he learned some computer skills here. What if he snuck onto a computer and covered his tracks?"

Duripi smirked. "He was barely a novice, and we're pros."

"Understatement of the millenium," Pijasiros added.

"The habitats have cameras at the entrances, right?" Will asked. Andreia had waved at something when they arrived at Katiki, probably a hidden camera.

"Why?" Duripi asked.

Andreia answered, "Yes, there are cameras outside monitoring the entry locks at Aux and Katiki. They were originally installed so someone on duty could open them when needed. Now, we use remotes and keypads, but the Council thinks the cameras are still needed."

"How long do you keep the exterior camera footage?" Will asked.

"Maybe three months before it's written over," Pijasiros said. "They're motion activated, with a person-sized threshold so they don't go off every time a fish passes by."

"So you should still have recordings of Galen," Will said.

"If you're wondering whether or not we looked at the camera where he left from," Duripi replied, "of course we did. We're not idiots. Didn't tell us anything other than confirming he took a sled."

"I figured. Did you check the other cameras? I tell my students, if you're totally stumped on something, and your data doesn't supply answers, rethink your assumptions and look in new directions. Check every possible data source available."

Andreia half-smiled. "I knew an outsider might be helpful."

"I have to resume work," Yissharu announced. He nodded at Will. "Interesting to meet you."

Interesting? "Likewise," Will said.

Yissharu and Maia took seats at two of the computer workstations.

Duripi opened his palms. "Like Yissharu said, it was interesting." He looked around and left the room.

* * *

Andreia

After Duripi left, Andreia asked Zoze quietly, "Can you bring up the video from all the exterior cameras from the day my brother took the sled?"

Zoze's forehead scrunched. "I've never done that. I have no idea where it's stored."

Pijasiros turned from his nearby computer and made an argumentative popping noise with his mouth. "Sounds like someone should spend less time watching anime and more time learning the systems."

Zoze made an up-and-down motion with her fist. "Sit on it and squeal. Why obsess over minutiae when I can know something about everything?"

Pijasiros blew out a puff of air. "Your 'something' barely registers above zero."

"Mean humor is still mean," Andreia pointed out.

"She's the one who makes obscene gestures every time she talks. Do you want my help or not?"

"Of course I do."

Pijasiros turned back to his computer and brought up a window with a black background. His fingers flew across the alphanumeric keyboard, typing commands in Linux.

Rows of black rectangles, with camera IDs above, filled the big wall screen closest to Pijasiros. He typed some more, and all but four of the rectangles disappeared, the remaining ones increasing in size to fill the space.

"These are the cameras activated the day in question," he said. "Not many—three at Katiki and one here at Aux. This one was activated first."

The upper right rectangle displayed a sled exiting one of the locks, two Sea-Dwellers sitting atop it.

"Sealock 18 at Katiki," Pijasiros said. "Lock 19 at Katiki opened shortly after that." The upper left rectangle showed a similar scene.

Pijasiros typed some more. "It's two groups that went out spear-fishing. It looks like they returned well before Galen left, which is on this camera."

The lower left rectangle showed a young Sea-Dweller lying alone on a sled as it exited its lock. Andreia stiffened as she recognized Galen. He looked at the console instruments and drove off into the dark blue depths.

"No one tried to stop him?" Will asked.

"No one pays attention to who's leaving," Pijasiros said, "only to someone who's coming."

The guilt returned. "It was a whole day before anyone realized he'd left home," Andreia said. "I came from the surface as soon as I heard, but it was too late; the next day, the hurricane arrived and we had to shelter until it was gone."

"This is the last," Pijasiros said, "the Sealock 3 camera here on Aux. It activated about an hour after Galen departed Katiki."

The lower right rectangle remained blank.

Pijasiros typed some more. "Looks like there's no video after all. Maybe the sensor was activated, but there wasn't anything to record."

Andreia frowned. "Nothing useful."

"You're not giving up already, are you?" Zoze said, and pulled up another chair next to Pijasiros. "Can you check the other Sealock 3 sensors?" she asked him.

"Yes, I think I can search for water sensor alerts and cross-reference memory addresses for time stamps."

Andreia had no idea what he was talking about. She wasn't useless with computers, but neither was she near their level.

Pijasiros and Zoze stared at the computer and seemed to forget she and Will were standing behind them. "Score," Pijasiros said. "Lock 3 was opened when the sensor was activated. The camera should have shown someone entering or leaving, but didn't record anything."

"Does that camera normally work?" Will asked.

Pijasiros navigated to a file directory labeled LOCK_3_CAMERA_EXT. "There's no video data after the day Galen disappeared. An activation signal was sent to the camera on several occasions, but there's no corresponding data. It must be broken."

He double-clicked a file dated one day earlier. A video played of a sled with two passengers—one male, one female—approaching the lock, pausing outside, then entering it.

"It was working the day before," he said.

"Who's on the sled," Andreia asked, "out of curiosity?"

Pijasiros paused the video where the faces were closest to the camera. He zoomed in. "That's Basiipi and Tara. Two of our maintenance technicians."

"Rather a coincidence the camera stopped working the day Galen disappeared," Will said.

Pijasiros shrugged. "Someone's going to have to go outside and fix it. Or replace it."

Andreia froze. Will's right; it might not be a coincidence.

"Have you had this issue before, cameras not recording?" Will asked.

"Not on Aux," Pijasiros said.

"Could someone have disabled the camera? Or deleted the video files?"

Pijasiros frowned at him. "Why would anyone do that?"

Andreia's eyes darted around the room. *What if Will's right?* That someone would need full system access—in other words, someone in this room. Or Duripi, who'd suspiciously left.

"Forget it," Andreia said loud enough for everyone in the room to hear. *We need to talk privately.* She asked Zoze, "Can we get something to eat? I'm starving."

"Sure." Zoze led Andreia and Will toward the kitchen used by the communications team.

Once they were alone in the corridors, Andreia tapped Zoze on the shoulder. "What if someone in comms deleted the Sealock 3 video?"

Zoze stared at her. "Why would they do that?"

"Exactly what I want to know."

"Maybe check to see if videos from other cameras were deleted too?" Will suggested.

"Now that I know where it's stored," Zoze said, "I can do that. Although Pijasiros—don't tell him I said this—knows more about the computer systems than I do. He's been tinkering with computers since before I was born."

"Is he the only one able to delete camera footage?" Will asked.

"Anyone with root access on the servers could do it," Zoze said. "Why don't you two grab something to eat and I'll check from my room terminal?"

Andreia led Will to the kitchen and pulled a glass jar of pressure-cooked fish off one of the shelves, and a jar of sea lettuce out of the refrigerator. Will found plates and utensils. They sat at the metal table in the middle of the room, which had bottles of unlabeled condiments clustered on top.

"Seafood for every meal?" Will remarked as they ate.

"Not a lot of pasture down here to raise cows," Andreia responded. The jars weren't labeled, but the sea lettuce was fresh and the fish tasted like flounder.

Zoze still hadn't returned by the time they finished eating, so Andreia led Will down a white hallway to her friend's quarters, one of ten, with a shared bathroom at the end. The door was locked. She knocked.

Zoze opened the door and ushered them in, closing it behind them. Like most Mazi quarters, the room was small and efficient, with a bed and computer desk on the right, an open closet on the far side, and floor-to-ceiling storage drawers and shelves covering the rest of the wall space. The yellowish carpeting was faded and worn.

Andreia couldn't help but notice men's clothes mixed in with Zoze's on the floor and in the closet. Presumably Sama's; he and Zoze were a monogamous couple now. Sama had been one of Andreia's first sex partners, but it had never evolved into commitment. She'd been too focused on becoming the next Trader.

"I've been searching," Zoze said, "but haven't found any other instances of missing video."

"Would be nice if we could recover it," Andreia said.

"I thought that too, but whoever deleted it was thorough." She pointed at a window on the screen with a command bar and rows of randomly assorted letters and numbers. "Normally when you delete a file, assuming it's not just in the recycle bin, only the file reference is removed, so the computer doesn't know it's there anymore and can write over that space. But the data's still there until written over. I ran a data recovery program, but it looks like whoever deleted the video nuked it."

"Nuked it?" Will asked.

"Ran a program to overwrite the data with random garbage so nothing can be recovered. I can even guess what program they used." She clicked on an icon titled 'Data Shredder,' bringing up another window with various options. "Sama installed this, along with lots of other sick props." She turned to Will. "His father used to work down here. You might call him one of our infotech pioneers."

"But he's not here anymore?" Will asked.

"He maintains Katiki's systems now. Spits out programs and apps, too."

"It's an important job," Andreia told Will, "making sure our computers aren't infected by malware from above, and making sure the Land-Dwellers don't discover us. We have to hide our traces tapping the Internet cable too."

"That's one of my jobs," Zoze said. "And Maia's. We double-check each other to minimize any mistakes. Not that I make any." She glanced over her shoulder, a sign she was joking.

"What do Duripi and Yissharu do?" Will asked her.

"Content analysis, mostly. What the Land-Dwellers are up to. We all do that, actually. And we keep up with the latest infotech, reading academic papers and attending virtual conferences. That part's pretty boring, although Pijasiros—being the weirdo he is—loves it. He—his main land persona, anyway—even has an online professorship and publishes research papers."

"How did he manage that?"

"You'd be surprised how extensive our surface networks are," Andreia said.

"Can they find out who's behind the oil attacks?" Will asked.

Zoze tilted her head left and right, a sign of ambivalence. "Your people say Iran. You don't believe them?"

Andreia tried to get them back on course. "You couldn't find any other instances of deleted video?"

"Not yet," Zoze said, "and I'm almost done. Of course, it isn't kept forever. Storage is limited."

"The obvious question," Will said, "is why someone would go to the trouble to 'nuke' camera video around the time Galen disappeared. What are they hiding?"

Andreia's entire body tensed. "Do you think... No, never mind, there's no way."

"What?"

"Are you suggesting someone here was involved with my brother's death, and there was video evidence?"

Zoze shook her head. "Sea-Dwellers don't kill Sea-Dwellers. It's not in us, and I've never heard of it happening."

Andreia couldn't think of any examples either.

"Let's leave that aside," Will said. "I assume none of us deleted the camera video."

"I didn't even know how," Zoze insisted.

"And I presume Pijasiros wouldn't have helped us if he was the one responsible. What about Duripi? He left the room after I suggested checking the cameras."

"He and Pijasiros are intimates," Zoze said.

"Pijasiros might not have known. Let's not rule him out. Maia and Yissharu, what about them?"

"Maia's pregnant," Andreia mentioned. "It's all she thinks about, having a successful birth. She's been trying for years, and we have so few children these days."

"She's so different now," Zoze said, "all Bronze Age. We love her anyway, she's like our big sister."

"Maybe she'd rather not swim around outside," Will said, "but that doesn't mean she wouldn't delete camera video, say, on her husband's behalf. Speaking of which, is Yissharu from someplace else? He has a different accent."

"He's Karsk by birth," Andreia said. "But now he's Mazi like the rest of us. Even had his Karsk tattoo removed and replaced with ours."

"How did they meet?" Will asked.

"Online."

"Like a dating app?"

Andreia and Zoze laughed. "We don't have those," Andreia said. "But we have video chat."

"What are the Karsk like?" Will asked.

"Secretive," Andreia said. "Moving drugs is risky. And rumor has it, they sink the boats of the competition, and leave no survivors."

"Yeah," Zoze responded, "my mom thinks the Karsk have been hopelessly contaminated by their Land-Dweller dealings. That call to action they issued ten years ago? She claims it was an example of how working with ruthless Land-Dwellers instills the same sort of violent thinking."

"So now you're retroactively world-wise," Andreia said, "rather than someone who spent her childhood watching cartoons?"

"Ha ha. My parents talked about it a lot, how the Karsk would doom us all by getting the clans to fight the Land-Dwellers."

"Wait," Will said, "what's this? You planned a war against humanity?"

"Not us," Andreia said. "My parents told me our clan refused involvement."

"It was just talk," Zoze said.

"It completely fizzled," Andreia said. "No one supported such a foolish idea—we'd be completely wiped out—and the Karsk backed down. No one's discussed it since."

"What was their plan?"

"I don't think anyone developed a strategy. Didn't get that far." She glanced at the wall clock. "Let's get back to Galen. The Council's expecting us at six, and longer we stay, the longer we have to decompress."

"Maybe we can split the effort," Will suggested. "Someone look into Duripi—like what he was doing out of the room. Someone else look into Maia, and someone take Yissharu."

"There are three of us here," Andreia said, "but only two of us know the place. Will, why don't you accompany Zoze and talk to Duripi. I'll talk to Maia, and whoever finishes first can handle Yissharu. The quicker, the better, but it's more important to be thorough."

And if we find out who deleted the video? The more important question is <u>why</u>. Is it really possible one of my friends contributed to Galen's death?

Chapter 13

Andreia

Andreia pulled up a chair next to Maia, who was busy at her workstation. "Sorry to interrupt, but I've been wondering how it's going, if the tests have all been good."

Maia turned and smiled. "They have. Everything's normal, the healers tell me. We're very excited." Her smile faded. "I've been researching Land-Dweller medicine, though. They're much more advanced than we are, with all sorts of genetic tests."

"That's one of those technologies we could partner with humans on. We don't have their genetic disorders, but they don't have ours."

"It's too bad we can't trust them," Maia said. "Or better, if there were a lot fewer of them and a lot more of us. We wouldn't have to rely on their technology if we had tens of thousands of universities and research labs like they do."

"We have to do what we can." *Time to switch topics.* Andreia absolutely hated manipulating friends, but she needed Maia's sympathy and help. She thought about Galen and let her emotions flow, bringing genuine tears to her eyes.

As expected, Maia gave a look of concern. "What's wrong?"

Andreia rubbed away the tears. "I was thinking how much Galen admired you all and wanted to live here. He must have been headed here; I can't think of anyplace else he would go."

"To land?"

"He doesn't know anyone on land except me, and he was mad at me. When was the last time you talked to him?"

"Not since the last time you brought him over," Maia said. "I'm old compared to him. Zoze was his favorite."

"She lightens the mood wherever she goes."

Maia clasped Andreia's gloved hand. "You have to stop torturing yourself. Galen is dead and it isn't your fault. My opinion, he went off exploring and got in trouble somehow. We need to install face scanners or something so children—or teenagers—can't enter the sealocks without supervision."

"That's not a bad idea," Andreia conceded. "Will you mention it to the Council? If it's not just me suggesting, it's more likely to be taken seriously."

"Of course."

If Maia knew anything else, Andreia detected no signs. *I should move on to Yissharu.* Andreia stood and looked around the communications room, but didn't see him anywhere.

"I wanted to talk to Yissharu too," she said to Maia. "Do you know where he is?"

Maia paused before answering. "Outside. He's replacing the malfunctioning camera."

It wasn't malfunctioning, someone deleted the video. Andreia decided not to voice that, though. "Will he be back soon?"

"I have no idea how long it'll take. He'll have to decompress, he warned me, but didn't know how long."

Andreia flexed her fingers. We can't enter his sealock while he's decompressing, and we don't have time to wait for him.

* * *

Will

Like Andreia, Zoze had two keyboards, one with English letters and the other with Sea-Dweller characters. The pink-haired girl tapped furiously on the English keyboard after Andreia left.

"Aren't we going to talk to Duripi?" Will asked.

Zoze kept her eyes on the screen as she answered. "I don't have Andreia's skill set there. I'm looking through messages and activity logs for clues. I have admin permissions, like Duripi and the others."

Zoze typed some Unix commands, which brought up a list with user ID 'maziduripi,' process IDs, the terminal type and ID, start and end times, command lines, and other information. "He's on the system now—he's back in the comm center—but apparently not while he was out of the room. Maybe he had to piss."

"Does that rule him out as a suspect?" Will asked.

"If I was trying to hide by deleting camera footage, I sure wouldn't do it from my own account." She tapped a finger against her forehead.

Makes sense, Will thought. *They're IT pros, after all.* "Can you tell if someone's communicating outside the habitats?"

"The network is hardwired," she said. "Inside Aux and by cable to Katiki. The internal message system isn't connected to the Internet. If you have an account, you can access the Internet from certain terminals and send external emails—the Council does this to communicate with other clans—but we have firewalls, malware scanners, encryption, you name it."

"I assume Duripi has Internet access?"

"Of course, that's part of our job." Zoze resumed typing. "Looking for bubbles in the activity log, searching for odd times and activities." She started a program titled 'crawlncrunch' and turned to face him. "You're the first Land-Dweller I've ever met."

"That makes us even. You're the first person who's never met a Land-Dweller I've ever met."

"Nice rebound. So what's it like up there? Your media outlets make it seem dangerous—lots of murders and other crime. Do you carry a gun for protection?"

Will sighed. "Mainstream news producers think they need dead bodies to attract an audience. They have a motto, 'if it bleeds, it leads.' But no, I don't even own a gun. I live in a small town with less than two hundred people. It has no crime to speak of other than occasional shoplifting." He changed the topic. "You said you help Andreia a lot?"

"All of us help her, but mostly me. The trader is like the tip of an iceberg. Down here, we find sources for what the clan needs, run background checks, manage shell corporations and cryptocurrency, create fake identities, all that non-glamorous stuff that needs to get done. Andreia is our point person with brokers, lawyers, bankers… you wouldn't believe how big and convoluted the network is. Sometimes she meets them in-person, but only when something physical—cash or treasure for example—needs to be transferred."

A new window opened on the computer screen. "Activity analysis complete," she said. She scrolled through tables and text, too fast for Will to follow—not that he could decipher it anyway.

"Duripi likes to work odd hours sometimes," she said without turning.

"Doing what?"

"A lot of time on the Internet and a lot of time in a virtual macOS. I can't tell what he's doing inside it."

Will felt completely lost. "What's he doing on the Internet?"

Zoze flipped up her palms. "He uses Tor—we all do—which encrypts and anonymizes communication. There's no way to tell with the resources I have."

"So Duripi might be our culprit, but we don't have any hard evidence, only circumstantial."

She nodded.

"What about Maia and Yissharu?" he asked.

Zoze typed some more. "Nothing unusual. Yissharu uses a video chat program once or twice a day, and it's not the one the rest of us use."

"Why does he use a different program?"

"It's probably Karsk software. I assume he's using it to talk to his relatives, and their IT staff didn't think our chat program was secure enough. Which is ridiculous—I bet ours is better."

"I presume all his chats are encrypted and aren't recorded."

Zoze ran fingers across her opposite palm. "You got it."

"What now?"

"Keep an eye on them. They're friends of mine, though—doesn't feel right to spy on them."

* * *

Andreia

After speaking with Maia, Andreia popped into the adjacent work room where Sama was examining the air controller from Galen's sled. Cluttered tables and desks ringed the perimeter, with metal shelves reaching to the ceiling, overflowing with spare parts and equipment. Sama had opened the microcontroller box and run wires to an oscilloscope and a laptop.

Andreia closed the door behind her. "Find anything?"

Sama faced her with a grim expression. "The board was rewired." He pointed at different sections of the circuit board. "Everything's normal except the output signal to the oxygen level indicators. Those were disconnected from the CPU and rerouted. I'm getting a flat 5-volt signal for the reserve tank, which on the console would read as 100% full, and 3.3 volts on the primary tank—someone added a variable resistor and set it to mimic being two-thirds full."

A chill seized Andreia. "Someone deliberately emptied, or nearly emptied, the oxygen tanks, and made it look like they were mostly full? Who would do such a thing? When was it done?" Tears blurred her vision. "Why? Galen was a kid! You're talking murder, my little brother murdered in cold blood!" Her stomach contracted and she almost retched.

The door opened. Maia peeked in, her face rigid. "What happened? What's this about murder?"

I was too loud. Andreia wiped her eyes and held up a trembling hand. "Nothing. I don't want to talk about it now." She edged past Maia and hurried back to Zoze's quarters.

Zoze and Will stared as she entered, her anguish too powerful to mask. "What's wrong?" Will asked.

"Galen was murdered." She told them what Sama had found.

Zoze's jaw dropped. Will put arms around her. "I'm so sorry, Andreia."

Andreia held him and cried uncontrollably. "This keeps getting worse and worse."

Zoze rubbed Andreia's back, the sensation slightly comforting. "It doesn't make any sense."

"No, it doesn't. Galen didn't have an enemy in the world." She had to know why. More important, who. Her misery turned to anger, then rage. *Whoever killed my brother will pay!*

"What now?" Will asked. "Whatever you need, I'll help."

"Thank you." She collected herself somewhat, and turned to Zoze. "I have to tell Meltha I need more time here." She wiped the tears from her face.

Zoze set up a voice call from her laptop. Andreia didn't know who might have abetted her brother's murder and decided not to mention the evidence they'd discovered.

Meltha wasn't in her quarters or the Council offices, which was just as well. The woman could be as prickly as a sea urchin.

Andreia spoke with one of the other Council members. "I'm at Aux with Dr. Myers. We'll return as soon as we can, but will be unable to attend today's scheduled meeting. I apologize for the inconvenience."

"Why are you at Aux?" he asked.

"It's a long story." She left it at that and ended the call. She said over her shoulder, "Let's keep this investigation to ourselves."

She opened the chat program and messaged Sama, 'Until we know who's behind it, don't tell anyone what you found.'

'Maia and Pijasiros asked what the frenzy was about,' he responded. 'I told them someone tampered with Galen's sled, but we don't know who or why.'

Andreia cursed herself. She'd been too upset to be cautious. 'Don't let it reach any further. Especially beyond the comm team.' Maia would certainly tell her husband, and Pijasiros would tell his boyfriend.

She turned to Zoze. "Anything on Duripi?"

"Nothing solid."

"Let's talk to him," Andreia suggested. "Yissharu's conveniently unavailable, so I'll save him for last."

Duripi shared a room with Pijasiros on the other side of the hallway. The door was unlocked. Andreia entered, followed by Will and Zoze. Unlike Zoze's room—and her own quarters—Duripi's room was unbelievably neat and well-organized, with cubbyholes within cubbyholes.

Duripi was working at a computer desk, and turned to face them. "What is it?" His laptop screen was filled with Mazi text, and the big external monitor displayed engineering schematics, an oil platform on fire, and a document titled 'Fleet Tactics and Naval Operations.'

Will passed Andreia and stared at the monitor screen. "What the hell are you doing?"

Duripi slammed his laptop shut, turning the monitor black.

Andreia reached past him and opened the laptop. "Can you log back in, please?"

"You'll see my password. What's this about?"

Will spoke in a tense voice, "Do you have anything to do with the refinery attacks?"

Duripi stared at him, then laughed. "This is why I research in secret and use anonymizers." He shielded his keyboard from view and logged back in. "I'm writing the first Mazi novel."

Zoze pointed at the laptop screen. "That's what you do inside the Mac VM?"

"My writing program won't work in Linux," he said. "Have you been spying on me?"

Andreia scanned the text. It was full of dialog. And Duripi's face betrayed no indications of lying. "That's what you do at odd hours?" she asked.

"I get inspiration from my dreams, and have to get up and start writing while the net is full."

"You're writing about oil platform attacks and U.S. Navy combat tactics?" Will asked.

Duripi pressed his hands together. "It's alternate history. The premise is, we *Ahta* are more numerous and powerful, and rule the ocean, while Land-Dwellers rule the land. The Land-Dwellers are drilling for oil and spill a lot of it, and it pollutes an *Ahta* community."

"That doesn't sound like fiction to me," Zoze said.

"Yeah, but Sea-Dwellers being numerous and powerful is. It leads to war, and that's the part I'm working on now."

Will smiled. "Can I read it?"

"After it's finished and translated. I won't even let Pijasiros see it until then."

Mostly—but not entirely—convinced of Duripi's innocence, Andreia led Will and Zoze back to the comm room. Yissharu was the last remaining suspect.

Andreia watched him on the monitors as he examined every one of Aux's exterior cameras and cleaned the lenses. "I thought he was just replacing one camera," she complained to Maia.

"It looks like he's doing a complete inspection. It's been a while."

When Yissharu finally finished, he called the comm room from the decompression suite. "I replaced the faulty camera and inspected the rest. Did some cleaning and testing; all cameras should be fully functional now."

"They were already fully functional," Andreia muttered.

"It'll take four hours to decompress," his voice continued. "I'm catching some sleep."

Ugh. Andreia picked up the external microphone. "The camera you replaced, did you find what was wrong?"

"I have to test it in the work room," he said over the speaker.

Andreia lost patience and decided to throw him off balance. "There's nothing wrong with that camera. Someone deleted the video. I think it was you."

He paused before answering. "What? What makes you think that?"

"You left bubbles in your wake," she exaggerated. "The question is, why did you do it?"

Maia placed a hand on the microphone. "What are you talking about, Andreia?"

"Only someone here could have done it, and I've ruled out everyone else."

"Yishharu doesn't have root system access, so it couldn't have been him. And it wasn't me, if that's what you're thinking." Maia's eyes narrowed in anger.

Andreia's fists clenched. She stopped herself and took a long, careful breath. In truth, she had no evidence against anyone, and was too shaky to think clearly.

*   *   *

Will

Will suspected Yishharu or Maia had deleted the camera video, but had no conclusive proof. He returned to the residence hallway with Andreia and Zoze.

Andreia checked Duripi's door and one beyond it, but neither opened. "Looks like Duripi doesn't want to be bothered anymore, and Maia keeps her door locked." Her voice was tense.

They proceeded to the kitchen. Andreia examined the room thoroughly—Will guessed for recording devices—then asked Zoze, "There aren't any cameras or microphones in the kitchen, are there?"

Zoze stared at her friend. "Why would there be?"

"Are there any, like in storage or on unused devices, that we could use to monitor the others?"

"Sure, but I'm not going to spy on my friends. Besides, they're not easy to hide."

"What if you use existing cameras on laptops that don't get much use?" Will asked. "Can you disable the indicator lights?"

"Should be as easy as cutting a wire," Zoze said. "But don't ask me to install keyloggers or other spyware—I guarantee they'll find it."

Andreia waved a hand left and right. "I've got a better idea. Let's focus on Yishharu and Maia first. I don't think either is capable of murdering my brother, but that video wasn't deleted for the fun of it. If they talk, it will probably be in their room. There's a storage room next to it. I could run a microphone through the air duct and record what they say."

Will was impressed. "Did you learn this stuff as a trader?"

"No, it just seemed workable."

"I'll get what you need," Zoze volunteered.

An hour later, she returned with Sama and they proceeded silently to the storage room. Sama removed a microphone and a digital recorder from a carry bag. "These were the best I could find. The recorder has a voice activation mode."

Will fastened the microphone to the end of a broom handle and fed the wire to the recorder. He stood on a crate and unscrewed the air vent cover, then carefully pushed the broom as far as he could reach. By his estimation, the microphone was over the next room, although there was no guarantee it was over a vent.

"Let me see," Andreia asked. Will lifted her on his shoulders and she peered inside the air duct.

She hopped back down. "Close enough. Now we wait."

The four ate dinner together in the small galley at the end of the hallway, a simple meal of tank-grown mussels, seaweed, and various sauces—most of which Will found unpalatable. Andreia was quiet and picked at her food. Even Zoze said little.

After dinner, Zoze showed them a guest room. It had two beds and was crammed with stacked crates and clothes. Andreia collapsed in the nearest bed without speaking. Will found a blanket and took the other.

Without his medicine, he had trouble sleeping. Thoughts of the Sea-Dwellers raced through his head. They were simultaneously alien and familiar. And despite their claims of innate nonviolence, at least some were capable of murder.

Chapter 14

Andreia

Andreia woke the next morning to a knock on the door. In the other bed, Will stirred too. Andreia hurried to the door, not bothering to smooth her rumpled blouse.

It was Maia, who looked tired. "Call for you from Katiki."

"Let me guess, Meltha?"

Maia nodded. "This time, you are prescient. I asked what she wanted."

"My profuse apologies for inconveniencing the Council and my immediate return to Katiki?"

She smiled. "Again, correct."

"Tell her I'm on my way."

Andreia watched Maia walk away and turn into the corridor leading to the comm center. She waited another minute, then motioned for Will to follow her.

They slipped into the storage room and Will retrieved the voice recorder. They returned to the guest room and Andreia hit the play button. "I'll translate for you, just give me a chance to listen."

Maia spoke first. "You said Galen was fine when he left, and his death must have been an accident!"

"Not so loud," Yissharu responded. "Yes, he was fine. What are you talking about?"

"Someone sabotaged his sled—emptied the oxygen and rewired the circuits to make it look like the tanks were still full."

"What?" His voice sounded genuinely surprised.

"Please tell me it wasn't you."

"No! Who told you that?"

"Sama. Andreia was very upset, then Sama told me how her brother's sled was tampered with." She described the details.

"Does Andreia think I did that?" Yissharu asked. "She found out I deleted the video from when I went to meet Tareen."

Caught something! Andreia paused the recording and translated for Will.

"Who's Tareen?" Will asked.

"No idea." Andreia resumed the audio.

"She doesn't know for sure who deleted the video," Maia said. "She was bluffing. I told her you don't know the root passwords."

"Good misdirect. I swear by Great Leviathan I had nothing to do with Galen's death."

"I believe you. Do you know who did?"

"I don't know," he said, "and I have no desire to know. The waters are dangerous. Let's drop it."

The rest of their conversation was domestic, mostly revolving around their future child and how they could expand their quarters by annexing the adjacent storage room.

"We have to return to Katiki," Andreia told Will. "Let's put the recorder back and see what else we can learn. We can check it later." She decided not to tip off Yissharu and Maia by confronting them prematurely.

Will stared at the recorder. "When Maia said, 'when he left,' did she mean from Katiki or Aux? Or from someplace else?"

"Good question. We need to find out."

Andreia and Will repositioned the mic, ate a quick breakfast, and said goodbye to everyone. In the sealock, Andreia secured Will to the cargo platform again, placed one rebreather in her mouth and handed him the other.

Lying stomach-down, Andreia on the sled, Will on the towed platform, they exited the sealock. She ascended to forty meters—the same pressure as inside Aux—and headed for Katiki at maximum speed.

As they neared the halfway point, a finned shape emerged from the dark blue distance, swishing its tail back and forth. A shark. A big one. From its flattened, T-shaped head, a hammerhead. It was approaching at an intercept angle.

Andreia kept the same course—it was probably just curious, but if they tried to speed away, it would instinctively chase them. And sharks were at least twice as fast as her sled.

The shark closed the distance, its body undulating side to side. It was enormous—almost twice the size of her sled. Andreia's breath caught and her skin turned cold. *I didn't bring a speargun. Not that it could cause much damage to something this big.*

Will could no doubt see it too now. He's strapped down with no weapons. Defenseless.

The huge shark pulled close, matched their speed and direction, a pitch-black eye on one protruding end of its head trained on her, mouth full of sharp teeth half-open. Andreia pulled the dive knife out of her leg sheath. *Go away. Please.*

As if hearing her thoughts, it changed course, swimming away, but still in the same general direction the sled was heading. Andreia exhaled—she'd been holding her breath. She looked back at Will, whose eyes were wide behind his mask. He thrust a finger out toward his right.

Andreia spun her head in that direction. The shark was coming in fast— almost blindingly fast—for an attack. It opened its huge jaws, row after row of teeth framing a black maw.

Andreia threw the sled into neutral just as it arrived, causing the shark to overshoot. It swung its head around, but its momentum carried it past them.

Without the jets running, the cargo platform began to sink, dragging the sled down too. Andreia added more air in the ballast tanks to compensate. She twisted the throttle to half-speed and turned the sled toward the shark, keeping herself between it and her passenger.

The shark turned and came in fast again. Heart pounding wildly, Andreia pulled the rebreather out of her mouth, pointed it at the shark, and opened the valve, producing a cloud of bubbles.

She dodged aside as the hammer-shaped head burst past the bubbles, then drove her razor-sharp knife into the beast's gills. She gripped it with all her strength. The creature jerked away, though, and the damage was less than she'd hoped for. *Little more than a scratch.*

Nevertheless, the counterstrike buoyed her confidence. She swished the air-hemorrhaging valve in circles, producing a wall of bubbles between herself and the departing shark. *Go away or I'll really hurt you.*

The bad thing about the bubbles—besides squandering her air supply— was that she couldn't see either.

It appeared again, this time behind her, trickling blood. It swam almost casually over the cargo platform with Will. One of its black eyes stared in her direction.

Will had the good sense to remain motionless. The shark circled around him, then rammed the platform with its head.

The platform jerked to the side, Will still strapped on, probably panicking at this point. The connecting cable yanked Andreia's sled around, almost knocking her off.

A snapping sound carried through the water. Will's air hose detached from the sled, swishing back and forth and ejecting bubbles everywhere.

At this point, Andreia's ancestors would have prayed to Leviathan—the great Sea-God that slumbered at the center of the world. *That won't keep us alive.*

Andreia closed her air valve, ending the stream of bubbles on her end, and tensed her leg muscles. She banged her knife against the resin shell of the sled to divert the monster's attention from Will. An ancient, guttural roar came from her throat, echoing inside her closed mouth and radiating into the surrounding water. *Come get me!*

The giant hammerhead swerved toward her. Its mouth opened wide.

Just before it reached her, Andreia leapt at an angle off the sled. Again, the shark's momentum was too great to correct. *The smaller fish has a few advantages.*

As the shark passed overhead, Andreia plunged her knife into the uninjured gills on its other side. This time it went deeper, slicing through its gill flaps and spewing forth a cloud of blood.

The monster twisted its head violently, pulling the knife out of Andreia's hand. Its massive tail swung toward her. Andreia somersaulted out of the way, her webbed feet providing just enough mobility to dodge it.

With another head twist, the shark ejected the knife out of its gill flaps. Andreia watched helplessly as her knife dropped into the depths, sunlight glinting off the blade until it disappeared into darkness.

But the shark kept swimming away, its primitive brain apparently calculating that this food wasn't worth dying over.

The sled. It was still moving forward at a speed of four to five knots, Will trailing behind on the cargo platform, his air hose severed and trailing bubbles. He was undoing his straps. *How long before he loses consciousness and dies?*

Andreia swam as fast as she could, mustering every bit of energy she had. She was one of the fastest swimmers in her clan, and in peak condition.

Thankfully, the sled wasn't moving at full speed and wasn't far away. Andreia caught up to it, blew the spent air out of her lungs, and inserted the rebreather mouthpiece. She took a deep breath and swam back to Will with it.

Will had unstrapped himself. His eyes looked desperate. He sliced a hand across his neck, indicating that he had no air.

That's why I'm coming. She handed him the rebreather and he inhaled greedily.

Andreia examined his torn air hose. Unfortunately, the bioplastic had ripped—not something she could fix.

We'll have to share. She led him to the sled. According to the gauges, the tanks were nearly out of oxygen.

She placed Will's arms around her waist, unclipped the cargo platform, and rotated the throttle to maximum speed. With a whining noise, the sled lurched forward and water rushed around them. Will held on tight. Behind them, the cargo platform sank into the depths. She noted the position in case she was told to recover it.

Andreia kept an eye on the navigation computer and compass while scanning the surrounding water for signs of the shark. She tried to calm herself and lower her oxygen consumption as much as possible. Still, she had to periodically reach back for the rebreather. Will handed it to her, she took a deep breath, and passed it back.

When they reached the coordinates of Katiki—the bottom was too far below to actually see—Andreia slowed the sled. She couldn't reach the rear flaps with her feet while sitting up, so directed Will to tilt them down. She adjusted the front flaps and they began to descend.

They dropped down to the Trader sealock and entered. Andreia took great, heaving breaths as air displaced the water inside, then set the pressure to five atmospheres.

Safe. We're safe. The adrenaline was still coursing through her body.

Breathing heavily also, Will unzipped his drysuit. "Thank you."

Andreia pulled off her wetsuit. "We either got lucky or unlucky."

"We're alive. And it wasn't luck, it was you. No surface dweller could move in the water the way you did and take on a shark."

"I've never been attacked by a shark before. The reef sharks are a lot smaller. The open ocean… who knows what you might run into."

Will stepped close. As usual, he seemed mesmerized by her appearance in a bikini. *Land-Dweller men are all the same.* But even considering his swimming limitations, Andreia's heart fluttered. *He's a catch. Rugged-looking and fit. Smart, nice eyes and a nice smile.*

He kissed her, his mouth tasting like salt and canned air. But it woke something long-desperate inside her. She kissed him back and they threw arms around each other.

"If it takes near-death from a giant shark for a Land-Dweller to want to kiss," she said, "it's a wonder there are so many of you."

"I was worried you might still be mad at me for tracking you."

"I've moved on. I have more serious troubles, and you've been so supportive." She kissed him again.

She glanced at the analog clock and made some calculations in her head. "We'll have to wait here a while. For me, it would take 9-10 hours to decompress safely. But for you, a whole day. We were gone a lot longer than I planned."

Every problem presents opportunities. Something Stefan had taught her. Hurling aside social shackles, she gave Will her best seductive look. "We can speed up our decompression time with light to moderate exercise. It will increase breathing and blood flow, and outgas nitrogen from the body."

"What sort of exercise?"

She removed her gloves and ran a bare finger down his chest. "The best kind." She led him into the decompression suite and they embraced.

* * *

Will

Swimsuits off and hands exploring unexpected horizons, Will noted that Andreia had the same reproductive anatomy as a human female. *An absolutely stunning human female.* Then he realized he didn't have a condom. "Do we need protection?"

She looked in his eyes. "Do you have something contagious?"

"No."

"Neither do I, and I'm not in a fertile period. You couldn't get me pregnant anyway."

The statement brought him back to the new reality he found himself in. The Mazi seemed as human as anyone on the surface, though. And their differences were ones he wished he had. Underwater, he was handicapped.

Andreia pressed against him and he decided to quit playing scientist for a while.

* * *

Andreia

Andreia decided to spend the whole day with Will while he decompressed. *Everything's different.*

"I feel like you know more about me than I know about you," she said as they lay together on the air mattress.

"What do you want to know?"

"Your wife. I hope you don't mind me asking, what was she like?"

He sighed. "Her name was Yoselin. She was Cuban-American, grew up in Miami. We met at a party—we had mutual acquaintances—and hit it off right away. You could say I was smitten from the start."

He paused. "We got married, bought a house, were talking kids… then she got sick…"

Andreia touched his hand. "I'm really sorry. I know how you feel."

"It's been two years now, and still…"

She met his sad eyes.

"I've been trapped," he continued, "with Yoselin dying and watching the ocean die, and not being able to do anything." His expression softened. "But it feels so good to be here with you. It's like I was asleep and woke up in a whole new world."

With a fingertip, Andreia traced the empty spaces between Will's fingers. *We're the same, in so many ways.* "I'm glad I met you."

"You've changed my life," he said. "I feel hopeful again. I want to do whatever I can to protect your people and heal our ocean."

They held hands and kissed, sharing their breath and feeling buoyant enough to float to the ceiling. "Your hands…" he said.

"The price of living on land. My finger webbing was removed—it sticks out too much. I'll get replacement skin grafted on when I retire, but for now, my feet are freakish on land and my hands are freakish down here. That's why I had the gloves made."

He rubbed the contours of her feet. "Your feet are amazing. I've never seen someone swim like that."

Andreia was preparing for more nitrogen-purging exercise when the wall phone rang.

It was Meltha. "The meeting has been rescheduled for tomorrow morning. Please don't be late."

Leave it to Meltha to kill the mood. Considering earlier suggestions to kill or dissect Will, the Council presented as much a danger to him as that huge hammerhead.

Andreia scoured the closets for the finest clothes available—Mazi wore their best to meetings and ceremonies—but with muted colors as a sign of harmlessness.

"We need to prepare for the questioning," she told Will. "I'll be with you as a cultural interpreter, but let's go over their probable questions and some good answers. The Elders are difficult to sway, and you must be very careful. Most of all, you must convince them that you pose no danger to us, and won't share our existence with others."

"I'm on your side. What happens if they don't believe me?"

"Just speak sincerely. I'll be there to help."

Chapter 15

Will

When the decompression timer rang, Will and Andreia donned silk masks and exited into the corridor beyond. Andreia wore a flowing lavender dress, giving her an elegant appearance. Will wore a blue-and-white shirt and slate-gray flared slacks, not exactly his usual wardrobe.

Andreia drummed her fingertips together. "We should be careful our body language does not betray our, um, new closeness."

Will nodded.

"Some of the Elders will be hostile," she continued. "Like Meltha, although she hides it most of the time. And Xitaros—he's short, thin, and gray, and wears a necklace of shark teeth. He opposed my nomination as clan trader."

"Why?"

"He claimed I wasn't trustworthy. He's the King of Anal Warts."

"Sounds like it."

They entered a second corridor. "Kitane is this month's First Speaker, which is kind of like a rotating chairmanship in your country. She tries to be neutral, but it's best to act deferential—and to the others also. Mazi are taught from infancy to respect their elders. I try to at least give that appearance."

They followed a carpeted ramp down to an ornately decorated lobby, ending at two massive wooden doors carved with corals, fish, and curlicued seaweeds. Two male Sea-Dwellers stood attentively on either side, holding fancifully decorated—but sharp—tridents. *Ceremonial guards or the real thing?*

One of the guards extended forth a hand. "*Sint.*" He placed his trident in a silver wall bracket and approached Will, speaking unfamiliar words.

"They want to search you," Andreia explained.

Will let the guard pat him down. They didn't search Andreia.

"*Leita na intra,*" the guard said, and pulled open one of the doors for them.

Beyond, a large circular room was ringed by tiered stone benches, on which sat over a hundred men, women, and children, wearing bright, ornately-patterned silk clothes and ornaments made from shells, polished stone, and silver. The curving walls and support arches were painted with towering growths of corals, sea fans, and sponges; and fish everywhere, hundreds of species. It reminded Will of pictures of the Keys reefs back when they were still healthy.

Andreia scanned the room with wide eyes. She whispered to Will, "I thought only the Elders would be present."

"Why the change?"

"I'll ask."

The crowd eyed Will with curiosity, speaking animatedly to each other. More arrived, some pointing at Will as if he was an alien from outer space.

We'd do the same thing, he thought.

Several people came down from the benches and greeted Andreia with hugs and Will with spread-open hands. Andreia introduced a middle-aged couple to Will. "These are my parents."

"So you are the famous Dr. Myers," her father said in a quasi-Nordic accent.

He must be from another clan, but a different one than Yissharu. "I'm hardly famous."

"You're famous here. You're the first Land-Dweller to visit a Mazi home in hundreds of years."

"So it's happened before?"

"Taíno and Calusa traders," Andreia's mother said, "before the Europeans came."

Andreia then introduced her grandparents, uncles, aunts, and cousins.

"Thank you for allowing me into your home," Will told her relatives.

"You look like Land-Dwellers on television," an aunt told him. Her eyebrows rose. "Like on 'The Young and the Restless.'"

A cousin stared at Will's hands and feet. "How do you swim with those things?"

That again? "I wear dive fins."

A middle-aged man, impressively handsome and dressed in fine silks, opened his webbed hands and bowed. "I'm Stefan. Clan Trader before Andreia. I was her mentor."

Will mimicked the gesture and introduced himself. "From what I've heard, you made quite an impression."

Stefan smiled. "Glad to hear it." His smile faded. "Be very careful what you say here. Be honest, but careful."

The conversation was cut short by the loud blaring of a horn. Will turned and spotted a blue-robed man blowing into a conch shell.

Everyone resumed their seats. Andreia led Will into the middle of the chamber. They faced twelve elderly Sea-Dwellers wearing matching silk robes and all manner of jewelry. Meltha was among them. *The Council of Elders, I presume?*

Will's breath caught in his throat. He was the first Land-Dweller most of these people had ever met, and had the responsibility of acting as ambassador for the entire human race.

One of the Elders rang a brass ship's bell. The man with the conch shell banged palms against a set of decorated drums. An Elder in the front row, a stocky man with graying hair, stood and began singing in a deep, vibrant voice. "*Ita ahta muri tahn...*"

"That's the clan historian," Andreia said quietly. "We begin and end meetings with excerpts from the sagas." Her eyes gave a suggestion of rolling. "We're obsessed with the glory days."

"What's he singing?"

"I've never heard this one. I'll tell you later."

The bell sounded again and the historian sat. A silver-haired woman with braided hair and abstractly tattooed skin spoke in carefully enunciated English. "Welcome, Doctor Myers. I am Mazi Kitane, this month's First Speaker."

Andreia bowed to Kitane, then said, "I was told this was a meeting of the Council, not half the clan."

"Word spread, and subsequently everyone wanted to come. The prevailing sentiment was to open this... discussion... to all."

The Council members asked Will about his background, why he was spying on them, if he had told others what he learned, and if he was working with police or other authorities. Will had already given Andreia this information, and she'd prepared him for these questions, so the answers came automatically—and honestly.

"Scientists have this thirst for knowledge," he explained about his curiosity. "We want to know how the world works. It's a calling, at least for me." *Especially when discovering a new species of hominids.* "But I understand your desire for secrecy, and I will do everything in my power to prevent anyone else from finding you."

The elderly Council members peered at him, some scowling. "We should trust the word of a Land-Dweller?" one asked.

Will remained calm. "I will take any oath that you ask."

The First Speaker spoke in Mazi to the other Council members. Then she turned and replied in English, "We will discuss this possibility later." She stood and addressed the room. "Do any others have questions for Doctor Myers?"

"I do," Andreia said immediately. As mouths opened to object, she turned to Will. "Tell us about your research and what you've been doing for the ocean."

Will suppressed a smile. Andreia was playing attorney. "I was born in the Florida Keys," he began. "The ocean, reefs, and fish are as much a part of me as my arms and legs." He expounded on his work studying turtles and his past advocacy for marine life.

"Like you," he concluded, "we humans also rely on a healthy world ocean. It provides half the world's oxygen, contains 80% of life on the planet, absorbs 90% of the excess heat from our greenhouse gas emissions—which scientists are urging our governments to drastically cut—and it can solve our food insecurity problems if used wisely. Thus, it is in our direct interest to protect and restore it, and most of us agree when they think about it."

The faces and postures of some of the Council members—and most of the audience—appeared to relax.

But not the Elder named Xitaros whom Andreia had warned him about. "We cannot trust you," he spoke in a matter-of-fact tone. "You Land-Dwellers are destroying the ocean and driving us to extinction, victims of your insatiable greed and callousness." His voice began to rise. "Your history is drenched in the blood of your fellow humans and every other species that calls this planet home, and you revel in the fact! You won't stop until there is nothing but ash. Your species is utterly insane."

Will winced at the intensity of the man's venom. "While your observation contains some elements of truth, we are not all like that. I'm certainly not."

"It's in your genes. You are predators. Killers."

Racist—or speciesist—garbage. "You're focusing on the worst. Most humans are pretty decent most of the time."

"With so many of you," a Councilwoman said, "there must be a distribution curve of behavior. Even fish vary within their species."

Will smiled. Someone with possible knowledge of statistics. But it looked like the damage had been done. In the audience, most of the friendly expressions had vanished.

Will they let me return home after the week ends? Three more days. Or will they decide I'm untrustworthy and keep me here permanently? Maybe in a cage so they can study me? He froze. What if they decide to kill me?

He regained his composure. *I have to make myself more useful alive than dead.* "I was admiring the paintings on the wall." Maybe he and Andreia actually could make a difference. "I'd like to work with you to restore the reefs." *Might it be possible?* "You have knowledge we lack. I could publish it in scientific journals, share it at conferences and with my colleagues, which would help our efforts tremendously."

"Exploit us to help your career, you mean?" another Councilman said.

Will decided to ignore the dipstick gallery and address the First Speaker. "Whatever terms you decide, we can work together to heal the ocean."

The Speaker's eyes scanned the audience—or maybe the wall paintings—behind Will. Her face drooped in sadness. "How can growing coral colonies here and there compensate for the vast scales at which your people destroy the world? Indeed, how will these corals even survive when the seas are too hot and acidic?"

"Plant in colder water and areas of upwelling," Will suggested. He wasn't sure about the acidity problem. "We can work on it together."

"We will discuss it." The First Speaker then addressed the audience in Mazi. Half of them placed their hands together in an 'O' shape.

"Everyone wants to ask you something," Andreia told Will. She pointed at a middle-aged woman on the bottom row. "Siara?"

The woman spoke in Mazi.

"Can you ask in English? Will doesn't speak our language."

"I'm fluent in Spanish too," Will mentioned, "if that helps." It was practically mandatory in south Florida.

"I apologize," the woman said in heavily accented English. "I ask… what your people will do if they find us?"

Will wasn't sure. Most would probably treat it like contact with aliens. Governments and their generals and admirals would assess potential threats posed by the Sea-Dwellers and how to counter them. They'd search every square inch of the ocean bottom and keep them under constant surveillance. It was unlikely the U.S. or other nations would attack, though. The Sea-Dwellers weren't hostile—at least, they didn't seem to be.

"I'll help maintain your secrecy," Will told the woman, "but eventually your luck will run out and other humans"—he didn't like the term 'Land-

Dweller'—"will find you. Especially as technology continues to improve. I don't think anyone will launch a military attack, but your privacy may suffer. Certainly a lot of people would be curious, and want to come down and see you.

"It might be best if you were proactive, presented yourself to the United Nations as a sovereign nation or nations, and enlisted legal assistance, marked out borders where none could enter without permission. It isn't my area of expertise, but I would be happy to help in every way possible."

Andreia interrupted in soft tones, "That's a dangerous proposition. How would we announce ourselves without being overrun with tourists, fortune seekers, or conquistador types?"

"You don't have to disclose your locations at first. Maybe make a video about yourselves and appoint an ambassador?"

Meanwhile, the questioner looked at Andreia, confusion on her face. "*Panite, ma fimtava. Boritrasta na?*"

"Most of us don't practice English enough to understand you," Andreia told Will. "I'll have to translate your responses." She spoke in Mazi to the woman.

When Andreia finished, Will asked her, "You have Internet access. Don't you watch movies or television in English or Spanish?"

"They watch whatever they want on Aux, and of course I can, and whoever wants to visit my quarters, but the Council decides what we can copy to our internal network. There's an air gap for security reasons and there's also cultural preservation reasons. The Elders don't want us, they say 'polluted,' by Land-Dweller thought."

Andreia called on a lanky man next. He spoke in Mazi until she held out a palm.

She translated to Will, "He wants to know why Land-Dwellers have enough nuclear weapons to make the Earth uninhabitable, and nuclear torpedoes to create giant radioactive tsunamis. He wants to know what's next, a single weapon that will explode the planet? Such weapons are madness."

Will sighed. The Council seemed happy to allow negative information about humans past their cultural firewall. "Most people would agree. If you decide to announce your existence—in a careful way—you could express your worries to our public and thereby increase scrutiny of the issue.

Andreia translated, which led to animated conversations in the audience. "They're arguing whether coming out of hiding is a good idea," she told Will. "And about what might happen."

The blaring of the conch shell quieted everyone. The next question was from a girl who looked maybe six or seven years old. "What's your favorite food?" she asked in English.

The audience relaxed, many of them smiling. Will responded, "I love fresh lobster. And grouper, and snapper. If I'm lucky enough to catch them."

Andreia translated and a number of people nodded.

When the questions finished at last, the First Speaker ended the meeting. "I hope we have all found this meeting educational. The Council will deliberate on what we've heard."

* * *

USS Manassas
Persian Gulf

Capt. Dejuan Stallworth stood on the bridge of the USS *Manassas*, a Ticonderoga-class guided missile cruiser. Together with the rest of the carrier group in the Persian Gulf and an assortment of other assets, they'd been ordered to carry out strikes on Iran after their cowardly attacks on the U.S. mainland. There were no plans to land troops—Iran was much too big, with difficult terrain—but the task force commander had told him, "Shock and Awe's like lighting a sparkler compared to what we've lined up. We're going to bomb them back to the Stone Age."

They weren't alone—Saudi Arabia and NATO allies were launching their own attacks, all of them coordinated. It would be a shitty night if you were anyplace the planners had targeted. And once the allies achieved air supremacy, the punishment wouldn't end until Iran's military, leadership, and supporting infrastructure were buried in rubble.

The night was overcast and dark, and the water calm—perfect operational conditions. His ship and the others had gone dark, turning off their running lights and limiting electromagnetic transmissions. The crew was on high alert.

In the distance, the white flames of jet exhausts announced the launching of planes from the carrier. They climbed high into the sky, where they'd launch anti-radar missiles to help the cruise missiles penetrate the enemy air defenses.

Capt. Stallworth kept an eye on the mission clock. This wasn't his first rodeo, but it was his first missile strike while in command of a ship. He wished he had a cigarette, but his wife had made him quit, and he couldn't smoke on the bridge anyway—it would look bad to the crew if he broke his own rules.

When the clock hit 2 AM local time, he announced, "Commence firing." The strike officer repeated the command to the launch crew.

With a white flash and loud roar directly in front of the bridge, the first missile rose vertically from its below-decks tube. It trailed thick smoke as it climbed into the night sky and arced toward its target, an Iranian Air Force base. It was soon followed by more.

In the distance, bright flares revealed outgoing missiles from other ships. "See you in hell, motherfuckers," one of the bridge crew muttered.

* * *

Andreia

Andreia led Will back to her quarters. Surrounded by salvaged Land-Dweller artifacts, she embraced him again. "I feel like I threw you into a school of bloodthirsty sharks. But you did well." *Not good enough, but it could have been worse.*

"It wasn't that bad. And thank you for taking my side." He kissed her.

She kissed him back, wanting him to thrust away her remnants of loneliness. "I'm doing what's right. At least what I think is right."

"What happens now?"

She ran a bare hand down his leg. "They talk. Like they always do. They promised a decision by the end of your week here."

"What decision?"

Her hand froze. "Whether to trust you or not." *And whether to let you live.* "I'll do everything I can to make it turn out for you."

Will's forehead furrowed with worry. "And if it doesn't?"

I won't let them kill him. She whispered, "Then I'll sneak you back to the surface. They can't stop me." She slid her hands to his shoulders and caressed his tension away.

Abandoning words, they kissed and fondled, igniting a furnace inside her. She eyed the beaded-shell entrance to her sleeping room.

For a moment, she hesitated. Will was a Land-Dweller. If the clan found out... *Don't be a coward. Why should I live in fear and suffer for no reason? This man really cares about me.*

Resolute, she led Will to her bed and pulled off her dress. "This will be more comfortable than the sealock."

They held each other afterward, flushed and out of breath. They traced the contours of each other's bodies, his eyes liquid and loving.

"Where's your father from?" he asked.

"You have a good ear for accents. He's from the Widin clan. A long way from here. He's a painter—mostly wall recoats, but ample time for art. My mother's from here. She's a mechanic. One of the most important jobs—our home is old and under enormous pressure, and something leaks almost every day."

"It was nice to meet them. And everything seems to be working here, so your mechanics are doing a good job."

He's so nice. She kissed him, feeling giddy. *I made the right decision.*

"What was the historian singing about?"

"Oh, that. It was about the last time we were visited by Land-Dwellers, Calusa traders to one of our stilt villages. Before the Spaniards brought their diseases and guns."

"I'm sorry that happened."

She squeezed his hand. "Nothing to do with you."

"Is all your music like that?"

"Of course not." She sang him a Mazi classic of love and loss, lively in parts, somber in parts, then translated afterward. She started to apologize for being a mediocre singer, but his lips interrupted hers and they lay back down together.

He wasn't quite ready for an encore, so Andreia stood and pranced over to a footlocker. She pulled out a fine paintbrush, a ceramic cup, and two small jars, one filled with translucent jelly, the other with a white powder. She mixed a glob of jelly, a pinch of powder, and water in the cup, then returned to him.

"Here's something else I like to do for fun," she said.

"The temporary tattoos you were talking about?"

"Yes. We should scrub them off in the morning—some of the stodgier among us would disapprove." She dipped the paintbrush into the cup, and began painting curves and swirls onto his arm, rewetting the brush as needed. The designs gave off a faint green light.

"Bioluminescence?" he asked. "Like fireflies?"

"Sea pansy extracts. Hold still." She painted his face and torso, then handed him the brush. "Now you paint me."

"I'm not an artist."

"Everyone's an artist. It doesn't have to look fancy."

With the wetted brush, Will followed the curves of her body. When the cup was empty, Andreia switched off the lights, transforming their bodies into patterns of bright green lines. The designs she'd drawn were much more elegant than his, but she'd been doing this half her life.

She blew on his skin to dry the paint faster. He did the same for her, the sensation incredibly arousing. It wasn't long before they were making love again, two abstract creatures of green swirling lines.

* * *

Will

Early the next morning, Andreia called Will into her office room. "You have to see this."

"What is it?"

She scooted aside and pointed at her laptop screen. "Your country is bombing Iran."

Will had almost forgotten about the surface world and its periodic outbursts of violence. According to the article and videos, the U.S. and Saudi Arabia, supported by several other countries, had launched a major air and missile assault on Iran, overwhelming their defenses. Cyberattacks—no one claimed credit—had taken down much of Iran's communications and power grid.

"We are taking away Iran's ability to ever harm America again," claimed the U.S. president.

Will felt a surge of embarrassment that mass violence came so easy to human leaders, perpetuating an endless cycle. He searched for news about his brother Joe's aircraft carrier, which, last he'd heard, was stationed in the Indian Ocean.

No news. He opened a marine traffic site and searched for his brother's ship. Its track veered toward the Persian Gulf, then its position disappeared.

Will froze in panic. Had the ship been hit by something and sunk? Did Iran have missiles that could sink something as big as an aircraft carrier?

He shook away the thought. They'd probably just switched off their transponders to hide their location.

For the first time, he wished he'd opened social media accounts. He searched the web for public postings by Joe or anyone mentioning his ship. Nothing from his brother. His dad bragged on Facebook about big returns in Currentsea. But no posts about Joe.

Will looked up other naval ships. None showed up in the Indian Ocean or Persian Gulf. This pretty much confirmed that the fleet had gone dark.

* * *

Andreia

Andreia resumed control of her laptop. "We need to return to Aux," she told Will, "and check the voice recorder." She wondered if they could wire it to the intranet so she could listen from Katiki in the future. It would be more convenient, but given Maia and Yissharu's IT skills, risky.

Her computer beeped and Yissharu's narrow bald head appeared on screen. She answered the call. "I was just thinking about you."

He spoke in Mazi, "I heard what you and Sama discovered on the sled Galen took, how the air system was sabotaged."

"And the batteries drained," she said.

"Maia and I grieved over his death, and were shocked it wasn't an accident."

They had attended his funeral rite outside Katiki, along with the rest of the clan, but Andreia couldn't remember anyone's specific reactions.

"I know you want to know who's responsible," he continued, "as do we all."

Andreia leaned toward the screen, disguising her wariness. "And you found something?"

"I reached out to my former clan, whose reach extends throughout the Land-Dweller underworld."

"So I've been told."

"They found those responsible. That's all they would tell me. They asked if you would meet them here."

"Meet who, exactly?" *This Tareen person?*

"An old friend of mine. Listen, are you coming or not?"

Classic redirect. "When?"

"Tomorrow at mid-day. I'll reserve Sealock 6."

Yissharu seemed slightly nervous. Andreia decided to meet this friend of his, but enter Sealock 5 instead. "See you then. And thank you."

"Of course. Oh, are you bringing the Land-Dweller?"

Good question. "He's not allowed to roam around unescorted, so unless Meltha finds another chaperone, yes." She faked a frown.

Yissharu ended the chat. Andreia recounted the conversation to Will. "Do you want to come with me? We won't be there long."

"Of course." After a pause, he added, "We should prepare for trouble."

Chapter 16

Will

"Can we sit tandem?" Will asked Andreia in the sealock. He'd almost died while being towed.

"I thought you'd say that. You'll have to control the rear flaps, like you did last time. I'll signal when we need to ascend, descend, or level out."

"Got it."

They donned their wetsuits and gear. "Do you mind if I ask about something that's been bothering me?" Will said.

Andreia stopped and stared. "What?"

"The chest of doubloons in your room. I saw someone minting gold coins in the machine shop."

She sighed. "That. It increases the value of the gold twenty times. They're indistinguishable from shipwreck coins, of which we ran out. You'll keep it to yourself, right?"

Will honestly didn't care if they were counterfeiting Spanish doubloons. They were being sold illicitly, anyway. "I promise."

Will sat behind Andreia on the sled, feet awkwardly in the rear flap stirrups, arms around her waist. He instantly felt a stirring, but suppressed it. *Later, when we get back.*

The outer doors opened and they entered the dark blue water again. Andreia pointed her thumb up. Will pushed down with his feet, tilting the rear flaps up, and they ascended. As before, they leveled out at 120 feet and headed for Aux.

After half an hour or so, two bottlenose dolphins approached, then flanked the sled like stalkers. Will remembered how dolphins had watched him while his boat was above the Mazi habitat. Were these two working with the Mazi also? Maybe they were even the same ones—he admittedly couldn't tell them apart.

Andreia made clicking noises from her mouth. The dolphins responded with loud whistles.

Will tapped Andreia on the shoulder. When she turned, he pointed at one of the dolphins, wondering if she knew what they were up to. She shrugged.

The dolphins kept up with them, periodically surfacing for air. *Maybe the Mazi Council wants to keep an eye on us.*

Ahead and below, a massive shape rose from the depths, incredibly long, with almost crescent-shaped tail flukes, pectoral fins angled back, and mottled bluish skin. *A blue whale!* At a hundred feet long, they were the largest animals ever found on Earth.

Will had never seen one off the Keys. It was thick for a blue whale—maybe pregnant? It was rising without undulating its body or swishing its tail. And they were headed straight for it.

Andreia stiffened. She yanked the steering bar clockwise and the sled turned right. She twisted the throttle on the steering bar and they accelerated away.

The dolphins followed, then charged them, outracing the sled. One rammed them from below, throwing the sled off course and nearly causing Will to fall off. The other grabbed Andreia's right wrist with its teeth. It pulled her hand off the throttle and the sled slipped into neutral.

The whale caught up, opened its huge mouth, and headed straight for them. *Is it going to swallow us? Doesn't make sense.*

Andreia made a squealing noise and tried to pry the dolphin's jaws open. It didn't budge.

The speargun. It was strapped to the side of the sled. Will didn't want to shoot a dolphin—it was almost like shooting a human—but the one gripping Andreia could rip her hand off if it wanted. He reached for the speargun, but the dolphin behind him grabbed his arm. It didn't close its jaw tightly enough to pierce the wetsuit, but its grip was incredibly strong.

Ahead of him, Andreia pulled her knife out of its leg sheath. The dolphin released her and swam away, toward the surface.

The dolphin holding Will let go also. It lunged forward and grabbed the speargun with its teeth, tearing it free from the straps. It swam away with the speargun in its mouth. *Must be trained.*

Something clanked against the bottom of the sled, jolting it. They were dragged backward.

Will looked over his shoulder. A metal cable was drawing them into the mouth of the approaching whale.

What the fuck?

Andreia swerved the sled back and forth to free them, but it didn't help. She pointed at the controls, then somersaulted backwards over Will's head and kicked her way to the cable. She pulled on it, with no effect. She swam to the bottom of the sled where they'd been grappled.

Will had no weapons, but he'd watched Andreia operate the sled long enough to know how to pilot it. The control panel was simple—a lot like his boat, but with extra gauges like depth and air mix. No radio, though—not that one would work underwater. He scooted forward, grabbed the steering bar, and tried to keep the sled level.

The approaching whale mouth formed a massive black maw, a relatively thin row of plankton-filtering baleen lining the perimeter of the top jaw. It definitely looked like a whale, but whales undulated their whole body while swimming, using all their muscles. This thing was rigid. And of course, whales didn't spit out grappling hooks.

The sled lurched forward. *She must have pulled it out.* Andreia appeared from beneath, and swam to catch up. Will reduced speed to make it easier.

She grabbed onto the sled, sheathed her knife, and climbed onto the seat behind him. As Will resumed maximum speed, she pointed about thirty degrees starboard off the bow.

Will glanced at the compass. That was the direction they'd come from. He turned the sled and they headed back to the Mazi home.

Andreia tapped him on the shoulder and pointed behind them. The whale—which Will decided was definitely a submarine—had pulled in the cable and closed its mouth, but was still chasing them. And it was gaining on them. *Who are they? Did Yissharu arrange this?*

Remembering how Andreia outmaneuvered the big hammerhead, Will tacked the sled to the right, intending to take a zig-zag path to the Mazi home. The whale submarine changed course to match them, but lost a bit of ground in the process. When their pursuer was close again, he tacked left.

The submarine also turned left, but at a shallower angle. Will checked the compass. Rather than responding to the tacks, their pursuers were headed straight for Katiki.

So much for that idea. They'd guessed his tactic and destination. *What'll happen if they capture us? Is this what happened to Galen?* He could change course, maybe toward land, get as far away as possible. He turned and met Andreia's eyes.

She gestured with her hands and fingers, none of which were standard dive signals. She shook her head, apparently remembering he wasn't Mazi. She pointed at herself, then the steering bar. She wanted to take over. *Fine by me, you grew up driving these things.*

Will put the sled in neutral. He slid off the seat and they switched positions.

Andreia accelerated the sled, then held a thumb up and slowly raised her hand. Will pressed down lightly on the rear pedals. *The safe thing to do—be near the surface in case our air supply is knocked out.* What they'd do in that case, Will had no idea. They were much too far from land to swim to shore, and had no radio.

Behind them, the sub was still pursuing. They wouldn't dare breach the surface, Will assumed. Then again, it resembled a whale closely enough that even he—a marine biologist—was nearly fooled.

Andreia tried tacking, as Will had done. About thirty feet from the surface, she held her hand horizontally. Will evened the rear pedals and they leveled off.

They made incremental gains here and there, but the submarine was faster, and obviously knew their destination.

The artificial whale drew almost near enough to touch them. Andreia steered hard to the left and Will pushed down on the pedals. Too big to match the maneuver, the submarine glided past them.

The two dolphins returned. Neither was carrying the stolen speargun. Swimming faster than the sled, they rammed it repeatedly, knocking them off course. Will gripped the rear flap stirrups with his feet to keep from falling off.

The submarine closed the distance again. Andreia steered away, but the dolphins rammed the sled's bow and, almost touching, pressed their beaks against it. With powerful tail strokes, they pushed the sled in front of the artificial whale. Amid his growing sense of panic, Will admired the dolphins' tactical skills.

The whale opened its huge mouth. The dolphins fled. Water rushed inside the dark maw, sucking Will, Andreia, and the sled with it. *We're being swallowed!*

The turbulence knocked Will off the sled and twisted him around. The rebreather mouthpiece flew out of his mouth and he gulped salty water. *Don't panic. Don't panic.* He tried to reach the sled again, but the rushing water was too strong.

* * *

Andreia

While being sucked inside the artificial whale, Andreia lost her grip on the sled. She collided with a rope mesh, as did the sled.

152

She instinctively pulled her knife out of its leg scabbard. Clanks and clicks sounded around her and the whale mouth slammed shut, leaving them in complete darkness.

With the tremoring hum of a running pump, the water level inside the whale mouth dropped, leaving Andreia vertical against a net, the sled at her feet. She heard Will coughing and spitting up water off to her right.

She reached over and felt his arm. "Are you alright?"

"Yeah. Just some water down the throat." He coughed again. "Where are we?" His voice was raspy from the salt water.

"The Karsk have submarines for smuggling, I've heard. This could be one of them. I assume Yissharu or someone else in their clan told them to pick us up. They must be up to something they don't want anyone to know about." As she spoke, she started cutting a hole in the net.

"What do you think they'll do now?" Will asked.

Her stomach knotted in worry. *Good question.* A thought occurred—the sub crew might be listening to them. If they were smart. She whispered as quietly as possible, "They could be listening."

Then she spoke in a normal voice, "Sea-Dwellers don't harm other Sea-Dwellers, and they won't harm you, since you are a guest of the Mazi." She whispered again, "We're getting out of this net. Follow me."

Andreia slipped through the hole in the net and dropped onto a grated deck a few feet beneath. She moved aside and felt through the darkness for a wall.

A low thump signaled Will's drop to the floor. A second thump and a sharp exhale of air suggested his escape hadn't been as graceful as hers.

What if these people killed Galen? She was determined to find out, and make them pay if they had. Although she wasn't sure how.

The floor tilted downward. The sub was diving. It was surprisingly quiet—presumably electric motors driving impellers inside the hull. Andreia dropped into a crouch and scurried over to Will.

"Are you alright?" she asked again.

"Didn't stick the landing." Their hands twined together.

Andreia led him to a wall and felt her way along it. "I presume they want to talk to us," she whispered, "otherwise they would have just killed us out there."

"I don't have much to tell them," he whispered back.

The floor angle returned to horizontal. The submarine was leveling off. Andreia made some calculations. Judging by the elapsed time—a couple of minutes—they were probably around a hundred meters deep now.

She heard the opening of a metal hatch. Air blew against her skin, indicating that the submarine was pressurized. Overhead lights switched on, transforming pure darkness to blinding white and forcing her to squint. She heard Will ask, "Why are we here?"

"We must speak," came Yissharu's voice.

Andreia's eyes gradually adjusted to the light. They were in a big chamber with a curving roof and walls, painted to resemble a whale's mouth. *Swallowed alive like Mochlos from the sagas.* Sleds, diving equipment, gas cannisters, waterproof bags, and other gear were secured to the walls or hung from the ceiling in tight nets. A harpoon gun was fastened to the ceiling, protruding through the curtain of artificial baleen.

Their own sled hung in a big net in the middle, secured to the ceiling and floor by a system of cables and pulleys. A dome camera eyed them from the ceiling.

Just beyond the open hatch, Yissharu was flanked by two broad-chested Sea-Dweller men wearing padded blue body suits and bulky dark goggles. Rebreather mouthpieces hung at neck level, with tubes reaching back over their shoulders to a backpack. They pointed stubby automatic carbines at her and Will.

"Drop the knife," the one facing Andreia said in heavily-accented, bass-heavy Mazi.

Andreia's nostrils shut from fear. She forced them open. "Or you'll shoot me?"

"With a knife in your hand? Yes."

"Better do as he says," Yissharu said. "These guys are serious. Trained from childhood."

Andreia had no intention of fighting two armor-wearing soldiers holding automatic weapons. She laid her knife on the perforated floor.

"Step back, both of you," the soldier facing Andreia said.

She complied, as did Will. The soldier slung his carbine over his shoulder and retrieved the knife, while his buddy pointed his gun at them. The one holding the knife then bound Andreia's hands behind her back with a thick zip-tie. He did the same to Will.

Andreia exhaled slowly from her nose and asked, "Is that necessary?"

"Temporary precaution."

She looked at Yissharu. "Did these people kill my brother?"

His eyes flickered for a microsecond. "I'll answer all your questions if you come with me." He gestured toward the open hatch.

Andreia looked at Will, who pressed his lips together in apparent worry.

"The Turd-Thrower stays here," Zip-Tie Man said, using a derogatory term Andreia had never heard before. He grabbed Will by the bound wrists and pushed him over to the wall, then tied him to a wall bracket.

"If there's any trouble," he said, "we'll open the mouth and he'll drown."

Andreia locked eyes with Will. "I'll be back as soon as I can."

* * *

Will

Andreia exited the chamber with Yissharu and the two soldiers. The hatch closed and Will heard the sliding of lockbolts. The lights were suddenly extinguished, enveloping him in dank darkness again. *What are they going to do to us?*

The thick zip-tie was too tight for Will to twist his way out. He tried sawing it against the wall bracket, but the bracket was too wide and smooth. Smacking the zip-tie against it didn't work either.

Trapped, he went through the contents of the chamber in his mind, trying to devise an escape plan if Andreia later cut him free.

Thoughts of escape mixed with questions about their captors. What were they doing that demanded such secrecy and drastic action? It couldn't be just smuggling-related; the Mazi didn't seem to care about that. Neither could it be a planned attack on the surface dwellers—there were too few Sea-Dwellers to mount a serious challenge. The U.S. Navy could probably wipe them out without breaking a sweat. Perhaps it was part of some internal struggle among the Sea-Dwellers. If members of the Mazi clan had differing opinions and ideologies, it was certainly possible there were even greater differences between the clans.

All I can do is speculate. I need more information. Will returned to thoughts of escape. *Can we use the harpoon gun?* It was too high to reach, at least without water inside to swim through.

He remembered seeing a tool chest fastened to the inner bulkhead. It would likely have screwdrivers, wire clippers, maybe hammers…

* * *

Andreia

Yissharu and the two soldiers escorted Andreia down a narrow, low-ceilinged corridor lined with pipes and wires. It smelled like grease and fresh paint. They passed two doors marked 'STORAGE' in Karsk/Mazi symbols. Ahead were doors marked 'GALLEY,' 'TOILET/SHOWER,' and two marked 'QUARTERS.' The watertight hatch at the end of the corridor was marked 'BRIDGE.'

They entered a cramped galley with a shiny aluminum table and benches bolted to the floor. Just beyond was a kitchen with appliances, counters, and floor-to-ceiling cabinets. The Karsk sigil—a stylized fish impaled on the end of a trident—was etched into the table top.

The benches could probably seat four people per side. *Eight-person crew?* Andreia doubted this vessel could house much more than that. Even so, the odds of two against eight were poor.

Two more Sea-Dwellers, a man and woman in their thirties, stared at Andreia from the other side of the table. The woman was admittedly eye-catching, and dressed in fine silks. *Is this Tareen? Strange choice of clothes on a submarine.* The man, also somewhat attractive, but dressed in practical work clothes, had dark skin and small earlobes, placing him from one of the clans in the Indian Ocean.

"Please, join us," the woman said in a Karsk accent. Yissharu sat across from them.

"I can't sit down with my arms tied behind my back," Andreia said. She could, but it would be awkward. Regardless, it was a plausible reason to free her hands.

The woman looked at one of the guards. "You can cut her loose. We're all friends here."

We are? Andreia kept quiet, though, as the guard who'd taken her knife used it to cut the zip-tie.

Andreia shook out her wrists and sat next to Yissharu, even though his treachery made him repulsive. "So, we're all friends?"

"Of course. We're all Sea-Dwellers and our clans are neighbors. I'm Tareen and this is Rusos," nodding toward the man next to her.

Instead of engaging in introductory pleasantries, Andreia jumped straight to the point. "Did you kill Galen?"

Tareen didn't flinch. "Of course not."

"Are you from the Karsk clan like Yissharu?"

"Yes, we grew up together. And Rusos is my husband. We have two wonderful children."

Rusos smiled, and spoke in an unfamiliar accent. "Not on the sub, obviously. They're back home."

Andreia decided to press him for information. "Where's home?"

"The Karsk habitat off the Cayman Islands. It's a wonderful place."

"What brings you all the way over here?"

Tareen met her husband's eyes and he grew quiet. She turned back to Andreia. "I used to be a Trader, just like you."

Andreia didn't respond to the attempt to bond.

"In fact," Tareen continued, "I knew your predecessor, Stefan." She smiled. "We had some memorable times—this was before he took you on. The Land-Dwellers aren't totally useless; they wrote this guide called the *Kama Sutra*—"

Andreia held up a hand. "Yes, Stefan was quite the ladies' man." He'd played her too, although she'd gone along with it. Later, in moments of instructive honesty, they'd discussed the nature of deception and how best to master it.

"Anyway, Andreia, I feel like I know you, and I fully respect you."

Andreia examined Tareen's face for signs of lying, but didn't see any. Which, in the case of a Trader, was far from conclusive. She turned to Yissharu. She wanted to punch him so hard in the nose, he'd never breathe through it again. "I thought we, at least, were friends. Why did you delete the camera video and why did you have me kidnapped?"

Yissharu leaned away. "You weren't kidnapped. Tareen wanted to meet you, but not on Aux."

"Chasing us and shooting a harpoon into my sled isn't the way to make a good first impression."

"Sorry about that," Tareen said.

Andreia asked Yissharu again, "What about the video?"

Yissharu inhaled. "Even if I wanted to delete it, I have no idea where it's stored."

Liar. Andreia turned to Tareen. "What are you doing in Mazi waters anyway?"

"Just passing through. I do that a lot, going from place to place." She placed her hands on the table. "You live among the Land-Dwellers. What do you think of them?"

Why is she asking that? Andreia decided to answer honestly, since Yissharu—her *former* friend—knew almost everything about her. "There are billions of them." She thought of Will. "Some are more compassionate even than the best of us in my clan. Listen to recordings of the Dalai Lama some time. And some are so malicious, they kill their own kind for pleasure. You probably know about those. Most are in the middle, a lot like us. Generally caring, but not perfect."

"Are you implying there are malicious Sea-Dwellers?"

"That wasn't my intent." But interesting she'd say that.

"It sounds like you admire the Land-Dwellers."

A leading question? "Not particularly. But I don't despise them either." *Unlike some others in my clan.*

"They are destroying the world," Tareen said. "And with it, us."

Rusos spoke, "Look at how few of us there are now. We're dying off, just like the coral reefs and the rest of the ocean."

"You have two children," Andreia pointed out.

Rusos grinned. "I have strong sperm, apparently."

"Good for you. Back to Galen. What happened to him?"

Tareen's face hardened. "Your brother stumbled into a test by your U.S. Navy. We have a mole—actually, more than one—in the U.S. government." She opened a tablet computer and displayed a series of documents marked TOP SECRET. "Take a look."

The first two documents were budgetary, full of line items and dollar amounts. The third document, written on an official form, described testing procedures for 'PROJECT GORGON,' a toxin that would kill all marine life in a given area. Deployed in sufficient quantities, it could be used against hostile countries reliant on seafood. The background section focused on China, which accounted for nearly 40% of human fish consumption. Horror gripped Andreia as she read. *No wonder most of us think Land-Dwellers are evil; they constantly develop new, terrible ways to kill and destroy.*

The final document was a typed memorandum.

SPECIAL ACCESS ONLY
SUBJECT: LANCER 5 BRIEF RE:SEASPUR

LANCER 5 reported that an unknown submersible approached PROJECT GORGON restricted area following test #3. Upon strong recommendation of OMEGA 1, the SEAL Delivery Vehicle was sent to intercept. They returned with a foreign submersible in tow and an unknown male teenager (code name SEASPUR). SEASPUR was physically unusual, with webbed hands and feet. SEASPUR was interrogated and examined (ADDENDUMS 1-8), but refused to answer questions.

OMEGA 1 cited the extreme sensitivity of the mission and ordered the termination of SEASPUR. LANCER 5 objected on legal grounds, and as the submarine was under his command, SEASPUR was released. According to LANCER 5, a crewman reported that SEASPUR's submersible was mostly drained of battery power and oxygen to ensure SEASPUR was lost at sea, especially with a hurricane approaching. LANCER 5 objected (after the fact) to OMEGA 1, who said no such action was ordered or carried out.

The impersonal language amplified the horror. The U.S. government had developed a weapon to destroy all marine life and had murdered her brother to keep it secret? Andreia took a moment to collect herself, then scanned the faces around the table.

Tareen kept a grim face. Rusos looked as if waiting for Andreia's reaction. Yissharu kept his eyes on the tablet screen.

For the moment, Andreia decided to accept the horrific story—at least until she could glean more information. On the recorder Will had placed over their room, Maia had told her husband, 'You said Galen was fine when he left.' *Did she mean from this sub? Yissharu said he went to meet Tareen—probably why he deleted the camera video. They were up to something I—maybe the whole clan—would oppose.*

Andreia asked a different question, "You have spies with this kind of access?"

"We've cultivated quite a network among the Land-Dwellers over the decades. Partly to secure our financial interests, but mostly to keep a more accurate eye on the Land-Dwellers than relying on the Internet."

"Is that it as far as documents? The memo mentioned addendums."

"That's all we received." Her expression looked sincere.

"Did you identify the actual people who killed Galen?"

"Not yet," Tareen said. "Give us time. The true culprit, though, is the U.S. government, and Land-Dweller governments in general—they're all the same when it comes down to it." She leaned forward. "Their reign is coming to an end, though."

The last statement took Andreia by surprise. "Why do you say that?"

Tareen looked in Andreia's eyes. "Do you swear to the gods and your ancestors that you will not repeat anything I say to anyone, even your own family?"

Andreia didn't believe in actual deities or spirits, so she said "yes" without reservation. But thanks to Yissharu, they probably know everything about me. Why bother with an oath, then?

"We are destroying the ability of the Land-Dwellers to harm the ocean anymore," Tareen said.

It took a moment for the statement to sink in. How could a small group of Sea-Dwellers accomplish such a thing? Then again, the Karsk had drug cartel allies, spies in Land-Dweller governments, and plenty of money to buy politicians and other influencers.

Andreia recalled that ten years ago, the Karsk had proposed a war against the Land-Dwellers, but none of the other clans had agreed. *Maybe they went ahead on their own? Maybe recruited people in other clans too, like Maia? Were the Karsk behind the cyberattacks that blew up the ports and refineries? The news said it was Iran. Are some of their operatives Iranian?*

"It's us or them," Tareen continued. "The world is dying. The Land-Dweller population will crash once the world can't support their huge numbers and exponentially increasing resource extraction anymore. But it will be too late for us. We've modeled it; we'll die off first. That's why we have to stop them. It's an existential emergency."

"What exactly are you doing?" Andreia asked.

"Bringing down their rapacious economy."

"The whole global economy?" *Is that possible?*

"Yes. Some members of other clans are fighting the Land-Dwellers on a small scale, cutting trawling nets or attacking fish processing ships with underwater drones. But that does nothing to solve the problem; it is like a krill attacking a whale."

"So, how can you destroy the entire Land-Dweller economy such that it won't recover?"

No one answered. Then Tareen said, "Decades of careful planning and recruitment of key assets among the Land-Dwellers, along with developing and testing tailored computer viruses and social media bots."

Vague answer.

Rusos leaned forward. "The answers are in their academic literature. Just as the Land-Dwellers push ecosystems past their tipping points, to the point where they disappear entirely, so is their economy susceptible to pushing into a collapsed state from which it cannot recover. It's a matter of phase state physics and applying sufficient pressure. And we'll intervene as needed to keep them from climbing out."

"Our position becomes stronger each day," Tareen said. "A year ago, when prices were low, our organization invested billions of dollars—some of it cash from smuggling profits, the rest of it borrowed—in oil and gasoline options. After the export terminal and refinery explosions caused prices to spike, we closed all our options on the commodities exchanges. Not only did we make a ton of money, which will be invested in further operations, we screwed the oil companies and refinery operators, hurting the industry even more."

Andreia had a hard time processing the scale of their operations. "So you were behind the explosions?"

Tareen paused briefly before answering. "Me? No. If you examine the evidence, you'll see it was Land-Dwellers attacking other Land-Dwellers. Something they do every day."

In other words, the Karsk were behind the attacks, just not Tareen personally. And they left no trace. People had died in these attacks. People working their jobs, people with families. And collapsing the global economy could cause huge numbers to die from starvation and conflict. Andreia took care not to display traces of her doubts.

"It's not just the oil industry," Rusos added. "A semiconductor plant in China caught fire today, which will weaken the technology sector's supply chain."

Tareen continued, "It's a cause you'd be interested in, actually. We know you are on poor terms with the Mazi Council. Did you know they're thinking about having you replaced as Trader?"

"Who told you that?" Andreia knew she had enemies on the Council, but had thought they were a minority—they'd appointed her, after all.

"It's a simple matter of tracing the currents."

That wasn't a Mazi phrase, but Andreia guessed it meant the Karsk paid close attention to her clan. For some reason, it was important enough to them to plant spies on Aux.

"You have many admirers among the Karsk," Tareen continued. "Not just me. Your energy and initiative would be far more appreciated."

"It would help a lot," Rusos added, "to have more people with your experience handling Land-Dwellers."

Tareen edged closer. "You would no longer be ostracized, no longer isolated, no longer lonely. You'd be admired. You'd have more suitors than you had time for."

The offer sounded tempting. A few days ago, Andreia might have said yes. That is, if the offer was to ditch her clan and work as a Trader for the Karsk. Tareen was looking for spies and spy handlers, though. Like Maia and Yissharu.

Tareen met her eyes. Her face radiated the self-assurance of a fanatic. "You'll be saving our species—the most important cause there is, a cause that the Mazi Council is too self-absorbed to care about."

"And your brother deserves vengeance," Rusos added.

"You'll be a hero," Tareen said, "and everyone will recognize you for it. And you will be given whatever you need, whatever you want."

Andreia's first thought was to tell her to use a less harmful approach. The question was, would they let her go if she turned down the invitation? Would they believe her oath? She knew too much. She'd known too much even before. *And what about Galen? Did they try to recruit him, too?*

She settled on, "Isn't it dangerous? What happens to our species if the Land-Dwellers find out we're waging war against them? They outnumber us by 100,000 to 1, and they'll seek revenge."

"It isn't war, per se," said Tareen, "although I can see how our campaign might be construed that way."

Whatever helps you sleep at night, lady.

"There are risks involved," Tareen continued, "but they're low. Land-Dweller agents are carrying out all the operations, and we're insulated by multiple layers of operatives. No Sea-Dweller has had personal contact with any of the Land-Dwellers we're using; we only communicate through anonymizing software."

Andreia was skeptical this small group could outwit the intelligence services of the U.S. and other countries, but maybe Tareen was right. They'd been preparing for decades.

To further increase her survival odds, Andreia said, "I'm expected at Aux."

Tareen paused a moment. Rusos interjected, "Did you inform anyone other than Yissharu?"

"As a matter of fact, yes. The Council knows. I have to tell them my whereabouts as long as Will is with us."

"They don't trust you," Tareen said.

It was Will they didn't trust, but it was much safer for him if Andreia didn't mention that.

"Are you going to tell them about the submarine?" Tareen asked. "About our conversation?"

"I made an oath not to. I'll keep it to myself." Andreia made herself believe it so she wouldn't betray any signs of uncertainty on her face. And in fact, what would it accomplish to tell them?

"Good, we'll hold you to that."

Ominous wording. For survival's sake, she decided to accept Tareen's invitation—or at least pretend to. During her Trader apprenticeship, Stefan had taught her the arts of lying and persuasion. Of course, Tareen was a former Trader herself, so she had to know that also. Andreia hoped her skills were better and her experience more recent.

"If I decide to join your cause," she said, "to bring down the Land-Dwellers, what do you want me to do?"

Tareen smiled. "I could really use the help. Use your surface contacts to expand our network. Raise money. Monitor our Land-Dweller operatives. Recruit other Sea-Dwellers. We'll have to meet again to go over the details and how to maximize your impact."

"I can do all that," Andreia said, not knowing if she really wanted to.

Everyone stood. Tareen and Rusos clasped arms with Andreia, a sign of solidarity. Then Yissharu and the two soldiers escorted Andreia back to the mouth of the submarine.

Walking down the narrow hallway, Andreia weighed her options. It appeared that someone in the U.S. government had murdered her brother, although it didn't explain Maia and Yissharu's conversation about being 'fine when he left.' While she agreed that the destruction of the biosphere had to be stopped, the Karsk 'campaign' was the wrong response. It would cause terrible suffering on the surface, and the risks to her people were much greater than Tareen would admit.

But if she didn't pretend to go along, they might 'disappear' her and Will.

* * *

Will

The lights snapped on and the inner hatch opened. Andreia re-entered the whale-mouth chamber where Will was confined, again escorted by Yissharu and the two soldiers. Her wrists were no longer zip-tied. She met Will's eyes, but said nothing.

The Karsk left, shutting and locking the hatch behind them. The lights remained on. Their sled was still hanging from the ceiling. Will looked around and spotted a lever connected to the net.

Andreia hurried over to him and placed a hand on his heart. "It's okay."

He whispered, "Can you cut these zip-ties off? There must be something in the tool chest—wire clippers, box cutter, hell… even a nail or screw will do. They might be watching, though." He shifted his eyes toward the dome camera in the ceiling.

"That must be why they left the lights on, to see what I do. If I can't be sneaky about it, might as well be obvious." She waved at the camera. "Hey, if you're watching and listening, I'm going to cut Will's zip-ties. His arms are cramping."

She strode across the chamber and rooted through the tool chest fastened to the far wall. She returned with a wire stripper. "This should do it. Hold still."

She clipped the zip-tie binding his wrists. He shook out his arms in blessed relief. "Thanks. So what did they tell you?"

She knelt in front of him, legs touching his, her back to the camera and blocking both of their faces from view. "I was questioned by two other Karsk, a wife-husband team named Tareen and Rusos. They said Galen stumbled onto a top-secret test by your Navy and they arranged an 'accident' to keep it secret. They showed me documents confirming it all. As for the test, it was a toxin that would poison the waters off enemy countries." She went into details.

Will smelled bullshit. "That's utterly ludicrous."

Andreia studied his face. "There's more," she whispered. "The Karsk are trying to destroy the global economy. They claim it's the only way to prevent our extinction."

"What?" he whispered back. "How?"

In a louder voice, she said, "Why do you think it's ludicrous? I saw the documents."

She returned to a whisper. "They've been planning it for decades, and have Land-Dwellers on their side—presumably without knowing who they're really working for."

To continue the parallel conversation, Will said in a normal voice, "The U.S. signed a treaty more than 50 years ago banning chemical and biological weapons."

She scoffed. "Ask the Native Americans how well the U.S. government respects treaties."

"Fair point."

Andreia returned to whispering. "They're responsible for the oil attacks and more, and that's just the beginning. They made an ocean-full of money on the commodities exchanges, and it'll be used for further operations."

He said in a normal voice, "Can I see this so-called proof they showed you?"

She shrugged and matched the volume. "I'll ask, but it looked real."

He returned to whispering. "Did they purposely start a war between Iran and the West?"

"They didn't say," she whispered back. "Maybe Iran made a convenient scapegoat, or maybe it's another part of their overall strategy."

"Another thing," he said in a firm voice, "our government wouldn't murder a kid like that."

Andreia responded with a harsh laugh. "Next time we have Internet access, I'll bring up a thousand examples that prove you wrong."

"I do know," she whispered then, "based on the conversation, the Karsk have no qualms against ending all human life."

She raised her voice again. "I don't hold it against you personally, but Galen deserves justice, and our people must be protected from your Navy's insane plan to destroy the ocean."

As quietly as possible, Will said, "If we have to escape, we can lower the sled. It looks like the mouth can only be opened from the other side of that hatch. I don't see any controls on this side, although maybe we can force it open somehow."

Andreia eyed their surroundings. "In any case," she spoke in a normal voice, "I need to return you to Katiki before the Council loses patience."

"In case they don't let us go," he whispered, facing down, "we need to prepare."

Chapter 17

Andreia

Will pointed at a lever on the wall. "That appears to be connected to the net."

Andreia agreed and pulled down the lever. An electric motor hummed, and the cables and pulleys lowered the sled. She stopped it at arm's reach and untangled the skids, then lowered it the rest of the way. The net collapsed to the floor beneath it. Andreia pressed the power button and added air to the buoyancy tanks, so when the sealock began to fill, the sled would rise faster than the net.

Rusos entered the sea lock with the two soldiers. Tareen and Yissharu were not with them.

Rusos pointed at the lowered sled. "It looks like you're getting ready to leave."

Andreia made a show of rolling her eyes. "I assume you weren't planning to keep my sled. We have to return to Katiki before the Mazi Council enters a frenzy."

Rusos' expression turned grim. "We discussed your acceptance with our Coordinating Praesidium."

Will gave Andreia a questioning look.

"They decided there must be a test," Rusos continued, "before trusting you further."

A coldness crept through Andreia. "What sort of test?"

He pointed at Will. "We can't risk this man telling other Land-Dwellers about us. If you're serious about joining us, you must eliminate him. Otherwise, it was decided, you're both a liability."

Andreia's toes spread apart, an involuntary fight-or-flight response. She forced her feet back under control.

Will rose to his feet, either recognizing some of the words or interpreting their body language. "What's going on?" he asked Andreia.

The soldiers pointed their guns at him.

"Don't provoke them," Andreia told Will. She told the soldiers, also in English, "You're not going to shoot holes in the submarine, are you?"

One of the soldiers smirked. "We're not fools," he said in Karsk/Mazi. "We loaded frangibles. Won't penetrate the hull or ricochet, but will definitely take you down."

Andreia held out her hands. "This man poses no threat to Sea-Dwellers. And he is a guest of the Mazi clan. The Mazi Council has entrusted his safety to me. I cannot kill him."

Rusos looked uneasy. "That's part of the test," one of the soldiers said.

"To put aside prior obligations in service of the greater good," Rusos added. "And to demonstrate that we can rely on you."

They're as ruthless as a drug cartel. "Do I have to kill him? Can I just beat him up?" She kept her eyes off Will, not wanting to see his reaction.

The soldier who'd spoken before laughed. "No." He flicked a finger toward his comrade. "Espilon and I have killed lots of Turd-Throwers. Sicarios, mostly. It gets easier after the first one."

"And remembering they would gladly kill you if given the chance," Espilon added.

Andreia held out a hand. "Okay, can I borrow one of your guns?" If they were dumb enough to comply, she might be able to take them out. Although she wasn't sure she could shoot a fellow Sea-Dweller, even if they were professional killers.

The first soldier laughed. "Not a chance. Use your hands, strangle him."

Andreia looked at Will. Unarmed, she had zero chance against the soldiers. "I doubt he'll let me, and he's stronger than me. And what if his body is recovered? Strangling leaves marks on the neck."

"You wanted to shoot him before. That's a lot more obvious than strangling. Besides, we'll feed him to sharks afterward."

Will edged away from her, following the starboard wall of the mouth toward the inner bulkhead.

"Give me my knife back," Andreia told the soldiers, "and I'll do what you want."

The first soldier pointed at the tool chest fastened to the wall near the inner hatch. "Use a screwdriver. Show us what teeth you have."

Will met Andreia's eyes, then dashed to the tool chest. Andreia grabbed the wire strippers from the floor—a feeble weapon, but better than nothing—and ran after Will.

Will pulled out a big flathead screwdriver just as Andreia reached him. To their right, the two soldiers watched with amusement on their faces.

Will pointed the screwdriver at her. "I'm not going down without a fight." With his left hand, he reached into the toolbox again.

Andreia whirled around and with all her strength, kicked Rusos in the stomach, toward the two soldiers. He sprawled backward into them, knocking the closest one off his feet.

At the same time, Will hurled a handful of drill bits and bolts at the soldiers. Reflexively, they blocked their faces and the spray of hardware bounced off their padded blue armor.

Andreia hurled her wire strippers at the soldier still standing, Espilon, aiming below his outstretched arm. It hit him hard in the mouth, spraying droplets of blood.

Not waiting for the soldiers to react, Andreia dashed past them and leapt through the open hatchway, followed closely by Will. She slammed the hatch shut and spun the wheel in the center, which would hold the door closed and prevent water from leaking through. Then the security bolts would have to be slid shut to keep the soldiers from opening it again.

The wheel stuck before completing the rotation. She couldn't budge it, and against her will, it began turning back. Someone stronger than her was trying to open it from the other side.

"Need some help!" she told Will.

Will dropped his screwdriver with a clang, as well as a roll of duct tape he'd also taken from the tool chest. He grabbed onto the wheel. They strained to overpower the opposing force.

Slowly, they budged the wheel back toward the right. Muffled curses came from the sealock. At last, Andreia heard a click. She slid the security bolts home, preventing the wheel from moving again. The hatch wheel vibrated from efforts to turn it back, but it held firm.

Will picked up the screwdriver and duct tape, and pointed at the control panel for the lock. It had a pressure gauge with the needle at five atmospheres, a water level gauge with the needle at zero, a knobbed lever angled up toward the Sea-Dweller word for 'CLOSE,' and a red button marked 'PURGE.'

"Flood the compartment?" he suggested. "It'll keep them busy a while, if nothing else."

"Agree." The other lever options were 'SLOW OPEN' and 'FAST OPEN.' Andreia pulled the lever down to 'FAST OPEN.' *It won't kill them*, she rationalized. *They're Sea-Dwellers, and there's air tanks on the walls and sleds.*

A loud flushing noise came from the other side, accompanied by banging against the hatch.

"What now?" Will asked.

The door to the galley was open, meaning someone might be in there. Andreia pointed, then placed her fingers over her lips.

She whispered, "We have to take over the control room." She pointed at the closed door at the end of the hallway. She wasn't sure how many others were on the sub. It was only a hundred feet long, so there couldn't be very many. But anyone monitoring the sealock camera would have seen what happened.

"We can try to convince the pilot to take us to Katiki or Aux," she continued. "Otherwise, we'll have to figure out how to operate the sub ourselves. First, we need useful weapons."

She crept toward the open galley door, Will following. She peeked inside.

Yissharu was sitting at the table, eating soup. He noticed her. "You're back."

"Yes." *He must not know what's happening.* She entered the galley, Will following closely. Will shut the door behind them.

Yissharu eyed Will. "What's he doing here?" he asked in Mazi.

"We're hungry," Andreia said. She opened drawers beneath the kitchen counter until she found a fish-gutting knife.

"Why isn't he accompanied?" Yissharu said from the table.

"He is," she said, "by me. I'm on your team now."

Hiding the knife from Yissharu's view, she edged behind him, then thrust it against his neck while twisting his right arm with her other hand. "Don't move. I'd rather not kill you, but I will if you fight."

"You can't—"

"Shut up." She pressed the sharp blade against his skin.

Yissharu stopped moving. Andreia forced him to the floor and Will duct-taped him to the table.

Andreia found a big carving knife and handed it to Will. "If he lies, gut him."

Will nodded. "Gladly."

Andreia assumed he was bluffing, just as she was. She hoped Yissharu was suitably afraid of so-called inherent Land-Dweller violence.

They had to hurry. She stuck her blade against his larynx. "If you shout or scream, I'll make sure you never speak again. And the Land-Dweller will do much worse things to you. Got it?"

He nodded.

"And now, the truth," she told Yissharu in English. *Their story about Galen stumbling onto a Land-Dweller test likely contained some true elements.* She thought she could surmise the rest. "You left Aux to meet Tareen on this submarine around the same time Galen was arriving from Katiki. Galen saw the rendezvous, or was close to it, and your comrades captured him, perhaps like they captured me and Will."

Yissharu inhaled slightly, a sign she was at least partly right.

"Did you try to recruit him?" she asked.

He remained silent.

"You deleted the camera video," she continued, "because it showed you leaving Aux at that time, making you an obvious culprit. Tareen or one of your other comrades sabotaged Galen's sled because you couldn't have anyone find out about your war against the Land-Dwellers. Not just the Land-Dwellers themselves, but the Mazi clan, who rejected your war plan when it was first proposed."

Yissharu blurted, "None of that's true—"

We don't have time for this. Andreia held a hand over his mouth and snapped his right index finger. Yissharu let out a muffled cry of pain.

"You told Maia that Galen was fine when he left from here," she spoke in his ear. "But the sled was turned off and so its navigation data disappeared. Then Galen was given false information about where he was, and sent east into the approaching hurricane. To make sure he died, someone nearly emptied the oxygen tanks and batteries, but altered the gauges to indicate otherwise."

Yissharu stiffened, another sign she was correct. Andreia pulled her hand away from his mouth. "Who killed my brother? Who had access to his sled?"

"Who said I said that?"

Andreia yanked his right middle finger back, close to the breaking point. "Galen must have justice. I should just let Will kill you so we can get out of here."

"We need to hurry," Will insisted.

"It's a long story," Yissharu said.

"Summarize," Andreia said.

"Yes, Galen was here. Tareen talked to him, but decided he wasn't reliable enough to recruit. I did not sabotage his sled, I had nothing to do with it, and have no idea who did. I don't have that kind of expertise, and neither does Tareen."

Whoever runs and maintains the submarine probably does, though. Andreia decided to save his 'long story' for later and turned to Will. "Tape his mouth."

Will placed a strip of duct tape over Yissharu's mouth. "Stay put."

Andreia returned to the hallway, followed by Will. She pulled the galley door shut and they checked the head and crew quarters. Empty.

"Where'd you learn all those ninja moves?" Will asked quietly.

"Personal training from a retired Mossad agent. A Trader must be able to defend oneself, especially if female."

"Does he know you're a Sea-Dweller?" he said as they proceeded to the control room.

"She. No, you're the only one who knows. My hand webbing was removed, and I never take my shoes off in public."

Andreia tried to push down the handle on the watertight hatch to the control room, but it wouldn't move. Locked.

In case it was just jammed, she asked Will to help. Even with both of them straining, it wouldn't budge.

Andreia looked for an intercom, but didn't see one. No cameras either. She banged on the thick hatch with the back of her fist.

"Who is it?" came a muffled female voice in the Karsk dialect.

"Open the door," Andreia said, trying to disguise her voice—not that she expected it to help, since they'd only encountered men on her side of the hatch.

"I can't hear you through the door."

"Open it!" she shouted.

"Who is this?"

"We have a man injured," she lied, "and need help."

"The medical kit is in the crew quarters."

"Yes, but we need assistance."

A different voice, resembling Tareen's, said, "We know you're Andreia and the Land-Dweller. We know you trapped Rusos and the others in the sealock and opened it. I'm so disappointed, I almost cried."

Andreia doubted that. "They were going to kill us. We just want to go home."

"We need to make sure our people are okay," came the muffled response.

What are the soldiers doing now? They'd stopped banging on the sealock hatch. The mouth was still open as far as she knew—she hadn't heard the pumps activated. They had to be up to something. What if there was another way in and out of the sub? Katiki and Aux had lots of sealocks, not just for convenience, but in case of emergency.

"If you don't take us back to the Mazi home," she threatened, "I'll open all the hatches and sink the sub." She didn't know how to disable the safety mechanisms, but wasn't planning to follow through anyway.

"Threats are not necessary," the first voice responded. "We'll take you home."

Andreia didn't trust her. She turned to Will and spoke softly, "Go find something to hold the door closed on this end, in case there's another way in for the soldiers."

"Shit, I didn't think of that."

"Me neither, but if the Mazi had built something like this, there would be an emergency hatch somewhere. It might even be their main entry—flooding and emptying that whale mouth is wasteful for a single diver."

Will left, then returned with a thick electrical cord. He wrapped it several times between the outer wheel and a pipe running down the wall, then tied it. It looked pretty solid. And since the door opened inward, the Karsk couldn't batter their way through. They'd have to pry it open.

"If the soldiers re-enter the sub," Will said, "our chances of taking over are pretty slim. We should try to escape."

"They caught us last time."

"Then we'll have to delay them somehow," he said.

Andreia had superb spatial senses, and hadn't felt any change in direction yet. She pounded on the hatch. "I don't sense us turning!"

"You need to close the sealock first," the woman said, "and purge the water."

"You can still move with an open mouth. We saw you do it." It would be less hydrodynamic, but Andreia presumed the crew just wanted to reduce the risk she'd sink the sub. Of course, she had to purge the sealock anyway, or the inner hatch wouldn't open and she and Will wouldn't be able to leave.

"Turn the sub," she shouted, "then I'll do what you asked."

After a few moments, she felt the sub turn. "Now close the sealock," the woman—*the captain?*—demanded.

Andreia thought a moment. She was standing level to the perforated floor in the sea lock. As with Mazi sealocks, there was space beneath that floor, and from the shape of the 'whale', that space was about half the height of the upper mouth section. Probably it served as part of the sub's ballast system. *What's beneath the hallway and crew compartments?*

Andreia motioned for Will to follow her back down the hall. She whispered, "Have you seen any hatches in the floor?" She couldn't remember seeing any.

"No, why?"

"There could be a crawlspace beneath us. Maybe we can access the control room or engine room that way."

He stiffened. "We should look now. The crew—including their soldiers—could come that way too."

"Good point." The only hallway doors they hadn't checked were the ones marked 'storage.' First, she checked the gauges on the sealock bulkhead. It was still flooded.

She entered one of the storage rooms. It was lined with floor-to-ceiling shelves full of boxes, cannisters, and spare parts, secured by shelf lips and netting. No floor hatch.

"In here," Will said from across the hall.

She hurried into the other storage room, which looked the same except for a circular hatch in the floor with a wheel in the center. She opened it and peered inside. The space beyond was dark—a good sign that no one was in there.

Will found a small flashlight and swung it around. As Andreia had guessed, the space was lined with large batteries, pipes, and wires, with a crawlway between. Toward the bow, it ended almost immediately in a wall—part of the separation between the sealock and the rest of the sub. Toward the stern, it continued into darkness.

"I'll go first," she said quietly. Fish-gutting knife in one hand, she dropped into the crawlspace, not bothering with the short ladder. Will followed with the flashlight, which he needed more than she did.

The crawlspace was cramped and smelled like metal and grease. A faint hum came from the opposite end.

Eying the four long rows of batteries, Andreia suggested, "Maybe we can cut power to the motors and escape on the sled. Do you see a circuit breaker?

Or a diagram?" They couldn't cut power to the sealock pumps if they wanted to escape—they had to purge the water before they could enter.

"Look for the thickest cable," Will suggested. "One that heads back to the engine room."

There was no single main cable, but four thick cables ran along the low ceiling, connected to the individual batteries by smaller wires.

"Do you think I can cut it anywhere?" Andreia whispered to Will.

"They're connected in parallel. The further back we go, the more batteries we can disconnect, and the less electricity they'll have."

"What about the sealock?" she asked. "We need to keep the pumps operational."

He examined the wires and pointed forward. "They'll still be connected."

They crawled aft. Andreia stopped beneath a circular hatch in the ceiling. She whispered, "We're beneath the control room."

The rows of batteries continued another few meters, ending at a bulkhead. She heard faint humming on the other side. Presumably the motors or life support. She scanned the walls for a circuit breaker, but saw none. *Maybe in the bridge or engine room? They probably come down here as little as possible.*

"Think we could capture the submarine?" she asked Will, "or stick with the escape plan?"

"Let's cut the power and get out of here," Will said. "They have all the advantages."

Andreia agreed. They started cutting battery cables with their borrowed knives, both of which had wooden handles.

The rubber sheathing gave way easily. When Andreia's blade reached copper, bright sparks burst outward. On instinct, she pulled away and threw an arm in front of her face.

Will kept cutting. "Keep your hand away from the blade and you'll be fine."

She flushed. Instinct had overwhelmed reason. "I know that." She finished cutting the wire. The humming from the engine compartment stopped.

There were two more thick wires left. As they cut through them, the hatch wheel beneath the control room began to turn.

Andreia rushed over and grabbed the hatch wheel, trying to hold it still. Whoever was on the other side was stronger, though.

With her left hand, she grabbed the nearest severed cable, keeping her fingers well away from the exposed copper wires inside. She let go of the metal wheel and touched the wires against it. Sparks exploded into the air, stinging her hand. She averted her face to protect her eyes. On the other side, a man screamed in terrible pain.

"Let's get out of here!" She wrapped the cable around the wheel rim, holding the live wire in place against the metal. She'd grounded one of the rows of batteries, but that left three more, which most likely would provide enough power for the pumps.

They scrambled back to the forward hatch, Will leading. Andreia hoped the soldiers wouldn't be waiting for them when they emerged.

Will opened the hatch and peered out. "Clear."

They climbed into the storage room. Will peeked into the hallway. "Clear."

"What if there's another way into the crawl space? Like from the engine room?"

"Better block the hatch," he said.

Andreia scanned the shelves and pulled out a roll of thick wire. *Better than nothing.* "Help me with this."

"I got it." He wrapped wire around the hatch wheel and tied it to shelf poles on opposite sides of the room.

Andreia hurried to the sealock and pushed the lever upward to close the whale's mouth. She heard gears moving somewhere past the bulkhead. Then she hit the "PURGE" button to pump out the water.

Nothing happened. Then she heard a faint clank—possibly the mouth shutting—followed by the sound of pumps. The water level needle began to drop. Remembering how dark the chamber was when closed, she found the light switch and flipped it.

She hoped the two soldiers had indeed left the sealock. She also wished she could finish interrogating Yissharu. *He has to return to Aux some time, though. If not, there's Maia. And the voice recorder.*

Will joined her. "Won't be easy to open the crawlspace hatch now."

Terrible anxiety seized Andreia. "Do you think I killed someone back there?" *A fellow Sea-Dweller? Maybe not a soldier, but one of the crew?*

Will placed a hand on her arm. "Not necessarily. People survive lightning strikes, and that's way more current and voltage than those batteries could deliver."

"Thanks, Will." Even if she hadn't killed him, though, the man's shriek of pain meant serious damage.

A creaking noise came from the other end of the hallway. Andreia and Will whirled to face it. The control room door was being cracked open with a crowbar.

"Will the cords hold?" she asked him.

"They look pretty strong."

To prevent catastrophic flooding, Mazi sealocks were designed so you couldn't open the inner hatch if there was water on the other side. Andreia highly doubted the submarine was any different, but tried turning the hatch wheel anyway. It wouldn't budge.

A heavy-duty bolt-cutting tool protruded from the crack and edged toward one of the thick cords holding the door shut.

The color drained from Will's face. "Adaptive sons of bitches. We don't have long."

The water level needle reached halfway. At the control room, the bolt cutter closed around the cord.

Andreia pointed at the open storage room door. "If soldiers come out shooting, that's our only escape."

Will nodded. At the other end of the hallway, the bolt cutter snipped the cord in two. There was a thud as someone tried to force the door open, but the other loops continued to hold it in place. The crack widened, though.

The water level reached the ¼ mark. "Hurry, you over-clogged rectum," Andreia urged in Mazi.

The bolt cutter snipped the next loop. Another thud widened the crack more.

Can I get there in time and pull the bolt cutter out of their hands?

Will edged toward the storage room and pulled Andreia with him. "I know what you're thinking," he said, "It would be suicide."

The Karsk cut through the final loop.

The water level needle reached zero, and a click sounded. "About time!" She turned the wheel.

Behind them, someone pulled open the control room door.

Heart pounding, Andreia yanked the sealock hatch open. "Go!"

Will hurried through the hatchway. "Stop or I'll shoot!" a man's voice sounded behind them.

"Start the motors!" Andreia told Will. "I'm right behind you!"

She shoved the mouth lever down to 'FAST OPEN' and hoped the crewman wouldn't shoot another Sea-Dweller in the back.

The cracking of gunfire sounded behind her. Bullets clanked against the metal bulkhead and exploded into fragments. Pain erupted in her right cheek and hand. Nicks covered her wetsuit. Something hit her hard in the back, almost driving the breath out of her lungs.

Ignoring the onslaught of pain, Andreia whipped around and hurled her fish knife at the soldier at the other end of the hallway. It was the same man who'd bragged about killing lots of 'Turd-Throwers.' She doubted she'd hit him, but at least it might distract him.

Andreia jumped through the hatchway, hearing the clatter of her knife hitting metal. *Missed.* She slammed the hatch shut and turned the wheel. With the inner hatch closed, the whale mouth began opening. Water rushed into the sealock. No sign of the other soldier or Rusos—they must have all gone to another lock.

The Karsk wouldn't be able to enter the mouth now that it was filling with water. But they could close it and trap them.

* * *

Will

Amid the sound of gunshots, Will jumped on their sled and started the motors. He inserted one of the rebreather mouthpieces and shoved on his diving mask. Behind him, he heard the hatch slam shut. He hunched behind the visor and gripped the steering bar.

In front, the massive jaws of the sealock opened. Seawater poured in, crashing against the visor and over Will. He pressed his legs against the sides of the sled. In a matter of seconds, it was submerged.

The water stopped rushing in. Awash with bubbles, it circulated slowly around him.

Andreia swam to the sled. Blood streamed from her cheek and right hand. Her wetsuit was covered with nicks, and there was a ragged hole in the back, hemorrhaging blood from beneath.

Alarmed, Will tapped her shoulder and pointed at her injuries. She nodded and pointed at a compartment below the sled controls.

Will opened the compartment and found a small first-aid kit. He passed her two waterproof bandages for the small wounds she could reach, and applied a dressing over the apparent bullet damage on her back. It wasn't very deep—the soldiers had mentioned they loaded disintegrating rounds, and her wetsuit might have absorbed some of the momentum. But she was bleeding badly. They'd have to clean the wound and look for bullet fragments as soon as they could.

Andreia slapped on the other bandages and took over the driver's spot. The faux-whale jaws began closing again.

Will's chest tightened. *They're trying to keep us from escaping.*

The sled lurched forward, motors whining. The mouth continued to close. It didn't look like they'd make it.

Andreia ducked below the console visor. Will also ducked, pressing against Andreia and stretching his legs back. They passed through the closing jaws, rubbery imitation baleen scraping Will's back. They entered open water just before the jaws slammed together.

* * *

Andreia

Andreia's heart pounded as they squeaked through the closing submarine jaws. Her muscles shivered once they were clear. Will gave her a squeeze.

Andreia kept the throttle on maximum to get as far from the sub as possible. The depth gauge read 110 meters. *What was the pressure inside the submarine?* Presumably five atmospheres—the same as Aux—to accommodate Yissharu.

She signaled Will to tilt the rear flaps up slightly, and they gradually ascended. They had a big problem, though. She knew the coordinates of Katiki and Aux, but could only vaguely guess her current position. Without knowing where she was, she didn't know which direction to head.

As they continued away from the sub and upward, Andreia opened a storage compartment and pulled out a metal all-in-one tool. She unscrewed and pried off the console cover and handed it to Will to hold. Then she pulled out the sled's GPS, which contained a backup battery, and its wire antenna. Unfortunately, the GPS only worked on the surface; the signal couldn't penetrate water.

When they were 40 meters from the surface, she signaled Will to level off. Andreia pointed at herself and the GPS, then gave a thumbs-up for ascent. Since Land-Dweller SCUBA signals were primitive grunts compared to Mazi hand language, she then raised an undulating hand as far toward the surface as possible, hoping he'd understand.

Will shook his head and closed his fist, meaning danger. He was right, of course—she had been at five or more atmospheres for over three hours. But this was an emergency.

Not having time to argue the matter, Andreia cupped her heart and repeated the surfacing gesture. She shook out her limbs, exhaled until no more bubbles emerged from her mouth, and ascended slowly to the surface. She planned to minimize her time there to avoid the formation of nitrogen bubbles in her tissues.

The sky was overcast, obscuring the sun. No land was visible, not that she'd expected it. She held the GPS antenna as high as she could reach, kicking her webbed feet to add a few extra inches.

According to the coordinates on the display, they were 18 miles to the northeast of Aux and 26 miles from Katiki. Further than she'd hoped. The sub had taken them a considerable distance.

She dove back down to the sled, gave Will the 'okay' sign, and pointed the sled toward Aux, the closest refuge. She was feeling a little woozy. *Blood loss worsened by exertion?* And her knees and hips ached—a sign of decompression sickness. To counter it, she increased the proportion of oxygen flowing through her rebreather.

Will tapped her shoulder and pointed. A large mako shark was approaching from behind. Despite the bandage, Andreia was still leaking blood from her back.

Cursing silently, she headed for Aux at maximum speed. Unfortunately, Mazi sleds with two passengers were much slower than sharks. Especially deep-water sharks like makos. The shark caught up to them and opened its mouth as if to take a bite.

Andreia had no weapons left. She kicked it in the snout, triggering an eruption of nitrogen-induced pain in her leg. The shark veered off.

Behind her, Will brandished his big carving knife, but the shark had swum out of range. Andreia's leg throbbed with pain.

The shark returned for another pass. Will swiped at it with his knife, nicking its skin. It swerved away.

Andreia pulled out her mouthpiece and created a wall of air bubbles, then changed course and depth.

The shark didn't return, and Andreia turned back to their original course.

After a while, two dolphins approached from behind. *From the Karsk?* Andreia almost slapped herself. She'd taken the direct route to Aux, making herself easy to find. A mistake she might not have made without the injuries and blood loss. And the decompression illness might be worse than just joint pain—it could be affecting her brain.

She spoke to the dolphins. *Friend.* She wished she'd taken the time to learn their language better.

The dolphins responded with clicks and squeaks, roughly meaning *Follow us.* They turned and swam slowly the way they'd come.

I'm not that mentally impaired. Andreia declined their invitation. The dolphins made clicking noises and turned back toward them. They followed effortlessly, taking turns to periodically surface for air.

A sled approached from the distance, dark blue on top and light blue on the bottom, motors beneath rather than to the sides. Behind the thick forward visor was a single rider, wearing a padded blue body suit.

Andreia's skin turned cold and her leg joints ached even more. One of the Karsk soldiers, no doubt. Better one than two, at least.

The enemy sled emitted a series of beeps and blips, and the dolphins swam away toward the surface. Then their pursuer launched a torpedo.

* * *

Will

Will nearly panicked when he saw the torpedo head for them. It wasn't big, but neither were they. He tapped Andreia on the shoulder and made a swimming motion with his hand, away from the sled, which was unarmed. *Abandon ship.*

She shook her head and swerved sharply to the right and up. Explosions were much more devastating underwater than in air, Will recalled. They might not get far enough away by swimming. And what then? If he surfaced, he'd get the bends. A much worse case than Andreia was apparently suffering; he didn't have 200,000 years of evolution on his side.

The torpedo changed direction, tracking their course. Active sonar, most likely, which relied on emitting sound pulses through the water, detecting the echo, and calculating the distance and bearing of the target. But such pulses would bounce off air bubbles.

As Andreia had done with the shark, Will removed his mouthpiece and pressed the purge button in the center, blowing bubbles into the water behind them. He moved it around in an oval pattern, similar to the cross-section of the sled, hoping that the sonar reflection would fool the torpedo into detonating there.

Andreia was eyeing him. Keeping the sled at maximum speed, she reached forward and popped open the storage compartment. She yanked out the tarp that concealed the sled at her land house, and hurled it into the bubbles Will was generating.

Behind them, the torpedo exploded in a yellow flash. Knowing the danger, Will and Andreia clapped their hands over their ears and exhaled forcefully from their nostrils.

The shock wave passed through Will's body, rattling his sinuses and bowels. He vomited bile into the water, swallowed sea water, then threw up again.

When the blast wave passed, he took a deep breath from his mouthpiece, almost surprised to be alive. The sled appeared undamaged—the bubble trick had worked. And the tarp had given the torpedo something tangible to hit. *We make an excellent team.*

After a few minutes, the two dolphins reappeared. Will wasn't surprised; dolphins possessed excellent hearing and echolocation. *How are we supposed to escape them?*

The dolphins followed them on either side, at a distance of 20-30 feet. They made loud squeaks and clicks. Andreia made noises of her own, which grew increasingly angry-sounding. The dolphins responded likewise, and occasionally took turns dashing to the surface for more air.

After a while, the Kaisk sled reappeared. It slowly closed the distance, but did not launch another torpedo. *Maybe it only had one.*

When the sled was near enough to see clearly, the soldier lying on the sled pointed some sort of rifle at them.

Heart pounding, Will tapped Andreia on the shoulder and gave a thumbs-down signal. The deeper the water, the lower the speed and range of any projectiles.

Andreia nodded. With his feet, Will put the sled into a steep dive, while Andreia swerved it back and forth, creating a more difficult target. Will purged more air from his rebreather, waving it around and creating a screen of bubbles.

Rapid *pfff* noises came from behind. Long needle-like flechettes flew by, leaving trails of tiny bubbles. One punctured the left motor. Another hit the left pedal with a clank, barely missing Will's foot. The rest continued past them, then lost their momentum and sank.

Will continued the steep dive, moving his jaw to clear the pressure in his ears as needed. The Karsk dolphins abandoned the chase, the second not waiting for the first to return.

Two more flechettes hit the left motor. A grinding noise sounded from inside and it sputtered to a halt. With only one working motor, the sled was slow and difficult to steer.

Andreia sprayed a cloud of bubbles out of her rebreather. She pointed at Will, then the controls. *She wants me to take over.*

She inhaled deeply, then gently pried the carving knife out of his hand.

* * *

Andreia

As Will took control of their damaged sled, Andreia rose slowly in the water behind the screen of bubbles she'd created, ascending at the same rate. Then she flipped herself over to face downward, legs stretched above.

The Karsk sled passed through the bubbles below her, the soldier aiming his rifle at Will, who was maneuvering back and forth. The soldier was surrounded by low transparent siding, but was unprotected from above.

Fueled by adrenaline, Andreia swam down to the enemy as fast as she could, carving knife in her right hand.

The soldier shot a burst of flechettes at Will, but they slowed and sank before reaching him. At the last second, he spotted Andreia bearing down on him and swung the barrel toward her. The resistance of the water slowed the movement just enough for Andreia to reach him first.

She stabbed at the soldier, but he knocked her arm aside with the gun barrel. Her momentum carried her forward and she crashed into him. She slashed with her knife, grazing his face and drawing blood.

The soldier dropped his rifle. It remained attached to his tactical belt by a flexible cord. He unsheathed a combat knife strapped to his leg, and stabbed Andreia in the thigh. Blood billowed into the water, inky black at this depth.

Still in the grip of her adrenaline rush, Andreia aimed for the man's carotid artery and thrust her knife deep into his neck. *Die, you evil clump of shit!* She wiggled the blade to widen the wound.

Blood spurted everywhere. The soldier grabbed her wrist and twisted it. She lost her grip on the knife.

The soldier pressed a hand against the gushing wound, trying to stop the bleeding. It didn't help; his face turned rigid and pale. Now unpiloted, the Karsk sled began to slow. Will circled their sled around.

Andreia twisted the combat knife out of the soldier's other hand. She grabbed for it, but missed, and it plummeted into the darkness beneath them.

She tried throwing him off the sled, but even with such a ghastly wound, he was too strong for her. He pulled the blade out of his neck. Blood erupted from the wound in a massive cloud of grey. He slashed the knife at Andreia.

His attack was sluggish and Andreia knocked his arm aside. He swung again. Andreia grabbed his wrist and pivoted his arm toward his throat. The knife sank into his larynx. His torso jerked, then he stopped moving at last.

Andreia grabbed his rifle—looked like a useful thing to have—and unclipped it from its tether. She shoved the soldier off the sled, this time meeting no resistance. The body sank into the depths, trailing blood. In her mind, she felt Galen cheer.

Will approached the Karsk sled until the two were almost touching. They slowed to a near-stop. Will pointed at her right thigh, which was bleeding profusely.

Andreia reached past the forward vision shield and opened the bow compartment. A military sled, she hoped, would have good first aid equipment. A medical kit was on top, along with ammunition magazines, above toolboxes and hard-storage cases.

She opened a tube of clotting agent and squeezed the gel inside her thigh wound. The intense pain caused her jaw to clench and tears float from her eyes. Then she applied a pressure dressing inside her torn wetsuit and tied a thick support bandage around the outside. She handed Will another dressing and pointed to her back.

As Will replaced the old bandage, Andreia found a set of painkiller and stimulant syringes in the med kit. She jabbed a painkiller syringe into her thigh near the wound and pushed in the stopper. She injected a stimulant into her wrist. It took effect almost immediately.

There wasn't much else she could do, so she put the med kit back and closed the compartment door. As soon as Will finished, Andreia piloted the Karsk sled upward at a gradual incline. Like Mazi sleds, its controls were simple and intuitive. But the displays were fancy, with all sorts of computer graphics.

Will took a parallel course, almost within arm's reach. At forty meters depth, she motioned for Will to join her on the Karsk sled. With only one motor, Will's sled was too slow and difficult to maneuver, and was a liability.

Andreia filled the ballast tanks of the damaged Mazi sled and shut off the power. It sank into the depths. She recorded its position on the Karsk navigation computer so they could recover it later. Then she headed for Aux, hoping the worst was over.

* * *

USS Tarpon
Straits of Florida

On board the fast-attack submarine *USS Tarpon*, Sonar Technician 1st Class Dirk Hyun stared at the scrolling patterns on his upper and lower sonar screens, while listening for actionable signals through his headphones. The *Tarpon* was a newly-commissioned Virginia-class boat, which unlike traditional subs, placed the sonar workstations, combat control consoles, digital navigation table, command workstation, and pilot station in one big room where everyone could coordinate. The sonar supervisor, a Chief Petty Officer, watched Dirk and the other sonar operators from behind, monitoring all ten active screens at once. With the attacks on the Texas refineries and the conflict with Iran, the whole Navy was on alert.

Dirk's headphones, designed for durability as much as frequency response, emitted the semi-random white noise of the ocean. The screens displayed sound energy and frequency in different formats to help with detection, analysis, identification, and localization. Halfway through his eight-hour watch, he had detected nothing more interesting than distant ships or dolphins. *Boring as fuck job*, he thought, *but it beats flipping burgers, and pays better.*

The sound of a distant thud almost made him jump from his seat. On the monitor, the sound amplitude increased significantly. Then, nothing.

Dirk half-turned in his seat and called the CPO over. "Got an underwater explosion. Not a big one, but definitely an explosion."

"What and where?"

Dirk analyzed the clip. One nice thing about new submarines, they had incredibly advanced AI. It took mere seconds to crunch terabytes of data and deduce that the signal came from a relatively small detonation, the equivalent of less than a hundred pounds of TNT. After more thorough analyses, factoring in the Doppler effect from the sub moving, faint echoes off the sea floor, and more, Dirk pinpointed the location as 19.5 nautical miles off Islamorada, bearing 125 degrees. Not in a testing area.

"Good work, Hyun," the CPO said, then turned and spoke to the Conning Officer at the command console.

Chapter 18

Andreia

The Karsk dolphins didn't return. But the big mako shark did, approaching them at an angle.

May your teeth rot from your mouth. Andreia picked up the underwater rifle and fired a short burst. Unfamiliar with such a weapon, she overshot, but the noise and flechette trails were enough to scare it away.

Andreia could barely function. Only the stims and painkillers kept her from passing out, and Will had to take over steering. An hour later, they finally arrived at Aux.

They stopped in front of the Sealock 5 camera, and she signaled in hand language. She couldn't remember the code, even though she'd been here countless times. *Not a good sign.*

The sealock spiraled open, and they parked next to a Mazi sled. Andreia cheered inside when the outer hatch closed above them. *Safe!* The medication then seemed to fail all at once, overwhelming her with pain and fatigue.

Once the pump emptied the water from the lock, Will opened the Karsk medkit. "We'd better wash the wounds and look for bullet fragments. And change the bandages." He stiffened. "There's another problem..."

"Maia," Andreia realized. On the whale sub, Yissharu had admitted she was working with him.

"The Karsk may have contacted her and told her what's going on. Either she'll try to escape, or she'll help them from inside. Or both."

"I don't care if she escapes, but she could cause a lot of damage to our computer systems." She picked up the flechette rifle. "We have to confine her, right now." *I hope we're not too late.*

Will put his hands on the rifle and gently took it from her hands. "Agree. But you need serious medical help. Then I'll find Zoze and take care of Maia." Since Aux was pressurized, he didn't need to decompress.

"There's a medical bay here, and a healer—whoever's on this shift."

He brightened a little. "Perfect! Let's go."

A thought occurred. "Don't shut the sled power off." Andreia checked the inertial navigator for saved positions. Unfortunately, there were none preceding the chase. She wasn't surprised—the clans had long ago agreed to be diligent about keeping hidden from Land-Dwellers.

With Will helping her along, Andreia opened the door to the inner lock and hobbled to the wall intercom. She glanced at the posted codes and, with trembling fingers, typed the number for the medical wing. "This is Mazi Andreia. I'm in Sealock 5. I'm in need of urgent medical assistance. I've lost a lot of blood."

A woman—sounded like Thalassa—answered, "On my way."

Andreia turned to Will. "The healer should be here soon. She'll take me to the medical bay." The last of her energy gone, she slid to the floor, Will slowing her descent with his arms.

She looked up at Will's worried face. "Go stop Maia."

* * *

Will

The Aux communications chamber was a short walk from Sealock 5. Will brought the flechette gun to keep Maia from accessing it. It was his first time walking through a Sea-Dweller habitat unescorted.

At the cross-section between the corridor to the communications center and the ones leading to the rest of the habitat, a thin woman with short graying hair stopped mid-stride and stared at him. A canvas bag was strung over her shoulder.

Will waved uncertainly. "Are you the doctor, by chance?"

"Who are you?" Her eyes fixed on the gun.

"Will Myers. Andreia's, er, friend from the Keys, guest of the Mazi Council. On my way to help fix the Internet outage. The gun's Karsk, it's a long story. Andreia can tell you while she's recuperating." He hated to lie to a doctor, but added, "I don't think the gun's loaded, and don't know how to use it anyway."

The woman relaxed a little, but kept her distance. "My name is Mazi Thalassa. I am a healer. What happened to Andreia?"

He briefly described her injuries. As he resumed heading to the communications room, Thalassa hurried to the sealock.

In the circular communications room, Zoze, Sama, Duripi, and Pijasiros—but not Maia—were typing furiously on keyboards and shouting to each other in Mazi. They didn't appear to notice Will's entrance. On the walls, all the news screens were frozen.

I'm too late. "What's wrong?" Will asked.

Zoze and Sama turned to face him. "What are you doing here?" Sama said. He focused on the gun and cringed. "Why'd you bring that?" he half-shouted, sounding suddenly congested.

Duripi turned too, leaving only Pijasiros still focused on his computer. He stiffened, eyes wide.

Will regretted bringing the gun. He placed it on one of the curving desks. "It's Karsk. I just brought it to show you. Do you still have communications?"

"Where's Andreia?" Zoze asked in a tense voice.

"Didn't you see us on the camera and open the lock?"

"No, we've got problems here. Someone else must have let you in."

"Where's Andreia?" Sama shouted.

"She's injured. Waiting in the sealock for the healer. We were attacked by Karsk fighters. They tried to kill us. They're behind the terrorist attacks on the surface." He pointed at the gun. "There's a possibility they might come here after us."

"That's ridiculous," Sama said. "Sea-Dwellers don't invade the habitats of other clans. I've never heard of it happening. Besides, how would they—oh, Yissharu—well, we could change the entry code."

"I recommend doing that right now. Where's Maia? Her husband was with them."

"She switched shifts with me," Duripi said. "She's growing a baby, so we give her all the slack she needs."

At the same time, Zoze asked, "How injured? What do you mean, tried to kill you? None of what you said makes sense."

"Is she okay?" Sama added.

"She'll be fine," Will said. "Listen, Maia—"

Duripi interrupted, "The Karsk have weapons?"

"How'd you get it?" Sama asked.

Exasperated, Will let out a breath. "Yissharu led us into a trap. A Karsk submarine—it's disguised as a blue whale—"

Zoze's face relaxed. "You're pranking us, right? Or were you high on excessive oxygen?"

It did sound like an old fisherman's yarn, Will admitted to himself. "It's true. It's a pretty good facsimile. If you'll just let me finish, they intercepted us on the way here—"

"Why were you coming?" Duripi asked.

Pijasiros spoke over his shoulder, "Could you move your conversation elsewhere? I'm trying to work. The rest of you should be working, too."

Will took advantage of the black-clad hacker's interruption. He pointed at the frozen wall screens. "Is the Internet out?"

"We thought maybe the cable broke," Sama said, "but it's a software problem."

"I think I know what happened."

All heads turned to face him. *At last.* He decided not to blame Maia from the outset—she was their friend and he was an outsider. *And a 'Land-Dweller.'*

"Let me back up a step," Will began. "First, Sama, can you change the sealock password?"

"Already did. If you're brain-impaired, I'll just change it back."

"Thank you." He tried to be brief. "Andreia was investigating her brother's death, and we figured out who deleted the sealock video. It was Yissharu. Andreia wanted to question him, and he proposed meeting in person, here on Aux. The Karsk submarine I mentioned captured us on the way. Yissharu was on board, along with a pair of Karsk operatives he works for, and at least two soldiers."

Duripi gave him an odd look. "Soldiers? Like Land-Dweller mercenaries?"

"No, they were Sea-Dwellers. Yissharu's boss—a woman named Tareen—tried to recruit Andreia for their cause—"

"What cause?" Pijasiros asked.

"They're trying to destroy humanity. They've convinced themselves it's the only way to save the ocean. They're the ones who caused those explosions." He relayed what Andreia had told him.

Will left out the feeling that the desperation behind the Karsk terrorism might be justified. Humans had inflicted a lot of damage to the ocean and the rest of the planet in the name of economic gain. On the other hand, not everyone was guilty, and the consequences of a collapsed economy would hurt everyone, especially the most vulnerable. Innocent people would suffer and die.

"This is completely crazy," Duripi responded.

190

"According to Tareen, they've been planning it for decades." *Have to hurry this along.* "On the submarine, the Karsk tried to get Andreia to kill me, as a loyalty test."

Zoze's jaw dropped. "What?"

"We escaped, obviously. Andreia was injured in the process. The healer's taking her to the medical bay."

"You said she'll be fine?" Zoze asked.

"Are you sure?" Sama added.

"Yes, I helped treat her wounds. No organ damage apparent. Blood loss is the main problem." He froze. "Can you do blood transfusions here?"

"Of course," Sama said. "We're not primitive life forms, you know."

"I know. Just, I'm worried about her too. So she's in good hands?"

"Our healers know what they're doing," Duripi said.

Will returned to the immediate task. "The critical thing to address now is that both Yissharu and his wife Maia are part of a militant group that will do anything—including shooting and stabbing Andreia—to achieve their goals. Maia can access the computer system from her room, right?" Zoze had done so, last time Will was here.

"Of course," Sama replied. "Are you saying she disabled our Internet access?"

"Probably Tareen or Yissharu told her to do it." He waved a finger at their computer stations. "If you want to restore Internet access, you need to block Maia's network access and fix whatever she did."

The hackers spoke to each other in Mazi. Sama turned back to his monitors and brought up a new window, white letters on a black background. "She's online. But not running many processes. Nothing suspicious."

Pijasiros pointed at a window of command line text. "Someone set up a firewall to block all incoming and outgoing data. Easy enough to fix in theory…"

"But?"

"There's a ghost in our machines, no username, but root privileges. This new firewall supersedes ours and requires special access to alter. Even admin access isn't good enough."

Sama's eyes shone. "Fancy! Do you think Maia and Yissharu created invisible accounts?"

"Can't we pull her away from her computer?" Will suggested.

Ignoring him, Pijasiros kept typing. "I just disabled their regular accounts. Not that it matters. They probably set up backdoors and don't even need an account. We never considered this possibility."

From his workstation, Duripi inhaled sharply. "We've got more problems. I think the new firewall was just to buy time. Someone's deleting socket and API files and I can't stop them."

"What does that mean?" Will asked.

"It's how our computers connect to the Internet, all the protocols and packet processing."

Will picked up the flechette gun, trying to be subtle about it. "What's done can be undone. You outnumber Maia four to one."

"I can't believe Maia would do something like this," Duripi said. "Maybe the Karsk are doing it remotely."

Pijasiros blinked at his boyfriend. "We don't have Internet access, remember? Nothing at all's coming in."

We're wasting time. "Is there a master key for her door lock?"

"No such thing here," Duripi said over his shoulder.

Sama leapt out of his seat, causing everyone but Pijasiros to whip their heads toward him. He dashed into an adjacent room. Racks of computer equipment were visible through the open doorway. Cold air and the buzz of countless fans seeped out.

Sama began yanking out wires. "Have to air-gap the backup!" he shouted. "If this hacker—Maia, I guess—hasn't entered the system backup yet—"

"I doubt it," Duripi replied. "Whoever it is, is still tearing apart the installed system."

"We can restore it once the threat is neutralized. I'll copy the backup to a portable drive and keep the server air gapped until it's safe."

Holding the flechette gun behind him, Will said, "I need someone to come with me. Zoze?" She seemed the least busy, and he trusted her the most. "We can separate Maia from her computer."

She held up a fist. "Let's do it. If nothing else, it will confirm if you're right about her."

The most logical place to check was Maia's room, at the far end of the residential section. Unsurprisingly, the door was locked.

Will knocked, then motioned for Zoze to speak.

She rolled her eyes, then rapped out a rhythm with her knuckles. "*Des Zoze. Lito ne intra?*"

Maia's voice responded in Mazi from the other side. Zoze turned to Will. "She said she's not feeling well."

"I sense bullshit."

Zoze paused, then pressed her webbed hands together. "Agree. What now?"

Will had never been inside Maia and her husband's room. "Can you tell where her voice was coming from?" He had a rough idea, off to the right, but with a door in the way, he wasn't completely sure.

Zoze angled a finger to the right, confirming his guess. "Sounds like she's at their computer desk. Rather than sick in bed. Why?"

"Because I don't want to hit her."

"Wha—?"

Will motioned for Zoze to step away. He aimed at the lock, pointing toward the left, away from Maia.

"What are you doing?" Zoze whispered loudly.

"What's on the other side of her room?" Since they were well below the sealock entrance, it shouldn't be ocean water.

Zoze's forehead scrunched. "The aquaculture tanks."

Better that than people. Will pulled the trigger.

The sound was deafening—much louder than underwater—and echoed through the hallway. The acrid smell of burnt metal entered his nostrils. The burst left a hole in the door where the latch had been, the perimeter glowing red with heat. *Shit, this thing's lethal.*

Taking inspiration from cop shows, he kicked the door open, brandishing the gun. The room was a mess, with open drawers, clothes strewn about, and two large dry bags, at least half full, on the floor. Three holes formed a near-line on the far wall.

From a long table with two chairs and several computers, Maia stared at him with terror on her face. "Please don't kill me! I have a baby coming. Please!"

Will motioned toward the bed with the gun. "Go sit on the bed."

Maia hesitated, then turned back to the computer. "Just a second."

Will swiveled the gun toward her. "STOP!" "*Sint!*" he added, remembering what the trident-holding Mazi guards had commanded before allowing him to enter the council chamber.

She froze.

"Stand up!" Will had no intention of shooting her, but decided to take advantage of her obvious fear of crazed, gun-toting Land-Dwellers.

She stood, hands out, webbed fingers spread. "I'm doing what you want. Don't shoot."

"Lie on the floor, face down!"

She followed his command. "Can I lie on my side instead? My baby bulge—"

"Yeah, yeah. Just don't get up." Will met Zoze's eyes and pointed at Maia's laptop. He'd stopped her from locking the screen, which was filled with windows of Linux commands and file names. "See what she did," he suggested, "and if it can be undone."

Zoze hurried to the desk and sat in front of the laptop. She scrolled backward through the command window. "She deleted a lot of system files." Her voice was tense.

"Maia," Will said, "tell Zoze what you did and how to fix it."

From the floor, Maia said, "The files are irretrievable. I'm not stupid."

"No," Zoze responded in an uncharacteristically subdued voice, "just a backstabber. I thought we were friends."

"I'm sorry. I didn't hurt anyone, though."

Will felt not the slightest bit of sympathy. "Your comrades hurt Andreia and murdered her brother, not to mention all those people on the surface."

Zoze opened another window. "Disabling screen lock. I'll message the others, tell them what's going on, and send a copy of Maia's command history so we can coordinate."

"What are you going to do to me?" Maia asked in a trembling voice.

"Depends on how cooperative you are," Will responded. He couldn't possibly hurt a pregnant woman—or anyone who wasn't attacking him, for that matter—but she didn't need to know that.

Sama and Duripi rushed into the room. Their eyes widened. "What in the abyss—" Duripi blurted out.

Sama turned to Zoze. "We heard the noise. Are you alright?"

"Everyone's fine," Will said.

Duripi pointed at the holes in the wall and stared at Will. "Are you crazy? Maia's pregnant."

"She's fine. Can someone can check the other side for collateral damage?" *I hope I didn't damage anything important.*

"I'll go," Sama said. "Please get rid of that gun," he added as he left.

Out of caution, Will hog-tied Maia's wrists and ankles with electrical cords, as tightly as he could without cutting off blood flow. He searched her, but she didn't even have pockets, much less a knife or wirecutters.

"Duripi!" Zoze patted the seat next to her. "Since you're here…"

Duripi joined her and peered at the laptop screen. Zoze told him what she'd discovered. He looked down at Maia on the floor. "Why'd you such a thing? We're your friends!"

"I asked her the same thing," Zoze said.

Maia started to cry. "I know, I'm sorry, I had to do it."

Duripi scowled at her. "You had to? You had to betray our clan in favor of another? Your group almost killed Andreia! Our close friend!"

Maia kept crying and didn't answer.

"What do we do with her?" Duripi asked Zoze and Will.

"For the time being," Will said, "we have to confine her so she can't do any more damage."

Duripi nodded. "We can turn her over to the Council of Elders, and let them decide."

Zoze shook her head. "They'll exile her anyway. Save her the shame and let her go join her husband."

Maia wiped her eyes and looked at Zoze. "I don't deserve your friendship."

Zoze's face hardened. "You're right, you don't."

A message window popped open on the laptop screen. Zoze read it and turned to Will. "You shot up one of the aquaculture tanks. Water all over the floor, and some very distressed shrimp. Sama phoned maintenance and they're sending the aquaculture technician and some others over."

Will tensed, then relaxed. *Could have been worse. The technician could have been on duty.* "Sorry about that. I can help fix the damage."

Zoze responded in a tense voice, "I'm sure the people who know what they're doing have it under control."

Duripi started up the other computers on the table. He turned to Maia, still on the floor. "We need the passwords."

She didn't answer. Will poked her forehead with the gun barrel, keeping his finger well away from the trigger. "Passwords?"

She cringed and started to cry again. "Please don't do that. I'll do whatever you want."

Chapter 19

Will

Will kept an eye on Maia as Zoze and Duripi worked on Maia and Yissharu's laptops. Hog-tied and helpless, she cried quietly.

Although he felt like an asshole for doing it, Will pointed the gun in her face. "You owe Andreia an explanation. What happened to her brother? He was just a kid—imagine if it was your kid!"

She continued to sob. "Do you think I wanted him to die? In our clan, a child of one is a child of all!"

Will took inspiration from TV shows he'd watched growing up—which she might have seen also. "If you cooperate, we're prepared to show leniency."

Maia looked at him with red-rimmed eyes. "I should never have let myself get involved. I don't know who might have altered Galen's sled."

"Yissharu left Aux to meet Tareen," Will prompted, "and Galen saw the whale sub?"

"That's what Yissharu told me, that Galen followed him. Probably because of what he overheard earlier."

"What was that?"

She coughed. "Andreia had come to Aux a few days earlier and brought Galen. She was painting glow-lines on Zoze and Sama, and as usual, let Galen wander around—he got bored easily. Unfortunately, he overhead me speaking with Yissharu in the kitchen about the outpost."

"What outpost? I assume you don't mean Aux."

She shook her head. "The Karsk—some Karsk, anyway, and some from other clans—built a communications outpost northeast of here, about twenty years ago. Like Aux, only bigger. They tapped into the Internet cables, same as you."

"Northeast? I thought the Karsk home was on the other side of Cuba."

"It's separate." She exhaled. "Their home is spliced into the Cayman-Jamaica Fiber System, which is completely inadequate. There are six systems running through the Straits of Florida, with landings in the U.S., Mexico, and South America."

Zoze turned in her seat. "The Straits of Florida are Mazi territory, not Karsk. They built an outpost in our territory?"

"It's not in an area we use. I wanted to see it and meet Yissharu's comrades. We were arguing in the kitchen about it. He insisted I couldn't go there, that it was a security issue and that was that. And he said since I was pregnant, we shouldn't take any risks, and that was as important as the campaign. Then Galen stepped into the kitchen and asked, 'what campaign?' He'd been listening from the hallway."

"The campaign to destroy the global economy?" Will asked.

"To end the ability of the Land-Dwellers to harm the ocean. Galen didn't hear that part, and Yissharu made up a story, said it was a social media blitz for the Land-Dwellers to keep their trash out of the ocean. We were flustered, though, and I'm not sure Galen believed him. We did our best to make it sound as boring as possible, and suggested he return to Andreia and not wander around unaccompanied. But I think when he ran away from Katiki, it made him more inclined to follow Yissharu when he spotted him leaving Aux in a strange direction."

"Who decided to bring him aboard the whale sub?"

"Yissharu said it was a security measure. Tareen's order." She grimaced. "Yissharu mentions her all the time—Tareen this, Tareen that..."

"It bothers you?"

"They had relations when he was coming of age, and it makes me wonder if his visits have more than one purpose, especially since he says I can't come."

Will considered using that as a wedge, but for now, steered the conversation back. "Tareen had Galen brought aboard the sub. Then she questioned him?"

"Yes."

"And considered recruiting him?"

"At first."

Zoze stared at Maia. "Recruiting a 15-year-old for a war effort?"

"Their soldiers begin training as soon as they're weaned, so it's not unusual for them."

"Easier to brainwash?" Will asked.

"I suppose so. As for Galen, Yissharu said Tareen deemed him insufficiently reliable, and dropped the idea. They contacted their outpost and then they swore him to secrecy and released him."

"Where was he released?" Will asked.

"I don't know, you'd have to ask Yissharu. I do know they left the area around Aux. Yissharu was gone a long time."

Will changed subjects. "What do you know about the Karsk plot? About their operations?"

"Nothing. It's all need-to-know, and they decided I don't need to know anything. I don't even think Yissharu knows much."

"You must know where their outpost is, at least. Near one of the Internet cables?"

"Obviously. And less than a day's journey. And it's to the northeast. That's all I know; I haven't been there."

Zoze brought up a bathymetry map on the laptop she was using. "If we assume the Karsk station isn't much deeper than Aux, they've probably tapped the same cable we have, or the one near it."

Will looked at the map and brought up a drawing tool. He drew a narrow ellipse off the Upper Keys. "Somewhere around here?"

Zoze nodded and tapped her temple.

Duripi looked at it. "Definitely Mazi territory. Not cool."

Will pointed at a location south of the ellipse. Maia's confession supported Andreia's hypothesis. "Andreia told me Galen's sled was found here. A long way from Aux. Besides sabotaging the sled, the Karsk could have sent Galen in the wrong direction by saying the submarine had traveled west of Aux rather than east. Sending him east into the hurricane rather than west, back to Aux."

"How could you work with those psychos?" Zoze asked Maia.

"I didn't know!"

Will continued the questioning, but gleaned nothing else useful.

"I'm going to check on Andreia," he told Zoze. "Can you watch Maia? It's unlikely she can get out of those bonds without help, but just in case..."

"Sure." Zoze told him how to find the medical bay.

Not wanting to frighten anyone else, Will dumped out one of Maia's dry bags. Back in the corridor, he slid the gun inside and slung the bag over his shoulder.

The Aux medical bay wasn't far. It was brightly lit and smelled of disinfectant. The short-haired healer he'd met earlier—Thalassa—pointed to the patients' room.

Andreia lay on one of five cots, clad only in white stretch briefs. She was hooked to a heart monitor, blood bag, a clear liquid—presumably saline solution with antibiotics—and a drip monitor. The intravenous lines fed into a single needle in her right arm. A thick pad was secured to her thigh beneath porous bandage wrap.

Will knelt next to her and held her hand. "How are you doing?"

"Feeling better already. Thalassa's taking care of me. The good thing is, we heal faster than you. Almost makes up for our poor resistance to your diseases."

Will squeezed her hand. "I'd be dead if not for you."

She squeezed back. "Echo that. It was a team effort." She leaned toward him and they kissed. "What happened with Maia?" she asked then.

Will closed the window curtains and gave her a recap, including what Maia had said about Galen and where he thought the Karsk outpost might be.

Andreia's eyes narrowed. "Confirms my guesses. The more I hear about these people, the more I despise them. Although I hate to admit it, we need to inform the Council. When will communications be restored?"

"They're working on it."

Her eyes drifted down. "It's hard to believe, someone I've known my whole life being a traitor."

"I was a bit of an asshole with her," Will admitted.

"I'd have done the same thing. But she'd have known I wouldn't shoot her, and would have been less cooperative." Her face turned pale and she let go of his hand.

"What is it?"

She hesitated before speaking. "I killed a Sea-Dweller. Maybe more than one. His family will suffer terrible grief."

"You had no choice," he said. "He was trying to kill us. It was self-defense."

"I went straight for his throat until I was sure he had no chance to survive. What kind of person does something like that? I'm just like they are!"

"Not even close. It wasn't premeditated murder of an innocent child. That soldier—trained to kill—shot you and stabbed you." He made a small gap between his thumb and forefinger. "He came this close to killing us."

"I know. But we're born with this instinct against killing other Sea-Dwellers. It's powerful. It's why we don't have soldiers—though apparently we do, and we're capable of killing each other after all. We're just like Land-Dwellers. You were right all along." She began to sob.

Will held her close, avoiding her IV lines. He felt her pained heart beat against his chest, her ragged exhales warm against his skin. "Don't torture yourself. You did what had to be done, and now it's over." *For the moment, anyway. The Karsk aren't the type to give up.*

"The Sea-Dweller kills her own kind," she said, "and the Land-Dweller shows nothing but kindness."

He wiped away her tears. "I didn't show kindness to Maia."

"You stopped her without hurting her." She met his eyes, her expression soft. "I love you, Will."

His heart fluttered, then seemed to beat in time with hers. "I love you too. More than anything." He had entered a whole new world, and it was the best of all possible worlds, and he was in love with the best possible partner.

* * *

Andreia

Andreia snuggled against Will on the medbay cot. She'd never felt so strongly about someone, as if their separate lives had fused and transformed into something brighter than the sun. She wanted to hold Will forever, maybe rip out her drip lines and make love with him through the end of time.

But the outside world followed its own course, and had to be dealt with. Andreia sat up. "Can you remove these feeds without making a mess?"

He looked in her eyes. "Why?"

"The Karsk will see us as a threat to their plans."

Will nodded. "Can we keep them out of Aux? Sama changed the sealock password."

"Good move. But I wouldn't count on that stopping them. And we have to restore communications as soon as possible."

"I'll take care of it. You can't leave in the middle of treatment." He gave her a final kiss and headed for the door.

She opened her palms toward him, one of the see-you-soon gestures of the Mazi. "I'll join you as soon as I can."

As soon as the bags emptied, Andreia pulled out the needle and resealed the bandage to stop the bleeding.

Thalassa entered the room, probably alerted by one of the electronic monitors, and shook her head. "You need rest. At least a couple of days."

"Wish I could." Andreia threw on a linen robe hanging on a wall peg. "Thank you for your help." As a sign of great respect, she placed a fingertip against the end of her nose and bowed deeply.

Thalassa waved the bow away. She picked through a glass cabinet and gave Andreia three hand-labeled pill bottles. She pointed at each bottle in turn. "Antibiotics, twice a day. Healing accelerant, three times a day. Painkillers as needed."

Andreia pocketed the bottles in her robe, and headed to the communications center. Pijasiros was alone in the circular room, typing on a keyboard.

"Are communications back?" Andreia asked.

Pijasiros turned in his seat. "Not yet. Taking longer than we thought."

"Where's everyone else?"

He pointed at the open door leading to the server room. "Sama's in there, prepping a reinstall. Duripi and Zoze are in Maia's room, retracing what she and her husband have done, and fixing what they can. Will's in there, too."

"Thanks." Andreia followed the corridors to Maia and Yissharu's room. Inside, Duripi and Zoze were working on laptops. Will was searching through a pile of clothes next to two empty dry bags. They turned and greeted her.

Will hugged her. "How are you feeling?"

The doctor had injected her with painkillers before treating her wounds. They were starting to wear off, so she popped a white pill from her stash. "Doing a lot better than before. Where's Maia?"

"We moved her to the bathroom, where there's no computer terminals or jacks. Martis, one of the technicians, welded a latch on the door to keep her inside."

Zoze grinned. "She can't pull the 'I have to use the toilet, can you give me privacy so I can escape?' trick."

"I untied her," Duripi said, "so she can eat and drink."

"Isn't that risky?" Andreia asked.

"We can't risk her baby," Zoze said. "And there's no way to escape, we checked."

"Will told us about the Karsk crazies," Duripi told Andreia. "It's all so hard to believe."

"They almost killed us." Andreia showed them her bandaged wounds. "Yissharu must have alerted Maia, and she shut down your communications. They murdered my little brother... nothing's beyond them..." Her thoughts sank into an abyss.

Will squeezed her shoulder, then told the others, "They've caused massive destruction on the surface and spilled oil in the ocean. And they've just begun."

Andreia held Will's hand for support. "After Galen died, I poked and poked, and found a monster, like a bloodthirsty Leviathan. Maybe years of working with narcos poisoned their minds. Or maybe they were already twisted."

"Or both," Will said.

The image of sinking her knife into another Sea-Dweller's neck returned. She'd twisted the blade until she was sure he'd die. Worse, she'd felt vindicated as his body sank into the depths. She addressed her friends. "Did Will tell you I killed one of the Karsk? A soldier?"

Duripi and Zoze stared at her, so he apparently hadn't. Andreia told the whole story.

Zoze hugged her. "You did what you had to. It was you or him."

"That's what Will told me."

"You're a bad ass, my friend."

Andreia returned to the present. "We have decisions to make. If the Land-Dwellers find out who's responsible for these attacks, all Sea-Dwellers are at risk. Look what the Americans did to Iran."

"We have to stop the Karsk," Will said. "It's the only way. For both our species."

"Agreed," Andreia said. "Let's talk to the shift workers and decide a course of action. And send a messenger to Katiki."

"I'll do it," Duripi volunteered. "I don't have pink hair like Zoze, so they're more likely to take me seriously."

Zoze blew air in his face. "Whatever." She switched on Maia's portable printer and printed out a regional bathymetry map with a skinny ellipse drawn on it.

"We think the Karsk outpost is in here somewhere," she told Andreia. She gave Duripi the printout. "Don't forget to put this in a dry bag."

Duripi rotated fingers against his temples—a sarcastic 'I understand'—and headed for the door.

Will put up a hand. "Wait."

Duripi stopped. "What?"

"What if Maia and Yissharu aren't the only spies?"

The thought pained Andreia. "Then we have to uncover them. If we have to defend Aux, we need all hands. I'll study their reactions. To be safe, we should limit access to the computer systems. As for Katiki, we need them too. There's 150 Mazi there and only 16 here, not counting the traitor couple." She addressed Zoze, "I hate to ask, but maybe we should start combing messages and computer logs."

* * *

Tareen

It took the crew of the whale-shaped submarine *Trident* two hours to repair the battery cables and restore power to the motors. Espilon had been badly burned by the electrical discharge from the wire placed against the rear crawlspace hatch. The other commando, Kotan, had salved and bandaged his comrade's hands, then pursued Mazi Andreia and the Land-Dweller. Their dolphin auxiliaries returned with bad news—Kotan had been killed and Andreia had taken his sled.

Having no mechanical or engineering knowledge, Tareen and Rusos observed the proceedings in the control room. Like most of the sub, it was extremely cramped.

The pilot sat cross-legged in a hanging basket with a VR headset and touch controllers, receiving data from the external cameras and other sensors. The navigator sat beneath her at a touchscreen table, charting courses until his turn as backup pilot—it was hard on the eyes to remain in virtual reality more than a few hours at a time. The 'ear' operated the soundscape analysis and dolphin-influenced echolocation systems, and communicated with other vessels and the home base using encoded whale songs. The captain, Karsk Jadikira, had a swivel chair with a console, but usually stood. He wore augmented reality goggles and haptic gloves that were also linked to the systems.

"The outpost wants us to return and refit," Captain Jadikira announced.

"Then what?" Tareen asked.

"The Praesidium is meeting in the main conference room. You and Yissharu are to report there as soon as we arrive."

Tareen prepared herself for the broiling to come.

About an hour later, they docked at the *Silent Garrison* outpost, 34 kilometers southeast of Key Largo. Espilon was taken to the medical chambers. Rusos, who had served as Tareen's backup, went to call the children back at the home habitat. Tareen and Yissharu proceeded down corridors to the conference room.

They entered a scaled-down version of the assembly chamber in the Karsk home habitat, located off the Cayman Islands, which their clan had helped transform into one of the money laundering capitals of the world. The room was a flattened sphere with concrete bench seats and a speaker podium in the center. The walls were painted with anglerfish, giant isopods, and other creatures from the great trench that separated the Caribbean and North American plates, one of the deepest places on the planet. The home of Great Leviathan, the ancient myths said.

The seven members of the Coordinating Praesidium sat facing the podium. Mostly independent from the Caymans home, they were less formal here and no one wore ceremonial garments. The other attendees, sitting on side benches, were key personnel like Tareen.

Lanara, the middle-aged finance coordinator, stood. She held the golden trident that designated her as the Facilitator for this meeting. She tapped its base against the concrete riser, stilling the gathering. "Welcome, Karsk Tareen and...?"

Yissharu, who had been here before, gave a look of irritation at the slight. "Karsk Yissharu."

"Yes, of course. Everyone else has arrived. Let us begin." She went through an abbreviated homage to the ancestors, then turned to the cyberteam coordinator, a youngish but haggard-looking man named Itaka. "You are first."

Itaka stepped down from the Praesidium section and took a place behind the podium. He flipped through some note cards. "A brief update on the operations status. We are now in Phase Three. The identities of the Russian and Chinese hackers we employed against the port facilities and oil refineries have been leaked, along with emails discussing how Iran would be framed. The United States is the most powerful of the Land-Dweller countries, and being exposed for attacking the wrong country will cost them support. Thereafter, we will leak information pointing to elements within the Russian and Chinese governments, implicating them in a plot to bring down the West and create a new world order with China and Russia dominant."

"What are the risks we will be implicated?" Lanara asked.

"Zero," Itaka replied with a smile. "None of our Land-Dweller agents know they're working for us, or even that our people exist. We have been very careful."

Several others nodded. Itaka resumed his report. "The remainder of Phase Three is partially outside our control, as the Land-Dweller nation-states, factions, and companies must take action on their own. We have prepared computer viruses and an army of social media bots to deploy as needed to keep up the pressure. On the economic front, stock prices continue to fall. Companies are laying off workers and prices are rising. We are activating the blockchain bugs, which will crash all the cryptocurrencies except ours. Along with the declining stock and bond markets, this will make Currentsea the leading choice for Land-Dweller investment."

"And the final phase?" Lanara asked.

"Phase Four will begin when all the precursors are met, including market chaos and government frenzy. We have to remain flexible regarding timing." When no one asked further questions, he bowed to the other Praesidium members, signifying he was done.

Lanara returned the bow. "Thank you, Itaka, for the update. Tareen, you are next. What is the situation regarding the Mazi and their pet Land-Dweller?"

Tareen replaced Itaka at the podium. She gave an overview of Mazi Andreia's discovery of their plans to destroy the Land-Dweller economy, their unsuccessful attempt to recruit her aboard the Trident, and how Andreia and the Land-Dweller disabled the submarine and escaped. The Praesidium prodded her for details. She cringed inside when reporting Kotan's death and the loss of his sled.

Erebos, the trading coordinator and Tareen's chief, stood. "I thought Mazi Andreia was a Trader. You recommended her as a great asset."

Hiding her unease, Tareen nodded. "Yes."

"How did a civilian Trader overpower two highly-trained soldiers and an entire submarine crew? This monkey, does he have military training?"

Tatoku, the sinewy, stubble-headed man who coordinated the military forces, stiffened at the slight. Tareen waved Yissharu over, and ceded the podium.

Yissharu answered, "Will Myers has no military background, but he is proficient underwater compared to most Land-Dwellers. And Andreia received considerable self-defense training. All Mazi Traders do, since they're on their own most of the time, amid potentially violent Land-Dwellers."

"This is a disaster," Erebos said. "Will they tell the Land-Monkeys about us? Even telling other Sea-Dwellers could be a problem."

Tareen cringed inside at her chief's criticism. At least Yissharu was the one at the podium now.

Yissharu exhaled through his nostrils, presumably reopening panic-shut flaps. "Maia, my wife, is disabling Internet access at Aux, which will also disable it at Katiki."

"What if the Knuckle-Walker calls his people from the surface?"

Yissharu was silent a while, then suggested, "Should we involve our associates in Katiki, the Mazi home? They might be able to help."

"They do not know the campaign details," Erebos said, "only that we are doing something. It is best to keep it that way."

From his seat, Tatoku said, "We must neutralize the Turd-Thrower before he contacts others. And cut the Mazi Internet cable, and prevent them from repairing it."

Tareen stood. "Do you realize the consequences of such an action? Don't forget, none of this would have happened if you hadn't killed the Mazi boy—"

"He knew too much," Tatoku interrupted. "And it was arranged as an accident."

"He didn't know anything crucial," Tareen said. "If you'd let him go, like I suggested, Andreia wouldn't be mucking things up for us."

"And she never would have met Will Myers," Yissharu added, "and he never would have learned about our people."

"And now you want to follow one mistake with a worse one?" Tareen continued. "Attack another clan?"

Arudara, the gray-haired logistics coordinator, said, "We can repair the cable and pay reparations to the Mazi once the operation ends. Make it clear this is only temporary."

The Praesidium discussed the matter among themselves, then came to a decision.

Lanara banged the Facilitator trident twice against the floor, indicating she would now speak for the Praesidium. She called for Tareen and Yissharu to stand.

"Tareen," Lanara spoke, "you will take Yissharu and a contingent of soldiers to Aux on board the *Trident* and the *Swordfish*"—referring to the assault squad delivery sled. "You will cut the Internet cable leading to Aux and prevent it from being restored. Then you will enter Aux, detain its inhabitants, and determine what they know and whom they have told about it. The Land-

Dweller must be eliminated. It is an outrage the Mazi allowed our enemies to know about our people in the first place."

Tareen thought they were making a terrible mistake. They would be committing an act of aggression against their neighbors, something that hadn't happened for centuries. Their clan would become pariahs, subject to collective punishment by all other People in the global ocean. But the Coordinating Praesidium had made their decision.

Chapter 20

Andreia

Andreia sat with Will, Zoze, Sama, Duripi, Pijasiros, and the ten shift workers at two of the long aluminum tables in the Aux cafeteria—the closest the outpost had to a meeting room. The cafeteria was spacious enough to accommodate the whole clan if Katiki had to be abandoned. The walls were covered with underwater scenes and happy-looking Mazi families, the paint faded and flaking in spots.

Still wearing the hospital robe, Andreia stood, trying to convey with her expression and posture a sense of seriousness and confidence. She addressed her fellow clan members in Mazi, "I know everyone wants to know what's going on." She told them Maia and Yissharu had conspired with members of the Karsk clan to launch a war against the Land-Dwellers, that the Karsk had built a base in Mazi territory, that they'd murdered her little brother, and that they'd captured her and Will. "We were lucky to escape—they nearly killed us in the process."

Andreia scanned the gathered faces. The shift workers looked astonished at the news. "Maia cut off our Internet access," she continued. "We tried to undo the damage, but it looks like we'll have to do a system restore, which will take a while."

Sama stood and went into painfully technical details until Andreia gently cut him off. "Thank you, Sama."

Pijasiros addressed the room. "I deleted Maia's and Yissharu's accounts, and found their backdoors—at least some of them. To be safe, I locked everyone's account. To be reinstated, contact one of us at the communications center and we'll help you create a new password. And for now, Internet access is restricted to the communications room."

Thalassa peered at him. "You know we have to communicate with family at Katiki. Did you really have to disable our accounts?"

Pijasiros stared at her with amazement. "Absolutely. They may have been compromised; we're not passing over anything."

"There's a possibility," Andreia said, "the Karsk will come here to retrieve Maia and ensure we stay quiet about their plot. I'm happy to let Maia leave if the Karsk agree to let us alone. If they aren't satisfied with that… They may try to kill me again, maybe all of us."

Baktase, the middle-aged Systems Manager for this shift—a combination of mechanical and electrical engineer—peered at her as if her brain was oxygen-starved. "Sea-Dwellers killing other Sea-Dwellers? You must be mistaken."

Andreia had expected such a reaction. She untied her robe and removed it. Her undergarments were also med-bay issue and decidedly unsexy. She pointed at the bandage on her back. "This is the gunshot." She pointed at her thigh bandage. "This is where I was stabbed." She caught Thalassa's eyes for support.

"I treated her injuries," Thalassa said. "She speaks the truth, bullet fragments in her lower back and a knife wound in her right thigh."

Andreia put the robe back on. Will handed her the Karsk gun and she held it in front.

"This is one of their flechette guns," she said. "It's designed for underwater use, not inside habitats. They have other weapons too, like the one they used to shoot me in the back. Our best strategy is to keep them from entering Aux. We changed the entry codes—"

Baktase interrupted, "The Karsk are Sea-Dwellers like us. Entering another clan's home without being invited would be an incredible breach of protocol."

Andreia tried to stay patient. "They built a base in our territory. They clearly don't respect old protocols. We need new thinking."

"What if we can't keep them out?" a mechanic asked. "There's no weapons here, and none of us have combat training."

"I have self-defense training, and some experience fighting the Karsk. And we actually do have weapons here—spearguns and knives, for example. But you're right, we have some disadvantages. That's why we need to plan."

The meeting devolved into small clusters of conversation. "Can we move the webcams to monitor any potential breach?" Will asked Zoze.

"We don't have the wiring in place," she responded, "and there's no way a wireless signal can get through all the organometal and limestone separating the sections."

Andreia clapped her hands together, getting everyone's attention. "Can we agree not to open the sealocks for non-Mazi?"

After some discussion, the majority agreed.

"Great. Now if they're able to force their way in—"

"How?" the aquaculture technician asked.

"I don't know," Andreia said, "but they have explosives and who knows what else. We have to prepare for it." Unfortunately, none of the interior hatches or doors had security bolts. *We're so helpless.*

She turned to Martis, the young, short-haired woman who'd locked Maia inside the hackers' bathroom. "Martis, can you weld heavy latches onto all the sealock hatches to the interior? Take someone with you to help. Then we can work on the other doors. Make it as difficult as possible for any attackers to roam around inside."

The next request would be more difficult. Sea-Dwellers—Mazi, anyway—were generally violence-averse. "We should also gather potential weapons from the sealocks and storage closets. Then we'll go over defense tactics."

As she feared, there was an outcry of objections. "Are you expecting us to fire spearguns at people?" one of the technicians asked.

"If they're invading Aux and trying to kill you, yes," Andreia answered.

* * *

Will

Someone rapped rhythmically on the metal door, waking Will from a sound sleep. He was lying naked in bed with Andreia in the communications guest room, which was crammed with stacked crates and clothes. Before falling asleep, he and Andreia had found ways to please each other without aggravating her injuries. He'd held her close afterward, reveling in her body heat.

Will threw on his ill-fitting borrowed clothes—Sama had told him to help himself, but no one was an exact size match—and answered the door.

Zoze was standing in the hallway, her bright pink hair unkempt. "A cheery morning, my fam." She entered the room.

Still nude, Andreia sat up. "What is it?"

Zoze smirked. "I didn't interrupt, did I?"

"We were asleep," Will said, irritated.

Zoze displayed no signs of embarrassment. "I wanted to tell you we have Internet access again. And Duripi's back."

"What did the Council say?" Andreia asked.

Zoze placed hands against her cheeks. "They're skeptical and want more proof that the Karsk have an outpost in our territory. Duripi told them to go look for themselves, and apparently he wasn't very diplomatic about it."

"I should have gone," Andreia said.

"Duripi wasn't hospitalized with a knife wound," Will responded.

"Once we restored communications," Zoze continued, "Sama called his father, who's well-respected at Katiki. So now our Council is preparing a call to the Karsk Council."

"Did he mention Galen's murder and—"

"Everything."

Will turned to Andreia, admiring her smooth curves and brown nipples. *I'll never get tired of looking at her.* "Why don't you keep resting and I'll go see what's happening on the surface."

She smirked. "Thanks, Dr. Myers. Come get me if you need someone with more social skills than Duripi."

"I will." He gave her a quick peck on the forehead, then put on his germ mask and followed Zoze to the communications room.

On the way, Zoze attempted to give him a high-five. "FTW on bedding one of the flashiest women on the planet."

Will declined the high-five. "FTW?" He presumed 'flashiest' was a compliment of some sort.

Zoze rolled her eyes. "For The Win. As in congrats."

Will decided to come clean. "It's more than that. We love each other."

Zoze attempted a high-five again. "Triple that FTW, then. Andreia's one of the best catches in the ocean."

A little reluctantly, Will gently slapped her webbed hand. "Don't I know it. Keep it between us, though, would you? If word gets to the Mazi Council…"

"Totally down. Lips glued."

In the communications room, Sama, Duripi, and Pijasiros were busy at their computer stations.

"Any news about Iran and the global economy?" Will asked them.

"Shootings at gasoline lines," Sama said. "I can't believe a sentient being would murder another over a few gallons of anachronistic fuel."

Duripi answered too. "Looks like Iran was a set-up."

Zoze logged into one of the available computers and gave Will Internet access. She watched over his shoulder as he searched the news. What he found was frightening.

Someone, or some group, had posted the identities of more than two dozen cyberspecialists to an online document depository, along with a trove of emails and computer programs. According to news outlets, these cyberspecialists had arranged the sabotage of the oil ports and refineries and left digital fingerprints implicating Iran. Some of the hackers were apparently associated with Russian or Chinese spy agencies. The rest were apparently freelance, but presumably hired by the two governments, and these in turn had hired locals to help infiltrate the targets.

The world was in an uproar. Zoze pointed out that #AmericansBombWrongCountry, #WorldWarBegins, and #ChinaWillRuleTheWorld were the top-trending social media hashtags.

"Hashtag chill the fuck out, Land-Dwellers," she commented.

Will's joints stiffened. "This isn't a celebrity scandal. If this conflict gets out of control, whatever happens will affect you too."

She stared at him. "Thanks for the flashlight on a sunny day."

His anger settled a little. "Yeah. We have to do something, though. What if there aren't any countries at all behind this? Those Karsk fanatics are probably orchestrating the whole thing. Andreia said they're trying to destroy the global economy." Icy dread gripped him. "It might not stop there. It could lead to nuclear war. That might even be their goal, even though the ocean will be harmed too."

* * *

Andreia

Andreia's leg ached too much to fall back asleep, and her lower back itched. She downed another painkiller, changed the bandage, and put on presentable clothes. Then she joined Will and the others in the comm room.

"Things are getting worse on the surface," Will told her. "Documents were leaked that implicate Russia and China for the oil cyberattacks rather than Iran." He went into details, and said he suspected the Karsk for both.

"Tareen told me they've been planning this for decades," Andreia said. "So, nothing from them would surprise me."

"We have to stop them before it gets out of control, turns into a full-scale war."

"How?"

"Let everyone know how they're being fooled," he said. "We don't have to mention Sea-Dwellers. No one would believe it anyway. We can say it's a group of cyberterrorists trying to start a war, and no governments were behind the attacks. I want to get the world's nations to hunt for a group of terrorists instead of fighting each other. We'll need evidence to be convincing, though."

"And evidence that doesn't expose the Mazi," Andreia said.

Pijasiros swiveled his chair to face them. "Stop."

"What's wrong?"

"Why should we send messages to Land-Dwellers? The risk isn't zero, and it's not our fight."

Will frowned. "It *is* your fight. You claim to be peaceful, but you would condemn millions to death? Peace is more than refraining from violence, it also requires stopping and preventing violence by others."

Andreia displayed support, spreading her fingers and pressing the hands together.

"You know from observing us and meeting me," Will continued, "that we're sentient like you. It's true some humans act selfishly and harmfully. But harmful acts, once public knowledge, are almost always opposed by people who care."

"Land-Dwellers are more moral than the Karsk," Andreia added. "The Karsk have a cancer of the soul, so to speak, and it could spread to other clans if we don't do something."

Zoze pointed at her. "The Karsk tried to kill Andreia, our friend. I consider Will our friend also." She made a hole with one webbed hand and thrust her other knuckles inside. "The Karsk can go fist-ream each other."

Will smiled. "Thank you." He turned back to Pijasiros. "We have to stop them. They're an existential threat to both my people and yours—they killed Galen and tried to kill Andreia, and now they're attacking Aux. Beyond that, I've been thinking a lot while down here. We have the ability to heal the ocean with your knowledge and wisdom, and our resources and numbers. I want to do whatever I can to make it happen."

"You're merely one person," Pijasiros said.

"Two including me," Andreia said.

"And there are many more," Will continued, "including some in power. Alternatively, if you let the Karsk proceed with their genocidal plan, you'll be siding with them. If the Karsk are discovered—and I think there's a pretty good chance of that happening—my people will seek revenge. They'll lump all Sea-Dwellers together just as the Karsk lump all Land-Dwellers together, and the Karsk are in your territory, not that far from Aux and Katiki."

"No need to sling threats," Pijasiros said.

Will's voice grew tense. "I'm just stating the facts. Besides, if we don't intervene, the cyberwar could turn to a nuclear war. Think about what radioactive fallout and a nuclear winter will do to the ocean—and your clan."

"Who else thinks we should stop the Karsk?" Andreia asked.

Everyone but Pijasiros placed a fist against their heart. Then Pijasiros followed.

"Great, it's unanimous!" Andreia sat at one of the computers and called Will over. "What do you want to say?"

"Easier to write than dictate." He pulled up a chair and started typing on one of the English keyboards. Although she felt guilty about it, Andreia watched to make sure he didn't implicate her species.

Of course, he didn't. Instead, he invented a group of cyberterrorists with no name and loosely organized into small, secretive cells. 'This is not a state-sponsored group,' he added. 'Their only purpose is chaos and destruction.' He added the limited information they knew about the Karsk operation on the surface, and signed it, 'Concerned friend of an insider.'

"This group needs a manifesto," he said. "We can release it independently."

"What kind of manifesto?" Andreia asked.

"It would help to have some examples to draw from."

Zoze came over. "Lucky for you, Duripi and I find Land-Dweller conspiracy theories incredibly entertaining. We can write a manifesto. Like the ones by those Anonymous posers. But throw in some Discordian elements and some 'there is no freedom as long as there are governments' language."

Will pointed at his text document. "As long as it's consistent with this. And no QAnon or other antisemitic vitriol."

Zoze read through it. "Got it." She approached Duripi. "You're a writer. Want to help write a manifesto?"

"Sounds fun."

Andreia was surfing the net for supporting material when her browser froze.

"Internet's out again," Pijasiros said from his station.

"Something Maia implanted earlier," Will asked, "or something new?"

Pijasiros brought up a command window and typed for a while, then announced, "Not a systems issue. The connection's broken outside."

From the adjacent station, Sama sighed. "We're going to have to find the break and fix it."

Andreia froze. All the subdued noises in the room rose sharply into focus—the creaking of swivel chairs, the buzzing of computer fans, and the low hiss of circulating air. *The Karsk are outside.* "The connection's broken outside? Has this happened before?" She couldn't remember an instance.

"Rarely," Sama said. "Mudslides tore our splice loose a couple of times, but after the last time, I reinforced it and it hasn't happened since."

"The connection to Katiki's broken too," Pijasiros said in a tense voice.

"The Karsk are attacking," Will said, apparently reading Andreia's mind.

Andreia examined the camera feeds on the wall screens. The sun had set, and the water was dark. "Can we switch on the floodlights?" she asked.

"Sure." Sama typed on his computer.

On the video feeds, top-flattened cones of light cut through the darkness, fading at the edges. The lights were hooded to reduce the chance of being spotted from above, even though they were too deep for it to matter. The bottom was a monotonous expanse of undulating sand and silt. A tilefish passed by one of the cameras, but Andreia didn't see any divers or sleds.

"Can we get reinforcements from Katiki?" Will asked.

"They'd just be targets," Andreia said. "But we should tell them what's happening."

"I can go out and repair the connections," Sama volunteered. "Unless you think the breaks are being monitored."

"If I were the Karsk," she said, "I'd have soldiers stationed there. Or outside the sealocks. They won't let you fix it without a fight."

"We need to send our messages too," Will said, "to stop their war on the surface before it's too late."

"Same problem, we're cut off."

Will's forehead furrowed in thought. "Is there a two-way radio I could take to the surface?"

Andreia looked at Sama, who answered, "Since radios don't work down here, there's no reason to have one. Supposedly, we did have radio and television equipment pre-Internet, but that stuff was cannibalized for parts before I was born."

"Besides," Andreia said, "you can't go to the surface without a long decompression."

"I don't care about that."

"You know how painful the bends can be. It could also kill you."

"Stopping a global war is a lot more important."

Andreia admired his courage. Sama could probably build a radio if necessary, but any transmission would have to be short, before his position was pinpointed.

"What if we tap into the Internet cable somewhere else," Will suggested, "and run a new connection? Or... do you have a computer that works underwater at this depth? That would be quicker and safer."

Sama pointed at the open doorway to the repair room. "We have the test box. My father built it for cable work. Microcontroller board housed in a small pressure-resistant case with a keypad, screen, and wire and optical hookups. Limited functionality, though."

Zoze snapped her fingers. "Your test box has Netcat and a packet analyzer, right? And an onion router?"

"Yeah, all the usual network and encryption tools."

"Connect to the IP addresses and ports of whoever we want to contact, and send them a text message."

"Whom should we contact?" Andreia asked Will.

"I don't know, major newspapers? Interpol?"

"And how do you find their IP addresses while you're down there?" Duripi asked. "Ping random numbers until you find one that's useful?"

"URL to IP converter," Sama said. "I said the box has all the basics. We should probably search our page caches first, though, to make sure we get the spelling right."

Pijasiros suggested, "We should preload the IP addresses to save time at depth."

Sama pressed his hands together in agreement.

"And I'm coming with you," Pijasiros said. "You're the best cable tapper, but I'm the best coder."

This brought forth a howl of protests from Duripi, Sama, and Zoze. Andreia ignored them. "I should go with you two. I'll bring the Karsk sled and gun for protection."

"You're injured," Will said. "Let me go instead."

"Not a good idea," she said. "The Internet cables go down the middle of the Straits, a lot deeper than Aux."

"Where we're going," Sama said, "is on the slope. Not the bottom, but still 500 meters."

"That's deeper than any human has ever gone without an atmospheric suit," Andreia told Will. "The pressure would crush you. Even for us, it will be challenging." She'd never been that deep before, although Sama had. "We'll need to use a hydrogen-oxygen-helium mix, wear dry suits, and keep within eyesight of each other."

Will looked worried. "Promise me you'll be careful."

Andreia squeezed his hand. "We will. The trickiest part will be exiting the sealocks undetected." Another thought occurred. "And if the Karsk are nearby, keeping them from entering."

* * *

Flight Sea Hunter 11, above the Florida Keys

Petty Officer Second Class Deion Smith, a 28-year-old Sonar Technician, sat belted into his tactical workstation aboard an upgraded P-8 Poseidon maritime patrol aircraft. The big twin-jet aircraft had taken off from Naval Air Station Key West on Boca Chica Key and was headed to the site of an unexplained underwater detonation, 85 miles to the east.

The airframe was based on the Boeing 737-800, which you could tell from the plastic molding in the cabin, but the rows of seats had been replaced with computer stations, equipment racks, and sonobuoy launchers. A big magnetic anomaly detector protruded from the tail to detect metal objects like submarines. And if so ordered, they could deploy torpedoes, mines, anti-ship missiles, and depth charges.

There wasn't much for Deion to do until the sonobuoys—a brand-new model with unfolding solar panels—were deployed. To his left and right sat four other technicians at nearly identical-looking stations: keyboard, slanted panels with buttons and switches, and a monitor in a metal frame with carrying handles on either side. Deion figured if the plane crashed, his reinforced industrial-grade equipment would be more likely to survive than he would.

To his left, his friend Matt took off his headset and asked, "Coming to the barbecue? You didn't respond to the email."

"Yeah, I guess. Haven't run it by Latonya yet."

Their chat was interrupted by the pilot's voice over the intercom, "Approaching the target." The mission commander added, "All hands be on the ready."

"Short flight," Matt said, and put his headset back on. Deion did the same, and the whine of the jet engines disappeared.

"First sonobuoy away," the technician nearest the tail spoke through the headsets.

They flew in long ellipses, dropping a pattern of sonobuoys and listening in, with computers doing the initial screening. They'd be looking for magnetic anomalies and radio traffic too.

* * *

Andreia

Andreia, Sama, and Pijasiros marched down corridors to Sealock 5, which contained the captured Karsk sled and a Mazi sled. They donned dry suits—it would be cold at 500 meters, and they would be down a while. While Sama loaded the test box and cable tapping gear, Andreia reloaded the flechette gun and tied the two sleds together.

The wall phone rang. Andreia was expecting the call.

"The sled's on its way," Zoze informed her.

Zoze, Duripi, and Will had taped a note to the sled in Sealock 2, fastened the throttle down, and aimed it toward Katiki. If it reached Katiki, the note would explain what was going on. If the Karsk intercepted it, they'd have been diverted away from Aux, giving Andreia, Sama, and Pijasiros a chance to slip away.

Andreia and her friends waited a while, shut off all the interior lights, then opened the sealock. They'd turned the outside lights off an hour ago, and the water was absolutely black.

Andreia swam out alone, without the sled, looking and listening for any sign of the Karsk. She couldn't see anything at all, but from the direction the sled had gone, heard the distant buzzing of hunting dolphins.

She swam back into the sealock and imitated a series of shrimp clicks. The console lights of the Mazi sled switched on. Sama was piloting, Pijasiros in back.

Now able to see, Andreia hopped onto the Karsk sled. To stay hidden, they kept the spotlights off and dimmed the console lights until they were barely visible. Then they took the sleds outside and sealed the hatch behind them.

Sama took the lead. Roped behind him, Andreia added air to her ballast tanks and engaged the motors to assist their momentum. They headed southwest, away from the kilometer-long feed line that ran from Aux to the Internet cable.

Once well away from Aux, they turned south, hugging the bottom. They descended at a shallow angle. Sama had said he was bringing a magnetic detector to find the cable; the optical fibers were surrounded by steel strands and a copper power conductor.

After about ten minutes, they stopped. Sama switched on a headlamp and hopped off his sled, trailing his rebreather hoses and laden with equipment. Andreia hoped the Karsk weren't close enough to see the light, but as long as he kept it pointed down, it was unlikely. She shouldered the flechette gun just in case.

With his webbed hands, Sama scooped away sediment, revealing a 5-cm-thick black cable, presumably the same Internet cable the Mazi had tapped further northeast. He placed a thick transparent bag with a suction-cup opening around the cable, clamped it on, and inflated the bag with a spare hose from his rebreather, blowing the water out and creating a seal. The bag was studded with attachments, some connected to tools inside. He slipped his hands into gloves protruding inside the bag, and held an electric drill against the cable.

Long ago, back when they were sex partners, Sama had explained cable tapping to Andreia. The drill had a diamond tip to penetrate the polyethylene insulation and various layers of sheathing until a sensor indicated that it had reached the bundle of optical fibers in the center. Sama removed the drill and inserted a thin heat probe to melt a small section of inner polycarbonate sheath and protective petroleum jelly.

Finally, he attached the test box, which had their messages loaded, to a Mazi-designed splicing tool inside the transparent bag. With the manipulator gloves, he inserted the tool into the Internet cable, where it would grapple an optical fiber, splice it, and reroute the signal through the test box. The process was much simpler than attaching a permanent feed, which would require hookups to multiple optical fibers, burying a long line back to Aux, and carefully camouflaging everything.

Sama pulled his hands out of the bag gloves and signaled Andreia and Pijasiros that the splice had been successful, with minimal data loss. He'd told Andreia in the past that it was common on the Internet for data packets to become lost or corrupted, and the computers would just re-send them. Splicing—if you did it correctly—caused barely a hiccup.

Andreia signaled Sama, #Great job. When are you sending our messages?#

#Now.# With bare fingers and webbing trembling in the cold water, he slowly typed on the test box keypad. Pijasiros joined him on the seafloor to assist.

* * *

The Karsk outpost

In the circular, dimly-lit communications room of the *Silent Garrison* outpost, Norina received a cable tap notification. Their computers monitored all the cables in the Caribbean, especially for signs of another clan spying on them. If you knew what you were looking for, the pattern of data interruption was distinctive.

Norina pulled up the information tag. The tap was on the Internet cable used by the Mazi. She forwarded it to the *Trident* liaison, who worked in another chamber and relayed communications between the outpost and the submarine using variations of whale songs. She followed this with a chat message, 'Looks like the Mazi are trying to restore their communications by tapping a different spot.'

'Sneaky little crabs,' came the reply. 'Thank you, I will pass it along.'

Chapter 21

Will

Will typed furiously on one of the communications room computers, inventing more details about their fictional group of cyberterrorists. Once Internet access was restored, they could distribute it as appropriate. He paused periodically to think about what might come next if they managed to stop the Karsk. Could he convince the Mazi and other Sea-Dweller clans to reveal themselves in a dramatic manner, and work with humanity to heal the world? Maybe they could send ambassadors to the U.N.—Andreia would be perfect, if amenable—to secure guarantees first.

"Someone's at Sealock 6," Duripi announced from his terminal. His monitors were crowded with schematics, colored dots, and text windows.

"Are Sama and the others back already?" Zoze asked.

Duripi brought up a video on one of the overhead screens. They'd turned the floodlights back on. A woman wearing a blue body suit and bulky dark goggles had an arm extended past the camera's field of vision. "Doesn't look like them."

"It's the Karsk," Will said. "They're trying to get in."

"How?" Duripi asked. "We changed the entry codes."

On the screen, the sealock spiraled open. Five blue-armored soldiers and an unarmed Sea-Dweller swam inside.

Duripi stared at the sight. "What the…?"

"Maybe Yissharu programmed in an alternate code," Zoze said.

Duripi's face clenched. "I knew we wouldn't find all his backdoors. Traitorous parasite."

"Is the inner hatch locked?" Will asked. Martis had welded latches on all the interior entrances.

"All six are," Zoze said.

"I'm going to shut off the pumps," Duripi said. "They can't even enter the decompression suite if there's water in the lock." His fingers flew across the keyboard.

Zoze threw on a headset and brought up a window with "INTERCOM" at the top and an assortment of buttons and slider bars beneath, all labeled in Mazi. She tapped one of the buttons and spoke in her headset mic, "We have hostile intruders in Sealock 6." Her voice shook. "Lock all the doors with latches, block the others, and either ready a weapon or hide."

That's not much of a defense, Will thought. But they'd never had to deal with something like this before. He strapped on a dive knife and picked up one of the spearguns leaning against one of the curving computer desks.

"*Hatopo!*" Duripi shouted.

"What?" Will asked, hoping for a translation.

"I disabled the sealock pumps. Sealock 6 is still half full of water, which means the Karsk can't get any further inside."

Zoze bowed to him. "Mad props."

"Can you activate pumps independently?" Will asked. "Like if Andreia and the others try to enter one of the other sealocks?"

Duripi pressed his hands together. "If we see them on camera, certainly."

Will handed them each a knife and a speargun. "In case they get through anyway."

Duripi laid his on the floor. "Fight a squad of heavily-armed soldiers with a knife? Are you soft in the head?"

"Andreia and I used kitchen knives and random hardware to escape the whale sub." He pointed at the speargun and dive knife on the floor. "Those are much better weapons."

Zoze strapped on her knife. "Feels weird to have this on inside."

One of the red circles on Duripi's computer monitors turned green. "Sealock 6 pump's running again," he said in a tense voice. "They must have figured out how to override system control."

"Maybe they hotwired it?" Zoze suggested.

We are so unprepared for this. Andreia had done her best to organize them, but had told Will privately that she doubted any of the Mazi would use the weapons. Moreover, maybe that was for the best—it might get them killed unnecessarily.

"Can you bring up the Aux floor plan?" he asked Zoze.

"Sure."

The sealocks and their adjacent decompression suites were just below the ocean floor. Past the decompression suites, stairs led down to the rest of the habitat. Sealock 6 was right by Yissharu and Maia's room. *Maybe the Karsk are just here to free Maia.* If they were after him too, rescuing Maia might nevertheless be their first objective.

"Maybe we should weld the stairwell hatch shut," Will suggested. "And point one of your room webcams into the hallway in case they get in anyway."

The hallway from the Sealock 6 stairwell passed several living quarters, a shared bathroom, storage rooms, and a stairwell to Sealock 5, and terminated in a meal room and kitchen. A side passage led to the communications center and the rest of the habitat.

Zoze snapped her fingers. "Not a bad idea." She tapped the INTERCOM button on her screen again and spoke into her mic, "Martis, we need you and your welding gear right away. It's an emergency. I'll meet you outside the comm room corridor."

Carrying their spearguns, Will and Zoze hurried to the hallway intersection between the communications center, the hacker residences, the aquaculture tanks, and the "terraculture" chamber where fruits and vegetables were grown. Zoze closed the hatch to the hacker residences and turned the wheel to seal it. Unfortunately, there was nothing preventing someone from reopening it.

As they waited, Will heard a low thump coming from somewhere beyond the closed hatch. A few seconds later, another thump. "Can they smash their way in?"

Zoze's forehead furrowed. "Maybe if they brought a sledgehammer or battering ram."

Will heard more thumps. *They might even have a hydraulic door buster.* The hatches were pretty solid, though, designed to hold back 30 atmospheres of seawater.

The next thump was followed by a crashing noise. Zoze cringed. "Sounds like they broke through."

Shit! "What now?" Will asked. "We don't have time to weld the stairwell hatch."

Zoze pointed at the closed hatch in front of them. "Martis can weld this hatch shut instead. That way, we can confine them to the living quarters. Not that I want those sea monsters rummaging through my stuff."

Will glanced around for a way to keep the hatch wheel from turning, like they'd done on the Karsk submarine. Unfortunately, except for pipes and air vents on the ceiling, the corridors were bare.

"Where is she?" he asked. "We're running out of time."

"I'm sure she's hurrying."

"They'll probably focus on Maia first, and search the rooms."

"If Yissharu's with them," Zoze said, "he'll notice the new latch on the bathroom door."

Martis finally arrived, wearing thick coveralls and gloves, and wheeling an arc welder and portable generator. Zoze spoke to her in Mazi and pointed at the hatch to the living quarters.

Martis put on a dark-visored hood and got to work. Will and Zoze followed her instructions to help prep surfaces before she reached them, averting their eyes from the blinding white light of the torch. Will hoped they could finish before the Karsk soldiers headed this way.

* * *

Andreia

Lying on her sled, Andreia turned to check Sama's progress. He was hunched over the messaging box and rubbing his hands together.

They must be getting numb, Andreia presumed. Fingers and the connective webbing weren't as well insulated as the rest of the body. She signaled Pijasiros, #Can you take over?#

Pijasiros removed his gloves and took Sama's spot. Sama signaled Andreia, #Almost done.#

Andreia heard the faint whine of water jets approaching. She cupped her ears and turned her head. It was approaching from the northeast. *Who's coming?*

A powerful spotlight lit her up from that direction. She gripped the flechette gun and put her finger on the trigger, but didn't pull it. *I don't know who it is. What if they're Mazi?*

Her sled was parked on the bottom, with no protection against an attack from above. She jumped out and took partial cover behind it, rebreather still in her mouth. As the approaching sled neared, she noticed the motors were slung beneath, rather than to the sides. Between them was a torpedo.

It was Karsk, like her sled. She turned to signal Sama and Pijasiros, but they were facing the other direction, focused on their work.

Andreia imitated a dolphin alarm squeal and fired at the Karsk. The flechettes slowed dramatically after exiting the barrel, plinking against the sled visor and bow, but not penetrating. *Too deep for this thing.* The flechettes were designed to form a bubble of low pressure that reduced the resistance of the water. The deeper the water, though, the quicker this bubble collapsed, squelching the projectile's momentum.

The Karsk sled passed overhead, doing 10 to 15 knots. As it did, a trident jabbed at her, wicked barbs on the ends of the three prongs. With anxious kicks and twists, Andreia dodged the thrust. She tried to grab the trident, but her attacker pulled it out of reach.

The attacker was wearing Karsk-style blue body armor and had a man's face. Rather than using the sled oxygen supply, his rebreather was connected to a rigid backpack. He held up a curved shield with an engraved Kraken, seemingly strapped to his forearm, then shut off his lights and accelerated away. Andreia fired at him again, but didn't hear any hits.

Andreia's sled also had a spotlight, mounted atop the visor. She switched it on and scanned the darkness for the enemy.

She heard his sled approaching from the right and swiveled the light in that direction. Like a Land-Dweller medieval knight on horseback, the Karsk was speeding toward her, trident pointed forward as if to skewer her. He switched his spotlight back on, aiming it at her face and blinding her.

Andreia pushed off her sled and somersaulted to the other side, using it for cover. She aimed at the spotlight and fired another burst, emptying the magazine sooner than she'd hoped. With a shatter, his light went out.

The Karsk sled reached her, the soldier's face a mix of concentration and glee. He stabbed the trident at her. Andreia dodged to the right, evading the barbs by mere centimeters.

The soldier twisted the trident around and snagged her air line. With another twist, he yanked the rebreather out of her mouth. Andreia's heart hammered in her chest until she willed it to slow. She had plenty of oxygen stored in her body.

The enemy sled kept going, passing above and to her left. Wrapped around his trident prong, Andreia's air hose stretched until it broke. Residual air bubbles streamed out. She kicked toward the attacker as fast as possible to intercept, igniting pain in her still-injured thigh.

She couldn't reach the soldier, who was surrounded by thick transparent siding, but she managed to grab his sled's rudder. She couldn't see him, and tucked in her legs so he couldn't see her. So she could use her hands, she hooked her right arm around the bar holding the rudder to the sled hull.

Let's see if I can make this weapon useful. Carried behind and beneath the enemy sled, she slapped a new magazine in her flechette gun. She thrust the barrel against the right water jet's outflow exit, and pulled the trigger.

The echoing gunfire was followed by clanks from the motor. Pieces of metal flew out the back of the water jet. With thrust from only one motor, the sled turned to the right.

Still holding onto the rudder, Andreia fired into the left motor, emptying the rest of the magazine. That one ground to a halt, too. Andreia let go of the sled.

The sled's momentum continued to carry it forward, but not very far. Bubbles streamed out of the hull—she must have punctured one of the ballast tanks too. As the crippled sled sank, the soldier switched on its front, console, and bottom lights, illuminating a hemisphere of blue water and sandy sea bottom that transitioned to darkness. Squid and small fish swam into the light, looking for food. Andreia pulled another flechette clip out of her utility pouch and reloaded her gun.

The Karsk leapt off his sled, trident and curved Kraken shield held in front. Andreia fired a long burst, but most of the depth-slowed flechettes missed. He blocked the rest with his shield. They bounced off with barely a scratch.

The soldier gave a savage grin and planted his trident into the sediment beneath him. His expression turned to steel and he hand-signaled, #You killed my friend.#

#Just feeding the crabs,# she shot back. Her gun was practically useless at this depth, but maybe she could force him into a mistake.

The soldier pulled up his trident, pointed it at Andreia and charged through the water, shield up, legs propelling him forward with powerful strokes.

* * *

Will

As Martis finished welding the hatch shut, Will and Zoze picked up their spearguns. Martis pulled off her hood and wiped sweat off her brow. "I guess you'll have to find new quarters now."

As she checked her work, the hatch wheel vibrated slightly. It was followed by muffled voices on the other side.

Will pointed at the welded metal. "How long will that hold them?"

"Longer than if it wasn't welded," Martis replied.

Zoze snickered, but flexed her knees as if ready to flee. Will eyed the arcwelder. As a weapon, it could cause a lot of damage, but looked much too unwieldy.

They heard more voices and the clank of something heavy against the floor. "Can you hear what they're saying?" Will asked the others.

"Bits here and there," Zoze said. "Something about a hatch buster." She exchanged glances with Martis.

Martis spoke quietly, "If they're using something to pry it open, it won't work, since it's solid metal now."

"Still," Zoze said, "let's make waves."

They retreated to the communications center, Will covering with the speargun. Behind them, they heard a loud clang.

* * *

Andreia

The Karsk soldier swam rapidly toward Andreia, body lined up behind his curved shield, only his eyes peeking above. Andreia waited until he was within range, then fired at him. At the same time, he ducked behind the shield, so all she could see was that engraved Kraken. As before, the flechettes lost their momentum quickly, and either missed or bounced off, sinking to the bottom.

Her enemy was invulnerable behind the shield, but that meant he couldn't see her. She swam off to the right and circled toward the disabled enemy sled on the sandy bottom. She needed more oxygen, and that was the closest source—her sled was at least fifty meters behind in the darkness. With her thigh injury, there was no way she could outrace him that far.

The soldier peeked from behind his shield and saw she'd moved. Andreia fired another burst. Again, the rounds missed or bounced off the shield, but as soon as he hid his head again, she changed course, angling upward, hoping he'd lose track of her position.

He didn't. He spotted her again, planted his feet on the sea bottom, and sprang upward to intercept her.

Andreia shot at him again. The clip emptied. The remaining stash was on her sled, out of reach. Frustration mixed with a growing sense of helplessness. *Maybe I can grab more ammo from his sled.*

Andreia swam as fast as she could, suppressing the pain in her thigh. The soldier caught up and went straight for her gun, snagging it with his trident and yanking it out of her hands.

Andreia pulled her dive knife out of its leg scabbard. Her enemy backed out of range. He grinned again and signaled, #I have hours of oxygen. How about you?#

Alarm bells rang inside her brain. Her body had been burning through its stored oxygen and was nearly out now. Keeping eyes on her attacker, Andreia swam backward toward his sled, her only chance to survive.

The enemy lurched forward and stabbed at her face with his trident. Drawing from her self-defense classes, Andreia swung her left arm and knocked the three-pronged spear aside.

He rolled his weapon and shoved it forward, catching her armpit between two of the prongs. He tilted it up and turned it in a half-circle, flipping Andreia upside down.

She tried to escape, but the soldier was apparently a master of this weapon, and kept it pressed in place. He flipped her this way and that. She lost her knife.

Unable to free herself, Andreia fought desperately against a growing sense of panic. *I can't fight him, he's too good. I'm going to drown! Like Galen.*

Her enemy smiled. He was enjoying this. Did they enjoy murdering Galen too, or was it more business-like?

Now seething with rage, Andreia pulled her arm free of the prongs. She twisted her body and grabbed the trident shaft, planning to rip the rebreather from his mouth and plunge her thumbs into his eyes.

Her enemy's smile vanished. He swung her around, but she refused to be dislodged, and pulled herself way down the trident shaft. *I'll kill you!*

Her enemy smacked her in the head with his shield, then kicked her in the stomach. She lost her grip.

He withdrew his trident and swam backward. His head swiveled toward the Internet cable, where her friends were.

Andreia heard the faint whine of another sled. The enemy soldier left her and dove for his crippled sled. Feeling woozy, Andreia tried to catch him, but he was much too fast.

A darkened sled appeared within the lit dome of water, approaching quickly. It looked like a Mazi sled, with motors on the sides. Sama was on board. But not Pijasiros.

Andreia waved her arms. Sama swerved toward her. She gave the 'out of air' signal. Her lungs were burning and her head ached. She was so tired…

Focus! She remained absolutely motionless, trying to conserve the minuscule remnants of oxygen in her blood.

At his sled, the Karsk enemy traded his trident for a rifle, identical to the one she'd been using. Poor range and accuracy down here, but she and Sama had no shields or armor.

Sama reached her. He handed her the spare rebreather. She inhaled life-giving oxygen from the mouthpiece. Her body rejoiced.

#Thank you,# she signaled. Understatement of the century.

The soldier closed the distance, rifle aimed at Sama. *No you don't.* Andreia purged air bubbles from her borrowed rebreather to hide themselves.

She heard a rifle burst on the other side of the bubbles. A flechette wobbled past her head, its momentum robbed by the deep water. Metal plinked against the sled.

Retreat was the only survivable option. Andreia hopped on the back of the sled and pointed forward, signaling Sama to go. He twisted the throttle to maximum. She kept spraying bubbles from her air hose.

With two riders, Mazi sleds were limited to less than three meters per second. Before she was injured, Andreia could swim more than four meters per second underwater—she was one of the fastest in the clan, and much faster than any Land-Dweller, even wearing fins. But the enemy soldier was also fast, even with armor. They wouldn't be able to escape him.

Where's Pijasiros? Andreia reached in front of Sama and signaled, #where's our friend?# He pointed to the side, then gave the sign, #somewhere.#

A blue-clad arm reached through the bubbles and grabbed their rudder. The sled slowed as their enemy pulled himself forward, his shield attached to his back now. He looked like a blue turtle—a turtle with a flechette gun clipped to his chest.

With her uninjured leg, Andreia kicked their attacker as hard as she could. He wouldn't let go.

She kicked him again. He grabbed her leg, his grip too tight to shake. She kicked with her other leg, but it was like trying to dislodge a lamprey.

She heard another sled approaching, invisible in the darkness. Their attacker tried to pull Andreia off the sled, but she held on tight. He let go of her leg and unclipped his gun.

The dim lights of a sled cockpit appeared off at an angle. Their attacker glanced in that direction. Andreia took the opportunity to kick him again, this time in the face, knocking the rebreather out of his mouth. He winced.

The approaching sled switched on its spotlights, carving through the darkness and illuminating Andreia, Sama, and their tormentor. She could see it wasn't a Mazi sled. It was Karsk. Her energy faded.

The enemy soldier put his mouthpiece back in. Andreia kicked at his face again, but he blocked it.

The Karsk sled continued toward them, much faster than Sama's, which was now burdened with three people. The enemy grasping the rudder lifted his shield and faced the concave side forward, slowing them even more.

The other sled overtook them. To Andreia's great surprise, it rammed the enemy soldier in the side, knocking him well away from the sled. As it passed behind them, she saw the pilot's face. It was Pijasiros, aboard her captured Karsk sled. *You fooled both of us!*

Pijasiros shut off his lights and pushed the enemy soldier into the dark. Andreia heard the rapid cracks from a Karsk flechette gun, followed by plinks against metal. Her heart clenched.

A few seconds later, Pijasiros returned, seemingly unharmed, but with dents in the bow of the sled. Relieved, Andreia gestured, #Thank you#. The enemy soldier probably hadn't been injured, but he'd been knocked away.

#Let me lead him away from you,# he responded. He released a cloud of air bubbles from his rebreather. #Meet you at Wreck 83.# That was the closest shipwreck to Aux, about a kilometer west, a small Spanish galleon the Mazi had emptied over a century ago.

Sama held up his right index and middle fingers, one of the Mazi signs of assent. He changed course to the northwest, directly away from their enemy's probable position. Pijasiros followed, still releasing bubbles. Andreia stuck her rebreather back in her mouth and kept absolutely quiet.

Then, while Sama continued northwest—at least for now—Pijasiros turned directly toward Aux. Andreia lost sight of him. Assuming Pijasiros kept to the plan, he'd ensure the enemy followed his bubbles long enough for Andreia and Sama to escape, then push the motors to full speed.

Andreia squeezed Sama around the stomach. *I love you guys so much.*

* * *

Will

The banging against the welded hatch continued for a while, then stopped. Will pressed his ear against the comm center door. It was quiet beyond. "I think they may have given up."

"They try to bash through solid metal," Martis said behind him. "It won't happen."

"Great job!"

"Welcome to the Awesome Club," Zoze added. "I always knew you were awesome, but now it's official."

"The bad part is," Martis responded, "if you ever want to access your rooms again, we have to cut out the whole doorway and remake it. A huge job."

We should check to see if it's clear, Will thought. I should do it. I'm the target the Karsk want most, and I'm not really needed in the communications room. And I can show that humans can fight for the Mazi.

Speargun in hand—not that it could hold off a squad of armor-clad commandos—Will cracked open the comm room door and peered into the corridor beyond. It was empty.

He crept toward the corridor intersection. The hatch leading to the hacker residences and associated sealocks was still welded shut. No sign of the attackers on this side. He exhaled in relief, but for a moment, felt illogically disappointed that he didn't get the chance to fight for the Mazi.

The lights went out, leaving him in darkness. It grew quiet, too. *Wasn't it quiet before?* No—the faint sound of air exiting vents was gone.

Behind him, Will heard agitated shouts in Mazi. He felt his way along the wall back to the communications room, banging a toe against a hatch lip in the process. The sharp pain made him yearn for shoes.

The lights were on inside the comm center—apparently it had its own power supply or backup. The wall screens were out, and the computer screens were all black, with scrolling lines of green and white restart messages.

"Power's out in the corridor," he said. "The Karsk didn't get past the hatch, by the way."

Martis beamed and held up a fist.

"Where else?" Duripi asked.

"Only got as far as the corridor," Will said. "I wonder if the Karsk disabled the power."

Zoze got up from her workstation. "The comm center has its own geothermal tap and a roomful of batteries." She headed to one of the doors ringing the circular room. "It's supposed to be seamless, but all the computers are rebooting."

"It's not just the lights," Will said. "No air flow, either."

Martis held a webbed hand beneath one of the ceiling vents. Her face clenched. "You're right."

Will followed Zoze into the adjacent room. A horizontal metal drum, emitting a faint high-pitched whine, was bolted to the floor, connected by pipes and cables to a second drum and a vertical cylinder. Stacks of large gray batteries lined one wall.

Zoze checked an indicator panel. "No power interruptions here." Her forehead furrowed.

From the main room, Duripi called out, "Can't get in. My password's not working."

Zoze returned to her workstation and reported the same problem. "Yissharu must have gotten into the systems, like with the sealock. Slithered into the system, restarted our computers to kick us out, and changed our passwords or deleted our accounts."

Duripi grumbled in Mazi, then switched to English. "Let me guess, backdoors we couldn't find. I can't believe that poser's better than us."

"He's not bad. And who knows, maybe he talked Maia into helping again. She's as good as we are. Who knows what mischief they're perping now."

"We overcame Maia before," Will pointed out. She'd been able to cut communications, but the damage hadn't been permanent.

Zoze smiled. "And we have something they don't."

"Which is?"

"The servers and backups. Sama kept the backups air-gapped after Maia's earlier hack-o-rama."

"For all we know," Duripi said, "their changes are on the backups too. Yissharu moved in five years ago, and we only keep backups a year before we have to overwrite them."

Zoze's smile faded. "Solid point. If nothing else, these Karsk worms know how to plan ahead." She brightened. "We can wipe the machines and install a new operating system—we have downloads of every flavor worth having."

Duripi groaned. "The nuclear option. We'd have to rebuild years of modifications. And what about the life-support systems? Yissharu the Traitor apparently has access to everything."

"One step at a time. We can figure out what's been corrupted, quarantine it, and replace it."

"That's an oceanful of work. How long will the oxygen hold out?"

"We're blocked off from our quarters and the emergency supply there," Zoze said. "There's tanks in the shift quarters, but with the fans off, we'd have to move there, which means giving up on the computer systems." Her eyebrows raised and she moved a finger in a horizontal circle. "We can use rebreathers from the sealocks, at least for a while. Not locks five or six, but there's four others, and Sealock 1 is huge."

"Where does your oxygen come from?" Will asked.

"Electrolysis of sea water, powered by one of the geothermal taps. I don't know if the Karsk disabled that too, or just the fans." She turned to Martis. "Can you find out what's happening in the other chambers? See if we can get the air back on?"

"*Siv*," Martis responded. Mazi for "yes," one of the handful of words Will had surmised from context.

"I'll help," Will volunteered.

"If it seems like it'll take a while," Zoze added, "can you bring some rebreathers?"

"What happens when Andreia and the others return? Can we let them in?"

Zoze made a fist and pointed it down, a gesture Will associated with bad news. "We can't even log on. Another problem to figure out."

A voice came over the intercom, speaking first in Mazi, then in English. "You may have noticed the lights and air are out." It was Yissharu's faintly Cuban-accented voice. "If you want them restored, give us the Land-Dweller and the species-traitor Andreia. Will Myers, if you are listening, surrender and you won't be harmed."

Martis's jaw dropped. "They're threatening to kill us?"

Duripi placed his webbed hands over his forehead. "Yissharu was adopted into our clan. How could he?"

Because he's a traitorous spy. Stomach churning, Will turned to the others. "Are you sure you can fix the air? If not, I'm willing to give myself up." He didn't believe the promise of safety, but if they were all going to die, better just him instead.

Martis eyed him. Zoze spoke up, "Slam that down the chute. You're our guest. And they just insulted my BFF. Yissharu and Maia are the traitors. They can stuff sea urchins up their asses."

"Sounds painful," Will said, thankful for the support.

"Send the Land-Dweller and Andreia out the nearest sealock you can access," Yissharu continued. "We are monitoring them all. Once we have them in custody, we'll restore full power."

Will's fists clenched. *If I see that asshole again...* "If we run out of air," he told the others, "my offer stands." And maybe he could take out some of the attackers before they killed him.

Zoze put up a hand. "I've never been threatened like that before, and I'm not going to take it." She moved to a different laptop, which was covered with stickers of smiling vegetables. "This terminal's ultra-limited," she said, "but it doesn't require a sign-in."

She brought up an intercom program and tapped a green button with Mazi script. "Karsk invaders, go fuck yourselves!" She turned to the others and grinned.

Martis frowned. "You shouldn't speak for everyone."

"Would you seriously hand over a member of our clan to be killed? Or a guest of the Mazi Council?"

"I suppose not." She turned to Will. "Let's find the rest of the crew."

⋆ ⋆ ⋆

Flight Sea Hunter 11, above the Straits of Florida

They'd been flying for a while, a typical boring patrol, when Deion heard something from the deployed sonobuoys. It sounded like metal banging against metal. He increased the gain and listened to a replay. Definitely thick metal on metal, more pronounced than a slammed hatch or dropped tool. Low clank, upper frequencies highly attenuated. That meant deep water, and maybe a submarine hull surrounding the source.

He called the sonar supervisor over and ran a triangulation from all the sonobuoys within range. The program gave a direction of 222 degrees from the detonation they'd detected, at a distance of 13 nautical miles.

The thuds continued, every couple of seconds or so, same position. "What do you think it is?" he asked the supervisor.

"Don't know, but it ain't fish playing ping-pong." He went aft to talk to the mission commander.

Chapter 22

Will

Will followed Martis down a dark corridor away from the communications center. Like Andreia, the minimal light didn't slow her, and Will struggled to keep up without tripping over something. They turned right at an intersection and stopped in front of a watertight hatch that wouldn't open.

Martis banged on the hatch and shouted in Mazi, "*Ite Martis! Lito ne intra?*"

After a few seconds, it swung open. A fortyish Sea-Dweller man wearing coveralls, a vest with lots of pockets, and a tool belt greeted her. He eyed Will warily.

They entered a room full of lathes, presses, drills, and 3-D printers, dimly lit by electric lanterns. It smelled strongly of grease and chemicals. The man slid a metal bar through the inside wheel of the hatch, locking it in place.

Martis spoke with the coverall-wearing man in Mazi. She translated some of it to Will. "Air is out throughout the habitat. So are the lights—except in the communications center—and almost everything else connected to the network."

"Do you speak English?" Will asked him.

"I read it better than I speak," he replied in a heavy accent. "Manuals for electronics."

"A team of Karsk commandos—soldiers—invaded Aux. Yissharu is helping them, and took over the computer systems."

"I heard over the intercom." He eyed Will as if weighing his options.

"Then Aux still has power, at least?"

"Yes, the pumps and turbines are still operational. But not much else." He led them to a large chamber full of gas cylinders, pipes, and ductwork, lit by floodlights connected to bulky batteries. An older woman and a younger man had opened one of the control panels and were fiddling with it.

"Can we help?" Will asked. "Where are the problems?"

The man in coveralls pointed at a big pipe coming from one wall. "Seawater comes in here." He pointed at a grouping of pipes, valves, and metal tanks. "There, it is distilled into fresh water. Some is piped around the complex and some goes there"—he pointed at a complicated arrangement of more pipes, cylinders, gauges, and wires—"to split into oxygen and hydrogen. The distiller is working, but not the electrolyzer. Fans—which move air around Aux—aren't working either. And of course, the overhead lights are out."

Will considered himself somewhat mechanically astute, but he'd never worked with this kind of equipment before. "It's computerized?"

"Yes, it's supposed to operate automatically and keep the gas levels steady." He spoke to his colleagues working on the control panel. "*Mitre-ta?*"

They turned and responded in Mazi. They looked frustrated.

"Can you run it without computers?" Will asked.

The woman at the panel sighed. "We disconnected the line to the computer network, then tried a reset, which didn't work."

"Even tried unplugging it," the man in coveralls said.

"There goes my advice, then," Will said, only half-joking.

"We're trying to bypass the control board now, so we can operate it manually."

Martis spoke to him in Mazi, then told Will, "There's nothing we can do here. Beyond my knowledge. Let's start gathering rebreathers and oxygen tanks from the sealocks. I think there are some in the medical bay, too."

"While we're in the sealocks," Will suggested, "let's figure out how to let our divers back in without letting in more Karsk. We may have to weld more hatches shut, too."

Martis spread her webbed hands and pressed them together, one of the Mazi signs of agreement.

* * *

Andreia

Andreia and Sama met Pijasiros at Wreck 83, a small galleon the Mazi had salvaged over a century ago. Nothing was left but scattered cannons.

They flashed appreciation messages to each other, pupils fully dilated to see by the dim light from their sled instruments.

Andreia signaled, #Someone must tell Katiki what's happening.#

Sama responded, #You go to Katiki. You live there.#

#This is my fault. I must stay to help fix the situation.# Andreia traced Will's name in the water with her finger, then signaled, #I must stay for him too.#

Sama and Pijasiros looked at each other. #I'll go,# Pijasiros volunteered. #Promise me not to die.#

#We'll all grow old together,# Andreia responded, feeling incredibly grateful to be still breathing. She'd thought herself capable, but had been utterly humbled by an undersea warrior worthy of the sagas. Meanwhile, Pijasiros, who had never taken a defense class in his life, had been the one to save the day.

Pijasiros gave Sama his tools, then headed to Katiki on the Mazi sled. At top speed, he'd be there in about an hour. Andreia and Sama headed for Aux, Sama driving. They couldn't see in the dark water, but had entered the coordinates in the navigation computer.

After a while, Sama half-turned toward Andreia and signaled, #We're almost there.#

#I don't see the lights,# Andreia responded.

#They must have turned them off. I can tell we're close because the seawater intakes change the local currents slightly.#

Andreia hadn't known that trick, but she'd never lived here. #The Karsk could have disabled the lights or covered them. We should search for more enemies before entering.# She had no idea how many soldiers the Karsk had, or if they would actually dare to invade the home—even an outpost—of another clan. If they were capable of murder, though, they were certainly capable of home invasion.

#Unless they're stupid,# Sama signaled, #we'll never find them in the dark.#

True. #And if we use the sled lights, it will give us away. Let's assume the Karsk are here. They cut our Internet connection. If nothing else, the deceiver#—referring to Yissharu—#will want to retrieve his wife.#

#My companion's inside,# Sama signaled. #And others. We have to help them.#

#How?#

Sama shrugged. #I don't know. But the longer we're out here, the longer our decompression time.#

We need some semblance of plan. #Aux has six sealocks. The enemies can't cover them all.# *I hope.*

#If the Karsk are here,# Sama replied, #they'll enter through Sealock 5 or 6 to access our quarters. Another option might be Sealock 1, which is the biggest. Or maybe they'll use more than one entrance. I suggest Sealock 3, which is the furthest from those others.#

Andreia deferred to Sama's knowledge and gave an 'okay' sign. She continued to let him drive—no one knew these waters better than he.

Sama followed a circuitous route through the darkness, keeping his eyes on the inertial navigation readout and depth gauge, and occasionally stopping to feel the direction of the current. Then he shut off the motors and they glided to a halt. #Wait here.# He sprang off the sled, swimming forward.

He returned a minute later and piloted the sled a little further. They bumped gently against a solid object. In the dim light from the console instruments, it looked like a mound of rock, sand and mud. One of the camouflaged sealocks.

Sama pulled up a mud-textured flap, revealing a keypad. He typed in the code. Nothing happened. He kept tapping the keypad, then faced the camera. #Let us in,# he gestured.

The lock remained closed. Sama returned to the sled and signaled Andreia, #We're locked out.#

If the Aux crew had sealed the habitat, presumably they'd be monitoring the cameras. Zoze knew the team was supposed to come back in after sending their messages. Andreia traced an approximation of the Karsk fish-on-trident sigil in the water. #They're here. Let's move before they find us.#

As Sama restarted the motors, Andreia heard the rapid clicks of dolphin sonar, followed by the faint sound of water jets. They were too late.

* * *

Will

Will pushed an empty cart behind Martis down the corridors. They visited the medical bay first.

Like the machine shop, it was dimly lit by electric lanterns—probably fine for Sea-Dweller vision. Martis spoke in Mazi with the healer, Thalassa, who gave an expression of concern.

After a long exchange, Martis told Will in English, "She'll reserve the oxygen here and in Sealock 1 for the shift crew. We can take from Sealocks 2, 3, and 4."

Sounds fair. Will asked Thalassa, "Do you have a stethoscope we could borrow?"

She stared at him. "Why?"

"To listen for invaders, in case any of them entered those sealocks."

She nodded and opened a drawer, pulling out a stethoscope with an electronic console attached to the chestpiece. She powered up the screen and fiddled with the controls. "I set amplification to maximum." She handed it to Will and pointed at the display. "You can examine waveforms also. This is our one digital stethoscope. Please return it when finished."

"Of course."

Will and Martis proceeded to the nearest sealock—number 3. Martis had welded a heavy latch on the hallway side, but the Karsk had breached the one on Sealock 6.

Will placed the stethoscope against the hatch, but couldn't hear anything on the other side. The display showed only tiny random squiggles.

"No one there," he told Martis. "Unless they're being tricky." Which the Karsk certainly were. "We'll have to shut the hatch quick if I'm wrong."

Martis hesitated, then slid aside the thick bolt she'd added to the hatch. She spun the wheel.

* * *

Andreia

Andreia had always liked dolphins, but they made fearsome hunters. As Sama turned the sled throttle to maximum, she reached around him and signaled, ♯Go deeper.♯ The deeper the dolphins had to dive, the less tracking time they'd have.

Still facing forward, Sama nodded.

As they accelerated away from Sealock 3, Andreia signaled, ♯Pass by Sealocks 6 and 7.♯

Sama stiffened. Andreia added, ♯Just to see.♯

Andreia knew Aux well enough to judge where its compartments were positioned. From their speed and direction, they passed over the communications center, then over the hacker residences. No lights or shapes were visible in the darkness.

They left Aux behind, heading southeast to deeper water. The dolphin clicks grew louder, then emanated from either side. The water jet noise also drew closer.

Andreia's sense of helplessness returned. Their sled was too slow and they had no weapons. *At least we can draw away part of the Karsk force.*

* * *

Will

The decompression chamber for Sealock 3 was thankfully empty. Martis opened two of the unlabeled closets and they loaded cylindrical air tanks and rebreathers onto the push cart.

"Can the outer sealock hatch be unlocked manually?" he asked. "So we can let in Andreia and the others?"

"Yes, assuming you mean opening from the inside. And the inner hatch must be closed."

"So we just have to monitor the cameras somehow, to watch for them and not let in Karsk instead. Can we splice into the camera cables, plug them into a laptop?"

"Sounds like a job for Zoze or Duripi."

They gathered more air cannisters and rebreathers from Sealocks 2 and 4, then returned to the communications room. "This should last a while," Martis said as they unloaded the cart.

Will asked Zoze and Duripi about rerouting the external camera feeds.

"I can do that here," Zoze responded. "Unplug them from the camera server and run the cables to one of our test laptops." She went into one of the adjacent rooms.

"I will help Thalassa with Sealock 1 oxygen," Martis said, "then install more door locks." She extended a palm toward them. Duripi returned the gesture, and assuming it was good rather than bad, Will did also. Martis smiled and left with the empty cart.

"Will," Zoze called from the other room. "Need your help."

He entered a frigid room full of server racks, power strips, and cables. Red and green indicator lights, some blinking, dotted the towers of equipment like tiny windows. Computer fans hummed like insects.

Zoze was sitting at a small desk in the far corner, typing on a black laptop. It was connected to a docking station with a tangle of cables running from the back. She turned and waved him over.

"You've got quite a setup here," he said.

"Assembled over the years." She opened six video windows, all of them dark. "Looks like someone shut off the floodlights. Yissharu, I presume."

"Can you get them back on? I assume the Karsk are doing something they don't want us to see."

Zoze rerouted more wires and typed commands in a Linux window. The video window labeled CAM-6 remained black. Finally, a dark blue image appeared, with an expanse of sand and rock at the bottom. Zoze patted her stomach. "Victory is mine!"

Not turning, she pointed at the video. "Camera 6 covers where the Karsk entered. But I don't see any sleds or anything."

"Can you move the camera?"

"No, they're inside fake rocks."

"If it were me," Will said, "I'd park where the camera can't see."

Zoze slapped the back of her head. "You can tell how many covert ops I've participated in." She activated the rest of the lights.

The window labeled CAM-4 displayed a wide-open hatch. Blue-armored soldiers were entering, wearing goggles and rebreathers, and carrying guns and other equipment. Zoze practically jumped out of her chair. "Oh, shit, they're entering Sealock 4!"

"Same ones?" Will wondered out loud. "Or more of them?" *Hopefully not more, not that it really matters.*

One of the Karsk commandos pointed a gun toward the camera, slightly off-center. The video turned black again. The light, Will assumed, made a more obvious target than the hidden camera.

Duripi ran into the room. "What's going on?"

Zoze stood and faced him. "Looks like the Karsk are trying another entrance. Sealock 4." Her voice shook. "We have to contain them."

* * *

Flight Sea Hunter 11, above the Straits of Florida

Petty Officer Third Class Kate Oliver stared at her magnetic anomaly screen as the P-8 approached the site where Petty Officer Smith had pinpointed the repeated and anomalous banging of metal on metal. The pilot descended to a lower altitude to maximize signal strength for the magnetic anomaly detector in the tail. Like most of the equipment on board, it was newly installed and state-of-the-art.

Kate's display mapped the magnetic field variance as they flew, color-coded from deep red to dark blue, with green representing the region's natural field. The screen also displayed a changing vertical graph, a three-dimensional graph, and parameters like field strength and object length.

As the pilot began to fly circles, the vertical graph spiked, then dipped. On the map, a clover-leaf pattern appeared, shades of blue along one diagonal and shades of red along the opposite.

"Got a blip on the MAD, ma'am," Kate told the mission commander over her headset. "Weak but definite. About a hundred feet long." Much smaller than a full-sized submarine, but bigger than a mini-sub. She saved the 'Mark on Top' location and passed it to the sonar crew.

The distortion was smaller than objects she had practiced on, and fairly weak, meaning it was either mostly non-ferrous, or, like U.S. submarines, intentionally shielded or degaussed.

As the plane turned, the display showed more anomalies, even smaller and weaker than the first one. Older equipment might not have detected them at all.

Over the comm circuit, the mission commander ordered them back to the MAD blip. It had moved—not far, thankfully. *Gotta be a sub. What's it up to?* Could it be one of those types used by drug cartels? They'd detected a number of those before, and usually relayed the coordinates to the Coast Guard. The narco-subs were generally primitive though, not truly submersible.

Kate added a new 'Mark on Top.' She pinged the sonar team on the comm channel. They were only a few feet away, but some genius had installed a divider between. "Anything on sonar?"

"Hold on," Deion answered. "Maybe. Sounds kind of like a sink draining past a swirling toothbrush."

Kate heard Matt snicker. "Is that how you clean your toothbrush? Does Latonya know that?"

The sonar supervisor interrupted, "Let's focus, shall we? Smith, are you getting the same direction as the MAD hit?"

"Looks like it."

The pilot flew over the weaker anomalies then. They hadn't moved. *Parts of a shipwreck?* There was no shortage of shipwrecks in this hurricane-battered part of the world.

Returning to the confirmed contact—the possible submarine—the crew dropped more sonobuoys. Things were getting interesting! Kate couldn't wait to find out what was down there.

Chapter 23

Karsk special operations group

Karsk Jadikira, captain of the submarine *Trident*, listened with concern to Liadna, the sonar operator who doubled as communications officer.

"The Land-Dwellers dropped listening devices around Aux," Liadna said, "They know we're here."

"How is that possible? We've never been detected before."

"The US military spends a lot of money on sensors, maybe they finally designed ones sensitive enough."

Jadikira had a choice: continue the invasion of Aux, or flee. They'd rescued Yissharu's wife, but had not been able to recapture Will Myers or Mazi Andreia, who had dishonored the *Trident* crew, and more importantly, presented a danger to their operations. But the Mazi had apparently prepared for their arrival, and the operation had been much more difficult than anticipated. And the Mazi had also, most likely, transmitted a message over the Internet, which would make the entire mission moot.

The prudent course of action was to avoid increasing the awareness of the Land-Dwellers. "Tell the *Swordfish* to recall its assault team," he told Liadna. "Tell them that Land-Dwellers have arrived, and to set a course to Cuba using evasive maneuvers. We'll rendezvous at Point 17."

"Why Cuba?"

"To lead them to a rival Land-Dweller country instead of our outpost." He spoke to the rest of the *Trident* crew over his headset. "Prepare to recover our sleds. Navigator, lay in a switchback course to Point 17. As soon as the assault team is back on the *Swordfish*, we're leaving."

* * *

Andreia

The pursuing dolphin clicks and motor noises disappeared. Andreia tapped Sama on the shoulder and let him know.

#Where'd they go?# he signaled.

#The dolphins probably surfaced for air,# she responded. #I don't know about the sled.#

Sama changed course, from southeast to southwest. Andreia presumed the dolphins would find them again, but it would take longer.

When twenty minutes passed without signs of further pursuit, Andreia signaled, #Let's go back.#

Sama stared at her. #Why?#

#We're not being chased anymore. Our friends might need help.#

Sama gave her an exasperated look, then put the sled in neutral and rolled off. He pointed to the front of the seat. #You drive.#

#I honor your accomplishments.# She smiled and clasped his hands in solidarity, partly relaxing his grumpy expression. She sat in front and they headed back to Aux, ascending to reduce decompression time.

Aux's floodlights were on again—most of them, anyway. Andreia approached cautiously, avoiding the flattened cones of illuminated water and sand. She saw no signs of damage and no signs of the enemy.

She looked over her shoulder and signaled Sama, #Which entrance should we try?#

After a brief pause, he responded, #Let's try number one.# He told her the code, assuming correctly that she didn't remember. #Be careful.#

#Of course.# She passed well above Sealock 1. It was closed, and there were no sleds or soldiers within the lit area—not that she expected the Karsk to be that foolish.

Andreia dropped the sled behind the spotlight and camera, far enough that it wouldn't be seen. #I'll go greet the camera,# she told Sama. #Wait here.#

She took a deep breath and swam a circuitous route to the sealock. As soon as she reached the illuminated zone, she accelerated. *What if the Karsk are waiting for me?*

She exposed the keypad and typed in the code. The lock remained closed. She tried again, in case she'd mistyped it. Again, nothing happened.

She faced the camera and signaled, #Let us in.#

When there was no immediate response, she returned to the sled. #No response,# she told Sama.

#Maybe we should wait a little.#

Andreia moved the sled close enough to monitor the sealock. After another minute, it spiraled open. She held up a fist, then reconsidered her joy. *What if the Karsk captured the habitat and are bringing us in to kill me?*

If the Karsk were inside, though, wouldn't they have kept sentinels outside? *And tried to capture me immediately?* She decided to enter, and if she was wrong, she'd deal with it.

Only Mazi vehicles were inside the spacious main sealock—the big semi-cylindrical shuttle, which could be used either wet inside or dry, and three sleds, one of them partially disassembled as if for repair. It took a while to pump out all that water—one of the reasons she normally used smaller sealocks. The overhead lights weren't working, so she kept the sled lights on.

They proceeded to the decompression suite, built to accommodate up to fifty people. Unlike the smaller Aux entrances, it had two communal showering and changing rooms—one for women, one for men. The lights were not operating here either.

Zoze's voice sounded over the speakers. "Welcome back!"

Andreia rushed over to the intercom next to the exit. "What's the situation? Why aren't the lights working?"

"They'll be back up soon. We just got the air back on."

"You lost life support?"

"Karsk fish-fuckers broke in and took over the systems, but Martis blocked them from occupying the whole habitat. Then they gave up and left. We did it, we held them off!"

Surprise gave way to elation. Andreia hugged Sama. We survived! More than that, we defeated a whole team of super-soldiers!

"I saw you and Sama on the camera," Zoze spoke. "Where's Pijasiros?" Her voice sounded worried.

"He took a sled to Katiki to let them know what was going on. I assume the Internet connection is still out?"

"We couldn't exactly go out and fix it while the Karsk were attacking."

Sama spoke into the intercom. "Glad you're safe! How many were there?"

"Seven," Zoze replied, "including Yissharu. Wearing armor and carrying guns."

Will spoke next over the intercom, "Are you okay?"

Happiness flowed through Andreia at the sound of his voice. "Yeah, fine. We're both fine. We got the messages out."

"I assumed you would. Great news."

"How are you doing?" she asked.

"Relieved. And surprised they gave up, considering what fanatics they are."

Andreia was surprised too. The Mazi Council couldn't have confronted the Karsk Council while the Internet connection was cut. They'd long ago decided satellite phones were too risky. "Maybe the Karsk decided their effort was futile," she said.

Sama spoke again. "If the Karsk are gone, we can repair the Internet connection."

"They might still be nearby," Zoze said.

"We'll be careful."

Andreia closed the inner hatch and hit the exit button. The sealock began to fill with water.

"I have to pick up a length of connector cable from Sealock 5," Sama said. "I have everything else."

"Okay." She grabbed a speargun and two dive knives.

Except for the floodlit sections, it was still dark outside. Sama signaled, #I'm going to turn on the sled lights. We need light to do the repair work, and if the Karsk are still here, I'd rather know it while we're near the sealock.#

There was still no sign of their enemies. Which didn't mean much if they were being stealthy. Andreia gave the okay sign, though.

#If we're attacked,# he signaled, #I'll shut off the lights, then you swim for the sealock.#

Andreia gave the #message received# sign, meaning maybe she'd do that and maybe not, depending on the situation.

Lights on, they headed south. Still no enemies visible. They entered Sealock 5 and Sama retrieved a spool of fiber-optic cable from one of the equipment closets.

The connector entered Aux not far from the sealock, carefully buried beneath mud and sand. Sama seemed to know exactly where it was. At a painfully slow pace, they coasted away from Aux, hugging the bottom.

After several minutes, the sled lights revealed a small pit. At the bottom, the connecting cable was severed in two, perhaps by a dive knife. As Sama began reconnecting the ends, Andreia watched for enemies, speargun at the ready.

* * *

Will

Not long after the Internet connection was restored, Andreia called the comm center. "Sama and I are in Sealock 3. We have a six-hour decompression ahead. I'm exhausted, I'm going to sleep."

Six hours later, Will and Zoze met them in the hallway outside. Will threw arms around Andreia and they kissed.

She gazed into his eyes. "You're a wonderful sight."

"So are you." Their kiss grew passionate, and she held him tightly. He heard Zoze and Sama similarly engaged, interspersed with flowing words in Mazi.

"You got the lights back on," Andreia said.

Zoze responded first. "It took a while, but everything's working again. Thanks for fixing the Internet tie-in."

"Sama gets all the credit," Andreia said.

Zoze squeezed her boyfriend's crotch. "Hard as rock, my bae."

"In case the Karsk return," Will added, "the machinists are making stronger hatch locks. We also have to restore the hatchway Martis welded shut. It kept the Karsk from reaching the communications room, but the living quarters are sealed off."

"Next time—if there is a next time," Andreia said, "we'll be better prepared. What's the word from Katiki?"

"Pijasiros is back," Will said. "Asleep now. He returned alone. He briefed the Council, but they decided to wait until morning light to send reinforcements."

Andreia frowned. "Why even bother, then?"

"Pijasiros left for Katiki before the Karsk entered Aux. The Council didn't know about the forcible entry until we restored communications and called them. By then, the Karsk were long gone."

"Did he tell them the Karsk cut our communications and built a base in Mazi territory?"

"Yes, and that they kidnapped us and murdered Galen, and are waging a war on the surface. The Mazi Council told Pijasiros they would contact their Karsk counterparts when communications were restored. By now, hopefully that's happened."

"I'll call them," Andreia said, "and see if they did."

They descended the stairs to the rest of the habitat, Will and Andreia in the lead. "Things are getting worse on the surface," Will told her. "The Karsk are destroying the economy and people are hurting. Those port facilities and refineries will take years to rebuild. We're so addicted to oil, everyone's panicking. And it's not just the oil industry; there have been attacks in other sectors too. Stocks are falling, jobs disappearing, supply chains bottlenecked, prices rising..."

"Four of the top five cryptocurrencies crashed today," Zoze said behind him. "Their blockchains were corrupted, which isn't supposed to happen. Currentsea was the only major one not affected—supposedly because they have newer code."

My dad invested in Currentsea, he's probably doing fine. But cryptocurrency was just smoke and mirrors, and couldn't keep a physical economy afloat or workers employed.

Andreia stopped and glanced back toward her friend. "A lot of our transactions use cryptocurrency, and I've been too preoccupied to consider Currentsea. Do you think we lost it all?"

"Couldn't divest with no Internet access," Zoze responded.

Andreia made a fist, then opened it. "Good thing we're mostly self-sufficient, then. And have companies with accounts in dollars. And gold, of course."

They continued down the stairs.

Will opened the hatch at the stairwell bottom and they headed to the communications room. Andreia held his hand as they walked. "Are the Land-Dwellers going to war?"

"So far," he said, "it's only an information war. A lot of angry rhetoric blaming different countries for the port and refinery attacks."

"Military and spy agencies are in frenzy mode," Zoze added.

Will nodded. "There's talk of economic sanctions against this country or that, and some words about military action. But our cyberterrorist story is gaining traction, and the stakes are high enough that government agencies in the U.S. and elsewhere are looking into it."

"What happens when they find out your terrorist group doesn't exist?"

"I don't know. We should keep releasing clues to feed their investigations. It has to be more plausible than the story that China and Russia are behind everything."

"I think the Karsk are still active in cyberspace," Zoze said behind them. "There's been a massive uptick in malware attacks, a lot of them zero-day programs, infecting computers all over the world. If it's the Karsk, they'll be framing other countries to increase the tensions. And there's a plague of disinformation bots on social media, worse than usual. Reasons to fear, reasons to hate."

"One of the reasons I avoid social media," Will said over his shoulder. "Their algorithms isolate like-minded people into bubbles and radicalize them. Easy pickings for bad actors like the Karsk."

"Even MMO's are getting stirred," Zoze continued. "I was testing the Internet connection an hour ago—"

"Gaming?" Sama asked. "At a time like this?"

"Needed a break. If you'll let me continue, I was playing League of Wizards, and an NPC—a tavern server—tried to convince me to frag some players from South Korea sitting at another table. Claimed South Koreans were all cheaters. I turned the server into a toad, naturally."

"Naturally," Sama responded.

At the second cross-corridor, they took a right. "Do you think the Karsk are behind the cryptocurrency collapses?" Andreia asked. "And who's behind Currentsea?"

Behind them, Zoze snorted. "Current-sea! It has to be the Karsk, trolls that they are."

Will responded, "Just a pun, people would think."

"If the Karsk have been planning this attack for decades," Sama said, "they could have inserted Trojans in the blockchains back when they were first created, then waited for the right time to activate them."

They entered the communications room. Pijasiros and Duripi were sitting at adjacent workstations, watching a magenta-braided African-American woman speak at a podium. They turned to greet Andreia and Sama.

Zoze pointed at the screens. "That's Ronin. She's one of the best cybersecurity experts on the planet. Bad-ass script-fu."

"It's an emergency conference," Duripi said. "All the leading Land-Dweller cybersecurity professionals and companies are there. Just started; Ronin's giving the keynote."

"…Our governments need to sit down and take a breath," Ronin spoke into the podium microphones. "Knee-jerk reactions could escalate into something there's no going back from. We need to think logically and do some proper detective work, not just who wrote what, who deployed what, but who they were working with, who they were working for."

"Amen," Will commented. "Although we'll have to up our game."

Duripi clicked his mouse and a heart sign appeared on the screen and floated upward. "Don't worry," he spoke over his shoulder, "we have Land-Dweller personas that we've cultivated over the years." His heart sign was followed by others.

"We're big players in the Land-Dweller cyber community," Pijasiros said.

"This cyber-chaos group with no name," Ronin continued, referring to Will's made-up group, "is as likely as anyone else to have started this mess—assuming it's not another false flag. Maybe there are rogue government actors tied up in it too. My point is, we don't have the level of proof necessary to blame any government. Hasn't the unwarranted bombing of Iran taught us anything?"

"Finally," Will said, "a voice of reason."

"Maybe we can help the Land-Dweller white hats," Zoze suggested.

"We should," Will agreed. "Can we find proof the Karsk orchestrated this whole thing? Without giving away the fact they're Sea-Dwellers?"

"How?" Andreia asked.

"We can't exactly break into their stronghold and defeat their army of soldiers," Duripi said.

"Do we have to?" Will asked him.

"We only vaguely know where they're located," Duripi continued.

"Man-in-the-middle attack," Pijasiros suggested. "Tap their communications cable and intercept what they send and receive. Use that to hack their systems."

Will's knowledge of hacking was limited to the annual security training mandated for lab employees, but it sounded good. "Yes, let's do it!"

"Won't the Karsk know we're tapping the cable?" Sama said. "Somehow, they knew I was doing that yesterday, and sent someone to stop us. As for hacking them, I have a feeling they're as good as it gets."

"Not necessarily," Andreia said. "They hired—or duped—hackers in China and Russia. Maybe all, or most of, the programming was done by Land-Dwellers."

Zoze pushed open hands toward them, one of the Mazi gestures Will hadn't decoded yet. "Land-Dweller hackers don't know the Karsk exist, and Sea-Dwellers—except the Karsk, apparently—don't attack other Sea-

Dwellers. So besides random bot attacks, Karsk countermeasures might never have been tested before, and their IT team is probably focused on offense. Their systems might not be as invulnerable as they think they are, and they might not be paying as close attention as organizations that are attacked all the time."

"Solid point," Sama said. "I can work on eliminating the tapping signature. Or we could distract them, maybe a massive data glitch or DDoS attack."

"From what's been reported in news," Will said, "the Karsk used human hackers to carry out their attacks. We can recruit help too. This conference— is it virtual?"

"Hybrid," Duripi said. "I'm at it online. We attend a lot of hacker conferences and meetups—using Land-Dweller personas of course."

"If we can coordinate all those experts," Will said, "we can stop the Karsk and their plan without letting the world know about your people. Mingle and chat, push our narrative, agree with Ronin that the attacks must have been perpetrated by terrorists. Governments wouldn't cripple the world's oil production, especially oil-hungry ones like China. The cost of oil has skyrocketed, and that has to be bad for their economy."

Duripi and Zoze pressed cupped hands against their temples. "Solid thinking," Zoze added. "I guess to be expected from a professor."

"And with the Land-Dweller cybersecurity community on board," Andreia said, "we'll outnumber the Karsk." She looked at Will. "Your huge numbers can more than even the odds."

Zoze and Sama donned VR goggles and gloves. Pijasiros and Duripi remained at their keyboards. As the Mazi hackers networked with other conference attendees, Will and Andreia helped with ideas and tips.

"We're starting to play good defense," Will told the others. "But to overcome the Karsk, we need to go on offense." They had yet to score any points and the clock was running out.

* * *

Andreia

A few minutes after Andreia entered the comm room, they received a message from Katiki that a dozen Mazi sleds, each with two passengers, were heading to Aux to provide assistance. The sealocks couldn't accommodate that many additional sleds, so Zoze instructed them to anchor outside Sealock 1 and deploy camouflage tarps, then come inside.

With two riders per sled and the Mazi practice of keeping within sight of each other, Andreia estimated their trip would take two hours. "I'll meet them," she volunteered. Still tired, she then went to the medical bay to lie down.

Two hours later, Andreia went to the spacious Sealock 1 decompression chamber to greet the newcomers. Coming from Katiki, no decompression would be necessary, so she left the hatch open.

The alternate Aux maintenance crew entered first. After brief greetings, they dumped their dry bags on the floor and went straight to the showers. Surprising Andreia completely, her parents entered next. They rushed over and planted hugs and cheek kisses.

"What are you doing here?" Andreia asked, happy to see them.

Her mother looked Andreia up and down. "We heard you were hurt. But you look in good health. How are you doing?"

"Much better now, thanks to Thalassa."

Among the other arrivals were three members of the Council: Siaduare, the woman with flipper hands; Meltha, wearing an uncharacteristic wetsuit; and, souring her mood even more, Xitaros, her biggest detractor. Xitaros had brought along his nephew Theros, who was carrying two large dry bags. Theros was a large, broad-shouldered man in his thirties who worked as a cook. He'd been married ten years, but hadn't sired any children. From what Andreia had heard, he blamed his wife, even though typically it was the males who were infertile.

Andreia hid her distaste and bowed. "Welcome to Aux." As far as she knew, none of the three Council members had ever visited.

Meltha peered at her. "You're not wearing a mask."

Did these useless fools just come to harass me? Andreia stared back. "I have no infections. And Thalassa filled me with antibiotics." She turned to Theros and asked, "What's in the bags?"

He gave her a look of irritation. "Dry clothes, what do you think?" He opened the tops, revealing folded garments. "Mostly for the Council members."

Siaduare and—thankfully—Xitaros excused themselves and headed to the showers, followed by Theros with the dry bags.

"The Karsk attackers are gone," Andreia told Meltha, surprised she'd come in person. "At least for now. Did you contact the Karsk Council?"

"They claimed to know nothing about the Aux invasion," Meltha said. "They wouldn't even admit having an outpost in the Straits of Florida."

Andreia waved her hands in frustration. "Will and I were taken aboard a submarine with the Karsk sigil inside, and interrogated by at least two members of the Karsk clan. They implied that they have support from the Karsk home, and we know the submarine is based at an outpost from which these people conduct their war. The Karsk Council should be ashamed to lie so egregiously! Not to mention, their underlings murdered my little brother and tried to kill me!"

Meltha placed an age-spotted hand on her shoulder. "It makes me sad that a neighboring clan could be so evil. My colleagues and I are here to collect information and evidence before we decide what to do next."

No risk is too small for them to avoid taking action. "We should inform the other clans. The Karsk may not care what we think, but they might fear becoming pariahs. They've broken every Sea-Dweller custom I can think of."

"We must have indisputable evidence before doing that."

Andreia had expected such a response. "You'll have it. The Aux crew can tell and show you whatever you need to know."

"Thank you. Now, I must make myself presentable." She headed to the women's showers.

When everyone had rinsed and changed, Andreia led them to the cafeteria. "You can sit, eat, and we can discuss the situation."

She rounded up most of the current maintenance crew, who chatted with their counterparts from the other shift. She decided not to interrupt the communications team while they were working to stop the Karsk, and decided it was especially important to keep Meltha and Xitaros away from Will.

Clustered at aluminum tables, the thirty or so people occupied only a fraction of the cafeteria. Andreia sat with her parents and chatted about home. Two workers brought out jugs of water and small plates of marinated seaweed and clams.

"We're preparing a proper meal," the aquaculture technician announced. "So don't worry if you're still hungry."

"It's great to see you," Andreia told her parents, "but in case the Karsk return, everyone who isn't a metalworker should return to Katiki after the meal. The longer you stay, the longer you'll have to decompress afterward."

Her mother raised an eyebrow. "I assume that's aimed at us? I'm a mechanic, you know. Also helpful here."

"There are more mechanics here than we need." Then she admitted, "I'll worry too much if you're here. The Karsk aren't like other Sea-Dwellers. They're murderers."

As her parents ate, Andreia recounted her experiences and told them how misguided the Karsk war was, and that any Land-Dweller retaliation might target all Sea-Dwellers, not just the guilty ones.

"Come with us back to Katiki," her mother insisted. "It's safer there."

Is that why you came? "I'm the only one here with self-defense training." She decided not to add that she'd fought Karsk soldiers and barely survived. "I need to help defend the place and keep our communications open. You can help from Katiki, though. You—and whoever you can recruit—can pressure the Council to actually do something, and make the Karsk leave our territory and abandon their war."

Her parents finished eating. It looked like most others had, also. Since she'd been outside Aux at the time, Andreia prompted the maintenance crew to describe their experiences of the Karsk invasion.

Martis described how the invaders smashed through the sealock hatches, and that they'd finally been stopped by welding an inner hatch shut. "They gave up eventually. Maia left with them; maybe they got what they came for."

Baktase, the on-duty Systems Manager, spoke. "Karsk Yissharu took over the computer network"—disowning Yissharu as a member of the Mazi—"and shut off the air and lights. But everything's working again. The communications team did a great job."

"So did you," Andreia said.

Once the crew finished their stories and answered questions, Andreia stood and faced the Council members. Predictably, they were sitting together.

"We can show you the damage the Karsk caused," she said, "and take pictures. There may be camera video too."

"There is," Martis affirmed.

Xitaros stood. "An important factor has been omitted from our discussions." He paused, presumably for dramatic effect. Andreia waited for his conversational turd to drop.

"From what I've heard," he said, "the group that entered Aux is trying to stop the Land-Dwellers from destroying the ocean, and us with it. Why should we interfere with that?"

Siaduare pressed her flipper hands together in support.

The Council wouldn't care if all Land-Dwellers starved to death, but they certainly cared about clan safety. "We told you," Andreia said, "war is the wrong way to change Land-Dweller policies—it's much too dangerous for us. Especially since the instigators are operating from our territory." She let that sink in. "The clans—including ours—didn't latch on to this foolhardy plan of the Karsk the first time they floated it. Why should we now?"

Meltha nodded, taking Andreia's side for a change.

Xitaros continued, "We have no military force to fight further incursions by this Karsk group. But from what I've heard, they wanted to stop Will Myers from alerting his fellow Land-Dwellers. And for good reason—do we want their navy to use weapons of mass destruction against us?"

"They wanted me, too," Andreia reminded the gathering. "Because I wouldn't go along with their plan. Do you propose surrendering a clan member for execution? Someone who's committed no crime?" With a chill, she then remembered plunging a knife into a soldier's neck and twisting the blade. And electrocuting another. And torturing Yissharu for information.

Thankfully, all three Council elders shook their heads. None betrayed microexpressions of sympathy for such a plan.

"Of course we would not harm one of our own," Xitaros said.

"She's diverting us," Siaduare told him.

"We should negotiate with the Karsk," Xitaros proposed.

"You think we can trust them?" Andreia asked.

Xitaros continued, "We can hand them the Land-Dweller Will Myers in return for guarantees that they will never again invade our habitats, nor harm any member of our clan."

"Will is a guest of the Mazi," Andreia pointed out, "and is therefore under our protection."

"That can be revoked at any time," Siaduare said. "Xitaros has proposed a reasonable compromise."

Martis stood. "Will may be a Land-Dweller, but he helped us withstand the attack, and placed our clan ahead of his personal safety. We didn't surrender him then, and you must not surrender him now. I refuse to cooperate with such a thing."

Grateful for her words, Andreia invoked the Mazi sense of honor. "She's right. If we surrender Will, we besmirch our clan honor for generations."

Meltha stood. "You have a talent for arguing, Andreia. The full Council must decide such matters, not merely those of us here."

A groan escaped Andreia's lips. "Aux was invaded by Karsk soldiers from a base they have illegally placed inside our territory. They launched a secret war that risks destroying the whole clan. They killed my brother and tried to kill me. What are you going to do about it?"

Meltha's eyes narrowed, then relaxed. "It would help if we knew exactly where their outpost was. They should depart our territory and pay reparations for damage to Aux."

That won't stop their war. But it was a start. "Absolutely. They can leave us the outpost." That would disrupt their operations, and provide the Mazi suitable compensation for the insult.

Meltha gave a rare smile. "Yes, a more than suitable boon for our troubles."

"We must also stop their war before it endangers us and all other Sea-Dwellers."

Her smile faded and her gaze turned inward. "We will discuss that too."

Discuss? The Karsk war against the Land-Dwellers was the bedrock beneath all their troubles. Andreia turned to her parents and spoke quietly, "Please talk to Meltha when you return to Katiki. I'm well into adulthood, but she still considers me a mere child."

Chapter 24

Andreia

Andreia hugged her parents farewell outside Sealock 1. Half the visitors were returning to Katiki. The other half would remain to help fortify Aux in case of another Karsk incursion.

"I'll come back to Katiki as soon as I can," Andreia told her parents.

"Please be careful," her mother admonished her.

"I will."

Andreia then reported to the comm room to help Will, Zoze, Sama, Pijsiros, and Duripi organize Land-Dweller hackers against the Karsk cyberwar.

As they worked, Xitaros and his nephew Theros entered the comm room. Unfortunately, they hadn't departed with Meltha and Siaduare.

"Greetings," Xitaros announced in a loud voice. "May the ancient kings and heroes bestow their graces upon us."

Andreia and everyone else ignored him—except Will, who stared at Xitaros as if trying to guess what the Mazi words meant.

Xitaros let out a low whistle. "If I may have your attention for a minute."

One by one, the Aux hackers turned in their chairs to face him, irritated expressions on their faces. Sama pulled up his VR headset. "We're in the middle of conversations."

"Apologies for the interruption. I'll be brief. The Mazi Council of Elders has decided to station a Council member at Aux on a rotating basis. In case communications are lost again, that person can act as the voice of the Council until communications are resumed. I will be the first, and remain for two weeks."

Andreia sensed underlying reasons. More likely, they wanted closer oversight.

"Will this Council person perform any useful tasks while here," Zoze asked, "or just use up valuable oxygen?"

Andreia laughed inside at Zoze's insolent comment, but kept a neutral face. "There must be maintenance needs," she suggested.

"Yes," Sama said. "The floors can be mopped and the toilets scrubbed clean."

All the hackers laughed. Despite his punk-rock hair, it wasn't often that Sama landed such a blow.

Xitaros reddened. "This demonstrates exactly why our presence is needed. You have no respect for the clan, its traditions, and elders. Which is why you cannot be trusted to run the clan's communications without proper oversight."

Pijasiros displayed lines from a computer program on the wall screen facing Xitaros. "If you will, Lord Overseer, tell me if there are any errors in this code."

That evoked more laughter.

Xitaros's face clenched. "I am merely curious what everyone does here. There is no reason to insult me, and by extension, the Council."

And unfortunately, we can't stop the Karsk without them. "Everyone at Aux takes their work seriously," Andreia said, "and they're incredibly good at it. There's no need to micromanage."

Xitaros exhaled forcefully. "The decision has been made. Now if you'll excuse me, I must continue my rounds."

* * *

Flight Sea Hunter 11, above the Straits of Florida

Whatever they were chasing, Deion thought, was whisper-quiet. He wasn't picking up any propeller or engine noise at all, just faint water-churning noises that the computer identified as water jets from two separate underwater vehicles. One was slightly louder than the other. The monitor showed changing signal strengths from the sonobuoys, indicating that the contacts were moving.

The sonar supervisor was talking to someone on his headset. "Roger that." He addressed the team. "Not a test or exercise."

Changes in the Doppler pattern indicated that the sound sources were separating. Deion calculated their courses.

"Contacts heading different directions," Deion spoke over his headset. "Sierra One"—the louder one—"bearing 190 degrees. Sierra Two, bearing 155."

They flew past the contacts, then dropped an arc of sonobuoys ahead of them, positioned to track both contacts.

Deion bumped fists with Matt. "Two subs surrounded by one plane. How's that for bad-ass?"

"Let's not get ahead of ourselves," the supervisor told them. "That means two search boxes to tighten." He spoke over the main channel. "Contacts are moving apart. We could use tracking assistance."

The mission commander addressed the radioman over the channel. "Send an immediate request for backup, and give me the arrival time."

The contacts zig-zagged and increased their separation, but maintained the same general direction: toward Cuba.

"Two aircraft inbound," the radar operator spoke over the channel. "Speed, Mach 2. No transponder signals."

Cuban fighter jets, Deion thought. Cuba had only old Soviet aircraft, but a missile was a missile.

A few miles from Cuban airspace, an alarm went off. "Targeting radar active," the radar operator said. "They're lighting us up."

"We're over international waters," the pilot complained.

"Show the Cubans we have no intention of entering their airspace," the commander spoke.

The P-8 veered to the right, no longer approaching the coast. Deion kept monitoring the sonobuoys.

The sonar contacts maintained course, and entered Cuban waters.

* * *

Will

Will and the others helped draft a decision document at the online cybersecurity conference. It urged the world's nations to refrain from offensive actions, to investigate the cyber-chaos group, to work together to fight the onslaught of new malware, and to urge social media companies to stop the waves of disinformation. Concurrently, Pijasiros and Zoze dropped the new clues Will had written about the fake cyberterror group, and Duripi began crafting more. Based partly on the malware Maia and Yissharu had deployed against Aux, Pijasiros also dropped hints in GitHub about what to look for and how to counter it.

"We're finally fighting the Karsk," Will told the others. "But is it enough? They've been planning this war for decades, and we're just waking up."

Sama nodded. "They have the initiative. We don't know what else they have planned."

Will addressed Pijasiros. "What about the 'man-in-the-middle' idea you mentioned earlier? Tapping their communications. Can we figure out what they're doing in time to stop it?"

"With Sama's help," Pijasiros said.

Sama clasped his hands together. "I think I've solved the packet drop issue during the initial connection."

The scale of the problem weighed on Will like a thousand atmospheres. Even if they managed to stop the current attacks, the Karsk could just launch more. They needed a permanent solution. The fate of humanity depended on it. If the global economy completely collapsed, people would lose their jobs and savings, millions might die from starvation, authoritarianism would replace democracies, millions more could die from war and internal violence, and civilization itself might collapse.

Preventing that, he decided, was more important than prolonging the Sea-Dwellers' secrecy. He glanced at Andreia. *We might not be on the same side anymore.*

* * *

Andreia

Andreia and her friends examined a nautical chart on one of the comm room wall screens. The Internet cables were depicted by squiggly purple lines. More accurate delineations from Mazi surveys were overlaid in red.

"Aux only connects to one undersea cable," Sama said. "But there are six running down the Straits of Florida. We should at least check the two closest. The others are much deeper."

"We have two magnetometers," Zoze said. "But only two."

"Tie two sleds together like last time," Andreia suggested. "One follows the Internet cable and the other looks for the Karsk tie-in line. With only two magnetometers, we'll have to guess which side of the cable to search."

"There should be an additional signal at the tie-in," Sama said, "following the line to their base. At least, that's the case with ours. It'll be weak, so we have to monitor closely."

"Are we going at night again?" Pijasiros asked, his expression tense.

Andreia answered instantly. "We have to. We can't let them see us."

"Who's going?" Zoze asked.

"It should be me, Sama, and Pijasiros again. We know what to expect, more or less."

Zoze blew air from her mouth.

"We can't all go," Pijasiros told Zoze. "Someone needs to carry on the fight if we don't make it back."

Zoze, Will, and Duripi shouted protests against the possibility.

The telephone beeped. Duripi picked up the handset, then turned to Andreia. "It's for you."

Andreia took the handset. It was Meltha, calling on behalf of the Council.

"We are deciding what to do with Dr. Myers tomorrow," she said. "He must be present at the chamber tomorrow afternoon. That gives him adequate time to decompress."

Andreia's initial irritation gave way to fear. The wording, and Meltha's tone, sounded ominous. At least some on the Council, perhaps all of them, might have already decided it was too dangerous to let Will live.

"I'm needed here," Andreia said, "and Will can't return without me." *Maybe not true physically, but he can't face the Council alone.* "Our first priority is to deal with the Karsk threat." She decided not to share their operational plans.

"We contacted the Karsk Council of Elders again," Meltha said, "about the invasion of Aux and Yissharu's treachery. We provided the proof you and the others at Aux supplied, and demanded an explanation. As before, they denied any involvement; they said Yissharu is now Mazi, not Karsk, and they continue to claim they have no outpost in our territory. They conceded that their submarine passes through our territory, but only for routine trading."

"Do you believe them?" She hoped not.

"I believe members of my clan, especially when their information is compelling, over the word of strangers."

That's good. "What about appealing to the other clans for support?" With no military, the Mazi couldn't evict the Karsk by force.

"We are discussing the next steps. We obviously can't let this outpost remain in our territory. As for the other matter, I agree that you are needed for Aux's defense. Theros can bring the Land-Dweller here."

Andreia trusted Theros only a millimeter more than his human-hating uncle. "That's not necessary. We'll find someone else." *Stall for time.* "Besides, Dr. Myers is helping us here. He's facilitating discussions with other Land-Dweller experts to stop the Karsk terrorism above."

Meltha took an audible breath. "If the Land-Dweller fails to attend the hearing," she said, "it will look bad for him."

Andreia's muscles clenched. "Is that a threat?"

"A statement."

Stupid sea-hag! "Let us deal with the bigger issues first." She nearly slammed the handset down, catching herself at the last second.

Everyone was staring at her. "What was that all about?" Will asked.

Andreia cringed inside. *Did I make things worse for him?* And what if she was being paranoid? "The Council is deciding what to do with you," she said.

"And what do you think?"

"There's a small chance they'll accept your word and trust you won't reveal our existence. But the chance is greater that they'll never let you leave."

"I like it down here," he said, "but it would make my family and friends frantic. They'll never stop looking for me."

"That's why I think their most likely decision will be to arrange an 'accidental' death for you."

The stares intensified. "You think the Council would have him killed?" Duripi asked in Mazi.

Andreia answered in English so Will could follow. "Meltha floated the idea and Xitaros swam with it. There was also a suggestion to dissect him."

Will scrunched his face in disgust.

"I'm sorry," she told him, "I should have told you right away, but I talked them out of killing you initially, and thought we could continue that direction."

His eyes narrowed. "Still, you should have told me. My life's on the line."

Andreia cursed herself. "I know. I think deep down, I was denying my clan could do such a thing—you're such a good person—and maybe I was overestimating my persuasion skills. I won't let them do it—I told you that after the clan questioned you."

"Now you know why we don't live at Katiki," Zoze told Will. "They've got moray eels in their asses."

"Not everyone," Andreia said. "Mostly the Elders."

The anger on Will's face turned to hurt. "We've been through so much together. I thought we trusted each other."

Andreia placed hands on his stiff shoulders and looked in his eyes. "I was wrong not to tell you immediately. Your life is more important to me than my own, and frankly, I was being a coward." The ridiculousness hit her. "Willing to fight heavily-armed Karsk commandos, but afraid of my clan Council, and afraid what you might do once you realized the danger."

Will's face softened, but his eyes remained uncertain. "What do you think I might do?"

"I know you're on our side. But at first, I assumed you'd flee, and was worried you'd tell your people about us. You know what a catastrophe that might cause. Then I decided I would let you leave anyway, and try to talk you into protecting us. I won't let any harm come to you, you know that."

"Have I put you in danger?" he asked. "From the Council?"

She scoffed, but appreciated his concern. "The worst they can do is remove me as Trader. I'm getting tired of doing that, anyway."

Zoze wrapped arms around both of them. "Andreia made a mistake. But she loves you and she's faced death for you."

"Thanks, Zoze," Andreia said.

"You love him?" Duripi asked.

Andreia winced inside. *Zoze outed us—unintentionally, I assume.* She decided to own it. "Yes, we love each other." She kissed Will passionately, then looked at her friends. "Is that a problem?"

"Not with me," Duripi said.

"Not my business who you play hide the eel with," Pijasiros said.

Sama clasped and extended his hands in approval. "Will's one of us."

"Just don't tell anyone else," Andreia said. "The Bronze Age relics on the Council wouldn't approve."

Her friends spread their hands and pressed them together in agreement.

"Let's get back to stopping the Karsk," Will proposed.

"What about the Council demand?" Andreia asked.

"I'm worried about my life, obviously, but the Council also seems ineffective addressing threats like the Karsk. They trust the Karsk more than they trust me."

Zoze blew out a puff of air. "Those fossils waited more than ten hours to send reinforcements to Aux. They can go grind their asses on fire coral."

Will continued, "The rest of the clan outnumbers them by, what, ten to one?"

"Close," Andreia said.

"We could follow the example of human lobbyists. Get enough support on the Council and from other clan members. Apply pressure. You're the Trader—you know how to influence people. I'm not the most skilled at that, but a lot of my students were environmental activists on the side, and I've learned a lot about power shifting from them."

* * *

The Karsk outpost

In the semi-spherical conference room of *Silent Garrison*, the Coordinating Praesidium discussed the onset of Phase 4, the final part of their long-planned operation. Each of the seven SOC members had a particular expertise, but major decisions had to be made by consensus.

Erebos, who managed connections with other clans and Land-Dweller drug cartels, spoke first. "I transferred the poison to one of our Mazi supporters personally. He signaled it would be administered as soon as possible."

The others placed hands over their hearts in appreciation. Itaka, the cyberteam coordinator, said, "That sounds vague. Time is critical."

"I told him that," Erebos said.

"Especially after Tatoku's failures," Itaka added.

Tatoku, who coordinated the military forces, frowned. "We rescued Mazi Maia, our primary goal. You have no inkling of the power of random chance in such operations."

"I find it astonishing and regrettable," Itaka said, "that our team of trained and heavily armed commandos was defeated by a handful of maintenance workers."

The outpost coordinator, Minatos, tapped the gold Facilitator trident against the floor. "Our fight is with the Land-Dwellers, not with each other."

Itaka and Tatoku bowed to each other—only slightly, though.

Tatoku addressed the others. "The task force we sent to the Mazi communications post is now safely in Cuban waters. Cuba does not possess sufficient detection technology."

"What will the USA Navy do now?" Itaka asked. "Will they invade Aux? Will they find us here?"

"We're too deep and we're better shielded than the Mazi. As for Aux, the site is quiet now, and there is no sign of surface ships."

"For now, anyway," Lanara, the finance coordinator, said. "It was foolish to make so much noise."

"It was necessary," Tatoku said. "We didn't expect them to seal the hatches. Yissharu told us they had no interior locks."

Lanara turned to Itaka. "Phase 3 has culminated. But the Land-Dweller nations have only launched the first of the wars you predicted."

"We didn't foresee blame would be placed on a group that is most likely fictitious. Better than blaming us, but I wonder if it's the Mazi fighting us in information space." Itaka glared at Tatoku. "If so, we can thank the escape of Mazi Andreia and her Turd-thrower pet. They know about our operation, if not all the details. And the Mazi managed to restore communications. Your soldiers let us down in both instances."

Tatoku scowled. Minatos interceded, "Let us focus on the waters ahead and leave the detritus behind."

Lanara nodded. "Good news on the financial front. We now control the top cryptocurrency in the world. When we bring down the Land-Dweller banks and finance industry, Currentsea will be the only safe haven. We will then control the finances of the Land-Dwellers—whatever remains after the crash to come, anyway."

"Won't the Land-Dwellers investigate the Currentsea company?" Erebos asked.

"Possibly. But they won't find anything. There's nothing linking Currentsea to any of our other operations, and the ownership—on the surface, anyway—is legitimate."

"What if their governments seize the company? Or the currency?"

"It's decentralized. They can ban market trading, but not get rid of it completely. And we'll beat them to it, crash it when we don't need it anymore."

"There," Itaka said, "we must coordinate closely."

"Of course." Lanara updated the others. "We've invested and leveraged well, accumulated billions of dollars in key stocks. Itaka's group has infiltrated the exchange networks and can disable the trading brakes—the automated ones, that is."

"Our trojans and Land-Dweller stooges are ready to go," Itaka said.

"As soon as that happens," Lanara said, "we'll dump the entire portfolio. It will create panic and cause a tsunami of selloffs that can't be stopped."

"Our operatives will manipulate the exchanges to continue the panic," Itaka said.

"Won't their governments intervene?" Erebos asked. "And investigate afterward?"

"The sales will be automated. They will take milliseconds. And the damage will be long-term; no one will trust stock markets again. Their whole economy is based on wisps of trust in the system; take that away and they have nothing."

"What do we do with the money?" Tatoku asked. "It will be worthless when we're done."

Lanara smiled. "We convert it immediately to gold and strategic metals. Useful commodities to control."

"Status on the bank attacks?" Arudara, the logistics coordinator, asked.

"Almost there," Itaka said. His Sea-Dweller team and their Land-Dweller operatives planned to modify bank Domain Name System registrations, and had prepared programs to harvest login credentials from customers who thought they were visiting their account websites but were in fact being redirected to fake sites where their data would be captured. Simultaneously, they would activate trojans implanted in the cross-bank payment systems. Besides halting international payments, it would facilitate attacks on the banks themselves. Itaka's team would penetrate their databases and scramble them, which would plunge the financial system into chaos and obliterate the remaining trust in the whole economic system.

"The whole operation has to be timed perfectly," Lanara said. "The market manipulations, then the bank crashes, all in one day, before we bring down the communications networks and power grids."

"For that," Itaka told the Praesidium, "the software is in place and our operatives are standing by. We're using Russians again—without Chinese help, since China is one of our biggest targets."

"How long will power stay down?" Tatoku asked.

"Not long, I'm afraid. A day at most, and only the grids we had resources for. But it will interrupt efforts to address the financial damage we've caused. And attacking a nation's electricity grid will make its people demand a response. It will inflame the anger we've been stoking." Itaka grinned, not something he did often. "When Phase 4 is complete, the Land-Dwellers will be finished as a coherent threat. They'll be too focused on individual survival on continents ruled by famine, strife, disease, and death."

Chapter 25

Andreia

Two hours after sunset, Andreia, Sama, and Pijasiros departed Aux, each on a separate sled. They'd be gone a while, and possibly at significant depth, so they wore wetsuits and packed food and fresh water. Andreia took the captured Karsk sled and brought a speargun, two knives, and a wire-guided torpedo put together by the Systems Manager and mechanics. Made with the limited chemicals available, the warhead wasn't powerful enough to breach a sealock or a submarine hull, but the shock waves would incapacitate anyone nearby. Having learned from the last Karsk soldier she'd fought, they also brought metal shields, fashioned in the machine shop.

They roped the sleds together and matched velocities, Sama in the lead, Pijasiros to his right, and Andreia above. In case the Karsk had hidden cameras, they shut off their lights. By necessity, they kept their console indicators dimly lit, and had fastened cowling around them so only the pilot could see.

Sama followed the Internet cable with his magnetometer and compass, while Pijasiros used the other magnetometer to search for tie-ins. Andreia's job was protection. She hoped it wouldn't be needed—near the enemy base, they'd be greatly outnumbered.

They began at near-maximum speed, knowing the Karsk outpost was far. Andreia fell into a daze—there was nothing to see but blackness and nothing to hear but the faint whine of her sled's water jets. After a couple of hours, they reduced speed, so they wouldn't miss the Karsk tie-in, and to minimize their noise.

After another hour of mind-numbing monotony, Pijasiros yanked on the ropes connecting the three sleds. *He must have found the tie-in line.* In case of hidden cameras or microphones, they'd decided he wouldn't signal until well after passing it. Overly cautious, perhaps, since undersea cameras were useless at night, and at low speeds, the sleds were silent.

They circled back, approaching the tie-in line a hundred meters from the Internet cable, far beyond the range of any cameras near the intersection. Pijasiros tugged on the ropes again and they stopped. Thankfully, it was no deeper than Aux here.

They settled the sleds on the sandy bottom and scanned the dark water, ready to flee at any sign of danger. They were far from home, lurking in the shadow of their enemies. Andreia saw nothing in the distance, nor heard anything besides the flow of the water and the faint pounding of her heart.

Carrying bags of gear and hooded spotlights, Sama and Pijasiros hopped off their sleds. Andreia untied her sled and watched for trouble, periodically checking on her friends. With their lights on, she could see them, but beyond ten meters, they'd be invisible—at least to the unaided eye.

Sama uncovered the Karsk tie-in line. While Pijasiros aimed his light at it, Sama clamped on his glove bag and carefully drilled into the center. Then he inserted the splicing tool and hooked up his test box. He'd improved the process so no data packets would be lost, and had loaded every hacking tool he could think of—some of which they'd written themselves.

Sama and Pijasiros exchanged hand signals. They'd expected data from and to the Karsk outpost to be encrypted, employ authentication protocols, and use onion routing to hide the senders' locations. Their box, though, would forward the data to Aux and capture the encryption keys, which would be used to decipher the messages.

Sama handed to box to Pijasiros, who tapped on the keypad. After a few minutes, he turned to Andreia and held up two fingers. That meant the Karsk were using asymmetric encryption—combining a private key and a shared public key—to communicate. Pijasiros would have to phish the private key from the Karsk computers, which would take a while—assuming he could do it at all. When planning their attack, Pijasiros had talked about fake certificates, server impersonation, and rootkit injection to harvest the keys, but it was beyond Andreia's expertise.

After ten minutes, Pijasiros still wasn't done. Andreia signaled them to hurry—the Karsk might have roaming guards. Once they set up the connection, they could do everything else remotely.

Finally, Pijasiros held up a fist. Sama buried the test kit and connected a motion sensor. If someone unearthed it, a high-energy capacitor would discharge, frying all the electronics and any stored data.

They hopped back onto their sleds. Andreia reconnected her sled to theirs so they wouldn't get separated. They headed southwest from the tie-in to avoid the Karsk outpost, then changed direction to search for a tie-in to the other nearby Internet cable.

Andreia felt a tug on the connecting rope and stopped. They'd found a second tie-in. Sama and Pijasiros got to work. Andreia resumed sentinel duty, scanning the dark water.

Again, her friends seemed to take forever. After a while, a small squat object entered her vision from the probable direction of the Karsk outpost. It switched on two spotlights, illuminating her friends.

A drone? It had a camera lens in front, swiveling ear-like dishes, and a tube slung beneath. It was propelled by four tilting rotors. At least it wasn't trailing a cable, and was therefore on its own.

Andreia fired an untethered speargun bolt at it. The drone darted of the way.

It headed toward her. From the belly tube, it fired needle-like projectiles at her. She raised the shield strapped to her left arm, and the flechettes clattered off.

The drone was too close to use a torpedo on, and besides, an explosion would alert the Karsk. So far, the drone hadn't sent an acoustic warning, which her underwater-adapted ears would have detected. *Maybe it's too far from base.*

Almost as if reading her mind, the drone turned, extinguished its lights, and sped away.

Andreia accelerated her sled after it, keeping track of her position. Although risky, she switched on her lights so she wouldn't lose it. It didn't try to maneuver, probably programmed to return as fast as possible.

The sled was faster, and she began to catch up. She reloaded her speargun.

She rammed the thing, knocking it off course, then fired her gun at nearly point-blank range. The sharp metal spearhead pierced the plastic shell with a *thwack*. Its rotors stopped turning.

Andreia hauled the immobile drone onto the sled, and wiggled the spear around to further destroy its innards. She shut off her lights and headed back to her friends. Sama and Pijasiros stared at her when she arrived. #What happened?# Sama signaled.

#Let's go# she motioned back. She decided to dispose of the drone carcass far away from their tap.

* * *

Will

Will sat in the Aux comm room with Zoze and Duripi, helping recruit more hackers while waiting for Andreia, Sama, and Pijasiros to return. The Mazi habitats, originally so astonishing and alien, now felt like home. And Andreia's friends were his friends. Will had planned to keep working with them until Andreia returned, but by midnight, he could barely keep his eyes open. It felt like he had hardly slept at all since leaving the surface.

"Get some sleep," Zoze suggested. "Our quarters are still sealed off, but there are plenty of empty bunks in the emergency section."

"Where is it?"

"Do you remember where the cafeteria is?"

"Yeah."

"Entering from this direction," she said, "there's two hatches on the wall to the left. That leads to the emergency section. Most of that section is sleeping quarters. If you find yourself surrounded by empty aquaculture tanks, you've taken a wrong turn."

"Thanks. Is there a call box or something for when Andreia and the others return?"

"Not worth worrying about, they'll be decompressing for hours."

He'd forgotten about that. *Too tired to think straight.*

"About 12 hours if they follow the plan," Duripi added.

The twin hatches from the cafeteria led to a wide corridor with doors on either side, each bearing a stenciled number. The first door on the left opened to a storage room with racks of unlabeled plastic crates.

Will tried the opposite door, which led to a long room with rubber matting, four connected sets of triple bunk beds on either side, and storage lockers at the end. Each bunk was equipped with an inflatable mattress and pillow, folded sheets and towels, privacy curtains, two drawers beneath, and a narrow metal shelf. The room had the eerie feel of an abandoned bunker, complete with sad green walls, musty air, and flickering fluorescent lights.

The room could sleep 24, all crowded together. And it was only one room of many. Will felt isolated with this entire area to himself, and hoped Duripi and Zoze would sleep here also.

A door on the far wall led to a bathroom. When finished there, Will climbed into one of the top bunks and inflated the mattress and pillow. As with most of Aux, the room was chilly, so he borrowed a second set of sheets from the bed beneath. He had to climb back down to shut off the flickering overhead lights, then, with the room lit only by a faint red bulb over the bathroom door, he returned to his bunk and fell asleep.

Will was startled by the sound of a door opening and an influx of light stabbing through his eyelids. Without his medications, he was a light sleeper. Forcing his eyes open, Will initially had no idea where he was, and started to panic in the confined space. Then memory returned—he was on a top bunk in the Mazi emergency quarters. Was Zoze entering? Duripi? Andreia and Sama would presumably be decompressing.

The door closed again, returning the room to relative darkness, lit only by the dim red bathroom indicator. As Will debated whether to go back to sleep, he heard faint footsteps. The hair on his neck rose and his heart pounded. His eyes strained through the dim light to see who it was.

A figure popped up in front of him. A hand flashed. Something stung his neck.

Instinctively, Will pushed the figure—a man—hard in the face. He seemed familiar. The man fell backward onto the floor.

Will felt his neck and plucked out a syringe. It contained a milky liquid. Still inside—the plunger hadn't been depressed. At least not completely.

The figure, dressed in black, leapt up from the floor and pulled a big knife out of a leg scabbard. He was a big son-of-a-bitch, like an NFL linebacker. Will recognized him now—Xitaros's nephew Theros.

Theros stood and watched Will for a moment. Probably waiting for his drug—or poison—to take effect.

Should I play dead? Instead, Will called out, as loud as he could, "Help! I need help!" He wished he knew the Mazi word.

Theros winced as Will shouted. Will felt the syringe still in his hand. *My only weapon.*

The burly Sea-Dweller charged, knife in hand. Will had the advantage of higher position—nestled against the ceiling—and a protected space. He was like a lobster. Or a moray eel.

Theros tried to stab him from below, but Will backed out of reach. He shouted for help again. Even though he was a guest of the Mazi—supposedly a sacred responsibility—this clan member was trying to kill him.

Theros stepped up and planted feet on the bottom bunk, then stabbed at Will again, slashing him across the forearm. Searing pain knocked the breath out of his lungs. He inhaled and screamed, "Help!!"

Theros thrust the knife blade again. Will tried to block it with the inflatable pillow, which exploded with a pop. He hurled the remnants at Theros, then the sheets, trying pathetically to slow him.

As his attacker threw aside the sheets, Will remembered the curtains. He slid them shut. They were useless as a shield, but might give him a chance to strike back. His fingers closed on the syringe.

A hand thrust aside one of the curtains. Will grabbed the webbed fingers, then jabbed the syringe into the man's wrist. He depressed the plunger, pushing hard to pump in the viscous liquid.

Theros howled and jumped back to the floor, holding his wrist, which had a big—and probably painful—fluid bubble under the skin. Will had missed the vein, unfortunately. But maybe that would just slow the effects, whatever they were, not stop them.

Theros growled something in Mazi, then ran out of the room. Will started feeling woozy. *Did some of that shit get in my bloodstream?* His forearm was dripping blood, but it looked like the wound was shallow.

Will tied a pillowcase around the knife wound. He lowered himself out of the bed, keeping one eye on the door.

Theros didn't return. *Hope he's enjoying his medicine.*

Will tiptoed to the door. It had no lock. His best option, especially since he was bleeding and possibly poisoned, was to look for Zoze and Duripi. Or the doctor—although he might be treating Theros now.

Will opened the door and peered into the hallway. No sign of anyone. He decided to call for help again. His shouts echoed down the corridor.

A woman and man sprinted toward him. Martis and one of the other maintenance technicians. Will sat on the floor, too dizzy to stand anymore, the pillowcase around his arm soaked with blood. He pinched the skin of his neck to stay awake.

"Theros attacked me," he managed to blurt out. "I need a doctor."

* * *

Andreia

Andreia, Sama, and Pijasiros headed back to Aux, lights off. After a few minutes, Andreia heard the rapid trilling of dolphin sonar. She hoped it was just a dolphin looking for food, but there was a good chance it was one of the Karsk guards, maybe alerted by the drone battle.

Still emitting rapid clicks, the dolphin swam close enough to displace the water above Andreia, the waves brushing her hair and tickling her scalp. It returned and circled them, then swam off.

After a while, she heard buzzing from two distinct dolphins. *They must be Karsk.* So incredible were the echolocation abilities of dolphins, they would know they'd found three Sea-Dwellers, two on Mazi sleds and one on a Karsk sled. If they'd echo-sensed Andreia before, they'd recognize her body features, even in the dark.

Andreia cut the ropes tying her to the other sleds and moved away from Sama and Pijasiros. When the buzzing grew loud, she switched on the sled's floodlights, illuminating the two dolphins heading for her. Their eyes glowed in the glare.

Andreia pointed her speargun at them. Like other Karsk dolphins she'd encountered, they recognized the threat and swam rapidly away.

She piloted her sled back to Sama and Pijasiros. #Return to Aux,# she signaled them. #I'll stay here and delay the enemies.# Her teeth gripped the regulator mouthpiece. She'd been so happy to be alive, but how much longer would she last?

#We won't leave without you,# Sama responded.

Andreia had expected him to be stubborn about it. She embraced the gentle current caressing her hair. #You must. You have to decipher their communications, figure out their plans, and uncover their Land-Dweller operatives.#

#Pijasiros can return,# Sama signaled. #I will stay here with you.#

#No.# She pointed her speargun at him. #If you try to stay, I will shoot you myself.#

Sama gave up. #If you are not back at Aux by sunrise, we will rally the entire clan to search for you.#

#I will not be long. And I will not fight to the death. I will stop them from catching you, then flee.# Life was precious, existence a miracle. And Will would be devastated if she died, especially having suffered such a loss before.

She loved him beyond words and wanted desperately to spend the rest of her life—a long life—with him.

#See you back at Aux,# she signaled.

Her friends departed. She shut her sled lights off and piloted closer to the direction the dolphins had come from, but ten meters higher.

She heard the buzzing clicks of searching dolphins again. It didn't matter that she'd changed position, there was no escaping them in open water. When they drew close, she switched on her front spotlights. This time, the dolphins were followed by two Karsk soldiers on sleds. Her heart hammered. *Outnumbered and outgunned.*

Andreia decided to attack first. She fired her wire-guided torpedo toward the enemy sleds, hoping the Aux crew had built it correctly. It launched off the sled bottom with a high-pitched whine and streaked through the water.

The dolphins and sleds scattered. She maneuvered the torpedo with a joystick glued to the console, following one of the sleds. *Too bad I can't get both of them.*

The torpedo was faster than the enemy sled. It hit and detonated, an orange flash followed by a crashing boom and a fast-expanding sphere of bubbles. *It worked!* It was followed by a second, bigger explosion, presumably Karsk weaponry detonating.

At the same time, the other Karsk sled fired a torpedo at Andreia. Everything else disappeared from her mind.

She shut off the sled lights, rotated the throttle to maximum speed, pumped air into the ballast containers, and placed the sled into a steep climb away from the approaching torpedo. She forcibly exhaled the air out of her lungs and sinuses in preparation for the explosion to come.

Andreia repeated her bubble trick, purging air from the rebreather and swirling it to simulate the cross-section of the sled. To provide something to hit, she hurled the drone corpse into the bubbles.

A few seconds later, the enemy torpedo exploded behind her. The shock waves rattled her body. But the sled kept climbing. She patted its hull in appreciation.

She wasn't sure where the attacker was. She'd surely killed the other one. *Murder number two—I fired first.*

Andreia hoped to avoid close combat with the remaining soldier. She was too beat up, and the Karsk guns had a greater range than her speargun. Flight was the only survivable option. The hardest part would be evading the dolphins.

Keeping the expanding gas bubbles from the explosion between herself and the Karsk, Andreia leveled out her sled. She pointed the nose down and headed for the bottom.

She had no idea where her pursuers were, which was scary. With luck, the debris from the drone would convince the soldier he'd whacked her. But even if that was true, dolphin sonar profiling could easily tell the difference. And then they'd search for her.

Andreia leveled out the sled again before the depth gauge reached her prior depth. She didn't want to slam into the sea floor. *This sucks. I can't see shit and don't know the area.*

A barrage of rapid clicks announced that the dolphins had found her. She was doomed. Unless…

Andreia stopped the sled. With positive buoyancy, it began to rise. She felt the water move from a passing dolphin.

She switched on her flashlight and swung it around. One of the dolphins fixed a glowing eye on her, only a few meters away.

As fast as she could, she swung her speargun up and fired. The dolphin squealed, but couldn't move out of the way in time. The untethered bolt entered just above the left pectoral fin. *Forgive me!*

The dolphin made a shrieking noise and thrashed its body, blood gushing from the wound. Warm tears washed across Andreia's eyes and disappeared into the dark sea. *You're making it worse,* she wanted to tell it.

The wounded dolphin pounded its tail flukes against the water and hurried for the surface. The other dolphin charged Andreia. She raised her shield just in time. Its beak smashed against it, knocking her flat and spinning the sled off course.

The attacking dolphin bit her shoulder, teeth pressing down on the wetsuit. She dropped the speargun onto the semi-enclosed sled deck, and pulled out her dive knife. She poked the blade against her attacker's jaw, hard enough to draw blood.

It released her and followed its comrade to the surface, smacking her with its tail on the way up. *Her* tail—two mammary slits beneath.

Andreia felt terrible, but this was her opportunity to escape. She filled the ballast tanks with water and pointed the sled down. As it descended, she realized that her left shoulder and arm hurt too much to even lift.

Once along the bottom, she tacked right and left, occasionally scraping the sediment. Even if the Karsk had active sonar, she'd be nearly impossible to detect there. And hopefully the dolphins had more important things to worry about than trying to find her again.

Will the dolphin survive? The pair would probably seek help from the Karsk, who, despite being despicable, would hopefully treat a comrade. Congratulations, Andreia, you've murdered two Sea-Dwellers and grievously wounded a dolphin. You are the lowest of the low.

Andreia found a crevice and followed it. She'd be even harder to find now. She eyed the faintly-lit compass so she wouldn't lose her way. *What have I done?* Tears bled into the water around her. She was a killer. She would have to confess her sins to the Mazi Council and accept their punishment.

Chapter 26

Will

Will lay on a stiff cot in the Aux medical bay. Without any available blankets, it was much too chilly to sleep in. Thalassa had placed him in a tiny isolation room. She'd claimed complete ignorance of Land-Dweller physiology, and the only poisons she'd ever encountered were jellyfish stings.

Will's symptoms—primarily dizziness—were relatively minor, and already wearing off. Fortunately, he'd only received a small fraction of the syringe contents. He wasn't sure if it was meant to kill him, or just knock him out, like the drug Andreia had jabbed in his neck after he confessed to bugging her van.

He heard a commotion outside his room, a man shouting. He got up and peered through the large window in the door.

In the middle of the adjacent examination room, which was lined with metal cabinets and refrigerators, Theros lay motionless on a wheeled cart, still dressed in ninja black. His uncle Xitaros was yelling at Thalassa in the Mazi language and pointing at Theros. A mechanic stood behind the cart, gripping the push bar.

Thalassa felt Theros's pulse, then shone a penlight into one of his eyes. She shook her head and spoke softly in Mazi. Xitaros stared at the body. He placed a hand against his nephew's chest and began to cry.

Zoze and Martis came into the examination room and spoke with the doctor, also in Mazi. Then they entered Will's room.

"Did you kill Theros?" Martis asked him.

"He's dead?" Will wasn't sure how to process it.

"Yes."

"What happened?" Zoze asked.

"If he's dead, I'm sorry, but he was trying to murder me in my sleep." Will recounted the whole episode, step by step.

"Sounds like legitimate self-defense," Zoze responded. Martis agreed.

"See if you can find the syringe," Will suggested. "It may have traces of the poison."

Xitaros spotted Will through the door window and strode into the room. He spoke in angry Mazi, then stabbed a finger at him. "You murdered my nephew," he said in English.

"Your nephew tried to kill me in my sleep. If that poison hadn't been meant to kill, he'd still be alive."

Xitaros's face clenched. "I demand justice. A life for a life. It is our code."

Zoze's jaw dropped. "I've never heard that."

"That's because no Mazi has ever killed another Mazi. But Land-Dwellers are murderous by nature."

Will stepped within inches of the man. "You probably planned the attack! And sent your nephew to do it because you were too feeble and cowardly to do it yourself."

Xitaros's skin flushed red. He glanced around the room, possibly looking for a weapon. "You murdered my nephew, now you add dishonor. I will kill you myself!"

Zoze and Martis moved between them. "Let's all chill," Zoze said.

"There are procedures for disputes," Martis added.

"What's the procedure?" Will asked.

"Normally," Zoze answered, "they're talked out until everyone's good. If that's not possible, it's brought before the Council. That's not very common, though."

Xitaros waved his webbed hands. "Talking will not bring back my nephew, his life cut short by this murderous Land-Dweller!"

Zoze shouted at Xitaros in Mazi. Thalassa came in and shooed everyone out of the room.

"I apologize," she told Will. "You are a guest of the Mazi and in my care until you recover. I told Xitaros to let you alone, but he didn't listen."

Will was feeling better now—medically, anyway—but didn't argue the fact. His best-case scenario was a trial before the Council. And they might not care that he'd acted in self-defense. *And why did Xitaros try to have me killed? What if the whole Council was in on it?* As Andreia had warned, maybe they'd already decided it was too risky to trust he wouldn't reveal their existence.

Or maybe they secretly supported the Karsk and didn't want him to expose their plot.

* * *

Andreia

Andreia reached Aux an hour later than she'd promised. Which was certainly better than never. She guessed that Sama and Pijasiros would use the same sealock they'd left from. She chose wrong—the lock she entered was empty. There was a worse possibility—what if they hadn't made it back at all?

She hurried into the decompression suite and entered the number for the comm room. Duripi answered.

"This is Andreia. I'm in Sealock 3. Are Sama and Pijasiros here?"

"They arrived a while ago. Still decompressing, though."

Andreia exhaled in relief. "I've got a long decompression ahead, myself."

"There was some commotion here while you were gone," Duripi said.

"What kind of commotion?"

"That big sand shark Theros—Xitaros's nephew—attacked Will. Tried to inject some sort of poison."

Andreia's hands slapped against the wall on either side of the intercom. "Is he okay? Just tried, right? He's okay?"

"Yes, he's fine."

Andreia exhaled and slowly regained control of her muscles. "Can I talk to him?"

"He's resting," Duripi said. "I'll let him know you're here."

"Thanks. Thank you. Why did Theros attack him?"

"Only Leviathan knows."

Andreia thought a moment. "Has Katiki been informed? By someone other than Xitaros?"

"No, but we'll do that. Zoze knows more about it, I'll ask her."

"Tell her not to let Xitaros control the narrative." It was probably too late, but at least the Council could hear both sides. Of course, there was a chance they approved the assassination attempt, but that wasn't something to discuss over the intercom.

"We'll do our best," Duripi said. "After Xitaros's 'You cannot be trusted' speech in the comm room, poop from a sea cucumber merits higher esteem."

Exhausted and feeling wrecked, Andreia signed off. She peeled off her wetsuit and changed her bandages. After what felt like a fractured eternity of fighting trained killers, she was a mess, but at least she was alive.

She set the decompression timer to decrease from ambient depth to internal Aux pressure. She'd been at the bottom for seven hours, so she'd be stuck here half a day, unable to help Will or anyone else.

She barely managed to fill an air mattress before falling asleep.

* * *

USNS Surveyor, in the Straits of Florida

Dr. Ana Hernandez stood on the bridge of the surveillance ship *USNS Surveyor* as it approached the site of the latest underwater explosions. The boxy-looking, catamaran-hulled vessel was towing active and passive sonar arrays and carried a newly built unmanned submersible. The active array, a vertical line of sound projectors, transmitted low-frequency pings. The passive array, a horizontal line of hydrophones, picked up reflections of these pings. A submarine would show up like a deer caught in headlights.

The downside was that the enemy sub would detect the pings and know they'd been found. But given the attacks on the Texas refineries, the gruff *Surveyor* captain had told her, the Navy had no patience. They were also sending a fast-attack submarine, a destroyer, and support ships. Ana wasn't privy to the overall plan, but presumed they'd be deployed to intercept any subs flushed by the sonar pings. What they'd do then, she had no idea.

"Three nautical miles out," the young navigation officer announced from his station.

Looking at the radar display, Ana estimated they were about 20 miles southeast of Tavernier. Outside territorial waters, but within the Contiguous Zone, a relatively recent addition that extended the reach of U.S. law enforcement to interdict drug traffickers and other criminals.

"Slow to five knots," the captain announced.

"Slow to five knots," the helmsman repeated. Moments later, the ship slowly decelerated.

The navigation officer half-turned toward Ana. "Who are you with, if you don't mind me asking?"

Ana was dressed in a dark blue blazer, matching slacks, and a white button-down shirt, with a holstered sidearm on her belt. She might as well be wearing a neon sign stating 'Police Detective.' "NCIS, Office of Special Projects. I've been authorized to come along. There's a chance what you're looking for connects to a case I'm investigating." She left it at that.

The Navy had pored over the data collected by the P-8 off Islamorada. According to specialists Ana had talked to, the submarine's acoustic profile matched no known vessel. Apparently, it had never been detected before. Was it Cuban? If so, what were they up to? Cuba was a poor country, with limited resources following the collapse of the Soviet Union. And was the submarine linked to the webbed people who'd been found in the South China Sea and the Florida Keys?

Ana exited the bridge and hurried down corridors to the sonar station. There, Navy and civilian technicians stared at workstation screens, thick headphones on.

"Anything?" she asked the sonar supervisor.

"Not yet. But I wouldn't hang around after making a noise like that."

When they approached the site of the latest explosions, Ana returned to the bridge and addressed the captain. "Can we try the camera here?"

He let out a sigh. "I think whoever's responsible went back to Cuba."

"There might be debris."

The captain frowned, but had orders to assist her investigations.

"Slow to four knots," the captain commanded. He addressed the navigator. "Chart a course at new speed centering on the explosion site." Then he turned to Ana. "You can deploy your submersible."

Ana had assumed they'd reel in the sonar arrays and stop over the site to deploy the submersible, but apparently the captain thought sonar profiling was more important. Or else he was being passive-aggressive.

She made her way to the stern, where the remotely operated submersible was attached to a crane. The submersible was a 10-foot-long yellow cuboid with thrusters, lights, cameras, manipulator arms, and sample baskets. A cable connected it to a floating antenna that relayed commands and data. It was designed for deep ocean work; the 170-fathom depth here would seem like a puddle.

As Ana watched, the crane lowered the submersible into the water, then released it. Ana entered a trailer fastened to the deck, where a crew of three was working on laptops with attached flatscreens. The pilot, a thirtyish civilian woman with dark skin and a paisley head bandana, filled the ballast tanks, and the submersible sank toward the bottom. Another operator switched on its lights, revealing a sloping plain of sediment from several angles on some of the computer monitors.

"Starting the search," the pilot said, and began a grid pattern.

After a while, one of the video cameras revealed a torn scrap of hard plastic. "Looks like explosion damage," the camera operator said.

"Mark the spot and keep looking," Ana said.

The drone crew followed her directions. They found more fragments scattered over a wide area, and an area of disturbed sediment, presumably beneath the blast. The fragments included motor parts. No bodies.

"Let's look around some more," Ana said, "then collect samples."

Once done surveying this site, they'd pull in the submersible and remove the samples for analysis. Then they'd head to the next site, where the mystery submarine had been chased from.

* * *

Will

Zoze fetched a blanket for Will, and he managed to fall asleep. When he woke, the digital clock on his bedstand had advanced by five hours. Feeling relatively refreshed, he got up and went to the communications room. Zoze and Duripi were busy at adjacent computers, with multiple windows of system commands, program interfaces, and scrolling text.

"How's it going?" he asked.

Zoze turned in her chair. "Feeling better?"

"Yeah, for once it paid to be a light sleeper, otherwise I'd be dead. Did you find the syringe I was attacked with?"

"It was on the bunkroom floor. I gave it to Thalassa to analyze."

"We're receiving data from the taps," Duripi said. "And the hack worked—we're netting the keys to decipher it." He pointed at a block of random characters in one of the black-background windows, with the words BEGIN PRIVATE KEY above.

"It's mostly browser data they're receiving," Zoze said. "But some messages too. We're trying to figure out who the Karsk are talking to."

"It'll be challenging since they're using onion routing," Duripi said.

Zoze touched a finger to her forehead. "Detectives Zoze and Duripi are on it, though. With a little help from Pijasiros and Sama—they cached a laptop in one of the sealocks."

"The others are back, then?" Will asked.

"Decompressing." Zoze glanced at her screen. "Sama and Pijasiros will be out in five hours, Andreia in seven. She was gone longer."

Will decided not to call Andreia—she was probably exhausted and sleeping. He sat at the guest computer, which had limited access, and browsed the news.

Consumer prices were rising, goods were disappearing from stores, and some companies were already filing for bankruptcy. And disinformation bots were increasing exponentially on social media. In local news, the Miami Herald reported 'two to three' new underwater explosions off the Florida Keys last night. It gave few details.

Will told Zoze and Duripi what he'd read.

"We knew about the cyberattacks," Zoze responded, "but explosions?" She spoke into her microphone, "Sama, you there?"

After a pause, Pijasiros responded over the speaker, "He's asleep. Want me to wake him?"

"No, no. Did you blow something up?"

"What? No." He paused again. "You said Andreia's back. Maybe she got in a scuffle with the Karsk. She's got a talent for that, maybe she should be a full-time soldier."

"She doesn't like that sort of thing," Will said. "Maybe we should talk to her."

A high-pitched, cringe-inducing squeal came from the intercom. Zoze and Duripi jumped up from their seats as if under attack.

"What is it?" Will asked.

"Active sonar alarm," Duripi said in tense tones. "We're being profiled. Never gone off before. There's a manual somewhere, I forget exactly what to do."

Zoze found a red binder with Mazi script on the front and laminated pages. She flipped through it. "Don't make noise." She pointed at the intercom and rolled her eyes.

"Maybe that's why it's so high-pitched," Duripi said as he resumed his seat. "Won't penetrate the limestone and sediment above us."

Zoze continued reading. "Disable all sealocks so no hostiles can enter. Prepare for emergency evacuation. Close all hatches. Prepare to scuttle communications center." She turned to Duripi. "We have a self-destruct?"

"Not that I know of." He brought up a new window on one of his screens. "Sonar signal is low frequency, varying between 220 and 250 hertz, 5 second intervals. Source level estimated 215 decibels."

"Sounds like the Navy," Will said. He wished they were pinging the Karsk instead of the Mazi. "Maybe they're investigating the noise made during the Karsk attack. Maybe that's why the Karsk left."

Zoze cupped her hands. "Sounds legit."

"Can we turn the alarm off?" It was starting to give him a headache, and possibly panicking the other occupants.

Zoze closed the binder of instructions and returned to her computer with it. "On it. Then I'll read over the intercom what we're supposed to do." She addressed Duripi over her shoulder. "What are the chances they'll detect us?"

"We're beneath a lot of limestone and sediment here," Duripi said. "The problem is the sealocks. They're optically camouflaged, but made of non-magnetic organometal. Sonar pulses would reflect right off that, so when they built Aux, they added a sonar-absorbing coating—rubber and organoplastic with holes and bumps that scatter the signal. Never been tested against high-power sonar equipment, though. And the holes are probably all plugged with silt—who knows if it even works now."

"Shit-gobbling Karsk," Zoze grumbled. "This whole thing is all their fault." She muttered in Mazi—presumably curses—while she tried to figure out how to shut off the alarm.

If the Karsk were detected, Will decided, it might be for the best. As for the Mazi, he'd help them however could. Maybe not Xitaros and the rest of the Council, but certainly everyone else.

* * *

Andreia

When Andreia was finally able to exit the sealock, Will was waiting outside. They embraced, his body warm and sheltering.

"Are you alright?" he asked.

"I've been better," she said. "Sleep helped, broken though it was. And Sea-Dwellers have more blood cells than you, including platelets, so we heal faster. How you are you doing?"

"I'm fine." They kissed, a gentle but sincere 'I missed you' kind of kiss that morphed into a passionate 'I'm crazy about you and want you right now.'

Andreia pulled herself away. *Later. As soon as possible, but later.* "Where's Xitaros?"

"Ran back to Katiki like the coward he is. Took his nephew's body with him."

Andreia was disappointed. She had been looking forward to beating a confession out of the malicious worm. *He must have guessed that.*

"Obviously," she told him, "it's too dangerous for you to return to Katiki."

"Do you think the Council is behind Theros's attack?"

"Maybe. Or maybe just a subset. Xitaros has a lot of supporters, unfortunately. Even though Theros tried to kill you, the fact that he died at your hands will no doubt create more support for your demise." She changed topics. "Anything more about the Navy search?"

The alarm had woken her. She'd called the comm room and Duripi had filled her in about the sonar pings. Will had elaborated with what he knew about Navy procedures, having a brother in the service. She'd told them about her battle with the Karsk guards, but the torpedoes had detonated far from Aux.

"Seems like there was one ship and it left," Will said. "Either your sonar-absorbing coating worked, or they're combing the whole area and returning with reinforcements."

"Let's hope it's the former. If not, we need an escape plan."

"There already is one. A whole procedures manual."

Of course. Her ancestors were at least as smart—and paranoid—as the current generation.

They headed to the comm room, where the entire crew was working. They looked tired, but greeted her with hugs.

"We've decrypted orders from the Karsk," Sama said. He'd told her over the phone that their cable taps had worked.

"What's their plan?" Andreia asked.

Sama's lips curled down, expressing grimness. "They're planning attacks on banks and national currencies to drive people to their cryptocurrency."

"Both financial attacks and cyber-attacks," Will said.

"Some of their techniques are as old as the Internet," Pijasiros said. "Man-in-the-browser attacks, ARP spoofing, evil maid attacks, crap like that. But one of their groups is trying to scramble customer databases so the banks won't know whose money is whose. They hired two old, retired COBOL programmers to write the code; now they just have to install it."

"If it works," Will said, "it'll crash the financial system."

"And apparently they've gained access to some of the stock exchanges," Sama said. "We don't know which ones, or what exactly they plan to do."

"Judging by everything else they've done," Will said, "it'll be bad. Maybe disable the circuit breakers and start a barrage of short sells."

"Check out Mr. Stock Market," Zoze said.

"Just stuff my dad talks about."

Sama's eyes shifted up as if remembering something. "They also have operatives inside Swift, the… uh…

"Society for Worldwide Interbank Financial Telecommunication," Will filled in.

"Yeah," Sama continued. "It's what most banks use for cross-border payments. There's another one specific to China called Cips. We think they've accessed that also."

Will said, "I'm guessing the Karsk will frame China for the Swift attack and the West for the Cips attack."

"What's their plan after that?" Andreia asked.

"Currentsea," Will said, "which we confirmed is Karsk-controlled, will be the only investment refuge. If the Karsk wanted, they could use that power to control policy, like defunding the fossil fuel industry and curbing plastics, or investing in renewable energy and protection of nature. Since their goal is destruction, though, they'll likely buy whatever assets they want, then scuttle Currentsea. All that money will just disappear, and the world will enter a depression that makes the 1929 crash seem like a misplaced penny."

"Another clue they'll take the second route," Duripi said, "they're planning to take down communications networks and electrical grids too."

Feeling jittery, Andreia asked, "When's this all supposed to happen?"

"It's underway," Will replied in tense tones. "But still in the early stage."

"The good news," Sama said, "we know their general targets and have tracked down some of their operatives. Some of them are cybersecurity consultants or network administrators. Perfectly positioned for inside jobs."

"We're compiling what we know about them," Pijasiros said, "and we'll drop the info, along with all the communications we've intercepted, in a document repository and out them publicly."

"Then we'll let Ronin—that keynote speaker—know about it," Duripi added. "Anonymously, of course."

"And not just Ronin," Will said. "We have to be careful about who to trust, but cybersecurity heads at the targets need to know about the attacks so they can prepare. And agencies like CISA."

"What's that?" Andreia asked.

"U.S. Cybersecurity and Infrastructure Security Agency."

Andreia and Will—mostly Will—gave advice where they could, but the work was extremely technical. Her friends typed on command interfaces, examined readouts, ran hacker tools, and anonymously uploaded files into data hubs, working together closer than she'd ever seen. They messaged a long list of people and institutions they'd vetted as probably uncompromised, telling them what was going on, who the Land-Dweller operatives were, and what sort of attack they were attempting.

"We need to let the FTC and other regulators know about Currentsea," Will said, "that it's controlled by the terrorist group. Governments can prohibit its use if they're motivated."

Andreia and Will sat at one of the vacant workstations and, with Sama's help, found the locations of some of the Currentsea computer facilities and exchanges, scattered around the world. Unfortunately, they couldn't find any evidence that the Karsk had used Currentsea in their operations, nor any wrongdoing by its miners and traders.

After a while, Zoze announced, "That's the last of the uploads and warnings."

From the neighboring workstation, Pijasiros responded, "You can help pinpoint more operatives."

"On it."

Andreia was overcome with giddy admiration for her friends. "I love you all. You are awesome."

"Took you this long to realize that?" Zoze said over her shoulder.

Duripi shouted from his seat, "One of the people we warned is a mole! Sent a message, 'Someone knows what you're doing.'"

Heads turned, faces tense with concern. "Who?" Andreia asked.

"Don't know yet." He typed furiously. "If the Karsk respond, we can attach a ping and trace it."

"More important," Andreia shouted, "can you cut the Karsk communications before they warn their whole network?"

"Already prepping," Pijasiros said from his seat. "Operation Tsunami, here we go." He typed in a command window, webbed fingers a blur. With a final tap of the 'Enter' key, he turned and waved his hands in a flourish. "I told the boxes to stop relaying outgoing data and activate the sabotage routines of the rootkits we installed on the Karsk systems."

"What'll they do?" Will asked.

He grinned. "Overwrite everything in memory and attached storage with random garbage. That will include anything connected to the routers, and the routers themselves. It'll take them days to recover."

"The downside," Duripi said, "we can't monitor their communications anymore. All we can do now is hope the Land-Dwellers heed our warnings and take action."

Chapter 27

Will

The next day, Will and Andreia joined the Aux hackers at an invite-only virtual meeting of cybersecurity companies and consultants. The Aux team, via their human personas, had helped organize it.

Pijasiros, Duripi, Sama, and Andreia sat in a semicircle at adjacent workstations, each with two computers and four screens. Will and Zoze sat behind them with laptops to help coordinate, and texted suggestions and other thoughts. Zoze had loaned her Asian-American female avatar to Andreia, insisting they needed her persuasion skills.

The platform reminded Will of old adventure games—if the adventures were limited to finding the session you wanted to attend. Attendees moved their avatars around a 3-D virtual conference metaverse, navigating a realistic environment with multiple furnished theaters and common areas. The large plenary room made it possible to mingle with other attendees informally, while smaller presentation areas were dedicated to particular topics. Attendees could also chat privately.

The Aux hackers joined hundreds of other human-form avatars at the opening plenary session. Instead of sitting together, the Aux crew picked virtual chairs scattered throughout the audience.

Like in-person conferences, the plenary host, an esteemed cybersecurity professor, took the podium, thanked everyone for coming, and provided a general recap of the latest conditions around the globe, echoing media reports augmented by information Will and the Aux team had provided. "The purpose of this conference," the professor's avatar said, "is to forge a united strategy and battle plan to take down those responsible for the continuing cyber and kinetic attacks and prevent further damage."

Instead of a single hour-long keynote speech, eight speakers from different countries were given 15 minutes each. "This cyberterrorist group," a representative from Interpol said, "is behind the attacks on the world's energy infrastructure. Indications are, they're going after the global financial system next. Although law enforcement and appropriate agencies are already taking steps to apprehend over a hundred individuals connected with the conspiracy, we need your help."

A speaker from the World Bank added that without united action, the terrorists would succeed in their plan to effectuate "the greatest economic calamity in world history—far beyond the worldwide depression of the 1930's." He added, "we are perilously close to the tipping point."

A representative from China's Ministry of State Security denied that his country had anything to do with the attacks on the Saudi ports or U.S. refineries, and brought detailed dossiers on the Chinese individuals implicated. Will had insisted, via the Aux team, that the conference include representatives from China, Russia, and Iran, since the Karsk had framed their governments for the most devastating cyberattacks, and they ought to be given a chance to weigh in.

"We were also attacked," the Chinese representative said, showing slides of burned-out semiconductor factories. "In a spirit of radical openness, I have brought with me documentation on the testimony of numerous suspects we have detained. It is clear their acts of terror were not sanctioned by Chinese state organs, but motivated by personal gain and greed. All available resources are now dedicated to rooting out their entire network of cybercriminals."

A speaker from the Iranian Cyber Police angrily denounced the U.S. for attacking her country. "Your unwarranted aggression caused great damage to our country and once this crisis is averted, we will demand reparations."

Will winced inside. Iran's grievances, while legitimate, might torpedo the conference.

The plenary speakers then assembled at a long table on stage for the Q&A. Will texted questions to the Aux hackers, who raised virtual hands. They'd worked out a plan of action before the conference. When called upon, Duripi's nondescript male avatar suggested that financial institutions halt business until the malware was neutralized and the terrorist infiltrators arrested.

A representative from Swift, the biggest provider of financial messaging services, replied that they couldn't shut down operations without tanking the global economy. "And even for individuals—what happens when they don't get their paychecks, and can't use checks or credit cards to buy groceries?"

Predictably, a senior officer from the U.S. Cyber Command argued with the officer from the Iranian Cyber Police. The moderator stopped them and said, "This conference has a single, united mission. You can engage in sidebars on your own time."

Sama's avatar—a bearded man with glasses—asked the panel, "How will you find and stop the rest of the terrorist network?"

"A good question," the Interpol representative said. "Standard procedure—hundreds of computer devices have been seized and are being scoured for further leads. Emergency powers granted by many countries have made this rapid search and seizure possible. Suspects uncovered through this process will be monitored some to reveal the identities of their co-conspirators, who will then be rounded up."

Will was skeptical and texted the Aux team, 'The Karsk operatives probably operate in isolated cells, with no one person knowing the whole picture.'

Duripi repeated that to the panel when he was called upon.

"That's common practice among covert groups," a British intelligence officer affirmed. "But the exercise must be done. Someone will surely set a foot wrong and reveal a part of the network."

When it was Andreia's turn, she spoke in a confident, emphatic voice, and emphasized her avatar's words with hand gestures. "My name is Lila Song, I'm a security researcher. Some of you follow my research. I absolutely agree with the speakers that the problem is urgent. Every second counts if we want to avoid the biggest economic collapse in history. I pledge to spend every waking second to help stop it. We're the only defense. We must all work together, develop a plan, and plug in."

She looked around the virtual room. "Who's with me? The world needs us, and surely there's enough brain power in this room to outwit that unhinged gang of terrorists! And don't forget… if the economy collapses, we'll all be out of jobs, for who knows how long!"

A few others raised their hands. Then, presumably succumbing to peer pressure, more and more raised their hands, until every hand in the large room was raised.

"You all are awesome!" Andreia said. "Let's give ourselves a round of applause and wreck those psycho bastards!"

Even as an avatar, Andreia's charisma was infectious, and the attendees clapped their virtual hands or shook their virtual fists.

When breakout sessions began, each member of the Aux team selected different topics to spread their influence. Since they were sitting next to each other in real life, it was easy to coordinate.

The conference concluded at the end of the day, with a remarkably unified strategy to stop the cyberterrorist campaign through investigation, mitigation and counterattack.

* * *

The Karsk outpost

In the crowded communications room of the *Silent Garrison* outpost, Tareen struggled not to succumb to the atmosphere of panic. All communications with the outside were down, along with half the outpost's control systems. Technicians rushed around, swapping out parts, reformatting hard drives, and reinstalling operating systems. The meltdown had been sudden and unexpected. Connections to keyboards and external devices were the first things disabled by the mystery malware, making intervention impossible.

Under close supervision, Yissharu and his pregnant Mazi wife, Maia, removed storage drives from computers and performed other menial tasks. No one trusted them—especially Maia—but they were too valuable to imprison.

"A thousand deaths to the Turd-throwers and their technology," Minatos, the outpost facilities coordinator, complained. "They hunt us with sonar and submersibles, and somehow they entered our systems, too."

Tareen was the only one who responded. "How did they find us?"

"Too much noise." Minatos glared at her.

"I told you attacking Aux was a bad idea," Tareen reminded him.

"It's all Mazi Andreia's fault, that murderous glob of sea slime. She might even have purposely led the Land-Dweller navy to us. Her or her pet Turd-thrower. Now the entire operation is in jeopardy."

Tareen flinched. They should have killed Andreia and the Land-Dweller right away, but Andreia could have been useful. And of course there was the powerful instinct against killing other Sea-Dwellers. Which Andreia—polluted by living among Land-Dwellers—had disregarded. Following her murder of another soldier, the Coordinating Praesidium had called for her execution.

Minatos waved Yissharu and Maia over. "Do you think Mazi Andreia is working with the Land-Dwellers?"

Maia's face tensed. "You shouldn't have killed her brother," she muttered.

Yissharu displayed his broken finger. "Andreia has lived and worked among the Land-Dwellers for years. She hates us—although Maia and I had nothing to do with it—for killing her brother, and she is almost certainly seeking revenge. We made things worse by kidnapping her and telling her to kill the Land-Dweller. I have little doubt that she and Will Myers could be directing the U.S. Navy against us."

"Andreia and two others were discovered within our patrol perimeter," Minatos said. "Were they searching for us? We lost a drone, no trace of it. Did they destroy it? What else did they do? Could they have tapped our communications? We received a warning from a surface operative, then our systems went down. But other than the missing drone, we haven't found any signs of disturbance."

"The Aux communications team is very good," Yissharu said. "Better than ours, if this mess is their fault."

Around the circular room, eyes turned in his direction.

"I've been out with Sama," he continued. "He's an artist when it comes to cable work. And the others are equally skilled at their particular specialties. I learned a lot at Aux."

"So maybe they discovered our lines and tapped them," Minatos said. "Or maybe they didn't. We don't know one way or the other. In case they did, we need to keep searching, even if it means unearthing every meter of cable we laid."

He dismissed Yissharu and Maia, then told Tareen, "Come with me."

A feeling of dread roiled Tareen's stomach as she followed Minatos down pipe-lined corridors. Would she be blamed for the failures and punished? None of them were her fault.

They entered the domed conference room. Other members of the Praesidium were seated there, talking to two soldiers and Arudos, one of the communications specialists. "We should have taken the nuclear war option," Tatoku, the military coordinator, grumbled to the other Praesidium members.

A chill flushed through Tareen. She had been one of the chief opponents of starting a nuclear war between the Land-Dweller powers. The global devastation would have been uncontrollable, and the radioactive fallout and darkened skies would have caused great harm to Sea-Dwellers and the marine life they depended on. She would have to talk to the more reasonable members of the Praesidium to ensure they didn't revisit that option.

Holding the Facilitator trident, Arudara, the logistics coordinator, stood. The others followed.

"Tareen," Arudara said, "you will join Arudos and Thaito on an expedition to the surface to communicate with our operatives. Pherissa will rendezvous with the submarine and give them this message." She handed the female soldier a data stick. "Only Captain Jadikira can decode it."

The other assignees placed cupped hands together and bowed, accepting their orders. Tareen bowed also, wondering when she'd get to see her children again. But they'd invested so much in this operation, they had to see it through. Setbacks were an inextricable part of life.

And if the orders were to start a nuclear war, Tareen would do whatever she could to stop it.

"Gather what you need," the Facilitator said, "and depart immediately."

* * *

Will

The next morning, Will and Andreia entered the Aux communications room hand-in-hand, apprehensive about the future, but giddy with the joy of their union. Zoze and Sama were sitting at adjacent workstations. Duripi and Pijasiros were in their room, attending a 'white hat' working session to lay traps for cyberterrorists and identify their locations.

The big wall screens were full of press conferences in different countries. The volume was off, with English closed-captioning. Most of the officials were announcing arrests and thwarted cyberattacks. Stock market trading had been temporarily suspended "as a precaution."

"What's the arrest tally?" Will asked Zoze and Sama.

"Over 2,000 so far," Zoze said. "Although during events like this, governments tend to cast wide nets, encompassing just about anyone they don't like, especially in totalitarian countries."

"How many are actually involved, do you think?"

She shrugged. "It's not something the Karsk communicated."

"I think they've lost a big chunk of their Land-Dweller assets," Sama said.

"A lot of initial catches turned in others," Zoze said. "The rest were caught by honeypots."

Will had no idea what she meant. "What?"

"Traps set up to catch intruders."

Ah, like Duripi and Pijasiros are doing.

"An expected attack is a lot easier to prepare for," Zoze continued, "than an unexpected attack."

Sama rolled his eyes at his pink-haired girlfriend. "You might as well have said 'water is wet.'"

Zoze responded with an obscene gesture, then asked Will and Andreia, "Do you think any of the arrests will lead to the Karsk themselves?"

Andreia shook her head. "Tareen told me her group had no personal contact with their lackeys and only communicated through anonymizing software."

One of the wall screens was airing a speech by the UN General Secretary. Will couldn't find a control to unmute the screen, but the closed-captioning stated, 'Peace is the only pathway that doesn't end in a fall from a cliff. We must refrain from war in cyberspace and refrain from war in physical space. The first will surely lead to the second...'

The usual toothless words. Will sat at the guest computer and resumed composing messages for the hacker team to distribute, taking care to be consistent with their earlier releases and new information as it was aired.

He began with a statement to the press from the unnamed terrorist group they'd fabricated. Andreia sat next to him and helped. Chuckling at times, they wrote the attacks would continue until 'the steel-grey global order has transmogrified into a beautiful palette of freedom.' It concluded, 'The only good government is no government, without rules set by others. The only good economy is one without corporations and banks, where we work for ourselves, not for others. All chains shall be broken! In this new world of radical freedom, humanity shall finally start living!'

* * *

Andreia

When they finished writing statements to the press, Andreia suggested contacting the other Sea-Dweller clans and presenting a grievance against the Karsk. A unified front of the clans could pressure the Karsk to leave Mazi territory and end their war against the Land-Dwellers.

"As a Trader," Andreia told her friends, "I have contacts in all the regional clans. Clans beyond those, I can reach indirectly." She turned to Will, "Unfortunately, official inter-clan communications must go through the Council. For a matter of this importance, an all-Mazi meeting might be required, further delaying the process."

"We can't afford bureaucratic delays," Will said. "How much trouble will you get in for bypassing the Council?"

Andreia shrugged. "Not enough to prevent me from doing what's needed."

"May the Force be with you," Zoze said.

Andreia sat at a vacant computer and began writing her contacts in other clans about the Karsk invasion of Aux, their war against the Land-Dwellers, the danger to all Sea-Dwellers, and the actions needed to mitigate it. Once finished, she logged onto the Mazi internal network and composed a message to the Council members. She grew angrier with each sentence.

'The Karsk forcefully invaded a Mazi habitat and cut our communications. They murdered my brother, a juvenile. They attacked our guest, Dr. Myers, and tried to kill us both. They recruited members of our clan to commit espionage and sabotage for them. They attacked the Land-Dwellers without provocation and put all Sea-Dwellers at risk of discovery and retaliation.

'Ten years ago, the Karsk sought approval and assistance for their war, but were rightfully rebuffed, both by our clan and the others. Yet they proceeded anyway, thinking themselves above all other clans. Their war must be stopped immediately, before it's too late.

'We lack their capacity for violence. Therefore, I have taken the liberty of appealing to the other clans for joint action to force the Karsk to make amends and end their war. You must now add your voices to ensure our cousin clans know we are united.'

An hour later, Andreia received a call from Meltha. "You have no right to speak for all Mazi."

"I know, and that's why I wrote you afterward."

Meltha let out a huff. "Afterward is no substitute for beforehand."

"I apologize. Time does not favor us."

"Regardless, the Council is discussing your proposal."

Andreia decided to play to the woman's ego. "Fantastic! I knew you would recognize the importance of acting swiftly, before the Karsk cause us more harm."

"As I said, we are discussing it this moment. While you are on the line, there is another matter that requires your attention."

Andreia braced herself.

"The Land-Dweller Will Myers," Meltha continued, "has been accused of murdering Mazi Theros. He must immediately be returned to Katiki for a hearing."

Andreia had already decided it was too dangerous for Will to return. "Theros attempted to kill Dr. Myers in his sleep. He is lucky to be alive—"

"You may offer words of defense during the hearing. Do you plan to act as his advocate?"

Andreia had never attended the Sea-Dweller equivalent of a trial. She couldn't even remember one happening. *Stall for time.* "Yes. I need time to prepare."

"You can prepare while you're decompressing."

"That's not long enough. I need to study the protocols and procedures, and gather evidence. And we're needed at Aux as long as the Karsk remain a threat."

"And how long is that?" Meltha asked.

Andreia decided to take advantage of Meltha's impatience. "It depends on how long it takes the Council to appeal to the other clans about the Karsk. Surely you recognize the Karsk threat requires our clan's full attention. We can deal with other matters afterward."

"Of course," she admitted.

"Besides, we can hold this trial virtually. There's no need to waste time traveling to Katiki."

"I will float your suggestion. As for requesting joint sanctions against the Karsk, our clan must be assembled and consensus reached before we take such an action."

"I assume that will be today?"

"That is my hope." Meltha ended the call.

"What did they say?" Will asked.

Andreia took a calming breath. "It might help speed the process if others pressure the Council."

"Politicians on the surface are the same way," he said.

"There's another matter. You've been charged with murdering Mazi Theros. We're supposed to return to Katiki for a hearing."

"Why am I not surprised?"

Zoze and Sama had also been listening. Zoze scowled. "Those wrinkled fossils can stuff sea snakes up their pissholes!"

"Don't worry," Andreia told Will, "we're not going anywhere until we're ready. And dealing with the Karsk will take precedence. And if the odds are against us, I'll bring you home—really home. The Council is powerless on land." She looked at her friends. "That's not for sharing."

"Obviously," Sama said.

Andreia placed fingertips against her temples. "If we contest the murder charge, we need evidence to show that Theros carried out a premeditated attack."

"We have the syringe," Will said. He turned to Zoze. "Did Thalassa figure out what was in it?"

"She complained about the lack of lab equipment," Zoze said, "but thought it was a powerful neurotoxin, likely originating from Western Mana organisms."

"Western Pacific," Andreia translated for Will.

"And it was a disposable syringe," Zoze continued, "not the reusable type we use."

"This took a lot of planning," Andreia said. "How did Theros get a poison from the other side of the world? And where did he get the syringe? I'm the clan Trader, and he didn't get them through me. Maybe the Karsk provided them."

"Is there a way we can find out who ordered the attack?" Will asked. "Was it the whole Council? A subset? Just Xitaros? The Karsk had spies on Aux, why not on Katiki too?"

"They might not even be spies," Andreia said. "Maybe just useful idiots. Either way, we need to expose them if they're helping the Karsk."

"We can access Katiki's computers and camera data from here," Sama said. "Let's see what Xitaros and his sand-shark nephew have been up to."

On their computers, Sama and Zoze brought up camera databases, server logs, message and external email accounts, and command windows. With a little instruction, Andreia and Will combed through sea lock videos. Zoze and Sama started poring through messages and emails.

"We can look through Council notes too," Sama said. "My dad scanned all the old notes for posterity, and backed up their messages to and from other clans. I'll run a search for any mention of the Karsk or Xitaros."

Eventually, Andreia found a video of Theros—his face and body size were unmistakable—taking a sled from Katiki late on the night of the Karsk attack, well after the fight. He returned two hours later, just after sunrise. "Exhibit #1," she told the others.

"Nothing incriminating in saved messages or emails," Sama said from his workstation. "But I recovered deleted messages that were encrypted before transmission. We have a program that can find and recover the data, at least if it's recent enough not to be written over. And we have the keys to decrypt it."

"Theros doesn't use messaging," Zoze said. "Xitaros does, and from some of his messages, he supports the Karsk war."

"So is he a mole like Maia," Andreia asked, "or a useful idiot?"

"More like a general idiot," Zoze said. "Sounds like he was being played."

"Can I see what they wrote?"

"Sure." Zoze made room at her workstation.

There were only a handful of messages. "This is it?"

"The ones we could recover," Zoze said. "There could have been older ones, but the data overwritten."

The recipient was named Ancestral_Voice—probably catering to Xitaros's ancestor-worship religion. The grammar and word choice were subtly non-Mazi. The writer played to Xitaros's ego, saying, 'Together, we can end the threat posed by the Land-Dwellers and ensure our people have a safe, prosperous future.' Andreia suspected the writer was Tareen.

As Andreia read the messages, Sama said, "Netted something interesting in the Council proceedings from ten years ago."

Andreia turned to face him. "What did you find?"

"Xitaros was part of the minority back then who thought we should support the Karsk war. And guess who his main opponent was?"

"Who?"

"Meltha! She was the key to achieving consensus against the Karsk proposal. She's no fan of Land-Dwellers, but she insisted the safety of the clan had to come first."

Andreia was both surprised and not surprised. She continued reading. The day of Will's arrival in Katiki, Xitaros told Ancestral_Voice about it, and said it was unlikely the Council would let him return to the surface to communicate with other Land-Dwellers.

Ancestral_Voice had responded, 'The Land-Dweller cannot be allowed to tell others about us. Their military forces will exterminate our people, like the conquistadores, only more efficiently. Without question, he must be euthanized before this happens, or all will be lost.'

Andreia's stomach hardened. She'd suspected the odds were against Will from the beginning. Now she knew for sure. "Can you print these messages in case I have to defend Will?"

"Of course." Zoze moved her computer mouse and one of the laser printers started whining and clicking.

Andreia kept reading. After the Karsk attack on Aux, Xitaros had received a message to meet someone outside the habitat. It included a private web chat address where he'd receive the details.

Xitaros had responded that he'd have to send his nephew, who was in better shape. Andreia suppressed an urge to punch the screen. *Will's lucky to be alive.*

The response to Xitaros: 'Use the chat room!' There were no further messages.

Andreia translated the exchange to Will. His face grew angry.

"Did you retrieve the web chat messages?" she asked Zoze and Sama.

"We searched for it," Sama said, "but naturally, it had been deleted."

"What we have is good enough," Andreia said. "We have everything we need to feed Xitaros to the sharks and exonerate Will."

With the others' help, Andreia compiled a summary of their evidence and sent it to all the Council members except Xitaros, along with the supporting documents.

After a while, she received a reply from Kitane, this month's First Speaker. 'Thank you for the information you sent. We are examining it. There was some consternation that you accessed private messages, but I reminded the Council that our clan is a unified body, not a scattered mess of components.'

Kitane's message continued, 'Also, we assume you purposely omitted Xitaros from the distribution list. While understandable from your point of view, that is poor form. I forwarded your message to Xitaros. He denied your claims, but has already recused himself from the deliberation process regarding Dr. Myers's culpability.'

Andreia tried to reach Kitane by voice line, but without luck. She sent a message instead. 'As a tool of the Karsk, Xitaros must also recuse himself from the grievance deliberations and all other matters involving the Karsk. Please call me at the Aux communications room.' She included the number.

Kitane called half an hour later. "I received your message. Xitaros continues to deny your claims. He will not recuse himself from any deliberations except those concerning his nephew's death."

We can't let him sabotage the clan talks. "He must. He's been working for the Karsk at least ten years. I'll send the evidence." Even if Xitaros continued his stubborn resistance, his support and influence would drift away.

"As for the other matter," Kitane said, "when can we expect Dr. Myers? He must come in person."

Andreia struggled to keep her voice even. "As soon as the Karsk threat is ended."

At some point, the Council would tire of her delays and send people to collect Will. Then she'd have to return him to land. She'd promised he could return before classes started, anyway. But since they were saturated at five atmospheres, he'd need a lengthy decompression, and the Katiki team could just wait outside the sealock for him.

Then, there was the question of consequences. What would her punishment be for choosing a Land-Dweller over the safety of her clan?

* * *

Will

"Are we really returning to Katiki," Will asked Andreia, "after the messages you showed me?"

Andreia stood and placed hands on his shoulders. "I won't let any harm come to you. I can't stall them forever, though."

"What do we do about the Karsk?" His fellow humans would want him to do everything possible to stop the threat. "They'll keep trying to destroy civilization on land until they're stopped permanently. If we tell the US Navy about them—"

Andreia pushed out her gloved hands. "We have no right to make that decision on behalf of all Sea-Dwellers. It could lead to our extinction, and at the very least, would change our lives beyond repair."

Will understood, but the stakes were too high to back down. "And what about my people? Do we let the Karsk destroy the lives of eight billion people?"

"Of course not."

"Maybe we could trick the Navy into destroying them without revealing they're Sea-Dwellers."

She was quiet for a moment. "It's too risky. Let's keep this a Sea-Dweller matter. My clan and the others can pressure the Karsk into abandoning their war."

"Do you really think that will work? The Karsk are fanatics. And they've invested decades of planning and preparation."

"True," she said. "The Karsk tried to bring the other clans on board ten years ago, but no one supported it. They went ahead anyway. They apparently don't care what the other clans think. And they have covert support, at least among my clan."

"There must be something we can do. Besides rolling up their network on land, which they can replace."

"I told the Council to issue a grievance and evict the Karsk from our territory. I think the other clans will support it." Her eyes narrowed. "They should hand over their outpost as recompense."

Zoze and Sama each pressed spread hands together in agreement.

Will objected, "They'll just continue their terrorism from somewhere else."

Andreia met his eyes. "I'm not saying evict them and we're done, I'm saying evict them and buy time for a more permanent solution. For both our peoples."

Andreia sat at the computer she'd been using earlier and began typing. "I'm writing a joint request from the Aux inhabitants. I'll ask everyone to sign." She turned to Zoze. "Can you add your observations about the Karsk attack?"

Zoze wheeled her chair over. "Gladly."

When they finished, Andreia printed a hard copy and passed it around to sign. "I'll get everyone else on Aux to sign too."

Zoze turned to Will. "She'll have no problem. Charisma is one of her superpowers."

"Don't I know it," Will said. Still, he wondered, what were the chances they'd actually make the Karsk end their war? Especially the fanatics at their outpost? Their soldiers, from what he'd observed and heard from Andreia, seemed more likely to fight to the death than abandon their lifelong obsession. *We need a backup plan.*

When Andreia left to collect more signatures and Zoze took a toilet break, Will wheeled a chair next to Sama. He'd rather die than betray Andreia and her clan, but eight billion people—*holy shit!*—depended on what he did next.

"I was wondering," he asked Sama, "could you bring up a bathymetry map and show where you tapped the Karsk communications?"

"Sure. Why?"

"Do you remember where you buried the taps and what the directional orientation of their lines were?"

"Of course," he said. "I'm the main cable tapper. And even though we have navigation computers and compasses, Sea-Dwellers have an innate ability to find their way around underwater. As long as we aren't misled about our starting position like poor Galen."

"Yeah."

Sama opened a mapping program and loaded a detailed bathymetry background and red lines representing the undersea cables. With a draw tool, he placed four dots on the map.

"Probably the early Sea-Dwellers who got lost didn't get to pass on their genes." He smiled, but it quickly faded. "The Karsk can fool themselves they didn't actually murder Galen, but they did. They murdered a Sea-Dweller child, the most evil act imaginable."

"If their soldiers were to die in combat," Will said, "I assume you wouldn't be upset?"

"They're like a virus infecting our collective psyche. I wish we had an antibiotic."

You do. Will pointed at the mapping interface. "May I?" He wasn't exactly a geography systems guru, but knew enough for his research needs.

Sama slid his chair aside and gestured to the keyboard and mouse. With the drawing tool, Will connected the Karsk tie-in points and Sama's taps with lines, then extended the lines in the same direction. He pointed at the intersection of the two lines. "That's where the Karsk outpost is. More or less."

Sama stared at the screen. "So simple. But how does that help us?"

"We'll see." Depends on how well Andreia's plan works.

Chapter 28

Andreia

The next morning, Andreia and Will entered the communications room feeling cautiously optimistic. Thanks to the pressure from Aux, the Mazi Council of Elders had requested the convening by video of all 86 Sea-Dweller clans still in existence, ranging in size from a handful of individuals to over a thousand. Such meetings were extremely rare, but it had been centuries since a Sea-Dweller clan attacked another.

Since all Mazi communications were routed through Aux, Andreia and Will could observe undetected. The rest of the comm team had decided to focus on finding more saboteurs and roll up the Karsk network before they repaired their communications.

Fifty small boxes appeared on the overhead screen, each with a speaker from one of the clans. Almost certainly, the clan councils were sitting off-screen for consultations. Andreia wondered why the remaining 40% of clans had failed to show. *No Internet connection? Not interested? In on it?*

Kitane laid out the case for the Mazi clan, covering all the points Andreia had raised.

The Karsk, represented by a middle-aged woman named Iparane from their main habitat off the Caymans, denied responsibility. "It must have been a rogue element, no longer affiliated with the clan."

Kitane countered, "The clan is a unit. What one member does, all are responsible for."

"Not if they're on the other side of Cuba."

"If that is your position, then since this outpost is in our territory, you would not object to our clan taking control of it?"

Andreia raised a fist. "You go, Kitane!"

Iparane turned her mic off and looked off-screen, presumably consulting with the Karsk council. She switched her mic back on. "My understanding is that the area had been abandoned. There is no record of the Mazi using it for at least two generations."

The other Speakers asked questions, and seemed receptive to the Karsk position.

Frustrated, Andreia waved Sama over. "We need to intervene. Can you bring up the documents we sent the Council last night?"

"On it."

Andreia called the Mazi Council chamber from her computer. The Council assistant, who typed notes and prepared schedules, answered.

"I'm calling from Aux," Andreia said. "It might help our case if we let witnesses speak. Can you ask Kitane to let Mazi Sama represent Aux?"

The assistant spoke off-screen, then asked Andreia, "What do the witnesses plan to say?"

"They will describe the Karsk invasion of Aux."

As the Council deliberated, Sama told Andreia in a congested voice, "You're not really putting me in front of all the clans in the ocean, are you?" He looked terrified.

Andreia placed a hand on his shoulder. "I picked you because you live at Aux and I don't, and your father is well-respected on Katiki. But you can pass the mic to me and I'll use my Trader skills."

He exhaled through his nose, forcing the flaps open. "Gladly."

The Council agreed to let Sama speak, and ceded screen control. Fear returning to his face, Sama scooted aside and Andreia took his place.

"I am Mazi Andreia," she told the clan Speakers. "I will serve as Mazi Sama's voice."

Before anyone could object, she shared a document on screen. "This is an excerpt of a request by the Karsk Council from eighteen years ago requesting permission to build an outpost in an 'unused section' of Mazi territory. The request was denied, but the Karsk built it anyway and kept it hidden. The point is, it was an official request prior to the building of the outpost. The entire Karsk clan, or at least their representatives on the Council, planned it. They claimed a benign purpose, but their real purpose was to initiate a war against the Land-Dwellers from a position well removed from their home habitat, including accessing a different set of Internet cables. It wasn't a rogue operation."

Andreia's revelation brought forth a slew of arguing by video and chat. The randomly selected meeting Facilitator muted everyone but Andreia and asked for order.

Andreia fielded questions, then made an emotional appeal, describing her and the other Aux crew's experience of the Karsk invasion, including how she was almost killed. She shared photos of the damage to Aux.

The Karsk representative, Iparane, changed her defense strategy, claiming the Mazi granted them permission to build the outpost, and if the whole Council didn't support it, the Karsk didn't know that.

"You must be referring to your spies," Andreia responded, "like Mazi Xitaros. Not only did these spies not receive clan support, your clan knew that, because that was one of the reasons you recruited them. That and to keep eyes on us and manipulate us."

She shared evidence of Xitaros's duplicity—which she hadn't cleared with the Council, since he was still a member and had enough supporters to sabotage her entire effort. She concluded, "The Karsk committed an act of war against our clan, and furthermore, are endangering Sea-Dwellers everywhere through their war against the Land-Dwellers. The Karsk received explicit warnings not to pursue this war, but have done so anyway. They must leave our territory immediately and end their campaign. The outpost leaders must be imprisoned for everyone's safety and the Karsk must never again be allowed to access Land-Dweller communications." She returned control to Kitane.

Visibly angry, Kitane spoke, "You have seen the evidence. The Karsk must abandon their outpost, leave Mazi territory and make reparations for the offense. As the Aux representative stated, they must also abandon their war against the Land-Dwellers. The other clans told the Karsk ten years ago not to start this war, but they did so anyway, to the risk of all."

Many of the other attendees nodded in agreement.

Iparane smirked. "You said earlier, 'what one clan member does, all are responsible for.' We received assent from members of your Council, and have proof of that. It's not our fault you can't agree internally."

One of the clan representatives asked to see this proof. Iparane shared an email signed by Xitaros, Siaduare, and three other Mazi Elders, two of whom were now deceased.

Dismayed at the number of conspirators, Andreia sent Kitane a private message, 'Those three must be removed from the Council. They are traitors.'

Kitane responded, 'Later.'

As the deliberations dragged on, Iparane changed course yet again. "Our Council lost control long ago of those at the outpost. And we lost contact three days ago."

That was us. Andreia was happy to hear the enemy was still unable to communicate.

"We don't condone any of their actions," Iparane continued, "but consider this: they are acting to stop the Land-Dwellers from destroying the Great Ocean upon which we all depend. If you want our species to survive, you should support them in every way possible."

Andreia received Kitane's permission to speak again. "Your story keeps shifting, Iparane. That in itself is telling, is it not?" She didn't wait for a response. "All you accomplished was to anger the Land-Dwellers and put us all at risk. Your group also polluted the waters near the oil facilities they attacked. If you do not immediately put a halt to this insane operation, we will be forced to reveal your locations to the U.S. Navy. We do not have time for in-fighting. And if the Karsk Council are unable to contact the outpost, we would be happy to deliver the message in person."

The clans were unable to reach consensus, and many condemned Andreia's threat. "We must vote on the matter," the Facilitator ruled.

Kitane had to split the Mazi demands into five discrete sentences. Andreia waited nervously while the clan representatives signaled 'agree' or 'disagree' with their hands.

A sizable majority sided with the Mazi on four of the five sentences, deciding for the entirety of Sea-Dweller society that the Karsk had to immediately leave Mazi territory, surrender their outpost, abandon their war against the Land-Dwellers, and never again access Land-Dweller communications. By a narrow margin, the clans rejected the demand that leaders of the outpost be imprisoned.

Kitane floated a compromise on the rejected article: to imprison those responsible for the attack on Aux. This version passed.

Iparane consulted with her fellow Council members, then said, "We disagree with the collective decision, but will abide by it."

Will asked Andreia off-line, "Is that good enough? Will that really stop the more militant Karsk?"

Andreia held her breath, then said, "Their decision on imprisonment was worthless. The Karsk will just blame some low-level commander for the Aux invasion, and the leaders will be free to keep plotting. We'll have to remain vigilant."

The only way to be absolutely sure, unfortunately, was to kill everyone involved in the conspiracy. But the Mazi had neither the ability nor temperament to do that. *And even if we could, such a slaughter would mar us forever.*

Andreia deeply regretted the deaths at her hands. But it had been battle, and her brother had deserved justice. She took some small comfort that unlike some of the Karsk she'd faced, she felt no joy at the taking of life, nor even indifference. Only remorse.

* * *

USNS Surveyor, in the Straits of Florida

In the ready room of the *USNS Surveyor*, Dr. Ana Hernandez briefed the captain, navigator, and sonar supervisor as the ship prepared to return to the site where they'd recovered the underwater vehicle fragments. "The samples retrieved appear to match no known submersible equipment, and contain technology that we're still analyzing. More interesting, they contain anomalous carbon-chain compounds, like nothing seen. We also found pieces of a high-performance underwater weapon, also previously unseen. Needless to say, there's enormous high-level interest in learning who owned this equipment, and where it was developed."

The sonar supervisor, a fortyish man wearing the fouled anchors of a chief petty officer, sipped his coffee and gave her a look of concealed impatience.

Ana continued, "One notable feature is the electric-powered water jets for propulsion. Very quiet. Who knows how long they've been operating here?"

"The sonar profiles of the mini-subs detected by the P-8 are in the computer," the sonar supervisor said. "We'll be looking for a match."

"They have single-user vehicles too, like the one we recovered fragments of." She handed him a data stick and told him the password to unlock it. "They're even quieter, but here's the dimensions and a model of the acoustic profile."

She turned to the captain and navigator. "Naval Intelligence received information that the people using this equipment are behind the attacks on our oil refineries, the Saudi ports, and the Chinese semiconductor industry."

Ana was typically skeptical of unsolicited information, but the source had demonstrated insider knowledge of their past operations and what sort of underwater vehicles and weapons they used.

"They're affiliated with the cryptocurrency criminals," she continued, "who provide most of their funding." The bridge officers looked confused, so she summarized how the intelligence community had received information that the people who'd founded Currentsea had hacked their competitors and planned attacks on the larger financial system.

"We don't know why there were three underwater explosions here"—she pointed at an 'X' on a navigation chart—"whether they were tests, accidents, or some sort of factional infighting. But this terrorist group is trying to destroy the global economy and start wars, and it's imperative that we stop them."

"Our source inside their network said they have an undersea base here"— she pointed at another 'X'—"where they cache weapons and recharge their submarines from a geothermal tap."

"That's friggin' crazy," the navigator said. "We haven't even built things like that."

"I know, but it's consistent with what we've observed and the level of technology we found." She didn't mention the amphibious man they'd recovered in the South China Sea and the similar body recovered from the Keys, for which they had only photos. The crew didn't need to know. Her theory was these genetically modified people were working for the terrorist group, but had split into factions that were fighting each other. *There's so much more we need to find out.*

"We have our orders," the captain said. "Now they make more sense. Still seems crazy, though."

The *Surveyor* headed for the coordinates of the terrorist base. Once there, they'd profile the bottom until they found it. A P-8 would drop a circle of sonobuoys to track any movement of mini-subs or single-person vehicles. A submarine, destroyer, and other ships were positioned to intercept, and aid the *Surveyor* if needed.

* * *

The Karsk outpost

As the Coordinating Praesidium and key staff met in the conference room to discuss their contingency plan, the alarm system let out rapid high-pitched beeps. The overhead LEDs went out, replaced by dim red emergency lights.

Minatos, the outpost coordinator, hit the intercom button to find out what was going on. External communications were still out, but the internal system had been restored.

311

"Active sonar from the surface," the control room operator told him. "Our hydrophones detect a dual-propeller ship emitting low-frequency, high-intensity pulses."

"What's the probability they'll find us?" Tatoku, the military coordinator, asked.

"We should be undetectable," Minatos responded.

If discovered by the Land-Dwellers, the plan called for establishing a safe corridor, evacuating the base, scuttling it, and regrouping in Cuban waters. They'd practiced every step of this contingency, and the shuttles were pre-packed with essentials.

"And what do our sensors and dolphin scouts have to say?"

"Nothing. Yet."

Fifteen minutes later, the control room operator reported that sonobuoys had been dropped around them, and at least three other ships were nearby.

"They know we're here!" the finance coordinator said. "How?"

"The Mazi," Tatoku responded. "Who else? Our so-called useful idiots were idiots, but apparently not useful. We must evacuate and regroup."

Minatos waved a hand. "Let's not be hasty. It took years to build this facility."

Unable to reach consensus, the coordinators held a vote. All but Minatos chose to evacuate. Tatoku began mobilizing the garrison over the intercom.

"As soon as we finish off the Turd-Throwers," he grumbled then, "we should do the same to the species-traitor Mazi."

* * *

USS *Tarpon*
Straits of Florida

Commander Matt Nelson stood at the conn of the fast-attack submarine *Tarpon,* reading the decrypted message from the radio room on one of the monitors. A P-8 and the *Surveyor* had detected multiple sonar contacts headed for the Cuban coast—straight toward the *Tarpon*, which was running silent, all hands at general quarters. Their mission was to knock out the underwater vehicles and force their operators to the surface, where they'd be collected by Navy and Coast Guard surface ships waiting on the flanks.

Matt addressed the officer of the deck and the sonar supervisor. "Heads up. Received word, multiple contacts headed our direction, running deep. Non-friendlies. Same audio profile as Intelligence sent."

The OOD sat at the central console and forwarded the approximate locations and bearings to the sonar consoles, the combat control consoles, and the navigation table. Matt turned and watched the navigator plot an intercept course.

"Ditch the X-SUB," he ordered. The X-SUB was an expendable communication buoy connected to the submarine by a fiber-optic link.

The OOD picked up a phone and relayed the order to the radio room.

The sub's pilot and co-pilot were sitting in front of the captain at the ship control panel. "Pilot," Matt ordered, "ahead slow, bearing 015, down 10 degrees." Nice and quiet.

Staring at the digital controls of his navigation and trim screens, the pilot repeated the order back and nudged the black joystick. The floor tilted downward.

"Thermocline and bottom depth?" Matt asked the sonar supervisor.

"Thermocline 600 feet, bottom 2250."

"Pilot," Matt said, "level off at 1000 feet." The bogeys were beneath the thermocline and Tarpon's acoustics would be better there.

"Level at 1000 feet, aye."

Ten minutes after they returned to horizontal, one of the sonar operators said, "Got 'em. They're awfully quiet, though. Attempting to calculate course, depth, and speed."

From their intel, the targets would likely be small delivery vehicles with electric-powered water jets. Matt had two non-lethal options: first, blast active sonar at close range and deafen their quarry, who were supposedly exposed to the sea. Second, launch the squids - experimental torpedoes filled with dozens of self-propelled, squid-like masses that would disperse, then explode into sticky webbing. They were ideal against these targets because the webbing would clog their water jets and halt them.

He chose the second.

"Load squids in tubes one and two," he ordered. "Firing solution?"

"Still working on it," the fire control officer responded.

"Paint the targets," he told the sonar supervisor. It would give their position away, but they were in US-controlled waters, and it would enable more precise targeting.

The sonar operators lowered the volume on their headphone controls. "Six targets acquired," the supervisor said a minute later. He gave the distance and bearing.

Six? Matt hadn't expected that many. He told the combat team, "Fire, tube one! Fire, tube two!"

The fire control officer reported, "Torpedo one, course 005, unit running, wire good." The second torpedo followed a slightly different course.

After a few minutes, the officer announced, "Payloads activated."

One of the sonar technicians squawked, "Enemy torpedoes in the water. Two of them."

They can carry torpedoes? "Evasive maneuvers," Matt told the pilot and co-pilot. "All the power you've got."

The sonar supervisor shouted, "Two minutes to impact. They're small, but it won't be a love tap."

Matt ordered fire control, "Launch decoys. Then get a solution on the hostiles. Load lightweight torpedoes, all four tubes." These were faster and more maneuverable than their big anti-ship torpedoes.

The *Tarpon* turned and accelerated. "Decoys away," the fire control officer shouted.

"Got some hits with the squids," the sonar supervisor said. "Sounds like two of the targets are disabled."

The hull vibrated as one of the enemy torpedoes hit a decoy.

"Second enemy torpedo closing," the sonar supervisor shouted.

"Hard to starboard," Matt told the pilot. "Up 20 degrees." If the worst happened, it would be better to be near the surface. "Launch more decoys!" he yelled at fire control.

The *Tarpon* turned again and tilted up. "Decoys three and four away," the fire control officer said.

"Four more enemy torpedoes," the sonar supervisor shouted. "They're actively pinging."

Four! Matt cursed under his breath. The decoys couldn't fool the profiling of active sonar.

"Got a solution," one of the fire control techs said.

"Lightweight torpedoes loaded," the weapons officer added.

Another slight vibration, then a stronger one. The other torpedo from the first enemy volley had set off a decoy's proximity fuse.

Sweat dripping from his brow, Matt ordered, "Fire torpedoes, full spread!" They'd have to be turned, but that's what the wire guides were for.

"Torpedoes away," the fire control officer reported.

"Enemy torpedoes closing!" the sonar supervisor shouted.

The *Tarpon* was fast, but the pursuing torpedoes were faster. Matt told the officer of the deck, "Deploy another X-SUB. Call the flotilla commander and tell him we need assistance!"

The OOD relayed the order to the radio room.

"Two possible hits on targets," the sonar supervisor reported.

"Possible?" Matt responded.

"Two detonations at enemy positions, too much noise to analyze effects."

"Load more torpedoes!" Matt told the fire control officer. "Lightweight," he added. Too much was happening at once. *Six hostiles!* Sure, they were small, but that just made them harder to hit.

"Enemy torpedoes closing," he heard.

"Ping them hard," he shouted aft, "see if you can overload their receivers."

"Two more detonations at enemy positions," the sonar supervisor reported. After a few seconds, he added, "Two more."

Meanwhile, the *Tarpon* twisted and turned to evade the approaching enemy torpedoes.

An explosion rocked the boat, followed by another. Alarms rang. The submarine lost forward momentum.

"Breach in rear compartment!" came over the intercom speakers.

Matt hit the intercom button. "Damage control aft! Seal that breach!" He hoped the reactor hadn't been compromised.

"Propulsion's out," the co-pilot said. "We're dead in the water, sir."

Fuck! "Emergency surface! OOD, tell radio room we need immediate assistance!"

The pilot pulled the ballast levers, expelling all the water. The *Tarpon* shot upward toward the surface.

With a shrunken stomach, Matt felt like he'd failed his crew. But at least he'd keep them alive.

* * *

The Karsk outpost

As the alarms shrieked, the personnel at *Silent Garrison* grabbed what they could, stuffed it in dry bags, and hurried to the sealocks. The corridors were crowded, and the atmosphere reeked of barely controlled panic.

Tatoku and Minatos, though, headed to the outpost control room, trailed by their assistants. The control room and adjacent external communications center would be among the last to evacuate.

The red-lit control room was a compact hexagonal space with banks of equipment, monitors, and gauges on all sides, and a supervisor's post in the center.

"Two soldiers returned from the vanguard," the grim-faced supervisor said. "They were attacked by a large Land-Dweller submarine. Our soldiers knocked out the submarine, you will be pleased to hear."

Tatoku was indeed pleased, not just at the accomplishment, but that it would aid their escape.

"All the sleds were lost," the supervisor continued, souring Tatoku's mood. "The survivors returned by dolphin."

"Dual-propeller surface ship closing on our position," the sonar operator shouted from her station. "It's pinging us with sonar."

To escape, they had to sink, or at least disable, that ship too. "Send the second wave," Tatoku told the internal comms operator. "Tell them to destroy that ship at all costs."

The operator relayed his command.

Tatoku and Minatos examined the bathymetry map on one of the wall screens. Knocking out the enemy submarine gave them a clear evacuation path directly south. The Land-Dwellers had at least one aircraft—it had dropped sonobuoys around them—and they'd probably deploy it to cover the crippled submarine.

"Send the dolphins to disable the sonobuoys," Tatoku told the operator. "Tell the shuttles to head southwest, then disperse as planned and head for the Cuban coast." The shuttles were fairly big, with a capacity of two crew and ten passengers.

"We can still hold the outpost," Minatos claimed.

Tatoku glared at him. "The Land-Dwellers know where we are. We made a decision. We must abide by it."

316

Tears in his eyes, Minatos told the supervisor, "Initiate the self-destruct, 30 minutes."

The supervisor walked stiffly to a console, typed in a code, set the hydrogen tanks to discharge into the air vents, and armed the explosives. Thirty minutes from now, the explosives would ignite the hydrogen, rupturing the outpost chambers. 36 atmospheres of sea pressure would do the rest, collapsing their home and burying it.

With all his forces deployed, Tatoku exited the control room, followed by the rest. They hurried to the nearest sealock. The gauges next to the hatch showed that it was already open to the outside.

Tatoku, Minatos, and the others crowded into the sealock's antechamber. It filled with seawater and they exited into the spacious sealock. The outer blast doors had slid aside and the first shuttle was rising past them, into the deep blue ocean.

Tatoku and the others swam to the remaining shuttle. Tatoku took the pilot seat and inserted its rebreather mouthpiece—their shuttles were open to the water and therefore easier to use and maintain. As soon as everyone was on board, he hit a button to pump air into the ballast tanks, causing the shuttle to rise.

They'd barely cleared the outer doors when a barrage of explosions sounded from behind. Their second wave of soldiers battling the enemy, Tatoku presumed. He pushed the power stick to maximum and followed the other shuttles south.

The shuttle ahead of them exploded in a yellow flash. Tatoku expelled the air from his body just as the shock wave hit, rattling his shuttle and forcing it sideways.

A torpedo angled toward them from above and ahead. *From an airplane?* Tatoku swerved away. Without command, his aide in the adjacent seat released decoys from the stern.

The torpedo ignored the decoys and kept advancing. Tatoku could hear its sonar pulses as it neared. He took evasive maneuvers.

The end came before his senses could register anything.

Chapter 29

Will

Three days after the Navy battle with the Karsk, Will held on to Andreia's smooth stomach as she piloted her captured Karsk sled close to the surface, just beneath the wave movement. The water was dark, lit only by the moon and stars.

They'd already decompressed from five atmospheres to one in an Aux sealock. Since they'd been nitrogen-saturated, it had taken him two whole days. Andreia had needed far less time, but stayed to keep him company and sped the process with "light to moderate exercise."

The water calmed as they entered the reef zone. Andreia followed the channel into a canal, then turned into a side waterway lined with mangrove prop roots. She entered a small opening in the roots and settled the sled on the mucky bottom.

We're here. They climbed out of the water like amphibians and followed the narrow path through the mangroves. Mud squished between Will's toes and released a familiar rotten egg odor—hydrogen sulfide produced by anaerobic bacteria as they broke down detritus. Most people found the smell repugnant, but for him, it was a pleasant welcoming back to *terra firma*.

It was surreal being on land again, like returning from a moon mission. Will had been down among the Sea-Dwellers for eighteen days, but it felt like several lifetimes. He'd never be the same, that was certain.

The white cargo van and small off-grid house appeared as they'd left them. "Sorry I didn't get you back in time," she said.

Classes had started last week. Will had, via email, reluctantly claimed illness and arranged a substitute teacher. He wrapped arms around Andreia and kissed her. "It was well worth it."

Andreia laughed as she unlocked the front door. "I assume you want your wallet and phone back."

"And my keys. It's weird being back."

"Better or worse?"

"Different. Safer, though."

Andreia had chosen to return Will to land instead of delivering him to Katiki as ordered. "From what I've heard," she'd told him, "the majority of the Council has already decided against you. You wouldn't have received a fair trial in the current climate, and there's a good chance they would have disappeared you."

Andreia opened the safe and gave Will his things. Then she handed him her van keys, attached to a painted metal dolphin. "You can borrow the van to get home. I have to return to Katiki. I'll contact you when I need it back."

"What will they do to you?"

"They won't put me to death. I'm a member of the clan."

"But they'll punish you," he said.

"They can shove Leviathan's barnacled dick up their ass."

Will half-chuckled. Andreia and her friends certainly had a rich storehouse of curses. He toweled off and put on the dry clothes he'd left here. "Andreia, there's something I have to tell you."

"You want to marry me? I'm flattered, of course." She grinned, as if being playful.

It nevertheless took a moment for Will to recover. "No, that's not it. I mean, I would like to see you again. Every day for the rest of my life. But…"

"But what?"

He swallowed. He'd betrayed her trust and her people's trust. If Andreia never wanted to see him again, she had every right. "I passed along the location of the Karsk outpost and told Naval Intelligence what to listen for."

They'd heard—partly from their hydrophones, partly from Internet chatter, partly from patrolling Mazi-allied dolphins—that a battle had taken place around the Karsk outpost, with numerous undersea explosions. As Will had expected, the Karsk force had chosen to fight rather than surrender. A U.S. submarine and a destroyer had been disabled and a large number of Karsk vehicles destroyed. The fight had been followed by massive seafloor detonations—the Karsk had scuttled their outpost.

The Navy had responded like a poked hornet nest, sending everything available on a search-and-destroy mission. The Mazi were afraid they'd be discovered too, and had remained absolutely silent with minimal power while Navy ships were nearby.

"I'm sorry," Will said. "Lives were lost, and the Navy might find Sea-Dweller bodies and technology. I love you and your people—most of them, anyway—but as long as the Karsk outpost leaders are alive, they'll do whatever they can to destroy humanity. I couldn't let that happen."

"I know all that."

That was the last response Will had predicted. "You do?"

"I noticed you watching me and the others typing our passwords. Classic hacker trick—'shoulder surfing,' Zoze says it's called. But you weren't subtle enough. And Sama told Zoze you pinpointed the location of the Karsk outpost, and Zoze told the rest of us."

"And you let me do it anyway?"

"The clan councils mean well, but the Karsk fanatics didn't listen the first time, and there's no reason to think they'd listen now. Even if they left Mazi territory, they could set up elsewhere and continue their war. Zoze monitored you to make sure you didn't pass along anything that would compromise our clan—not that we expected you to. When it comes down to it, you had a right to defend your people from those shitholes. Besides, they were a threat to us, too. The world is safer without them."

"Who else knows?"

"Zoze, Sama, Pijasiros, and Duripi. That's it. They understand. What's more, they're not afraid to come out of the underwater closet, so to speak. We all know our technology isn't keeping up with yours—you outnumber us by 100,000 to 1. Land-Dwellers have already discovered us; they just haven't realized the truth yet. But they will. We can't hide forever. Which is just as well; we can't heal the ocean by ourselves. But we want the revelation to be on our terms, have to make clear that we're not all warmongers, and have to bring the rest of our species around to the idea."

"I presume some of the Karsk militants survived," Will said. "But hopefully their core team and their operational plans were wiped out when their vehicles and base were destroyed. And now the Navy knows what to look for and will search in earnest, like the cybersecurity community has."

Andreia relocked the house and returned to the sled, Will accompanying her. "You could have asked," she said. "Didn't you trust me?"

"Of course, but I didn't want any blowback to fall on you."

She stopped at the water's edge, face dappled by sunlight reaching past the dense canopy. "A nice gesture, but unnecessary."

"And I wasn't as sure about the others," he admitted.

"They're my friends."

"I know, but remember, two of your friends were moles."

She sighed. "Yes. But my true friends proved themselves."

"This isn't goodbye forever, is it?" He felt like he'd ruined her life.

She rolled her eyes, then smiled. "Of course not. You have my van keys. There's only one set."

Will realized he'd been holding his breath. Her smile resuscitated it.

Andreia shifted on her feet, then stepped forward and embraced him. "Don't worry, my love is a stubborn thing."

They embraced, Will savoring the salty smell of her hair and the feel of her moist skin. When they drew apart, Andreia said, "One more thing. Buy a gun and learn how to use it. We made some people very angry."

Then she dove into the water and didn't re-emerge.

* * *

Andreia

Andreia stood alone before the Mazi Council of Elders in the circular Assembly Chamber, surrounded by the wall murals of reefs in their former glory. Xitaros was absent, having been removed by his peers, along with Siaduare and another co-conspirator. Xitaros was now working in sewage reclamation. *They let him off easy*, she thought.

"Why, Andreia?" Meltha asked. "Why did you side with a Land-Dweller over your own clan?"

"I didn't. The Council isn't the whole clan. You were going to have him killed, weren't you?" She scanned the gathered faces. "How many of you wished Theros's assassination attempt had been successful?"

Several twitched facial muscles in response. In slow tones, Didekaso, the new First Speaker, spoke impassively, "Xitaros and his nephew acted on their own, with help from the Karsk. He confessed everything, but still claims it was necessary."

"We shouldn't have interfered," a Councilman in the back grumbled. "We could have been rid of the Land-Dwellers. Things are worse than ever now."

Another spy or just a sympathizer? Andreia started to respond, but Meltha interrupted.

"Will Myers is now free to tell the whole world about us," she spoke in stiff tones. "Do you know what danger you've put us in?"

"Zero," Andreia said. "Will loves our people—the Mazi, anyway. It's the Karsk who put us in danger, and Will was instrumental in stopping them. Couldn't you show some gratitude?"

She'd rehearsed a grandiose speech about Sea-Dwellers ending their fearful isolation on the bottom of the ocean and announcing themselves to the Land-Dweller media. Then, they could help humanity clean up their mess. First, they would have to teach Land-Dwellers how to share the planet, and set aside areas exclusively for Sea-Dwellers. Maybe even include some islands, like the 'good old days' 25 generations ago.

But her words would be wasted. The Elders were too stuck in their ways to listen to such heresy. She'd have to convince young people instead, and prepare the way for a more enlightened generation.

"You may wait outside while we discuss the matter," Didekaso said. One of the two ceremonial guards stepped toward Andreia, but she signaled, #I know the way.#

She sat on a concrete bench on the other side of the carved wooden doors. What would the Council do to her? The clan needed her—she was the only trained Trader besides Stefan, who'd retired. And she knew things about the broader world that no one else did.

Half an hour later, she was escorted back into the chamber. Didekaso leaned on the golden Speaker trident for support and spoke, "It is the consensus judgment of the Mazi Council of Elders that Mazi Andreia, having recklessly and willfully put the entire clan at risk, be permanently banished from the clan, without the possibility of return."

A chill swept through Andreia. Her knees shook, and threatened to buckle and spill her to the floor. There was no punishment more severe than exile, and the Mazi had not invoked it for generations.

"In recognition of your past services," Didekaso continued, "you have one day to say farewells. Then you will report to Sealock 1 and have your clan tattoo removed."

Andreia had witnessed the removal of Yissharu's Karsk tattoo before it was replaced by the Mazi cross-and-circle. A Council member had used an electric sander to remove the tattooed layers of skin. They'd given him a local anesthetic to reduce the pain—but according to lore, exiled clan members were given no anesthetic, and a knife was used instead, causing permanent scarring.

"Then," the Speaker said, "you shall leave our home and never return."

Andreia's stomach clenched and tears blurred her vision. "I've done so much for the clan. How could you?"

Didekaso ignored her. "Further, it is the decision of this Council to cease further trade and other contact with Land-Dwellers. It is far too dangerous."

Andreia rubbed the tears from her eyes. "How are we supposed to keep up with technology, or obtain things we can't make ourselves?"

"We have machines and 3-D printers. There is nothing we can't make ourselves. There is no need to pollute our minds or live dependent on our enemies on land. We are Mazi, proud inheritors of all the seas between…"

Andreia tuned him out. She'd been exiled. She might never see her family and friends again. Every atom of her body wanted to shout and scream and wail and beg for mercy.

She couldn't stop the flood of tears and the trembling of her limbs, but otherwise she stood her ground. She would say her goodbyes, but depart before anyone had the chance to carve her skin. She would take a sled and whatever she needed for a decent life with Will, the man who made her whole.

And eventually, the political currents would shift. Then she would return.

Chapter 30: Epilogue

Will & Andreia
6 months later

Will flipped the wahoo steaks on the grill bolted to the aft deck of *Eden's Gateway*, appreciating the calm, sunny day. He and Andreia lived aboard the 53-foot dive yacht full-time, making it hard for any surviving Karsk zealots to find them. Will had taken a sabbatical from teaching and was researching reef restoration full-time, part of a huge multidisciplinary project.

Andreia emerged from the spacious living quarters, trailed by Zoze, Sama, Duripi, and Pijasiros, each lugging a dry bag full of electronics, medicines, food items, and comic books—the last mostly for Zoze. The Mazi Council had ended trading with the surface, but the clan still needed things they couldn't make, and the Aux crew had decided to fill the gap.

Their friends had arrived about an hour ago from the ocean below, and had exchanged their swimsuits for clothes and hats from the closets. Although this wasn't the first time Andreia had met friends or family since being exiled, this was the first time above water.

Andreia strode up to Will and kissed him, forgoing words. They kissed at every opportunity, still euphorically in love. To Will, everything seemed so bright and full of promise when she was around. Especially lately.

Andreia wore a loose white blouse and a lightweight skirt, and a wristband of linked cowrie shells Will had given her. He wore a matching wristband Andreia had made, a traditional Mazi engagement custom. He'd introduced her to his family and friends; none suspected she was other than human. They hadn't decided on a marriage date yet, but would need two separate ceremonies. Like other Mazi, Andreia's relatives and friends were prohibited from going ashore.

Zoze and Sama had matching sea serpent tattoos. Zoze had a noticeable pregnancy bulge beneath her borrowed T-shirt. Her hair was now purple instead of pink, and Sama, the baby's father, had switched from green to orange. The couple plopped their bags on the deck and eyed the steaks.

"If you're still hungry," Will said, "there's plenty more." The five-foot long wahoo had been a beast to catch, nearly stripping the line from his reel and fighting ferociously for over an hour.

"Your boat is amazing," Zoze told him. "So much room inside!"

"Thanks. Andreia bought it used, at a bargain price." To pay for it, and cover their other expenses, he'd sold his house and boat, and Andreia had sold the Trader outpost and the gold and other valuables there. The global economy had somewhat recovered, but the price of gold was still high, almost compensating for the stratospheric fuel prices.

"How's your research project going?" Sama asked.

"I wish we could credit the Mazi and other clans," Will confessed. The Sea-Dwellers had lived among ocean ecosystems for tens of thousands of years, and knew everything there was to know. "I'm just applying your knowledge of reef species and systems and telling the modeling and microbiology teams what to look for. We can stop the coral diseases and breed heat-resistant varieties, for example, and with your understanding of how everything works, create new reefs further north and in thermal refugia."

"We have to reveal ourselves eventually," Andreia said. "But taking credit for things isn't our way. We'd just want respect, and assurances our knowledge would be used for the good of the planet."

Duripi and Pijasiros sat on the bench seat against the rear railing. "Andreia showed us your armory," Duripi said. "Expecting trouble?"

"It's hardly an armory," Andreia said. "Just a few weapons in case enemies find us."

The Karsk war council had been wiped out and their land network broken up, but the force that had attacked Aux was still unaccounted for. No one had heard from them, but Will assumed they were still alive and would be eager for revenge if they found him.

"Aux and Katiki have armories now, also," Pijasiros said. "And the Council has us training in case we're attacked again."

"We watch all your posts," Zoze told Will. "Andreia's become quite the influencer!"

Both Will and Andreia had been posting near-daily undersea videos on all the popular social media platforms, showing reef life, the stresses it faced, and restoration techniques. Andreia had a lot more followers—over a million already and climbing fast—but she had the looks of a model, swam with grace—and without a mask—and had been taught incredible charisma powers. She just had to keep her feet covered.

"It's weird being in the public eye," Andreia said, "after hiding in the shadows all those years."

Zoze spread her webbed fingers. "I wish I could do that, but we've been forbidden from interacting with Land-Dwellers in any way." She frowned.

"We still monitor the Internet, though," Sama said, "and can create fake personas when we need to."

"It's whale shit, the Council exiling you," Zoze told Andreia. "Almost everyone thinks so. Sama and I are thinking of leaving the clan."

Andreia blinked. "What? You didn't tell me that before."

"Us too," Pijasiros said. Duripi nodded.

"There's a better way," Andreia countered. "Stay. Join with others and fight for a better system, one where everyone has an equal voice. Worst case, Aux can declare independence from Katiki, but it's better to change Katiki, too."

Zoze clasped her hands together in support. "I like it." She exchanged glances and nods with the others. "You'll help remotely, right?" she asked Andreia.

"Of course."

"Step 1," Duripi said, "change the Council of Elders from a decision-making body to a purely advisory one."

"Who will make the decisions?" Sama asked.

"Everyone." Duripi massaged his temples. "Some research and testing might be needed to come up with a good system."

Will gave him a thumbs-up. It sounded like the scientific method.

"And why should the council be limited to elders?" Andreia said. "One of you should be on it, to represent Aux and the younger generations."

Zoze smiled. "And reverse Andreia's exile!"

The wahoo steaks were now white and flaky. Will put them on a platter and turned off the grill. They ate in the wood-paneled dining room, which was lined with saltwater aquariums used in their research. Andreia had jokingly announced earlier that the fish and crustaceans inside weren't a help-yourself sushi buffet.

After they sat down to eat, Andreia flipped up her palms. "Thanks again everyone for coming."

"*Grazi itas merid*," Will repeated in Mazi.

Their friends stared at him. "You even got the pronunciation down," Zoze said.

"I've been teaching him," Andreia said. "Anyway, we have an announcement. More than one, actually."

326

Will began with the global conference. They'd defeated the Karsk, but the fundamental problems remained—the accelerating climate and nature crises, the dying ocean, and the impending collapse of the planet's ability to support complex life. And as with the Karsk, the problems had to be solved—at least for now—without revealing the existence of Sea-Dwellers.

"We're speaking at this year's U.N. Ocean Conference," he said. "The organizing committee loved the proposal Andreia and I put together on behalf of the Florida university system. I'm giving one of the plenary addresses, about filling the massive gaps in our understanding and protection of the ocean, and a blueprint for the way forward. The ocean and nature deserve inherent rights and should have the same legal protection as people. Ecosystems and species must have the right to exist, thrive and regenerate."

"Spoken like a Sea-Dweller," Duripi said.

"Some humans—Indigenous people, for example—feel the same way, but not enough yet. Before industrialization, it was obvious how much we rely on nature, but most of us have forgotten that." He squeezed his fiancée's hand. "Andreia is also giving talks."

"How's the documentary coming?" Duripi asked.

"Doing final edits," Andreia said. "Thanks for all your help."

Andreia's full-length documentary illustrated the decline of the ocean with video clips, photos, and data obtained from Sea-Dweller clans around the world. Like Will's U.N. speech, she was also showing how to fix it.

"Sea-Dwellers aren't the only ones suffering," Andreia continued. "I won't mention us, of course. But humans also can't survive without a healthy world ocean. Humanity must stop destroying the ocean, the land, and the atmosphere, and repair the damage they've caused before the world becomes completely unlivable."

"The Land-Dweller Jacques Cousteau warned about the ocean dying decades ago," Duripi said, "but look how much worse the world's become anyway."

"I'm dedicating the rest of my life to this fight," Andreia said, "the biggest fight that matters to us." She kissed Will again. "My wonderful fiancé, too."

"Look at you," Sama said. "From representing our clan to representing the entire world ocean."

"We're calling for a Rights of Nature Treaty and an ambitious and binding Ocean Recovery Treaty," Will said. "We've laid out the essentials, and are recruiting influential signers."

Pijasiros leaned toward them. "What's the other announcement?"

Andreia backed up her chair and stood. She lifted her blouse, revealing a slight stomach bulge. She placed a hand against it. "You're not the only one who's pregnant, Zoze."

Her friends stared, seemingly unable to speak. Will held her hand.

"Who's the father?" Zoze asked with a straight face.

Andreia blew air at her. "Will is, dummy."

"That's impossible," Duripi said. "You're different species. It's never happened in recorded history."

"How often has the opportunity arisen?" Will asked. "And how many interspecies couples would have written it down for everyone to know?"

"Even if they did," Andreia added, "plenty of Elders would want to destroy such heretical evidence."

The thought of raising a family with Andreia filled Will with more joy than he'd ever thought possible. At the same time, he was nervous. Would the baby live? Would it be healthy? What if there was a complication requiring a hospital visit? But according to a midwife in the dive club, Andreia's pregnancy was proceeding smoothly so far. Despite what they'd been told, Land-Dwellers and Sea-Dwellers were fundamentally compatible.

"It was a surprise," Andreia told everyone. "We're even less different than I thought."

Will raised a glass of water—he'd given up alcohol. "There's a human custom called a toast. It's a type of collective celebration."

Andreia and their friends raised their glasses.

"To friendship, to love, to the kinship of all, and to our collective home, our world."

Dear Reader,

Thank you for reading! If you enjoyed this book, please consider taking a moment to leave a review at your favorite retailer and/or book review site. It will greatly help other readers discover the book.

Thanks!

T. C. Weber
https://www.tcweber.com/

ABOUT THE AUTHOR

T. C. Weber grew up in South Florida and spent summers fishing and diving in the Keys. His first published novel was a near-future cyberpunk thriller titled *Sleep State Interrupt* (See Sharp Press). The first book of a trilogy, it was a finalist for the 2017 Compton Crook award for best first speculative fiction novel. The sequels, *The Wrath of Leviathan* and *Zero-Day Rising*, are also out. These were followed by *Born in Salt*, a character-oriented alternate history novel that pits an Illinois farm boy against a ruthless fascist government. Published in 2022, *The Survivors* (Solstice Publishing), is a post-apocalyptic cli-fi horror novella in which a young mother is forced on the road and struggles to survive a living nightmare. *The Council*, also published in 2022, is a satire of local government. More works are on the way.

Mr. Weber is a member of Poets & Writers, the Science Fiction & Fantasy Writers Association, the Horror Writers Association, and the Maryland Writers Association. By day, Mr. Weber works as an ecologist, and has had numerous scientific papers and book chapters published. He currently lives in Annapolis, Maryland with his wife Karen. He enjoys traveling and has visited all seven continents.

For book samples, short stories, and more, or to contact the author, visit https://www.tcweber.com/

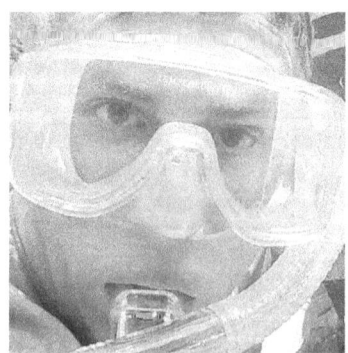

www.ingramcontent.com/pod-product-compliance
Lightning Source LLC
Chambersburg PA
CBHW070913260626
47162CB00007B/2657